A REALLY GOOD DAY

a novel

by

JAMES HOSEK

Dedicated to my wife, Laurie.
Merry Christmas

PROLOGUE

It was a crazy idea. It was insane. It was stupid. Why even consider it? No one here was going to blame him. A nice easy five-wood to the halfway point, then on the green in two. A two-putt would insure him the win. That was what a smart golfer would do. That was what a sane person would try for.

"How far?" asked Scott Hanover.

His friend and caddy, Paul Bauer, looked a bit confused. "How far to where? The sand trap?"

Scott chewed on his lower lip. He looked at the crowd of people. He never imagined this day would end like this. He looked over at Sally Gina, snuggled warm against her mother. He found Andrew Patterson, his expression was half frustration and half confusion. Things certainly hadn't gone his way today.

"How far over the water?"

"To the green?" asked Paul. "That's crazy."

"I know."

"That's insane!"

"I know."

"It's stupid!"

"Exactly," Scott agreed. "How far?"

"Three hundred and fifteen yards in the air, and Scott old buddy, I've seen you do some amazing things today, but you ain't got that swing in the bag."

"Sometimes you just have to go for it."

"Listen. Lay-up with the five-wood and get on in two. A good putt and you tie the record. On the other hand, you put your drive in the water you're back here hitting three and kissing it all good-bye."

Scott looked over at the ball sitting on the tee, the yellow rubber ducky logo smiling at him.

"Don't even think about it, Scott," Paul warned.

He held out his club to Paul. Paul chuckled and took it. "You're an idiot," he said with a big grin.

"No argument here," agreed Scott.

Paul slipped the club into the bag and pulled out Scott's driver. Over the club head was a gopher doll holding a plastic golf ball. Scott took the club with the cover on it. A murmur began rippling through the crowd. He knew that everyone was thinking the same thing. This guy is going for it.

He raised the club above his head and a cheer broke out. The polite silence had been transformed as everyone realized what was going to happen. History was going to be made, one way or another.

To his right, Scott heard a group break into the most appropriate song he could imagine.

I'm alright,
Nobody worry 'bout me.
Why you got to gimme a fight?
Can't you just let it be?

The words and music from the Kenny Loggins song that graced the closing credits of "Caddy Shack" spread through the mass of people like a fire. Scott bounced his driver with the gopher cover to the beat feeling a surge of adrenalin flowing. This was his day. His moment.

He returned to the tee and pulled the cover from his club. He draped it across Paul's outstretched arms like he was giving his coat to a butler. He turned forty-five degrees to his left to face the flag on the distant green. He stretched out his right arm with the driver, lining up his shot. As if on cue, the singing and clapping from the crowd faded out and was replaced by a respectful silence.

He set his club behind the ball and lined up his feet in the direction of the hole. No practice swing this time. He'd use whatever was there.

He closed his eyes for a moment and pictured the ball sailing across the pond and rolling onto the green. He could do it. He knew he could. He felt it. Something had given him the confidence or perhaps the stupidity to take the shot and he wasn't going to ignore it.

He looked at the ball, at the yellow duck with the orange feet and beak and black beady eyes. The song, "Rubber Ducky" from Sesame Street ran through his head for a moment.

Rubber ducky, you're the one...
He smiled even more.

"What water?" he said to himself as an impromptu prayer. The eighteenth hole at George Dunne National Golf Course was a four hundred and fifty yard dogleg left around a large pond. In order for this to work he had to imagine that the water wasn't even there.

As he drew back the club starting the motion that would end with his ball leaving the tee for the last time that day, everything seemed to go in slow motion. His back swing, the uncoiling of his body, the ping as his driver hit the ball. He found himself facing the far off green with his club hanging over his left shoulder. His ball lifted higher and higher, further and further. No one spoke. No one breathed.

This was how it was going to end. One way or another, this day came down to this one shot.

Even from where he stood, Paul could tell that the ball, Scott's best drive of the day, didn't have enough to make it. He muttered almost to himself, "It's wet."

People lined up along the left side of the water hazard had come to the same conclusion. A few shouts of "No, no," rang out across the water.

Scott could see the ball was going to be short. He closed his eyes willing it to just go a little further.

The day hadn't started out like this. Seven hours ago he was just a low-ranked amateur wondering how he'd even gotten into this whole mess. Now the whole world was watching and holding their breath with him, wondering if this was how it was going to end.

CHAPTER 1 – THE DAY BEGINS

1

Scott had never been a morning person. The only thing that could get him out of bed this early was an equally early tee time. Looking out the bedroom window at the approaching sunrise he wondered why he had never just taken time to enjoy this moment of the day before.

He turned and looked at the glowing red numbers on his alarm clock. He had been standing at the window for ten minutes. It hadn't felt that long. The truth was he should be excited but all he was feeling was the biggest case of nerves he ever had and some well-deserved guilt.

One week earlier he had been informed that his alternate status in the regional tournament of the Northern Illinois Amateur Golf Association was being upgraded to active. Joe Caulkin, the golfer who originally had the spot, had broken his wrist chopping wood. It wasn't that Scott had played all that well but he had an amazing putt on the eighteenth hole that put him in third place until the disqualification of the second place finisher for having an extra club in his bag moved him up.

Now he found himself not only having to prepare to compete with the top local amateur golfers in Chicago, but also trying to convince his wife that it was the absolute last time he'd play before their child was born. He had promised the same thing before the previous tournament, convinced he would go no further.

Sarah eventually did relent and allowed him this last fling before the delightfully terminal condition of fatherhood overtook his life.

"Scott?" muttered the soft voice of his wife from the bed. "What time is it?"

"Six forty-five," he answered. "You can go back to sleep."

"No I can't," she said. "Being pregnant means having to go to the bathroom all the time. Didn't I explain this to you already?"

"Right, come to think of it you did," he replied.

She slipped out from under the sheets and went down the hall. The sky had brightened and the bedroom was bathed in the glow of early morning.

After a few moments Sarah's arms slipped around his waist from behind and she nestled her chin on his right shoulder. Scott tilted his head back so their cheeks touched. "You're sure you'll be okay?" he asked.

"Hey," she chided, "you were the one begging to go. Getting cold feet?"

"I don't belong out there," he answered.

"You'll have fun," she answered. "You and Paul will go out and do your golf thing for five hours, grab a beer and still get home in time to get started on that list of things we need to get done before the baby comes." Scott cringed at the last part.

But she was right. They would have fun. Scott and his friend Paul Bauer couldn't help but have fun when they were on the golf course together.

Scott snuggled closer to his wife. "These guys I'll be playing with today all shoot par. I've only broken eighty twice!"

"Eighty sounds good," said Sarah. Scott smiled at her comment.

"Par is usually seventy-two for eighteen holes. And this is a tough course. Paul and I played there last year and I think I shot a ninety-five. I just hope I don't embarrass myself."

Sarah pulled away and grabbed his hand. "Come back to bed. It's cold in there without you."

"I don't think I can sleep."

"Then just lay next to me."

Scott turned to face her. He kissed her lightly on the lips and let her lead him back to bed.

She muttered in a half sleepy voice, "In a half hour I'll make you a good breakfast and you can go to play with your friend, Paul. You'll do fine."

Scott snuggled up behind his wife, reached over her pregnant belly and took her hand. She was asleep in less than a minute. He listened to her slow even breathing. His apprehension returned without Sarah's reassurance. Hopefully he could keep his score to no higher than ninety. That was just one over par every hole. That would be a score he could live with.

2

"Sally," screamed Jason Bernard over the noise of the shower. There was no immediate response so he shouted louder turning his wife's name into two distinct syllables. "SAL – LY, where is my green tie."

"What?" she finally shouted in return over the rushing water.

"My green tie."

"I can't hear a word you're saying?" she shouted back.

"Never mind," he returned.

"What?"

"NEVER MIND!" he shouted again, louder.

Jason looked through the closet again, searching through each one of the hundred or so ties in his collection. Not that it mattered that much today. Lucy Penndel had been assigned to cover the Chicago Marathon. Both baseball teams were out of the play-offs so it was the top sports event in Chicago today and Jason wasn't going to be there. With a lot of the best marathoners running it was going to be as much of a psychological race as a physical one. They expected a fast start and one of the runners to set a world record today.

Jason had covered the marathon for the last five years for the USA Sports Channel in Chicago. This year he was condemned to reporting on an amateur golf tournament in the south suburbs. He wouldn't even have any live reports, just a video camera and one cameraman. He'd then have to spend the afternoon editing the whole six-hour ordeal into a one minute twenty second segment to be aired on the nine o'clock report.

Lucy Penndel had been hired to try and widen the sports network's female demographic. There were some rumors she had slept her way to the Marathon assignment; she was very attractive and young, but Jason had been assured that since marathons were as much as a woman's sport as a man's, the execs thought it might boost their ratings and not to worry, big things were in line for him.

If this was their idea of big things Jason was seriously considering putting on one of his wife's dresses. What's more, he hated golf. Not only was it boring but only the wealthy could afford to play the really nice courses. He personally didn't even consider it a sport. The idea that people would use carts to drive from shot to shot just seemed to prove his point.

He found the green tie he was looking for hanging on the last hook. It was still stained from the tomato sauce that he meant to have cleaned out the last time he wanted to wear it. He grabbed a red tie with gray diamonds. The shower had stopped and Sally had come back into the bedroom.

"Did you find it?" she asked.

"Find what?" asked Jason, distracted by trying to knot the tie around his neck.

"The green tie." She ruffled her hair with a towel as she said it, bending over to let the long blonde strands hang straight down. The towel wrapped around her chest barely covered her behind in this position and he took the opportunity to whack her sharply on the butt. "Can't hear me my eye," he muttered not too softly.

His whack caused her to squeal as she stood up, her hair flipping back to reveal her sinister grin. Despite her nasty prank, he allowed himself to become infected by her beautiful smile.

She looked at him and shook her head watching him trying to tie his tie. "What would you do without me?" she asked. She took the tie from his hands and undid his loose knot. She pulled the tie under his collar and expertly knotted it, snugging it tight around his neck. She kissed him quickly. "You're going to be late," she admonished.

"Doesn't matter," he replied. "Just that silly golf tournament."

"Oh, is Tiger Woods playing?"

"No," he chuckled. "Just amateurs. But the winner gets a chance to play in a Pro-Am PGA event. The station thought it would be nice to get some coverage of a local guy who would be going to play with the professionals."

"Are you going to be gone all day?"

"Pretty much. I might make it home by seven o'clock. It really depends on what cameraman I get and how good he is. Alf is going to be at the Marathon. I have no idea who I'll be assigned today." Alf Redding was Jason's usual cameraman on his assignments. Lucy Penndel had insisted on him for the marathon and Jason felt it wouldn't be fair to force Alf to suffer at the golf tournament too.

"Well don't think I'm going to be having any fun at the rummage sale. I'll be haggling with people over fifty cent coasters and trying to keep Cecily Waterston from putting too high a price on some of the chatch we've collected." She slipped into her walk-in closet to pick out a dress, her towel tossed out behind her.

Jason looked at his watch and frowned as he saw he was going to be late. "I got to go," he called after her.

"She peeked her head around the doorway. "Are you sure?" she teased.

"Yeah, I'll be late. But tonight..."

"You know we really need to talk about something related to that," she began.

Here it comes again, thought Jason. "Sally, there's too much pressure at work now. With me losing the Marathon assignment I have to work even harder to keep my position. I know you want kids, sweetheart."

"It's okay," Sally sighed. Jason felt the disappointment in her voice. He had put her off for years and could tell she wasn't in the mood to fight about it now.

"We'll talk tonight," he promised.

"Alright," she answered, the door of the walk-in closet closed behind her. Jason looked at his watch. He knew she was in there crying, frustrated by his delays at starting their family. He wanted to go in and hold her. He knew she hadn't pushed the issue as hard as she wanted. She was patient but he wasn't sure how much longer that would last. His job required he work most weekends and vacations were short and far between. But he wanted to make sure his job was stable before he made the commitment to raise a family. Wasn't that important too?

He checked his watch again. He had to leave. There was no time now to spend on the long conversation he knew was ahead. He would make it up to her tonight, flowers, chocolates, and reservations at Morton's. Maybe in a year he'd feel confident enough start a family. Things would be better then.

3

Andrew Patterson sat comfortably in his leather wing back chair. An unlit pipe hung from the corner of his mouth. In his left hand he held one of his Pierre Cardin golf shoes. With his right hand he carefully dabbed a dull spot with some Kiwi shoe polish and carefully buffed the shine back. He had already tightened the spikes and evened out the laces. Perfection graced his every endeavor.

He could conceive of nothing that would deny him a victory today at the Northern Illinois Amateur Regional Golf Tournament at the George W. Dunne Championship Golf Course.

Andrew Patterson had achieved success in everything he pursued. He worked hard to get where he was. He had obtained his MBA from the University of Chicago and had used his business expertise to start a software company, then a property management firm, and most recently an Internet consulting firm. Two years ago he decided he needed something different. He wanted more recognition for his accomplishments. He wanted a certain degree of fame. Not to where he couldn't walk outside without some photographer harassing him, but more where people might recognize him on the street and solicit an autograph.

He settled on golf as the perfect vehicle for this goal. It required skill and athleticism, but not the physical stamina required of other sports. It was something he could work on and perfect with his usual approach. He researched the game thoroughly. He sought out the top golf instructors and the best equipment and practiced until his body and mind had united to produce a consistent swing. He analyzed the technical factors of the game; when to use a particular club, how to read a course, and most importantly, how to manage it. He perfected every aspect of the game.

Today would be the culmination of his efforts. If he won, he would have a chance to play in a PGA Pro-Am tournament. If he did well enough there, the prospect of turning professional would not be all that distant. As a professional golfer, he would be in a position to obtain the fame he desired.

He set down his shoe, leaned deep into the chair and sighed. He looked at his desk on which sat his putter. It was like no other golf club ever made. The head was a solid piece of jade. The shaft was gold plated. Next to it was a dozen of his personalized Callaway Tour golf balls and a bag of eighteen wooden tees.

He had been over the course in person several times and in his mind hundreds of times. He knew which holes to go for it on and which to play it safe for par. He wasn't a gambler on the course, but he had every shot planned in his head. If all went as planned he would shoot five under par for a total of sixty-seven. Of course, there was always the possibility he might sink some long putts he hadn't planned on, place a few approach shots close enough to the pin for a tap in birdie, but a sixty-seven would win the tournament.

His only major competition, Joe Caulkin, had carelessly injured himself and was out of the running. He could taste the victory. It would be so easy. No one else was in his league.

He stood and placed his golf shoes carefully into a gym bag. On the desk beside the golf balls was the enlarged course layout he had obtained from a scorecard. Every shot was clearly marked. Tee shots in blue, fairway shots in green, and putts in red. Every club was noted. He had a printout of the National Weather Department Forecast. Low winds, 5-10 mph from the southwest, temperatures in the high sixties to low seventies. A beautiful fall day.

To celebrate he planned on taking his fiancé, Cecily, to dinner at the Palmer House. She never attended his tournaments. He was quite sure she would be terribly bored with it and she had promised to help out with the rummage sale at her church.

He picked up his putter and carefully wiped a few fingerprints from the shaft with cheesecloth before sliding it into the velvet case Cecily had fashioned for him. He fastened the studs over the head and slid it gently into the center of his golf bag. Next the balls and tees went into their own compartment.

Andrew smiled to himself. Very few things he could think of required such attention to details and reliance on everything going perfectly as golf. That was why he loved it. Today would be a perfect day.

4

Jake Fischer fumbled for the crumpled pack of Camels on his nightstand. In the process he knocked off the nearly empty gin bottle spilling some of the remaining liquor on bedroom's gold, shag carpeting. He looked at the bottle and the wet stain next to it. Well, it wouldn't be the last stain in his life, he thought.

He shook the pack, encouraging one of the remaining cigarettes to pop out the opening torn into a corner of the top. Once enough of it was protruding he put the cigarette up to his lips and sleepily pulled it out. He could almost feel the cool drag of smoke that would soon bring reality back into his senses.

A little more fumbling on the nightstand retrieved a book of matches. As he opened them he noticed they were strangely soggy. He had a vision of them falling into the toilet the night before as well as the remembrance of his scheme to dry them out overnight.

With little hope he pulled one limp, gray-headed cardboard match out and dragged it along the lighting strip. The head crumbled off without even a sulfurous smelling spark.

He let the cigarette drop from his mouth onto the floor along with the gin bottle.

"Alright," he conceded to no one in particular, "I'll quit."

He pulled himself up with a groan as much as with his muscles. A tear in his dirty t-shirt revealed a portion of his potbelly. He noted that he had slept in his pants and was still wearing his socks. He barely remembered Gina helping to pull off his shoes. How had he let himself get so drunk last night? They were supposed to be celebrating her birthday and he had promised himself to go easy on the booze. Obviously he had broken one more promise to himself and to Gina.

She had known him when his life made more sense. Jake had been there for her when she was recovering from an attack by a mugger that nearly claimed her life and he knew she felt an obligation to help him as he struggled with his own life altering tragedy. He wondered how much longer she would hang around, waiting for him to get things back together. Whereas Gina's injuries affected her mentally and physically, Jake's were purely psychological. At times he hoped she would leave him. With the last remnant of his former life gone, nothing would stop him from sliding completely into his own self-destruction. Maybe Gina knew that.

A year ago things were quite different. Jake was on top of the world. His career was taking off and he was even considering proposing to Gina.

Jake was a sports agent. He wasn't quite a Jerry Maguire. He didn't set up Tiger Woods with Nike or Michael Jordan with Gatorade. He worked with a smaller scale of athlete. He was able to find unknown sports figures and find an endorsement that fit them to a tee.

He connected Al Gregory, a beach volleyball star, with an LA laser eye surgery clinic. The result, a 300% increase in surgery appointments in one week from two five hundred dollar a month billboards on Venice beach, tripling the money Al had been taking home on the volleyball circuit.

Then there was Mona Dirk, the bowler. Not an attractive woman, but she allowed a local Duluth, Minnesota microbrewery, Lewis Grand Brewery, to enter the bowling alley bar market with their brands. The deal effectively quadrupled overall sales within three months, forcing the brewery to double their production facilities and making Mona the Lewis Grand Brewery savior.

For the last year he hadn't signed a single new client. He hadn't really tried. He'd even let his top existing clients jump to other agents as his apathy worried them enough to sever their ties. The agency he worked for, Frasier and Frakes, would have fired him long ago if his friend and boss, Jonathan Jones, hadn't convinced them to give him time to recover from the Finley account. When Jake's savings had run out and his commissions had dried up, Jonathan had advanced him some cash, enough to keep up his rent and also his drinking. But Jake knew that wouldn't last much longer. Jonathan was a good friend, but he couldn't keep risking his career in the hopes Jake would get back to where he was.

It had been a long year, but not long enough to cleanse the guilt Jake held on to. He had found a skateboarding phenom named Brad Finley, a high school senior, who was Jake's ticket to bigger and better things. When a photo shoot for a Nike ad ended up with the teenager paralyzed from the waist down, Jake blamed himself. Brad's parents blamed him too and their lawsuit against Nike was like a nail in Jake's coffin.

The ringing phone shattered his head like a piece of glass. He snapped out of his self-destructive reminiscence and checked to see if the answering machine was on then remembered he had broken that a week earlier when a spilled can of beer had shorted it out.

He fell back on the bed and pulled a pillow tight over his head. The muffled sound persisted. He counted twenty rings before starting to think that maybe someone was really interested in getting through to him.

He sat up and took one more shot at shaking the cobwebs out of his brain. He took a deep breath and let it out as he picked up the phone. "Fischer," he answered.

"Thought you were dead, Jake," said the voice on the other end.

"I'll get back to you on that," he answered recognizing Jonathan Jones' voice on the other end.

"Well I hope you're not because I have something for you."

Jake sat up a little straighter. "Something?"

"Jake I need to know you can get back in the game. It's been a year, buddy, you have to do something."

"I don't know," answered Jake. He was sure Jonathan didn't want to hear that but he wanted to be truthful with his friend.

"It's right up your alley. Frakes has a big client interested looking to find a different face to sell their product. They feel that having an overpaid professional isn't appealing as well to the masses as they'd like. They want an unknown. A rising star who will get rich and famous because he uses their product."

"Who are we talking about?" asked Jake in confusion.

"The client or the athlete?"

"Either."

"The client is Callaway."

"The golf guys Callaway?" asked Jake.

"The golf guys Callaway," answered Jonathan. "They are looking for Cinderella."

"I don't suppose you have a glass slipper?"

"Andrew Patterson."

"Who?"

"Exactly. He's the top rated amateur golfer in Northern Illinois, perhaps the whole state. He took up the sport two years ago and has won every tournament he's played in. Suppose to be a real character as well."

"So Callaway wants him?"

"He's playing in the Northern Illinois Amateur Regional Amateur Golf Tournament. The winner gets to play in the next Pro-Am. You sign him up and we ride him to a $500,000 contract when and if he turns pro."

"If?"

"He will. He's been shooting towards this goal for two years, perfecting his game, advancing in the rankings."

"No one's thought to sign him yet?"

"No one but us knows Callaway is looking to go this direction."

"Sounds too easy," commented Jake.

"I need to know I can count on you. I spent an hour convincing Frakes you were the guy to do it. That it would snap you out your slump. Believe or not, he still remembers the Jake Fischer from a year ago and is willing to give you a shot at it."

"When is the tournament?"

"That's the thing. It starts in an hour. I tried calling last night and your machine isn't picking up. Anyway, it's at the George W. Dunne National Golf Course."

"An hour?"

"Yeah. It's down in Oak Forest so you need to get moving. There will be credentials for you at the starters table." Jonathan paused for a moment. "Jake, I got to ask," Jonathan started.

"I know. And I am all right now but a few hours ago it would have been questionable."

"Please do this Jake. It may be your last chance."

Jake felt a spark of determination ignite in him. If he could do this, he'd no longer be disappointing Jonathan and Gina. Two people who loved him dearly and whom he loved as well. Screwing up might be the last straw for Gina. And that would be the last straw for him. He kindled the spark and let a small flame begin to warm his resolve.

"I'll be there Jonathan." He started to hang up the phone but quickly put it back to his ear, "Jonathan?"

"Yeah, buddy."

"Thanks."

"Nice to have you back."

"Nice to be back."

CHAPTER 2 – DRIVING RANGE

5

"Where the blazes is my camera man?" shouted Jason Bernard. His voice echoed through the parking garage of the USA Sports Channels Chicago offices. He had parked his green convertible near the row of white Ford E-150 vans that were used for remote taping and sometimes live broadcasts. He had phoned Ed Furley at dispatch from his cell phone on his way in and was expecting to have the van already warmed up. All he saw was a girl with a long red ponytail sitting on the bumper of a blue Honda Accord wearing a black leather jacket.

He pulled out his cell phone and cursed the "no signal" message flashing on the display.

"You Jason Bernard?" asked the girl.

"Who are you?" he answered holding back none of his frustration.

"Ellen Burke. Call me Ellie. I'm your cameraman."

"You?" blurted Jason with disbelief.

"Yeah. You want to drive?" she asked launching from the bumper of the Honda towards one of the camera vans.

"Drive? I don't even know where the place is."

"You never played Georgie 'Done Me Wrong?'"

"What?"

"The Golf Course. The NIAGA tournament. Right? It's at George Dunne."

"I don't golf," answered Jason as he headed for the passenger side door.

Ellie stopped in her tracks. "You don't golf? What kind of sportscaster are you."

"The unlucky kind, apparently," Jason muttered halfway under his breath.

"I can't believe you don't golf. Everybody golfs nowadays."

"Do you golf?"

"You bet. I'm not that good but I still have a fun time. I love to watch tournaments. This is the first time I ever covered one. Should be a blast. This guy Andrew Patterson is supposed to be a great golfer, destined for the PGA tour. And he's a heck of a character."

"Just what I need, a golfer with an attitude."

"Shouldn't you be interested in all sports?" asked Ellie as she pushed the unlock control on her remote key chain for the van.

Jason opened his door, brushed some crumbs from his seat, slid in and answered, "I am interested in all legitimate sports."

"You have to be a real athlete to be good in this game," argued Ellie.

"I haven't seen so many pot bellies in one place since the I stopped by the White Sox dugout last year."

"I dare you to put a fist in Tiger Wood's belly," she countered.

"I just don't see the excitement in it," added Jason.

"Well, when I play I find a challenge with every shot. And when I make that one great shot of the round that I never thought I had in me, I know I'll be back next week to try it again." She started the van and began to back up.

"Maybe we can skip the end. Get some tape on a few holes, a few comments from Patterson and do some editing back at the studio. Hey, we could be done in time for lunch rather than dragging this out all day." Jason figured that would be enough effort to expend on this assignment. And getting home early would win him back some points with Sally.

"We might miss something exciting," argued Ellie.

"Somehow, I seriously doubt that," answered Jason.

"Here I thought I lucked out by pulling this assignment."

"Listen, Ellie. I should be covering the Marathon. No one is going to care about some regional amateur golf championship in Chicago. This spot will be the first to be cut if something more interesting comes along. We'll get some tape of this Patterson guy do a quick interview with him and voila we're done. Okay?"

"Geez, what a grouch."

"Just work the camera, Ellie. I'll decide what we shoot."

"Okay, Mr. Bernard. I just think..."

"Ah, ah, ah," warned Jason, not wanting to hear any suggestions that might ruin his plan for the day. "See if you can get any information on the radio about the Marathon, would you?"

6

"You have to even out your brain," said the voice behind him.

Scott sighed and relaxed his grip on the club. He had been warming up at the driving range and just couldn't seem to find his perfect swing. He was hitting good shots but he knew he could do better. He turned to see who was offering up the advice.

An elderly man, still in pretty good physical shape was leaning against the wall of the pro shop. He wore a maroon cardigan sweater over a knit golf shirt. A few strands of thinning gray hair sprayed out from the edges of a baseball cap emblazoned with the Northern Illinois Amateur Golf Association logo. "You're thinking too much with one side of your brain. You're analyzing yourself too much and concentrating on the details rather than how the whole swing should feel."

"How do I stop doing that?"

"Come here," he motioned. Scott stepped over and shrugged. "Untie your left shoe."

"What?"

"Untie it."

Scott was confused but he thought he'd humor the guy for a little while. He leaned his driver against the club stand and untied the soft spike golf shoe on his left foot.

"Good, now tie it again."

"What is this, some sort of philosophical lesson in life?"

"No, I want to demonstrate something," answered the man. "When you tie it cinch down the laces nice and tight. Make it noticeably uncomfortable, almost painful if you can."

Scott tilted his head with a confused expression but resigned himself to following the instructions. He pulled on the laces until he could feel the sides of the shoe squeezing his foot and the laces biting across the top. He finished with a nice bow and stood up.

The man walked over to Scott's bucket and pulled out one of the stripped range balls. He placed it on the rubber practice tee then handed Scott his club. "What's the farthest you ever hit a drive?"

"A few inches over a three hundred yards," answered Scott, honestly. No Tiger Woods but not bad for an amateur.

"Do you remember what it felt like? I don't mean the swing, but the sound of the ball hitting the club face perfectly, then the ball taking off from the tee and slowly rising into the air, almost as if it had helium in it and would never come down."

Scott chuckled. That was exactly what it had looked like. "Yeah, I do."

"Don't think about the swing, just the ball floating off the face of the earth." He stepped back, out of the range of Scott's back swing. "Go ahead."

What the heck, thought Scott. Nothing else was working. He set up his stance standing about a yard from the ball. He gripped the end of the club with his left hand then wrapped his right hand around the shaft right below it, his right pinky overlapping the left index finger. His thumbs pointed down the top of the shaft to the head of the driver. He lined up his feet and laid the club head on the mat. He rocked on his heels setting his balance and letting his hands drop to a comfortable position in front of him. The picture of his ball lifting with an upward trajectory as it sailed out past the fence at the end of the range filled his mind. He wiggled his left shoe a little, trying to adjust to the unusual tightness. He started his back swing then paused a fraction of a second before bringing the club around to meet the ball. He heard the precious "plink" as contact was made and he let the club swing over his left shoulder as his eyes watched his ball sail with perfection.

It rose and rose and rose.

Scott stood mouth gaping open as it landed by the 275 yard flag and continued to roll up to the fence at 300 yards. Range balls typically took 20 yards off a good drive. If he had been hitting one of his Pinnacles it might have made it 320 yards or more.

"Now what was the last thing you remember before you swung?" asked the man.

"My stupid tight shoe."

"Not the mechanics of your swing? Not where your club should be or keeping you arm straight or remembering to bend your wrists?"

"No. My stupid shoe. Where the heck did that shot come from?"

"You stopped overpowering the right side of your brain with details and gave yourself over to the left half and let your natural ability take over. I can get almost anyone to swing like that, Although I must admit it usually takes then ten or twenty tries. You nailed it the first time around."

"So I just need to keep my left shoe tight?"

"No, that's just a way to interrupt your normal brain sequence. Once you feel it, it can come again very easily. Try again."

Scott placed another ball on the tee. Without a second thought he started his back swing and watched a second ball follow almost the same trajectory as the last. He turned around grinning. "Who are you?"

"Oh, sorry," apologized the elderly man, "Ted Lange. The tournament hired me to help out anyone who might need a quick lesson at the driving range." He extended his right hand and Scott shook it.

"Scott Hanover."

"I know. I saw you play two weeks ago at Indian Boundary. That shot on the last hole was amazing. You knew you nailed that fifty-foot putt as soon as you hit the ball."

"It was a lucky shot."

"Perhaps," answered Ted, "But luck isn't a bad thing."

"I suppose not. So, Ted, you're helping everyone hit like that?"

"No. Most people are too set in their ways, especially at this level, to want to make any changes."

"Well, I'm not at this level."

"You're close."

"You were at that tournament. I only made second because of a disqualification. I'm only here today because some guy broke his wrist. I'm a real fish out of water around here. I just hope I don't embarrass myself around these other guys today."

"You know what really separates them from you, Scott?"

"Three thousand dollars in golf equipment?"

"Well there is that," laughed Ted. "But it's how you approach the game. You're not here to keep from embarrassing yourself, but to have a fun time. If you don't do well you go home, look forward to the next time you go out and maybe do a little better. You play against yourself."

Ted leaned a little closer to finish his thought, "To most of these guys this is a make or break tournament. A chance to play with the pros. If they flub a shot they'll think about it for years. They'll beat themselves up the rest of the game and spiral into a real mess."

"I can do that without the pressure of a tournament," joked Scott.

"I suppose you can," laughed Ted. "But those guys let the game play them, rather than playing the game. It's become a job to them. They've stopped loving it. You still love to be out there no matter how well you play."

"Still, I don't really have a shot. Most of these guys shoot well under par."

"Not all of the time," corrected Ted. "I bet if you took their top 18 worst holes over the last year they'd be shooting 120 something."

Scott laughed. "Yeah, I suppose."

"Tell me, Scott, have you ever had a birdie?"

"Yeah lot's of times."

"More than eighteen?"

"I hope so."

"Ever make an eagle?"

"Once. Nailed a chip shot on a par five once."

"Okay, we take your best holes and put them together, you can shoot a fifty-three."

Scott laughed heartily at the possibility. "You have me there, Ted."

"You said you had a lucky putt two weeks ago. Imagine if you put together fifty some lucky shots in a row."

"That's be like rolling a snake eyes fifty times in a row. The odds against it are astronomical."

"But the chances aren't zero." Ted started another tack, "You know about the bell curve?"

"Sure."

"Well, if you plot out all of you scores they would group around your average, most clustered in the middle but a few high scores and low scores spread out at the edges, fewer the farther you get from your average."

"Right."

"Well, statisticians can calculate the percentage of scores that will happen at any particular point. Heck there's even a small chance someone could score a thirty-six on any particular course. What I'm trying to say is that if you play long enough you're bound to put together a real good game at some point, just like you have real lousy games occasionally."

"I don't think I've played long enough," added Scott.

"Just like rolling fifty snake eyes in a row with the dice. The odds that you do it the first time out are the same as at the millionth time."

"So today could be my day to shoot a thirty-six."

Now Ted laughed. "Maybe. But just imagine having eighteen of your best holes. An eagle. Maybe a few pars. Heck even with a bogey or two you would be more than competitive with these guys."

"That'd be nice."

"All I'm saying is that it's possible. Just keep your brain even and have fun."

"That I can do, Ted. I must say it's been very nice to meet you. You've taken the edge off today for me. I think I will have a good time."

Ted shook Scott's hand firmly again. Looking down at Scott's left foot he said, "Better loosen that lace up before you lose circulation."

Scott chuckled again.

"Oh, and Scott, have a really good day."

"I will," said Scott. He replayed his last two drives in his head and thought to himself again, I will.

7

"Sorry I'm late," shouted Paul Bauer as he came jogging up the driving range. He clapped a friendly hand onto Scott's shoulder. Even after the jog Paul wasn't out of breath. His brown hair was cropped to its usual buzz cut, his beard and mustache trimmed to a neat van Dyke. "Hey, I just saw some guy nail a drive all the way to the fence,"

"That was me," said Scott.

Paul froze in his tracks. "You're kidding."

Rather than answering Scott placed a ball on the tee and whacked it with confidence. It sailed almost as far as his first drive with Ted's instruction. He turned back to find Paul staring with his jaw hanging open. "I've been able to knock out at least half of them that far, none shorter than 250 yards and that's with these cruddy range balls. I still don't have full control of the direction but hey, on the drive I don't have to be that accurate."

"What did you do, sell your soul?"

"That guy over there gave me a quick lesson." Scott pointed to Ted Lange who was now giving pointers to another golfer on the range.

"That's Ted Lange," said Paul.

"You know him?"

"He was on the senior tour a while back. I saw him at the local tournament two weeks ago when you sank that putt. I heard he hurt his back a while ago and had to quit the tour."

"Nice guy," commented Scott.

"So what exactly did he tell you?"

"To tie my shoe," laughed Scott.

He explained the whole encounter to Paul and how he had spent the last ten minutes practicing his drive with the new mental technique. It was starting to get grooved into his swing. If only he had figured it out a month ago he'd feel a lot better.

"Well, you're going to be up soon. You're in the first threesome to go off."

"You mean I placed that low in the standings."

"Sixtieth out of sixty is as low as you can get, Scott."

Tournaments that did not use a shotgun start usually had the poorest players first so the real battles for the title would be played out later in the day.

"Who am I golfing with?" asked Scott.

"Jerry Spaulding and Pete Baldwin. I don't know either of them but they both have single digit handicaps." Paul was close to being in that league. If he hadn't blown a hole in his own local tournament, Scott might be caddying for him. Thankfully Paul seemed to not harbor any ill will concerning the twist of fate. He was pulling for Scott and was impressed by the drives he was seeing now.

Paul Bauer had been a fairly good athlete during high school and college. Baseball. Bowling. Golf. Even a little bicycle racing. He had a natural ability pick up a sport and become good at it, sometimes really good. The two had been friends since grade school and made an effort to get together on weekends for a round whenever they could. Since Paul's two kids had started school he had been out golfing more but prior to that he was not out all that often.

Scott knew a similar fate faced him once his first child was born in a couple of weeks. He really hoped to take home some good memories and hopefully not finish dead last as his handicap predicted.

Scott unfastened the Velcro on the glove from his left hand and handed his driver to Paul. Paul smiled and took it. His job as caddy had just officially started. Unofficially, he had taken some time last week to walk the course, checking out the fairways and greens. Measuring some distances and making a few notes to help them along.

Paul stopped as they exited the practice area and set Scott's golf bag down. "I have something for you," he said as he pulled a black golf glove and a pack of green tees from his pocket and handed them to Scott. "I had hoped 'Zorro' would be able to make an appearance in the tournament today, but maybe you'll do me the honor of using these."

"Zorro" was Scott's nickname for Paul when he was on a particular hot streak on the course due to the black golf glove he always wore. The green tees were another part of his signature golf equipment.

Paul preferred the color green as a psychological ploy to help his game. The ploy, however, was aimed at his golf ball, not him. He believed that if a ball was sitting on a green tee it would think it was just sitting on the grass and wouldn't be worried that a club head was about to smash into it at over a hundred miles an hour, squashing it flat like a pancake and then allowing it to explode from its face with a burst of energy.

"I also had a few of these made up," added Paul. He pulled a sleeve of golf balls from his other pocket and handed them to Scott. Scott looked a little confused. "Open the box, stupid," instructed his friend.

Scott laughed when he saw what Paul had done. Each of the balls was imprinted with a custom logo. A large yellow rubber duck with an orange beak, orange webbed feet and silly grin was stamped over the Pinnacle logo. "Duck" was Paul's nickname for Scott because he usually found himself hitting balls into the water. "Quack, quack." Uttered Scott with a laugh. "I got three more sleeves in the car. That should hold you for eighteen - I hope."

Scott put his right arm over Paul's shoulder as they headed for the starter's table. If nothing else it would be a fun day.

8

Jake pulled into the parking lot of the George W. Dunne National Golf Course next to a USA Sports camera van. Must be a bigger deal than he thought if they were going to be covering the tournament. Couldn't hurt to have some tape of Patterson running on the ten o'clock news to run up the golfer's stock a little.

His Geo Metro sputtered into the space and died before he had a chance to shut if off. A new car would be first on his list of priorities after he received his commission. He'd be able to pay off all of his debts. Start things over. Make up a lot to Gina.

He stared at the steering wheel for a good long time, considering doubling back to the liquor store on 159th street for a six-pack of Budweiser. He knew he could function well on a couple of beers and it would sure help take the edge off today. He was beginning to feel some doubts. His earlier confidence was sputtering.

He slumped back in his seat, his fingers tightly grasped around the steering wheel. He glanced at the rear view mirror and adjusted it to reveal his reflection. Three Advil had reduced most of the pounding in his brain to a dull throb but his face still showed the effects of a year of abuse.

He hadn't been able to find a totally clean set of clothes and settled for the least stained, least wrinkled shirt on his bedroom floor. He chose a wide tie to cover some of the spots and a tweed sports coat to cover the rest. His brown slacks also needed a good laundering but he settled for letting them steam while he took his shower.

Gray hairs has started to salt his head and his hairline had given up nearly an inch to his forehead in the last year. He needed a haircut. Maybe even a teeth whitening. Time for those things later.

He took a deep breath and found himself staring at a corner of a white card or something sticking out from above the passenger side visor. He reached over for it and pulled it out. It was a photograph, a picture of him and Brad Finley in London, taken right before the accident. Brad was giving the thumbs up with his left hand and had his right hanging over Jake's shoulder.

Why had he put that photo there? He didn't remember doing it. He found himself wondering what had happened to Brad. He hadn't heard anything from Brad or his family after the accident and had made no effort to find out himself. Brad Finley had put his life in Jake's hands and Jake had failed him, not only as an agent, but also as a friend. As sobriety dusted away the cobwebs of his brain, his shortcomings came back to the forefront and he began to realize what an utter jerk he had become over the last year. Even he didn't like himself all that much anymore.

The thought of drinking a beer suddenly became revolting to him. Whatever his reasons for putting the picture there in the first place, its effect had been to put his life in perspective. He was getting a second chance today. Hopefully it would start a string of second chances.

He opened the door, stepped out of the car, and took a breath of air. Twelve hours without a cigarette. The longest he had gone in fifteen years. Already he could smell things that had until now been buried deep in his memory. The fresh cut grass of the golf course was the first thing he noticed. The pull of the hot coffee brewing at the starter's table was next. A cup of coffee would certainly help shake the morning dew off his brain.

He glanced towards the practice range to his right. Although he couldn't see who hit it, a shot sailed to twenty yards from the far fence and bounced up to a stop next to it. Jake wasn't a golfer but he knew the game and he knew that was a decent drive. He hoped to see whoever hit it playing on the course. Maybe it was even Andrew Patterson.

9

"Name," asked the man staring at a clipboard at the starter's table as Andrew Patterson stepped up to sign in. The man wore a red-jacket with the Northern Illinois Amateur Golf Association patch stitched on the left breast pocket. A plastic laminated name tag was pinned to the lapel.

"Patterson," said Andrew.

The man scanned his roster list and at the end found Andrew's name and made a heavy X next to it. "You're in the last group. You tee off in about two..." He stopped in mid-sentence as he looked up to hand Andrew his player's envelope. He gathered himself after digesting Andrew's appearance and continued. "...hours." He held up the clipboard for Andrew. "Sign here," he instructed.

Andrew was unphased by the stares he was receiving. His outfit was acceptable golfing attire, if perhaps a century out of style, but he liked it and that was all that mattered. He signed in, smiled and walked away. A few chuckles and whispered comments followed him.

In the envelope he found a paper number for his caddy, Eric Peters, to pin to his back as they traversed the course today. Eric had caddied for Andrew before and had adequately met Andrew's needs. Mainly someone to carry his bag and stay quiet. He glanced around to see if Eric had arrived yet.

A smile creased his lips as he noticed familiar figure nearby. Standing fifty feet away with his left arm in a cast held up by a blue sling was Joe Caulkin. The broken arm was the reason why Andrew was so confident this tournament was his to win.

Joe shook his head when he saw Patterson approaching. Undoubtedly the man was coming over to express his insincere condolences for Joe's misfortune. Joe was thirty-five years old. He was physically fit, six foot and a hundred and ninety pounds. His blonde hair curled loosely around his head and his bright blue eyes almost matched the fall sky.

He had taken a sabbatical from his job as a Physical Education instructor at Northeastern University to work on his golf game. He hoped to someday go pro, perhaps not until he was eligible for the senior circuit, but he wanted a taste of the big time. His accident couldn't have come at a worse time. He knew the second the log fell on his wrist that the bone had broken. He had broken the same wrist in high school and he remembered the feeling and the pain.

"Tough break," joked Andrew.

"Lucky break for you," answered Joe.

"Well, your time will come, Joe," said Andrew, a smirk in his voice.

"You know you don't necessarily have this won yet, Andrew. Anything can happen. Ask David Duvall sitting in a sand trap on seventeen for five shots."

"I always play it safe. That's why I win, Joe. In fact, if you want to take the field against me in a little wager, I wouldn't be opposed to a little friendly action."

"The whole field?" asked Joe.

"Why not. I'll have it in the bag by fifteen no matter what."

"Shall we say a thousand dollars?" asked Joe.

"Why not five?" retorted Andrew.

"I thought you wanted to keep it friendly?"

"If you're too afraid..." said Andrew.

"You know you're a jerk Patterson."

"I can live with that," he answered.

"You may have the technical aspect of the game mastered but there is more to this game than hitting a ball with precision. You haven't learned that part yet. These other guys may not be as skillful as you but they have the heart to be a winner and sometimes that's all it takes." He reached out his right hand to seal the deal. "Five thousand it is."

Andrew took Joe's good hand and shook, trying not to grimace at Joe's vice-like grip.

"Just bring your checkbook to the clubhouse after the eighteenth," said Andrew. He glanced towards the clubhouse and spotted his quarry that had been his aim before Caulkin distracted him. A medium height, blonde-haired boy was staring out over the first hole, his hands in his pockets as he took in the view. "Eric," shouted Andrew Patterson as he stomped over to his waiting caddy.

10

Joe chuckled and flexed the fingers of his left hand. There was hardly any pain now. The doctor said the fracture was non-displaced and Joe had begged for a removable splint so he could still try to play. His wife had joined the orthopedist in convincing him that another day and another tournament awaited him. Today he would hope that pompous jerk Patterson would get a taste of the muse.

The muse was Joe's name for the fickle golf god that afflicted his life. Perhaps goddess was a more accurate term for no one other than a woman could tease a golfer so much. A sudden gust of wind here and chipmunk hole there could destroy an otherwise perfect shot. Of course it worked both ways. A poorly hit chip shot could strike the pin and fall into the hole with an awe-inspiring perfection. A drive slicing into the woods could bounce off a tree and land smack in the middle of the fairway with a clear shot to the green.

Andrew Patterson was technically one of the best golfers Joe had seen in a while, but he seemed to lack any humility. Joe had played against Patterson twice and lost both times. Patterson seemed intolerant of other people's mistakes and never seemed to make mistakes himself. Joe was hoping for the muse to intervene today. He had five thousand dollars riding on her.

"Is it bad?" asked a female voice from his left. Joe turned to see a smiling, red-haired girl with a video camera riding on her right shoulder.

"Is what bad?"

"Your wrist."

"Oh, that," realized Joe.

"You're Joe Caulkin, right?"

"Yeah."

"We're," she gestured to a well-groomed man with a sports coat and tie a couple yards behind her, "here to cover the tournament. Anything to say about the game today."

"Sure," he answered. Ellie introduced herself and Jason. Jason shook his hand and smiled, saying nothing. "He's a little crabby," commented Ellie. She turned to Jason. "Do you want to ask Joe some questions? He was supposed to be in the tournament today."

"What for?" asked Jason.

"Background? Color? Human interest?" she suggested. "Fine, I'll do it."

"Whatever," said Jason.

She handed Joe a small microphone that was attached by long cord to her camera. He clipped it to his jacket. She hefted the camera up so she was looking in the eyepiece and smiled.

"Tell me, Joe, who do you think is going to win today?" she asked first. Jason shook his head. What a waste of time.

"Well," started Joe, "Andrew Patterson is favored by many since I won't be swinging any clubs today, but all these guys are top amateurs. They wouldn't be this far if they weren't."

"So you think Patterson can do it?"

"Well, someone is going to have to have a pretty good day to beat him, or he's going to have to run into some bad luck."

"I guess anything's possible," she added.

"You bet. For example, the guy taking my spot is playing today not only because of my clumsiness," he explained, lifting his cast for emphasis, "but because he put together a pretty good game and the second place finisher was disqualified. All it takes is a twist of fate for the unexpected to happen."

"Who is taking your place?"

"Scott Hanover."

"So you think he can beat Patterson."

Joe laughed. "That would be a miracle. I checked the standings and it seems that he's ranked last out of the golfers playing today."

"Well, maybe someone else can give Patterson a run for his money."

"That's what I'm hoping," said Joe. Hoping her statement had more meaning than she intended. "Ted Lange might have some ideas who to watch today."

"Ted Lange is here?" she asked letting her camera drop.

Jason had to interrupt, "Are you done with this spot?" he asked.

"I'm done, Mr. Bernard," Ellie answered.

"Ted's at the driving range, helping the golfer's work out any last minute problems."

"We should talk to him," suggested Ellie, "He was on the Senior tour. He'd have a good idea whom to watch." She pointed over the practice area. "The driving range is over there."

Jason looked out across the parking lot to an area fenced on the back and right sides with a line of tall pines on the left. Tiny white balls were sailing from unseen practice mats with an irregular rhythm.

"I'm not walking all the way over there," he complained. "I'll be in the clubhouse up there. Talk to him yourself if you want. I'm going to find myself a cup of coffee."

"What a great idea," agreed Ellie, "I'll take my black, two sugars." Before he could open his mouth to give a sarcastic reply, she was bouncing down the sidewalk to the driving range with the camera and her shoulder bag.

I would have to get a nutty camerawoman he thought.

He decided to get her the coffee. She was after all doing most of the work and he decided it would be to his advantage to keep her happy. If she shot a lot of footage now, maybe she wouldn't complain too much if they left early.

11

Ted was excited to have the pretty red-haired girl set up her camera to interview him. It brought back the old days when he was on tour and those were good times.

"So," started Ellie, "I know Andrew Patterson is the favorite, but who else looks good to win."

"Well on paper, one has to assume Patterson could easily take the win today."

"How about off paper," suggested Ellie.

"Statistically, anyone of these guys has a chance."

"Even Scott Hanover?"

Ted chuckled. "Yeah, even him. How do you know about Mr. Hanover?"

"Joe Caulkin explained that his accident was the reason Hanover was playing today."

"But seriously, Scott Hanover has an advantage that few of these top amateurs can claim."

"What's that?"

"When I saw him play two weeks ago I had the sense that he wasn't on the course to compete against any of the other golfers there that day, but to play against himself. Trying to hit the ball a little straighter and farther with every shot. Happy with the good shots, and determined not to repeat the bad ones. A golfer like that is bound to have a good day every once in a while. He's in a different place than most of these guys. They want to win. He wants to play."

"Interesting assessment, Mr. Lange."

"Call me Ted."

Ellie let down her camera and shook the old golfer's hand. "Thanks for the interview. You going to watch the round?"

"I'll be here until just before the last group tees off so I should see most of the tournament."

27

"Well, have a good day," said Ellie. She turned and started walking back up to the clubhouse. Despite having to work with a sportscaster who seemed to hate golf she was determined to do a thorough job today. One never knew when a bit of tape would come in handy and she brought a lot today. The chill of the morning still seemed to be clinging to the day despite the rising sun. She hoped Jason Bernard had her coffee.

CHAPTER 3 – FIRST HOLE

12

"Attention golfers," announced the voice over the loud speakers. "Would Scott Hanover, Gerald Spaulding, and Peter Baldwin please report to the starter. You will be teeing off in five minutes."

Paul grabbed Scott's Bag and stood up. "This is it. Boy I wish I was teeing off with you."

"I wish I was carrying your bag, you have a better chance against these guys than me," answered Scott

"Ah, there's always next year for me. I'm going to miss golfing with you after Sarah has the baby," lamented Paul. "Is she going to come out to watch?"

"Watch golf?" answered Scott. "She leaves the room whenever I put a PGA tournament on TV. It's a good way to get some time to myself," he laughed.

Scott signed in with the red-jacketed official holding a clipboard and noted he would be teeing off second, after Peter Baldwin, alphabetical by last name. The official was overweight and balding. His head attached to his shoulders without the benefit of a neck and his collar remained open under his red tie.

Paul and Scott walked over to the tee and joined the other two golfers with their caddies. "You must be Scott Hanover," greeted one of the men. He was short, maybe five foot four and had thick dark hair and thick, dark-rimmed glasses. He wore a gray sweatshirt over his golf shirt. His smile made him squint as his lips parted slightly from his oversized teeth. "I'm Pete Baldwin," he introduced himself, "this is Jerry Spaulding."

Scott's grip shifted over to the other man and he almost had his hand wrenched off of his wrist. Jerry was about Scott's height but blonde haired and very athletic. He looked more like a baseball player or even a basketball player and golf was probably a hobby sport for him. His muscles on his arms bulged the knit cuffs on his short-sleeved golf shirt. The chilly morning seemed to have no effect on him.

"This is my friend and caddy, Paul Bauer," Scott introduced.

The handshakes were exchanged again and the official announced quietly to Pete, "You're up."

Pete took his driver from his caddy and pulled a ball and tee from his right side pants pocket, the tee already gripped onto the ball, ready to be pushed into the grass in the tee box. Scott and Jerry took up their position to Pete's right and Scott took a look down the first fairway.

It was the first of four par five holes and relatively straight and hazard free until you reached the green where two sand traps guarded each side. Along the fairway there was little danger of ending up in the woods on either side for the first three hundred yards, but then the trees closed in, coming into play on the second and third shot.

Jerry took a couple of practice swings then stepped up to address the ball. Scott remembered the old Honeymooner's episode when Ed Norton was trying to teach Ralph golf and when addressing the ball tipped his hat sincerely at it and said, "hello, ball." He chuckled to himself quietly, trying not to disturb Pete's concentration.

Pete had a pretty short back swing and as soon as he hit the ball his squinty face dropped into a frown. The ball had sliced, veering to the right of the fairway into the taller cut grass of the rough and rolled behind an eight-foot pine tree. Scott said nothing as they passed each other exchanging positions. What could he say? He hoped his shot wasn't as bad as that. At least Pete hadn't lost it in the trees.

Scott pushed his tee into the ground and placed his ball on it, measuring the distance to the ground by the thickness of his knuckles. That gave him his perfect tee height when he used his driver. The ground was soft and yielding, probably watered the night before in preparation for today. This course was the nicest of all the Cook County public courses and it showed in its maintenance.

He rotated the ball on the tee so that he was looking square at the yellow rubber duck Paul had had printed on the ball. He smiled at it and looked at Paul. "Go Duck," Paul said.

He stepped back and used his driver to mark an invisible line through the air from the flag on the green to a position three feet behind his ball. He would position his feet parallel to that line to set up his aim. It didn't always insure a straight shot, but he had learned long ago not to trust his ability to walk right up to the ball and place his stance. More often than not his toes formed a line that led far left of where he wanted to aim. His ritual drew a confused look from Jerry and Pete but he was determined not to let them intimidate him. They were better golfers so he wanted to make sure he had taken every step to guarantee he had a good game.

Scott stepped up to his imaginary line and looked down at the ball again. He set his left foot just to the left of the ball, his right foot a shoulder's width away. As he tilted his head back to stretch his neck he noticed a girl with a red ponytail about fifteen yards away on the cart path leading down the fairway. She had a large camera hoisted on her shoulder and appeared to be taping him. Perhaps she just wanted to make sure she had a good angle for when the top-ranked players made their start in an hour and a half or two.

Scott took a deep breath and his love for this often-frustrating game was invigorated by the fall scents. For some reason he was taken back to his first golf swing on a course while he was home on summer break from college. He played a little nine-hole course with his brother and Paul. It was just after sunrise and the grass was still damp with dew and it was chilly. Sunlight was starting to warm the distant green, burning off the morning fog, and the starter gave them the go ahead to begin their round. Paul and his brother Rob had been golfing for years and Scott wanted to take it up to spend more time with them. When they had informed him they would be arriving at the golf course at five thirty in the morning he almost decided to sleep in.

He had carried a two-dollar golf bag filled with an odd assortment of one-dollar clubs Rob had picked over from flea markets. The ball was one that had been reclaimed from the woods but still appeared in good shape. The tee was brand new, bought in a pack of twenty from the golf course coffee shop for fifty cents. The round of golf cost four dollars.

As he stood on the tee he took a few practice swings, the club head never quite covering the same patch of grass twice but he figured that was as good as it would get and stepped up to the ball. When he swung the head of the club caught the edge of the ball which popped it off forty-five degrees to the right disappearing in the woods.

"Mulligan," Paul had offered as he tossed him another ball. Mulligans were free shots handed out in casual games to prevent an embarrassing start.

Scott topped the second shot but it managed to go straight about fifty yards.

Thus began an affliction that would get him out of bed at five in the morning most weekends that summer.

His mind returned to the tee. He had no idea how long he had just drifted away. No one seemed to be hurrying him and any tension he may have had was gone. No Mulligans today, he told himself.

His body seemed to pull his club back almost involuntarily. His head remained frozen in position, staring at the yellow duck. As he reached the top of his back swing he knew he had the shot nailed. He brought the club back around and the ball went sailing, his eyes reflexively following its path. The ping of the club head echoed once from the trees. Scott held his driver dangling over his left shoulder, watching the ball, too afraid to take his eyes off it for fear it would drop and he would lose it. The golfers and caddies clapped, impressed as they watched the ball land precisely in the middle of the fairway, bounce a few times then roll to a stop.

"Nice one," commented Paul. Scott pulled his club off his shoulder keeping his eyes on the ball. Paul took it from his hand. He turned and saw the red-haired camerawoman staring with disbelief at the shot. Her camera was pointing slightly down but he thought maybe she had taped the ball sailing out.

"I'd say three hundred and ten yards," whispered Paul as he slid the club into its slot in Scott's bag.

"Whew," muttered Jerry Spaulding. His head was nodding from side to side. He slipped his tee into the ground near where Scott had shot. Without much fanfare he set up his shot, waggled the club in his hands for a second or two, and almost too quickly to see, drew it back and slapped the ball down the right side of the fairway almost as far as Scott's. "First time I've been out driven in a while," he commented to Scott as he handed his club to his caddy.

"Lucky shot," was Scott's answer.

Jerry looked back down the fairway and smiled. "I'll take lucky over good any day." Scott and Paul laughed at the saying. They had exchanged the same sentiment with each other many times.

Jerry patted Scott on the shoulder and the three golfers and their caddies started walking down the dewy fairway. The loud speaker from the clubhouse announced the next group starting. A few spectators wandered along behind them, staying to the path cart. The camerawoman picked up a Styrofoam cup of coffee from the ground next to her and sipped it as she followed the fans along. She looked back once to the clubhouse but shrugged her shoulders and walked on.

Ellie had returned to the clubhouse earlier and was surprised to find Jason Bernard waiting for her with a cup of coffee. When she suggested she go out and get some footage of the early golfers he agreed eagerly. She was sure he wanted her out his hair and it looked like she was going to do all the work today. She shrugged it off and went out to the first tee. Scott Hanover's drive was a thing of beauty. She decided she would follow his group, at least for a while.

Paul pulled a club out of the bag and handed it to Scott. It was his seven iron. Scott looked a little confused at Paul. "I can make it to the green with my three wood, Paul," he whispered.

"You can make it to the sand trap, Scott. Get it up to a hundred yards and then close to the pin for a one putt. You got eighteen holes and a great chance to birdie this one."

Scott knew Paul was right. Risky wasn't smart and he needed to play smart today.

The short pine tree blocked Pete's shot to the green. He chipped it out at a forty-five degree angle onto the fairway and ended a few yards behind Scott's ball but slightly in front of Jerry.

Jerry had what looked like a three iron out. He would likely try for the green and probably had the control to do it. Or was he taking a risk after being out driven by Scott?

With the same quickness of his tee shot he powered the ball off the short fairway grass toward the green. After watching his ball for a moment he snarled loudly like an angry lion. The ball bounced then rolled into the sand trap to the left of the green.

Paul was grinning and nodding. That was likely where Scott was headed if he tried for the green in two. Scott was beginning to realize the value of his friend's advice.

Pete looked to also be trying for the green but favored a three wood. His shot took off straight for the pin. Unfortunately, he hit it better than he wanted to. The ball bounced on the back of the green and rolled down a slope out of view. Scott saw a hedge visible over the edge of the green and suspected it may have stopped the ball's continued progress. Pete's grunt signified a similar assessment of his shot.

Scott walked over to his ball took a few practice swings. He knew it probably looked pretty amateurish to Spaulding and Baldwin and he tried not to feel embarrassed. He slid his feet forward a few inches and placed the club head behind the ball. He didn't look at the ball this time but instead at an imaginary ball directly in front of and next to his actual ball. That would help assure his swing would follow a trajectory that would bring the bottom of the blade of his golf club under the ball. His back swing pivoted perfectly around his spine and as he brought the club around his ball was lifted into the air followed by a divot of dark green grass which itself sailed a good fifteen yards. The ball landed, bounced once, and ended up about one hundred yards from the pin. Perfect position for his pitching wedge.

None of the players were on the green yet but Scott felt he was in the best position. On a par five you're expected to take three swings to get on the green and two putts to get it in the hole. If Scott could get his chip shot near the hole and sink the ball with one putt, he'd have a birdie to start out the tournament and an incredible psychological lift.

Paul said nothing as they walked towards Scott's ball. He'd never seen Scott hit two shots in a row so well. He noticed the pony-tailed redhead walking along the cart path on the right side of the fairway. She was getting set to tape Scott's approach shot. The side of her camera had a USA Sports logo decal. He wondered if he and Scott might show up on the 9:00 sports wrap-up. He'd have to ask his daughter, Mary, to set up the VCR. She was the only one in the house who understood how to use the machine.

Paul looked behind them. It seemed like there was more of a crowd around the tee than when they left a few minutes earlier. He pulled the pitching wedge from Scott's bag and handed it to him. "Be the ball," he encouraged, reviving the famous quote from Caddy Shack. He watched as Scott lined up the shot standing behind the ball and drawing his imaginary line. Scott set his feet and took a practice swing.

Paul looked around. Everyone was still, waiting to see what Scott did. The camerawoman was poised and ready to tape Scott's swing. He looked back at Scott who seemed to be in a trance. As his body began the swing Scott seemed almost surprised by what was happening. He stopped short of a full back swing then the club swung down on the back of the ball. A divot flew ten feet ahead but the ball was lofted into a high arc. Paul thought he could see the yellow duck spinning in the air. It was going to hit the green, no question. The pin was near the back of the green and the green itself sloped toward the fairway. Scott's ball landed two yards to the left of the pin, bounced up about a foot leaving a dark dent in the ground and landed another few inches closer to the hole.

"How did you do that?" asked Paul.

Scott stood staring at the green, his mouth hanging open. "I have no idea."

"That's a doable putt, Scott."

"Definitely doable. A gimme almost," Scott added.

"I don't think they'll give it to you," commented Paul. Gimme's were putt's that were so close to the hole it wasn't worth the effort to sink them. They were strictly forbidden in stroke play, especially in a tournament.

"You're probably right. I guess I'll have to use that putter after all."

"Don't want to let it feel left out, Scott," pointed out Paul.

"Not at all," agreed Scott.

The other golfers and caddies had wandered past them, nodding their appreciation of Scott's shot, all secretly wishing they were also on the green. The redhead came up to them. "You're Scott Hanover," she announced.

"Yep," answered Scott. He looked at the logo on the side of her camera. "You're from USA Sports?"

"Ellie Burke," she introduced herself, holding out her hand. Scott shook it.

"Practicing your camera work for the top golfers later on?" asked Paul.

"Yeah, I guess, but you never know when you'll catch something good." She patted her camera. Her shoulders and upper arms were muscular from hauling the equipment around. "You're having a great hole."

"Best one today." They all laughed at the joke.

"I wish I could put together three shots like that," she added.

"Believe me, Ellie," said Scott, "This is not how I usually play."

"Well, you're a lot better than I am. That's why I have this day job, you know."

"If my wife wasn't convinced this was my last round of golf for the foreseeable future, I don't think she'd have let me out today. I should be home trying to figure out how to put that crib together in our nursery."

Ellie looked confused.

"Scott's not a real golfer either," explained Paul. "He's an architect with delusions of golf grandeur and about to become a father."

"Congratulations," said Ellie.

"Thanks," said Scott.

Ellie looked down towards the green. Jerry Spaulding seemed to be muttering curses to himself in the sand trap and Pete's caddy was carefully parting branches of the hedges behind the green in a search for his player's ball.

"Well, today your showing these guys who the golfer is," she commented.

"Wait 'til the next hole," offered Scott.

"I just might," she answered, smiled, and walked back to the cart path to head for the green.

Scott and Paul walked up the fairway and onto the green. Scott replaced his ball with a tiny copper coin, smaller than a penny, then stepped back to allow the other golfers to play their next shots.

Jerry's ball was half buried in the sand and that was the cause of his earlier curses. His shot was made tougher by the presence of the other bunker on the other side of the green. He'd have to hit the ball just right to get it to stay on the green, let alone get near the pin.

In his quick play style he pounded at the sand with the club and the ball popped out. It landed a foot away from the pin and kept rolling until it was on the fringe of the green, three inches from the other trap. He still wasn't technically on the green but the ball was putt-able and he still had a decent shot at par and maybe even a birdie if he made the putt.

Pete's ball fared even worse trapped under the shrubs. He managed to pop it out somehow and made it onto the green, but the ball continued to roll assisted by the downhill slope until in was on the apron in front of the green, twenty yards from the hole.

Pete wandered around the green, putter in hand, shaking his head from side to side. Still a remote chance for par, thought Scott. Pete was aiming for the hole, but only hoped to get it close. Too far and he'd have a downhill putt for par. To little and he might still be five yards out. He hit the ball with deliberate force. It rolled up the unseen undulations of the green, veering to the right, ending up almost exactly opposite the hole to Scott's coin.

Jerry took more time lining up his putt that he did with his other shots. The slowness of his putting stroke was in stark contrast to the speed of his other swings. He putted the ball off the narrow fringe surrounding the green. It passed so close to the hole it veered to the left, as if some force in the dark depths of the hole was trying to pull the ball in. He ended up only twelve inches away from the cup and with a casual, almost careless single-handed swipe, knocked the ball into the hole. He was in with a par.

The red-jacketed tournament official indicated that Scott was furthest from the hole so he readied himself for the putt. He walked off the green to the left and Paul followed him. The ground sloped away and he was able to view the green almost at tabletop height. The left to right slope of the ground was certainly more evident. "Breaks pretty good to the right," said Paul.

"Still doable," said Scott.

"Oh yeah."

Scott walked up to his coin and carefully placed the ball in front of it, the duck facing to a point six inches to the left of the hole. If he wanted to get it in, he'd have to take the slope of the green into account and allow for some downward roll. The key was to hit the ball just hard enough so it's trajectory would intersect with the hole, but not too hard that it would roll right through the break.

He lined up the ball midway between his feet and placed the putter between him and the ball. He drew the club back a few inches swung it in a practice arc, judging the speed he would need to hit it just right. He did this three times then he stepped forward to line up the center of the putter with the ball. He twisted his head to the left, his eyes following the imaginary trajectory the ball should take to land in the hole then twisted right, his eyes coming back to the ball. He did this three times as well, making very small adjustments to the angle of the putter to make sure it was aimed to the spot he had picked out to the left of the hole.

With the same motion he used in his practice putts, he drew the club back then pushed the club into the ball. This is where years of playing miniature golf as a kid paid off. The ball bounced off the putter, the yellow duck rolling along the green. The ball's speed seemed to remain constant as it approached the hole, the slope of the green adding speed where the friction of the closely cropped grass slowed it down. As it approached within a foot of the hole it turned slightly, angling directly to the hole, and landed inside with a satisfying plunk.

"Yes," Scott almost whispered. What a great way to start. He could bogey the next hole and still be shooting par!

"Bir-die," said Paul drawing out each syllable with pride.

Scott pulled out his ball and walked off the green past Pete Baldwin. Pete was shaking his head in disbelief. He lined up his putt, not taking nearly as much time as Jerry and Scott had. He hit the ball strong and although it went straight for the hole, it went right over it ending up a yard and a half away from the hole. He looked like he wanted to pound the green with his putter. He resumed his stance and retook the shot without the ball, trying to adjust in his mind the strength of his swing to let the ball drop satisfyingly into the hole.

His sixth shot was almost too light. The ball rolled up to the lip, quavered for a moment before dropping in. Pete's caddy gave him a pat on the back and took his putter.

Paul noticed a tournament official talking into a walkie-talkie and making some notes on a clipboard. Probably an update to the clubhouse on how the three had finished up. He looked back toward the tee. The next group was already waiting halfway along the fairway to hit their balls on the green. The third group was waiting on the tee itself. Plenty more birdies coming today, he thought. His great hole would be lost in a sea of others, but what a great way to start the day.

13

Jake Fischer was starting his second cup of coffee. He could feel the surge of caffeine still fighting through the lingering effects of the alcohol from the night before. His morning coffee had usually followed his first cigarette and today he could taste the delicious flavor of the drink he had usually consumed out of habit. A habit that was perhaps just as strong as his addictions to smoking and alcohol but one he knew he'd allow himself to keep.

Earlier, the official at the starter's table had eyed Jake with a questioning leer as he rummaged through the stack of credentials, wondering if Jake Fischer was really suppose to be there. Jake had smiled and tried to smooth out his hair as best as possible. He pulled his jacket closed in the front to better hide his dirty shirt and curled his left fore and middle fingers into his fist to bury the nicotine stains. He realized his appearance didn't present him in his best light. He hoped his offer of a contract would be taken seriously by Andrew Patterson, once he found him that was.

A badge was now clipped onto his lapel and he used it to cover a stain on his jacket he hadn't noticed earlier. He took some time to study the pairings for the tournament and get some idea when Patterson would be teeing off.

Between the tees for the first and tenth holes was a series of four-foot by eight-foot plywood panels, each painted green with white lines drawn on them to create giant scorecards. Large green placards with the players names carefully stenciled in white hung on small hooks on the left sides of the enlarged scorecards. A separate board was reserved for the top ten players at any given point in the tournament.

Jake's knowledge of golf was limited to watching an occasional game on television and a few rounds he had played years before that had convinced him it wasn't a game tailored to his particular temperament. In addition he could name a couple dozen professional golfers. His limited experience had instilled an admiration for those players who had the skill to consistently send the ball where they wanted over distances greater than three football fields. Like many sports, however, his ability to play or even understand the intricacies of the game were not necessary to successfully recruit an athlete. He found the best way to get in good with a player was to compliment them and let them talk. Athletes usually loved to talk about their sport and Jake would let them.

Right now he hoped his sports agent skills would do their trick on Andrew Patterson. The only description he had of his quarry was that he was "quite a character." He noted on the information sheet he was given that Patterson was in the last threesome to tee off. The other two golfers were good, but not as impressive in their statistics as his target. Jake needed to be able to appeal to Patterson's ego. Making sure Andrew knew that Jake knew he was the best golfer out there seemed a good place to start. He wanted Patterson to want Jake as his agent as much as Jake wanted him as a client.

Jake took his nearly empty coffee cup back into the clubhouse. Another refill was in order on this chilly morning although the temperature had risen a little since he'd arrived.

He noted another man wearing an official credential pass on his lapel sitting at one of the Formica and metal tables in the tiny dining area near the food counter. He was much more neatly dressed than anyone else, with a glaringly white, pressed shirt and a red and gray patterned tie. His sports coat looked equally perfect. He was sipping a cup of coffee and holding a cell phone to his ear. He shook his head with a frustrated grimace as punched the END button on the phone.

Jake worked his way over to the table. "Mind if I grab a seat?" he asked. The man waved at an empty seat across from him. His badge identified him as Jason Bernard of USA Sports.

"Be my guest," Jason said.

"I wouldn't think this would be the type of event USA Sports would send a reporter to," observed Jake nodding at Bernard's press pass.

"Me either," answered Jason. He glanced at Jake's badge, squinting slightly to read the information. "Foreman and Frakes, eh?"

"Yeah."

"You're an agent?"

"Yep. Jake Fischer," he said, extending his hand.

Jason shook it and suddenly realized something. "Don't tell me, Andrew Patterson," he almost spat.

"He's my quarry."

Jason grabbed the thin plastic coffee stirrer and set a small whirlpool into motion in his cup. "Some company wants an amateur golfer to sell goods?"

"Callaway," answered Jake. "They want a Cinderella."

"Well, from what I've heard, they might be getting an ugly step-sister, Mr. Fischer."

"Please, call me Jake."

"I'm Jason," he answered smiling for a moment. "Are you a golfer, Jake?"

"Nah. But I've found I don't need to live a sport to sell it," answered Jake.

"If you can call this a sport," muttered Jason.

"I take it you're not hitting the links every Sunday?"

Jason laughed at the observation.

"How'd you end up here?" asked Jake.

"It's a long, unpleasant tail. I'm suppose to be out covering the Marathon but I seem to be a victim of demographics or some other sort of nonsense," explained Jason.

Jake seemed confused but sensed it was better to leave the explanation alone.

"I just got off the phone with a cameraman friend of mine and some college kid is out challenging the Kenyans early out of nowhere. There might be a surprise upset, not to mention a story out there today." Jason sipped at his coffee. "So why does Callaway want a Cinderella?"

"There are hundreds of millions of dollars out there waiting to buy the newest ball to add ten yards to your swing. If you want those dollars to buy your balls to have to give them a good reason. You get an amateur golfer who gets a shot to play a Pro-Am tournament, everyone is going to want to know what ball he recommends because who knows, they could be next."

Jason laughed this time. "Did you used to sell used cars in another life?"

"Naw, but it's nice to know you think I have an alternate career if this one falls through." Jake was glad to see Jason smiling. His idea of getting Patterson on the news would be much easier with Bernard on his side. "Have you seen this Patterson fellow?" he asked.

"Yeah. You'll get a kick out of his outfit. Knickers and a funny cap. The whole nine yards if you don't mind me mixing my sports metaphors."

"Well, I guess it must be part of his charm," suggested Jake. He wondered if such a quirk would hurt of help Patterson's ability to endorse a product. He concluded that the more memorable a person, the better.

"Well," began Jason, "the affiliate office in Chicago thought it might be nice to provide some local coverage for whoever ends up going to the Pro-AM. Sounds like Patterson is a lock. Once he tees off we'll get some footage of him doing his golf thing, maybe a few quotes, get the heck out of here for a quick edit and I'm home for a nice dinner with my wife."

"Nothing else worth covering out here?"

"Who said that was worth covering. I'll probably get bumped if something more interesting comes up, which as things are, seems very likely."

"Well, I'll keep my eyes open for any newsworthy sports scoops for you," offered Jake. Jason gave another chuckle.

"Good luck," answered Jason. His gaze suddenly fixed at a point over Jake's left shoulder, "speak of the devil," he said, "there's your boy." He nodded to a place outside the Pro Shop.

Jake turned around and immediately found the scene that had caught Jason's attention. A tall, middle-aged, interestingly dressed man was having a very animated discussion with medium height, casually dressed, younger man. The discussion seemed to concern where in the extremely large leather golf bag each of the golfer's clubs should be placed. The caddy seemed properly impressed with the placement of the clubs and also the proper way to insert and remove them. Each club seemed to have its own custom head cover and the putter was in a full-length sleeve. The older man's costume did exude a certain air and it had a strong odor of pretentiousness, even through the glass of the pro shop window.

A dark red leather pair of soft spiked golf shoes contrasted greatly with the green and purple argyle socks. Halfway up his thigh, the green and yellow plaid knickers screamed all the way to his blazing white belt. From there, argyle took over again in the sweater combining a pattern of dark red and bright orange diamonds with yellow stripes splitting the diamonds into smaller shapes. His shirt was lime green and open at the collar. A coat of arms decorated the left breast of the sweater. In his left hand, the stem of a white-brimmed brown pipe held by the bowl helped to emphasize the golfer's points. The golfer wore spectacles rather than glasses, thin wire frames with large loops over the ears. He topped it off with a plaid Scottish tam complete with a white and maroon pompom plopped on the middle.

Jake turned his head back slowly to look at Jason. "How's that for charm," offered Jason. "Meet Andrew Patterson, my friend."

It was Jake's turn to chuckle. What had Jonathan sent him into? He turned back to observe the scene again. Patterson gave his caddy a final admonishment and turned on his heel, his pipe now jutting from his mouth as he nodded in disbelief of the boy's apparent ignorance. Jake got up from the table to chase after the flamboyant golfer.

"If you see a redhead with a ponytail and a television camera, don't tell her where I am. I'll find her when I'm ready," said Jason.

Jake thanked Jason for the information. The two men shook hands and Jake went outside. Unbelievably, his prey had vanished. He turned to the caddy to see if he might know to where his boss had disappeared. He might also be able to give Jake a better impression as to what Patterson was like. The more he knew the better and it seemed like there was a lot he needed to know.

14

Sally Bernard followed the noise to the basement of the grade school building. Already several dozen women were emptying boxes of donated items onto the unfolded tables and sorting through them. Most of the items had been set out over the previous week, but donations had been coming in every day and there were always some last minute pieces to sort and price.

A few of the women greeted her as she came in but they quickly resumed their work. The doors would open to the public in less than an hour and everyone felt the pressure to be ready.

The Northfield Methodist Church Woman's Auxiliary Rummage Sale was a widely popular biannual event and consequently, the biggest fundraiser for the church. Many other groups had tried to copy it but over the years, the NMCWA had built up a loyal core of people who solicited and gathered items for the sale. No one else could match the selection and quality they garnered twice a year and most had given up on trying to compete.

Sally headed for her section of the basement. She called it the living room because she was in charge of things to be sold that people would likely put in their living rooms. There was a large area of furniture containing everything from sofas to rocking chairs, several with "sold" signs on them as the Woman's Auxiliary members had first choice of all the items and many took the opportunity to single out the prime pieces for themselves. There was also a central area of coffee tables, also for sale, each decorated with knick-knacks and chatch also available. Each item had a small rectangular sticker with an amount on it. As a rule, nothing at the sale sold for less than twenty-five cents but usually the lowest she priced an item for was one dollar. From her years of experience she knew how much an item had to be priced to get it to sell. Price it too high and you had to pack it up to be marked down in six months. Too low and you were in danger of risking not breaking the previous sales record. One of her little tricks to help get rid of little pieces was to group two or three with a larger item and selling them only as a package. It seemed to work well and others helping with the sale had started to copy her strategy.

Sally found herself still fuming over Jason's unwillingness to discuss starting a family this morning. Every year it was the same excuse. His career needed his full attention right now but soon. She loved him and knew he wanted a family. They had talked about it often before they were married and she wondered if there was something else keeping Jason from pulling the trigger. She sometimes thought she might get pregnant "on accident," but dismissed the idea, realizing that Jason might resent her for taking on the decision alone.

Cecily Waterston was already there and had an office storage box filled with bric-a-brac and other last minute items to be priced. Sally winced as she hoped against hope Cecily would not put her customary five dollar price on everything. Cecily's philosophy was that people would be willing to pay those prices to help support the good work at Northfield Methodist Church. Sally knew that where the money was going was of less concern to the buyers than getting a great bargain on that "crystal swan that was just like the one aunt Edith had when I was a child."

Cecily looked up from her work, a polite but small smile, careful not to ruin her perfectly applied makeup. Never mind that she was adjusting it every fifteen minutes with her compact makeup kit anyway. "Hello, dear," she said. Dear was drawled out like a line spoken by Katharine Hepburn in an old movie. Sally had thought when she first met Cecily Waterston that her mannerisms had to be an act, but she quickly came to realize that that was how she was. Even down to the pointing pinky when she drank tea (not coffee) at the Auxiliary meetings.

"Hello, Ceci," greeted Sally shortening the name to "see-see" knowing that although it annoyed Miss Waterston to be addressed with such a nickname, she would say nothing. "More things to price?"

"I've got this batch, dear, but I think there's another box of coasters on that sofa over there." "There" was drawled nearly as severely as dear. Sally knew that coasters offended Cecily almost as much as "Ceci" did. Sally chuckled and headed over. She would check Cecily's pricing later as she rearranged the distribution of items on the tables.

"Hello, Sally," called a bright voice from nearby. Anne Matterly approached her with her legal sized clipboard, checking off a few items as she approached. "Everything set over here with you girls?"

"Just the usual last minute pricing," assured Sally.

"You know I am counting on you to sell at least five thousand dollars worth this year. We're definitely looking at another record if everyone does their part."

"We should have no problem with this selection," guaranteed Sally. She looked over at Cecily who was glancing over the items surrounding her with her ever-present expression of incredulity that people actually wanted this old stuff.

"Excellent, excellent," approved Anne. "You know everyone coming is looking to buy something," she reminded the ladies.

Sally smiled to herself as she accepted the Anne's slogan for perhaps the twentieth time this week. Anne considered every unsold item a failure, even though it was rare that something would survive two rummage sales in a row. There was perhaps a ten percent leftover after each Saturday free-for-all but that was mainly due to the fact that there no chance that anyone coming would get an opportunity to see everything, and often times second chance items, as Anne called them, were snatched up early in the next sale.

Anne checked another box on her clipboard and headed to the next section filled with kitchen items.

"What does she think we are, incompetent?" asked Cecily, assuming Sally had the same impression of the matronly sale supervisor.

"I'm quite sure she doesn't, Ceci. Ever since her husband died five years ago this sale has been her reason to go on."

"Sad, I'm sure," commented Cecily.

Sally held her tongue and turned back to her box of items.

"Oh," started Cecily a short time later, as if just remembering something important, "I will have to leave early this afternoon. Can you handle the pack-up without me?"

"Early?" questioned Sally.

"Yes," she answered. She put down the last item she had just plastered with a five-dollar sticker and carefully adjusted her white cashmere cardigan sweater. Its brightness accented by the pearls around her neck. Her too perfect figure was slightly improved by the tightness across the mother-of pearl buttons. Her distinctive red lipstick, pale, perfect complexion and neat, dark hair gave a Snow White quality to her beauty. Although Cecily's attire seemed more appropriate for a Saturday afternoon tea, Sally not only didn't mind, but counted on her appearance to help sell some of her five dollar items to men too distracted to notice they were getting ripped off until their wives yelled at them later.

"Andrew is playing in a tournament today and we planned on going out to celebrate afterward. He has reservations at the Palmer House and I need to get myself ready."

Sally glanced over Cecily again. She seemed more than ready for a dinner at the posh steakhouse but she shrugged her shoulders. "Fine," she answered. "It shouldn't take too long"

In Cecily Waterston's eyes Andrew Patterson was perfect. If he said he was going to win then by God there was no question it would happen.

"What is he playing in?" Sally asked politely.

"It's some sort of golf thing. Only the best players in Chicago get to play he's told me. He says he'll be able to play with professionals after this. It's ever so exciting for him," she explained with her own matching degree of excitement.

Sally turned to face Cecily as she realized what she was saying. Andrew was playing in the golf tournament that Jason was going to cover today, the one that had him in such a bad mood. "Really," drawled Sally, half imitating Cecily's mannerisms. "I do believe Jason will be covering it for his station today."

Cecily was confused for a moment before somewhere uncovering the fact in her mind that Sally's husband worked for the local affiliate of a television sports networking. "Oh, how exciting for Jason. Perhaps he can get Andrew a tape. You know a memento."

"Maybe," agreed Sally. If only Andrew would lose today and Jason caught it on tape. That was something she wouldn't mind delivering to Cecily.

CHAPTER 4 – SECOND HOLE

15

Since Scott had the low score on the previous hole, he had earned honors at this one and was the first to tee up. This hole was a par four. A good drive would get him a hundred and forty to a hundred and fifty yards from the pin, From there a shot onto the green would position him for a decent chance at par. Par would be acceptable. He knew his limitations and two birdies in a row was a rare event. Even one over par, or a bogey, would leave his total score even at par for the first two holes. He'd still be at a great position to shoot a personal best.

As Scott stepped up to the tee, he noted a kid holding a pole with a white sign on top. It had places for five golfers' names. Three were listed now each followed by two numbers. Hanover was at the top with a –1 and a 1 next to it. Then Spaulding with and E for even and a 1 followed by Baldwin with a +1 and a 1. He wished he had a camera to get a picture of that! The first number was their current status with regard to par and the second which hole they had just completed. Scott was one under par and Pete one over.

Scott placed his ball near the right gold tee box marker and stepped back to line up his swing. He would aim a little to the left side of the fairway since his shots tended to fade meaning they veered to the right. Even if he hit it straight, he'd still have a playable situation. To the right was a stretch of forest and he definitely wanted to stay out of there.

He drew his imaginary line back from the ball then lined up his feet parallel to it. The quiet was noticeable but not distracting. A cool breeze brushed his hands and the smile on his face. He took a practice swing and the club seemed to pass through a perfect arc ending up over his left shoulder with the follow through. A swish through the air emphasized the speed of the club.

He stepped forward four inches and started to bring the club back again. His wrists bent slightly at the top of his back swing. The memory of his muscles from the practice swing took over and he swung the club through the ball. It took off with a perfect trajectory and then he saw it. The end of his club was in the wrong position. He had opened it up, turning it clockwise. The result of his error was quickly apparent as the ball veered to the right. The spin caused by Scott's twisted club head had taken over from the raw velocity of the shot ending up with a very significant slice. The ball hit the grass traveling almost perpendicular to its intended path and rolled out of sight behind some trees. At best he was still perhaps two hundred to two hundred and fifty yards from the hole assuming he could find his ball. Worse yet, the large trees to the right side of the fairway would now provide a difficult obstacle to the green.

He stood frozen, his club hanging over his left shoulder, his eyes closed with disappointment, ready to give it all up. Who was he kidding? One good hole, yeah. A par round? In your dreams, bucko.

"Mr. Spaulding is up," announced the official. Scott looked quickly for his green tee but it had flown out of site when he hit the ball and he left the tee and handed the club to Paul.

"I saw where it went, it opens up behind those trees, I think you have a shot," Paul half whispered and they stepped back to a safe distance.

"Maybe," agreed Scott glumly. "Darn. I really didn't want to bogey this hole, Paul."

"Just get it on in three and you'll make the up and down," said Paul. Up and down referred to the neat trick of still being able to finish a hole in par, even though you didn't make it to the green in regulation, that is the par of the hole minus two strokes for the putts.

Jerry's drive was perfect this time and he was no more than a hundred and thirty yards from the pin. Pete followed him with a similarly great shot, perhaps ten yards behind him. Both of them seemed to be shaking off the last hole and moving on. While everyone else moved down the fairway, Scott and Paul trundled off to the right.

Paul was correct; the trees did recede back to leave a small meadow of tall grass. After a minute or so of looking, Paul gave a quack and Scott joined him to study his lie.

The ball was visible, but just. A good whack might get him to the fairway, but he'd be lying two and likely still behind the other golfers. They'd be waiting to hit their second shots while he still was hitting his third. Even though a line of trees stood between him and the hole, Scott wondered if he might not have an alternative.

"Pop it out with the seven iron," suggested Paul.

"I'm thinking seven wood," answered Scott. "If I can get it to roll up through the trees, I might be left with just a short chip to get on the green instead still being two hundred yards away."

"A seven wood won't cut through the grass, Scott, you just need to get it over to the left on the fairway and get a good shot at the green."

"I can get it out with the wood. I've done this before."

"Okay," conceded Paul, "it's your game." He pulled the large headed club from the bag and handed it to Scott.

Scott lined up a shot and took only half back swings when he practiced the shot. He didn't need to get a lot of distance from the club, just to hit it out of the tall grass into something playable. Each practice swing ended up with the club knocking down a bunch of grass. With little of the confidence that had been with him on the last hole he smashed at the ball. The tall grass caught the club as he swung twisting it and sending the ball off to the right, this time barely getting above the ground. It found the asphalt cart path and rolled a bit before settling in the grass on the far side of the path. He was now behind the line of trees he had hoped to avoid and nowhere closer to the fairway he needed to be on.

He handed the club to Paul, afraid to look at him lest he get the "I told you so" stare.

"At least you're out of those weeds," offered Paul, trying to find a positive spin to put on the situation.

"Closer to the hole," added Scott stating his golf motto that he had developed on his first day golfing. It was his theory that any shot that got you closer to the hole was a good shot and he was closer to the hole, even though he was left with a tougher lie. He was still further from the hole than the other golfers and would have to hit his third shot before Spaulding and Baldwin would hit their second.

As he got up to the ball he started to grin. He saw a small break in the line of trees, perhaps fifteen-feet wide that gave him a straight line to the flag on the green. He'd have to keep the ball low but if he hit it straight he could still get on the green in three and have that chance at par.

"Grass burner please," he asked Paul, referring to his three iron. The club had slightly more loft than his putter. That would keep the shot low over the grass and hopefully out of the tree branches.

"Are you sure?"

"Do ducks quack?" answered Scott.

Paul pulled out the three iron from Scott's bag. "Aim for the tree," joked Paul, hoping to relax his friend. It had been another of Scott's golf theories that one never hit what they aimed for. Therefore the easiest way to miss hitting a tree was to aim straight for it. Scott chuckled at the comment and seriously considered doing just that, but he had made this shot dozens of time before. A nice easy back swing with the ball near his back foot so the club face would hit the ball when it was nearly perpendicular to the ground, keeping the ball low and out of danger.

He took two practice swings, confident he had just the amount of back swing to make it on the green. He stepped up and flawlessly duplicated his practice swings. It took only a fraction of a second for the ball to whack one of the trees to the left and bounce off to the right. Once again the cart path was there to help his ball roll, this time down hill. He watched as the little white orb followed the path beyond and to the right of the green.

"You didn't aim for the tree," pointed out Paul.

"No I didn't," agreed Scott and he laughed. "Should have aimed for it."

"Like I told you," said Paul. The banter was light and the mood had shifted. They were now just two friends playing the game they both loved, rotten shots and good shots together, enough good ones to make it worthwhile and enough bad ones to keep it fun and interesting.

Scott handed Paul his three iron and they started off down the path to his ball. Pete was lining up his shot and easily made the green, ten yards to the right of the pin. Jerry's rolled a little off the back of the green, but both could be in the hole easily in two more strokes for pars. If Scott landed his next shot on the green and one putted he'd have a five, one over par or a bogey. Two putts would give him a double bogey but he would still be only one over par and that was still a good start for him.

Scott's ball was on the path next to the grass. The rules allowed him some relief and after getting a nod from the official, he picked the ball up, walked a yard up and while holding it at arms length, let it fall onto the grass. Paul handed him his pitching wedge. "It slopes to the back and left side of the hole," he advised.

Scott nodded and casually stepped up to his ball. The girl from USA Sports had her camera ready again and was just off the back of the green. He hoped he wouldn't hit her. Wouldn't that be great? The clip would definitely show up on a sports blooper reel.

He lined up the shot a little to the right of the pin to leave him a slight uphill putt. He took only one practice swing this time, an easy, slow, back swing not quite as full as his regular swing. He stepped up to the ball and repeated the same stoke, the club picking the ball nicely out of the rough and sending it soaring high into the sky. Scott could see that despite his careful aim, the ball was headed slightly to the left of the pin. Hopefully he might catch some downhill action to roll it closer to the hole.

It seemed to stay up forever and Scott watched the one good shot he'd had this hole. He stood facing the pin, still frozen in his follow through position, his club hanging over his left shoulder, his weight balanced on his left foot.

Paul had sensed it almost the moment Scott hit the ball. It was like the ball knew where it wanted to go. With a soft thud it hit the green just past the fringe and started to roll, and roll and roll.

Scott's club slipped out of his fingers onto the grass behind him as he watched the ball plink against the flagstick and drop into the hole. He realized he had been holding his breath and it escaped with a sudden gasp.

"It's in the hole," Paul said in a perfect Bill Murray impersonation. "Caddy Shack" had provided a lot of good quotes for golfers, and none was sweeter than, "it's in the hole."

"Yes it is," said Scott.

Some from the next group of players on the tee joined the applause from the spectators and players around the green. Without having the ball near the fairway or even using a putter, Scott had parred the hole. A disaster had turned into a miracle and now he was still one under par.

Ellie slowly lowered her camera as she shook her head. She'd never seen anything like it. This guy was either extremely good or extremely lucky and she suspected the latter. She thought about pulling out her cell phone to get Jason Bernard out here to watch this guy, but realized it wouldn't do any good. He was here to do the least amount of work and get on to his next assignment. Well, she'd keep following him. Maybe this guy wouldn't turn into a story, but for now it sure beat sitting around the clubhouse.

Scott picked up his club and handed it to Paul. Together they walked up to the green and the sight of the ball in the hole made it real. He picked it out of the hole and held it tightly in his hand. His grin was huge. He could muff the rest of the shots today and nothing would take away how his felt now. He would tell the story of this hole for months, even years to come, as a highlight of this amazing day.

Jerry Spaulding gave him a pat on the back and added a "good shot" as he walked past. Scott thanked him and he and Paul took their place by the other caddies as Jerry and Pete finished the hole. They both ended up with pars but nothing as dramatic as the hole Scott turned in and they knew it. The official with the walkie-talkie made his report and the threesome headed for the next hole.

16

Sarah Hanover hauled the tall and wide but relatively thin box out of the front closet where it had sat for the last two months and pulled it into the living room. She looked at the picture on the front and smiled to herself. In a couple of weeks the baby pictured in the crib would be theirs. She was so looking forward to it. With a sigh she remembered why she was doing this by herself today. Scott was out at his golf tournament and likely he and Paul would make a full day of it. Well, if he wasn't going to put this darn thing together, she would. It couldn't be that hard.

Sarah never could understand the attraction that golf had for Scott. As far as she could tell, it caused more frustration than anything else. She was always picking up golf magazines that Scott had left lying around. Each one promised to take ten strokes off your score and eliminate that pesky slice. If they were able to do what they said, then why did they have a different article on the same subject every month? Shouldn't all the golfers be hitting the ball perfectly and having their best score on every round by now?

But he seemed to love it nonetheless. Scott and Paul would come back and regale her with stories of missing the hole by an inch or almost nailing a goose with a drive. For those few hours they had problems unrelated to the rest of their lives that ended after eighteen holes and a beer. They could spend all that time together and discuss nothing deeper than the latest golf equipment, little tricks and tips from their magazines, how beautiful the course was this particular time of year.

Perhaps her feelings were related to her own frustration. In a way she was jealous of his golf time. She had nothing comparable. It seemed whenever she got together with her friends they all seemed to do was just complain about their lives and their kids and their husbands. They never seemed to be able to leave it behind like Scott and Paul could. Men had a different way of interacting with each other, Sarah thought.

She pulled open the flaps at the top of the crib box and started to remove the pre-assembled side sections. The resemblance to a jail cell struck her as she lined each piece up against the sofa. Her baby would be a prisoner for a couple of years.

When she was a kid, cribs were much more dangerous than today. The bars were too far part and the mattresses too soft and it was too easy for tiny fingers to get caught in the mechanical workings. Yet she and her two sisters had survived those old cribs just fine. Her mother couldn't understand why Sarah wanted to buy a new crib when she had a perfectly good one sitting in the basement that Sarah's father could set up for them in a few minutes. Sarah tried to explain the safety features that the newer cribs had incorporated in the last thirty years but her mother clicked her tongue in disgust. "It was good enough for you girls, it ought to be good enough for my grandchild," she insisted.

Sarah thanked her for the offer and ordered the crib from a web site after a few weeks of research. Scott complained about the cost and was almost ready to get her old crib from her parent's basement but she convinced him it wasn't safe and she really wanted something better for their baby.

He had been promising to set the thing up for over a month now but one thing after another delayed it and now it was this stupid tournament. If only that stupid guy hadn't broken his wrist, she complained.

Well, he could have his golf game. She would show him she had the ability to accomplish this task without him and when he came home tonight and saw the crib in the baby's room, he'd have to be impressed. Oh, he'd shake it and test the assembly a little, but he'd have to give her his approval and she'd have a little bit of guilt to hold over him for putting the project off for so long that his poor pregnant wife had to do it herself!

The instructions were printed in about sixteen different languages and finally she located the tiny square in the huge fold out sheet that had English printing. It was full of spelling and grammar errors; likely the product of some poorly paid Chinese translator but she soon had the twenty or so parts sorted out.

She took a little break and poured herself a cup of decaffeinated coffee from the pot in the kitchen. She flipped on the television for a moment and there was live coverage of the Chicago Marathon. Apparently some unknown runner had taken a large initial lead, but most of the commentators said he lacked the stamina to keep it up and the well-trained and experienced Kenyans would overtake him soon.

Talk about more boring than golf. At least in golf there were eighteen holes. With this it was two plus hours of one race that likely would come down to the last few hundred yards anyways.

She turned off the television and selected the CD of prenatal songs on her iPod. She set it into the speaker adapter that Scott had gotten her on their last anniversary. The songs were said to train your babies mind while it was still in the womb. She figured every little bit of help was needed to combat any quirkiness that Scott's genes had inserted into their baby's brain.

She grabbed the tools she had rounded up from Scott's workbench and started to assemble the crib. It went together relatively easy and within twenty minutes she was rolling the crib back and forth on its castors. She covered the mattress with the pad and Sesame Street sheets she had bought a couple of weeks before. It boggled her mind that sheets less than a sixth of the size of her own bed sheets could cost twice as much. This was one little expense she would keep from Scott.

Jubilant in her accomplishment and anticipating the surprise on Scott's face she wheeled the crib down the hall. The Baby's room was across from theirs. She opened the door and started to pull the crib in behind her. She stopped and shook her head in disbelief. She covered her eyes and soon she was laughing.

Sarah Hanover, Master Carpenter, in her first project for her unborn child, had made a simple yet important mistake. The crib was wider than the door. A few futile attempts to twist the crib in different angles were made before she was ready to give up.

She could just imagine the laughter from Scott if he had been here right now and she was laughing with him. Oh well, live and learn. She looked at her belly and told her ripening child, "Don't you go and tell your daddy. This'll be our little secret."

Maybe Scott would have made the same mistake. She was half tempted to put it back in the box and insist he assemble it himself tonight. The disassembly and reassembly in the baby's room didn't take as long as the first time around. She rolled the crib next to the diaper changing table and stood back to admire her handiwork.

God, she suddenly thought. What if it's a boy and, and... She almost couldn't bring herself to imagine it. What if he liked to golf too?

The sudden pain in her abdomen startled her. It wasn't as intense as she had been warned labor pains could be but she wondered if that was what it was. Had she exerted herself too much? The doctor had told her that even though she wasn't due for a couple of weeks, the baby could come at any time.

The sensation quickly faded and it seemed like nothing had changed.

"That was interesting," she said to herself. Still, Scott would be home by dinner. It was unlikely anything would happen before tonight if she really was starting labor.

17

Andrew Patterson's caddy had a white handkerchief out and was wiping the leather of Patterson's bag, working out some invisible stains for the perfectionist owner. "Hi," said Jake. "You must be Andrew Patterson's Caddy." He held out his right hand.

"Hi," answered the boy. He took the hand, smiled and quietly resumed his work.

"Tough boss, huh?"

"I suppose."

It was going to be a little harder than he thought. "I'm Jake Fischer."

"Eric Peters," announced the boy without looking up.

"So, you think your boss is going to win today."

"He does," Eric answered.

"What do you think?"

"Hey, I'll take any chance I can get to caddy in the big leagues."

"You a golfer?" asked Jake, changing tack but keeping in mind the boys last statement.

"Who isn't?" he answered.

"Yeah, I guess so. You think you'll be in this tournament some day?"

"Maybe. I mostly play so that I can be a better caddy. You know, apply my experience to help the golfer. Mr. Patterson ain't like most golfers though."

"How's that?" prodded Jake.

"He's got every shot already worked out. He gives me a list of what club he's going to use on every shot and I have to give them to him. I don't ever try to give him any advice."

"Does he need it?"

"I've caddied for dozens of golfers. Even Tiger Woods needs some advice from time to time."

"But Mr. Patterson doesn't like that."

"No, sir. He pays well and he says if he wins, I'll go with him to the Pro-Am. Once you get to caddy on the pro tour that's where the big bucks come in. Heck Tiger Woods' caddy made nine hundred thousand dollars that one year. Not bad for a bag carrier."

"Wow," said Jake in awe.

"Yeah. Now I don't think Mr. Patterson has a chance in the pros, but there is always someone looking for a new caddy. I just got to be in the right place at the right time is all."

"Sounds like a plan," agreed Jake.

"You a reporter?" asked Eric. It was the first sign of curiosity he had expressed up to this point.

"No, I'm a sports agent." The reply seemed to be the first thing Jake said that got Eric's attention.

"You're looking to sign Mr. Patterson?" asked Eric with no small degree of incredulity.

"I have a company that might be interested in him, if he wins," said Jake. His comment evoked an unexpected response from the caddy. Eric began to laugh.

"That is a good one, mister," he managed to say between chuckles.

At this point Jake, thoroughly confused but intensely curious waited. He sensed there was more to come.

Eric's amusement faded and seemed to focus his attention on his duties with Andrew Patterson's clubs. He turned back to Jake, "Have you seen Andrew Patterson yet?" asked Eric.

"From inside the clubhouse a few minutes ago. I came out to see if I could get a word but he disappeared. I had hoped you might know where he was," answered Jake.

"He always disappears before a tournament. I have no idea what he does. But if that company wants a winner, well Mr. Patterson has never lost one yet. Still, I can't imagine seeing him on a TV commercial driving a Buick like Tiger Woods. He just wouldn't fit, you know?"

"You don't think he'd be good at that, eh?"

"Well, maybe if you were trying to sell pipe tobacco to pretentious snobs, but I hardly doubt that's a market worth pursuing," added Eric.

Jake's agent instinct automatically made a note of the suggestion. To Eric it might not seem like a potentially grand idea, but to Jake, that was just the kind of direct connection he used to be able to make. Used to, he reminded himself, before the disaster with Brad Finley.

Before he could reclaim that life he would have to regain the trust of those he had disappointed during the last year. His job today was to get Patterson for Callaway and then move on. It was a way to jump start his life and career.

"If you see him, tell him I'm looking for him." Jake pulled out a business card from inside his sports coat and handed it to the caddy. "Have a good day, Eric."

"I'll see you around."

Jake let out a long sigh as he looked around for the bright splash of color that would give a clue as to Patterson's whereabouts. A familiar desire began to fill Jake's thoughts. He glanced at his watch. It hadn't been that long. Surely he could last the day. Fortunately there was nothing to be had here. This was a Forest Preserve golf course and no alcohol was permitted. Still, there was that liquor store he passed on 159th street and at least an hour or two before Patterson even got to the first tee.

He sat on the low stone wall in front of the clubhouse and buried his face in his hands. Was he sweating? Was he beginning to have physical withdrawal symptoms or were they entirely psychological? He imagined Gina and took strength from his desire to make things right with her. He was here after all. He was trying.

He lifted his head and saw a skinny, older man walk briskly past him. He was dressed in yellow and red plaid long pants and had a yellow golf shirt on. The ensemble was topped with a yellow cap. He had some cardboard placards and was headed for the large plywood scoreboards.

Most of the cards he carried were numbers but he also carried larger ones with player names on them, presumably for the leader board. Jake assumed that the running list of placements in the tournament would change frequently. As with most tournaments, the lowest ranked players began and were quickly washed off the top ten as the better players took to the course.

Jake stood and walked over to the space in front of the scoreboard and watched the scorekeeper slide a placard labeled Hanover into the first place spot and put a −1 followed by a 2 next to the name. Hanover was one under par and had finished the first two holes. Five other names followed, the second in a tie with Hanover but only after on hole. He wondered how long this Hanover guy would last. At least another two threesomes, he figured.

The scores for the individual holes went up and Jake saw two fours go next to Hanover's name. From what Jake knew about golf, if Hanover could keep that kind of scoring up, he might stay in contention, but there must be a reason he was starting in the first group.

"Interesting start," commented a man who somewhat startled Jake. He had come up next to him while Jake had been studying the board. His left arm was in a cast and was suspended by a blue sling. He had a beige baseball cap on and tan slacks. He wore a red and white-stripped golf shirt under his tan jacket. He looked to be about thirty-five and had a deeply tanned face that was staring enviously at the scoreboard.

"Don't tell me it's a golfing injury," joked Jake.

The man laughed. "No, carelessness. A log fell on my arm while I was chopping some firewood."

"I assume you're not playing today, just an interested onlooker?"

"You could say that. I'm Joe Caulkin." He held out his right hand.

"Jake Fischer," returned Jake. They shook.

Joe held up his casted arm, "cost me a spot in the tournament today," he continued.

"I'm sorry to hear that," Jake said sincerely. "It sounds like the winner is going to have a chance to go pro."

"Well, play in a Pro-Am tournament. Going pro takes a lot more than one win in a regional tournament."

"Did you have a chance?" asked Jake.

"Actually, yes."

"Really?"

"Now it looks like Patterson has the field to himself, unless something unusual happens."

"You think someone could beat him?"

"I got five thousand reasons to hope someone does."

Jake looked perplexed.

Joe explained, "I bet Patterson five thousand dollars, him against the field that he'd lose today."

"Regretting that bet are you?" realized Jake.

"A little, but that arrogant jerk sucked me into it. I doubt the anxiety will affect him any, but it will certainly keep my blood pressure up today."

"Five grand is a lot," commented Jake.

"Well, there are fifty-nine other golfers out there today. One of them may have it in them."

"You know Patterson well?"

"Not really. We've played twice before. He beat me both times but I had a couple of bad holes. Stupid mistakes. He's a good golfer, but he doesn't know how to play golf."

"Excuse me?"

"He can swing a club and read a green with the best, but to him, it's a project – a job – a task. I truly believe he has no fun when he golfs. He's here to win a tournament. Anything less will be a tragic disappointment."

Jake mulled over Caulkin's assessment adding it to Eric's. Neither of them had high regard for Patterson. Should that tell Jake something? Was he heading for a disaster with this assignment? Still he didn't want to let Jonathan down. He was sticking his neck out giving Jake this chance and he didn't want to blow it. He'd sign the golfer and let Jonathan work out any potential personality conflicts.

"Now, Scott Hanover," mused Caulkin.

"Off to an early and doomed lead, eh?"

"Well, based on his scores all year, he's sixtieth out of sixty."

"Not much of a chance to win your bet there, I guess."

"No," agreed Joe, "but he does play golf, in every sense of the word. I saw him make a putt that he himself didn't know he could make a couple of weeks ago. No one could have made it unless they just walked up to the ball and said, 'what the heck, I'll give it a shot.' He could come in sixtieth today and be ecstatic just to have gotten the chance to play."

"Sounds like a great guy."

"He is. His wife is expecting soon. He mentioned to me that it was unlikely he'd get out to golf after that. But maybe he'll be out here someday with his son or daughter, giving them his gift for enjoyment of the game."

"I guess that is the key, you really need to enjoy the game," agreed Jake. The essential truth of those words grabbed at Jake. He was beginning to believe Patterson wasn't what Jonathan or Callaway had envisioned but he'd follow his orders. There was time for selectivity when he was fully back in his game.

Joe pulled a little disposable camera out of the sleeve of his sling and snapped a quick picture of the leader board. "I'm sure Scott wouldn't mind a souvenir of that," he said, nodding at the neatly displayed board."

"Good idea," agreed Jake.

18

Ellie Burke watched as Scott Hanover retrieved his ball from the hole. He had a genuine expression of disbelief as he looked to make sure it was his ball he was holding. She checked the battery on her camera. It was still at about seventy-five percent. With the spare she had in the shoulder bag she ought to be able to follow him the whole way through the front nine. There were more batteries in the truck she could retrieve at the turn to continue taping, unless that stuffed sport-coat, Bernard, wanted to leave after getting his shots of Patterson. She was half tempted to let him take the truck back with whatever Patterson footage they took and she'd get back to the editing room on her own later. This was what golf was about; turning a disaster into a par with just one lucky shot. Of course the luck could turn the other way at any point, but right now, she had that amazing shot on tape. Hopefully she'd be able to get Bernard to work it into his report.

She watched as the other two golfers putted out but didn't tape their shots. They were good players but this was a relatively short par four hole and a good player should par it. Scott Hanover was not as good as these guys. That much she could tell from his first three shots on this hole. But for some reason, he was playing better than he usually did. That much she could tell from his expression. She seemed certain Hanover was going to have a good day and decided to make sure he'd get a copy of whatever she was able to tape of his game today.

She watched as the scorecard holder made the changes updating the standings so far. Two of the players from the following threesome were added, one right under Hanover with a birdie as well on the first hole. A humming from her hip distracted her attention. It was her phone vibrating. She looked at the caller ID and it read USA REMOTE 12. That was Jason Bernard's phone for the day. She pulled it out and stayed back as the rest of the group headed for the third tee. She pressed the SEND button. "Hello," she answered.

"Where are you," asked Bernard.

"Just getting some tape of the first group. A guy just sank a chip shot from seventy-five yards away," she answered softly. She wasn't sure the officials would allow cell phone use during play so she wanted to be as unobtrusive as possible. That was why she had set it to vibrate mode in the first place.

"Amazing I'm sure. I just need to know you'll be here to get some shots of this Patterson guy when he tees off."

She glanced at her watch. "That won't be for at least an hour and half," she answered.

"Just be here. I'll want to tape a little interview too. Just a few questions. I can't wait to get out of here."

"Don't worry," assured Ellie. She pressed END before she could hear any more whining from "the talent." Most reporters Ellie enjoyed working with. They were excited about the events they were covering and would jump at the chance to highlight the unexpected. Most clips that showed up on blooper reels were camera operators keeping the camera running when they didn't need to. She could envision a short spot featuring Hanover's four shots on this whole as a quick example of a golfing alchemist turning lead into gold.

The group was on the third tee already and Hanover was getting ready to make his tee shot. She pulled her scorecard she had grabbed from the clubhouse and jogged up to them. She looked at the layout of the hole on the map illustrated on the back of the card. The hole was a par three next to a small pond. It was the shortest hole on the course she noted. These could also be the most challenging, she thought.

19

Andrew Patterson was standing on the cart path leading away from the eighteenth green. The path twisted through the woods a bit effectively hiding him from the view of anyone around the clubhouse. The path was paved in asphalt and imprints from the golf cart tires crisscrossed the surface.

The thought of golfers using a cart to play the game made him shudder. If one was going to play this game, they should do it right, he thought. It was well that the PGA had prevented that one golfer from using a cart on the tour. Walking made stamina a part of the overall challenge to the round. You didn't have to be in great shape but one should be able to walk seventy two hundred yards in four or five hours without dropping from a coronary.

Visiting the last green was a ritual Andrew had started with his first tournament a year and half ago. Not even his caddy knew he did it. It was a private moment and one that he would remember as he teed off on the final green in five or six hours. He saw himself standing on the tee, a crowd of anxious spectators waiting to see him finish with another win to his credit. Some might think him odd or eccentric, but he didn't let that bother him. He was playing against the best amateurs, less one, in the Chicago area. They were the ones who needed to be impressed with his ability. Probably all of them had been playing longer than he had and some were certainly jealous.

He would par this hole but left room for a birdie attempt. The tee shot would have to be just the right distance. Too far would end him in one of the bunkers to the far side of the left turning dogleg that surrounded the largest water hazard on the course. He would tee off with his five wood and place the ball two hundred and twenty-five yards out then follow up with the same club to get him safely on the green in two. Even if he was just off the green two shots to get in the hole was a conservative estimate. He wasn't interested in making a mistake and turning the score into a bogey.

He pulled his pipe from the pouch hanging from his belt. He was here to relax. To prepare himself mentally for what lie ahead. That was truly one of his strengths. He'd seen many players let a bad shot affect their game and literally self-destruct. Andrew would never let that happen.

He dipped the bowl of the pipe into the pouch of Dunhill Durber tobacco and tamped it down just right with his thumb. He retrieved a stick match, stooped down, and struck it against the cart path. He watched the flare of the sulfur and slowly stood up. He lit the pipe taking short puffs to draw the smoke into his mouth, and then exhaled, blowing out the match. He didn't smoke his pipe often and when he did it was in private like now. The aroma of the burning tobacco hung in the still air of the protected, woody area around the green. He wondered if the scent would still be here when he returned.

He figured he'd relax here for forty-five minutes or so, find Eric and warm up a little at the driving range before heading off on his round. He looked forward to collecting his five thousand dollars from Caulkin at the end of the day. He had sensed Joe's reluctance to make the bet. It would take some sort of miracle for someone to beat him today. Andrew didn't believe in miracles.

CHAPTER 5 – THIRD HOLE

20

"Mr. Hanover, you still hold honors," the tournament official informed him. Scott Hanover stood off to the side of the tee for a moment. It seemed like the exhilaration of the previous hole had completely erased the long water hazard lining the right half of the hole from his memory. Paul had removed Scott's six iron from the bag and held it out to him.

"Scott," Paul muttered, trying to shake him from the trance. "It's not there, no water balls today, buddy."

Scott smiled. "No water balls today," he echoed.

Water balls were so named by amateur golfer because you wouldn't mind losing them in a water hazard if you happened to hit a bad shot from the tee. Why send a brand new two dollar Top Flite XL 7000 to an early watery grave if you had a slightly used Titlist you fished from another water hazard that wouldn't be missed? Scott had an early predilection to hitting balls into the water, hence his nickname, Duck. The name still stuck with him as Paul had reminded him earlier with the special duck logo balls.

At some point Scott realized that the balls he used as water balls were probably a previous golfer's water ball. Maybe there was a reason it had ended up in the water in the first place! Perhaps they were damaged or waterlogged or just plain bad balls. Why not use your best ball if you needed to clear the water on a tee shot? Hitting someone else' castoff was just asking for trouble.

It wasn't a bad way to approach life either. Why put your worst foot forward in the worst situations hoping to cut your loses if things went badly. You needed to approach each situation in life with your best foot forward. Step into the future with confidence and the best outcome was assured.

Scott reached into his pocket and retrieved a ball and a tee. Some golfers skipped the tee when teeing off with an iron but Scott sank his nearly flush with the ground, letting his ball sit above the ground a quarter of an inch. It made it easier to get under the ball with the club.

He set his ball and then stepped back. The safest shot was to aim at the left side of the green, keeping the water hazard along the right as far out of play as possible. Unfortunately this would end him up on the opposite side of the green from the pin. If he aimed for the pin then the ball would have to travel a good distance directly over the water.

Paul stepped up behind him. "Do you think you can do it?" he asked, reading Scott's mind.

"Not after the tee shot on that last hole," he answered.

"Don't remember your tee shot, remember your last shot," advised Paul. "Just hit it nice and easy and keep to the left."

Scott nodded in agreement and lined up to face the left side of the green. With any luck he'd have a little slice or fade and the ball would end up on the center of the green no more than five yards from the pin. At worse, he'd chip on with his second shot and get himself close enough for a one putt.

He stepped up just short of the ball and took a practice swing. The club swished the air, barely brushing the shortly cropped grass of the tee box. He took another practice swing and it felt just as mechanically sound as the first. He stepped up to the ball. He took a deep breath and exhaled. Then he released the hold on the club and leaned back into his stance. Something was missing and he knew what it was but did he dare? Here?

He turned to Paul. "You're dying to say it, aren't you?" he asked.

"Well," equivocated Paul, "it is appropriate for the hole if not the situation at large.

"I think I need it, Paul."

"Are you sure?"

"Go ahead."

Paul looked around at the confused onlookers, rather embarrassed but not as embarrassed as he soon would be. "Quack," he quacked.

Scott laughed and shook his head. "Just what I needed," he said.

"Yeah," thought Paul. "It had to be done, buddy."

"What are you doing," asked an annoyed Jerry Spaulding. "Hit the ball already."

The official shushed him and shot Scott a warning glance as well. Scott composed himself. He prayed this ball would not end up someone else' water ball. He took one more practice swing and stepped up to his ball. "Quack," he thought and pulled the club back. A part of his mind was thinking what he needed to do to keep the ball straight but he wasn't aware of it. His six iron should put the club out there between a hundred and sixty-five and a hundred and seventy yards from the tee. The club swung down with the same mechanical precision of his practice swings. As he hit the ball, Scott let his eyes follow it out over the left side of the fairway to land precisely where he had aimed. It hadn't pulled the least bit to the right and he had a long fifteen-yard putt to make a birdie. A fairly easy two putt for the par.

Paul took the club and patted his shoulder, "you're dry, Scott" he assured him.

"Dry as can be," agreed Scott.

"It'll be a tester," pointed out Paul referring to the long putt Scott had just left himself.

"I studied all night," Scott said.

Jerry Spaulding nodded his approval at the shot took his turn at the tee. He was using a seven iron, confident he had the distance to reach the green comfortably.

He didn't use a tee and place the ball carefully on the ground. With perhaps too much confidence he wound up and swung. A huge clod of grass obscured the flight of the ball for a moment. The grass landed twenty yards out and the ball plopped nicely in the middle of the pond.

Paul whispered to Scott, "he used a water ball."

"Most definitely," agreed Scott.

With grim determination, Jerry pulled another ball from his pocket and let it fall onto the teeing area. He lined up and swung for the second time, this time the ball soaring in a beautiful arc right for the pin. It stuck and gave a slight bounce to finish no more than six inches from the hole.

He shook his head from side to side staring at the small white speck on the green. It that had been his first shot he would have birdied the hole and likely tied Scott for the lead. As it was he was sitting three, having to take a penalty stroke for going into the hazard and he would sink the ball with his fourth shot.

Pete took a little more time getting ready with his shot and he landed on the far right side of the green inches away from the water but in good position to attempt a birdie himself. Pete's caddy took the outstretched club exchanging it for a putter as the whole group started walking for the green.

When they reached it, a nod from Scott and Pete told Jerry it was okay to play his shot out of order. Normally, the player furthest from the hole would hit first, but Jerry just needed to tap it in and his was done. His caddy lifted the pin and before he took two steps Jerry had knocked his ball in with a careless one-handed putt.

Ellie Burke shook her head at Spaulding's cavalier attitude to the putt. She had seen many golfers miss a short putt doing just the same thing. A tournament like this was not the place to take a double bogey for no reason. She walked around the green to the back right, near the path to the fourth tee to set up to tape Scott's putts.

Scott was obviously next. Although he had little hope of sinking it, he took the time to read the green carefully. Despite having made it to the green in one shot, the water hazard was still in play behind the hole. If he judged the speed of the green wrong, he could roll right past the hole and into the water. If he hit it too softly, he'd have no chance of making par.

Paul stood behind him as they both eyed the shot. "Just hit it in," was Paul's only words of wisdom. "Be the ball," he added, once again quoting a famous line from Caddy Shack.

"Be the ball," echoed Scott.

He took his time and lined up his putt and took his three practice swings to fine tune the speed of the putter. He stepped up to the ball and sighed out a deep breath. He remembered a tip he had absorbed from watching a golf tournament on television once. The pro advised not following the ball when you hit it as that could throw the direction of your club face off.

He pulled the club back even with his right toe and pushed it through, keeping his eyes focused on the spot where the ball once was. His club ended up a few inches past his left toe and he stood frozen.

The crowd around the third green had become automatically silent as Scott putted. As he stood looking at the grass he realized how un-silent it really was. There were subtle noises all around, ignored by his conscience mind most of the time but at this moment he was aware of every single one of them; leaves on a tree to his right rustled with wind, a sparrow chirped behind him, a muffled cry of delight could be heard from a golfer on the first or second hole, a ball plunked neatly into a cup.

A ball plunked neatly into a cup?

Scott slowly turned his head to the left. His ball was not visible. Had it gone in or was it so far of course that it wasn't even on the green anymore, perhaps into the water after all. Then he saw Jerry Spaulding on the far side of the green.

He was standing next to the camerawoman muttering in disbelief. Ellie was smiling. She let her camera fall and gave Scott a thumbs up.

Scott walked across the green to the hole. He looked in at the yellow duck on the white ball sitting calmly at the bottom waiting for him to pull it out.

"You should always take my advice," said Paul still holding the flagstick in his hand.

"What's that?" asked Scott.

"I told you to just hit it in."

It wasn't as far as his putt two weeks before but sinking a putt that long wasn't a common experience for him. He thought he just might stop watching all his putts from now on.

Pete took the time to compliment him on the shot and lined up his own putt hoping to equal Scott's score on the hole, if not the way he did it. His putt broke to the left. Head hung with disappointment he walked over and with more care than Jerry had shown, tapped the ball in the final eight inches or so for a par.

"You taped that?" Scott asked Ellie. She nodded and patted the side of the camera. Scott smiled. The man with the walkie-talkie was making his report. The board with the leading scores was now up. Scott still led with a −2 after three holes. There were two other players at −1, one after one hole, and the other after two holes. Jerry and Pete were fourth and fifth with Es after their names. Scott could bogey the next two holes and still be shooting par for the round. If he could only keep from having a disaster hole he'd finish with a nice respectable score, a great way to end the golf season. Who knew, in four or five years when the kid was in school, he'd start coming out again with Paul. Maybe enter some more tournaments. For the first time he wished Sarah was there to share it with him. He knew she didn't care much about golf, but maybe she'd be proud of how he was doing so far. He hoped the tape from the redheaded camerawoman would turn out okay. Without it who would believe he was playing so well?

21

Jason dialed the number into his phone again and waited about five rings before it was picked up. "Yeah," muttered the voice on the other end, seemingly angry at the disturbance.

"What's going on?" asked Jason.

"The kid is still leading. Don't you have anything better to do than keep bothering me? Aren't you supposed to be covering some golf tournament?"

"Well, my camera girl is off get useless footage and the best guy isn't due to tee off for another two hours. I should still be in bed. What were they thinking sending me out here so early?"

"Maybe Lucy just wants you away from the Marathon and got Keith Kelly to hide you as far away as she could."

"I think you're absolutely right. By the time the leaders finish the marathon and Lucy gets her story this thing will likely just be getting started. There won't be even any scraps for me."

"With this high school kid out of nowhere they have another team getting some background on him right now, you know, track coach, neighbors, other kids. It'll probably eat up most of the evening report."

"Tremendous," said Jason, "This god-awful tournament will hit the garbage can as soon as I walk in the door. Why am I wasting my time?"

"Maybe you can get nine holes in?" joked the man on the other end.

"Ha, ha. If you weren't such a great cameraman I'd hang up on you."

"Well, I'm going to have to hang up on you. It looks like Lucy is going to have us move to the next location. Later, buddy."

The cell phone went dead in Jason's hand. He slipped it back into the inside pocket of his jacket and crushed the empty paper coffee cup in his hand. He glanced at the scoreboard outside and quite a few golfers and other onlookers had gathered to see the latest postings. About a dozen golfers had scores to post and the numbers were starting to fill the board. Most seemed to be pointing at the placard listing the leader so far, "Hanover, S." His score was posted as –2. Not bad, he thought for just three holes.

Then he saw it, suspended from the ceiling in the far corner was a thirty-five inch television not doing anything. He walked up to it, reached for the power switch and turned in on. Maybe he could catch a glimpse of the marathon and this out of nowhere kid who was making the Kenyans sweat. At least it would take his mind off this miserable day.

22

When Jake first saw her, he thought he was having a hallucination, maybe some withdrawal symptom from the alcohol. A red convertible had pulled into the parking lot and slid illegally next to the last car in the row nearest the clubhouse, partially blocking the driveway. The car was different but the woman getting out was all too familiar. She wore a lemon yellow suit over a white blouse. Her hair was cut short and her legs were cut long. It was Karen Blakely, another of the agents that worked for Frasier and Frakes.

Horror gripped Jake and he backed up past the scoreboard. He was pretty sure she hadn't seen him. He cursed himself for perhaps the hundredth time for not ever getting himself a cell phone. He looked around and saw the payphone by the pull carts lined up on the far side of the clubhouse amazed that they still had one but then he realized these courses were mostly frequently by the senior golfers, the group least likely to have cell phones.

He walked over, leaned into the booth and dropped two quarters into the coin slot and dialed Jonathan's office number. "Hello?" answered Jones.

"What is she doing here?"

The silence on the other end told Jake that Jonathan knew exactly whom he meant by 'she.' "Jake, I just found out about it. I'm glad you called. When are you going to get a cell phone?"

Jake interrupted the inquiry. "This isn't some competition, is it? Tell me she's just a huge golf fan and is here to watch the tournament."

"April found out I was sending you and went to Frakes. She convinced him this was too big a deal to trust to you and Frakes had her send out Karen as a sort of backup. I'm sorry."

"So In case I mess up she steps in?"

"She won't bother waiting, she'll just go right for him. You need to get to him first. Tell me you've talked to Patterson."

"I've talked to his caddy. The great one himself has disappeared."

"Hey if you can get him first, you get the deal. Frakes will have to let you be his agent."

"This stinks Jonathan. Karen Blakely being here doesn't do a lot for my confidence."

"Jake, you have to believe me. I want this for you. I know you can do it. Sign Andrew Patterson and we can rub it in April Weinstein and Frakes' faces. This is what you're good at, my friend."

Jake hung the phone up firmly. What was the point? Patterson was never going to sign with him. Karen Blakely was his style. Jonathan should never have sent him here.

Anger and frustration wiped away the remains of his earlier resolve and the overwhelming desire for the numbness that could only be found at the bottom of a bottle of vodka overtook him. He'd go to his car. Find a liquor store or grocery store or even a drug store. Any place that could sell him booze this early in the morning.

He rustled back past the crowd at the scoreboard. He looked towards the parking lot. There was his little GEO metro. A far cry from Karen Blakely's Mercedes convertible but it fit him just fine. With single-minded determination he walked down the sidewalk past the starter's table through a crowd of golfers and caddies. As he reemerged he found himself almost colliding with a neatly dressed woman in a yellow suit. "Sorry," he muttered automatically before his brain registered the situation.

"Hey, watch where you're going," cautioned the woman. Her expression of annoyance turned to glee as Karen Blakely recognized Jake. "Well," she continued, "already signed mister knickers?" she asked jokingly.

"Hey, you want him, he's all yours," Jake answered.

"Jake, honey, with you on the case, there was never any doubt." She turned to head for the starter's table. Undoubtedly Frakes had phoned ahead and her credentials were waiting for her.

He turned and continued for his car. He loosened his tie and pulled it off. He felt his pockets and located his car keys and licked his lips, tasting the burning, numbing liquid that would soon be anesthetizing his throat and his soul.

He stuck the key in the door, popped the lock and opened it. He sat down, and with his hand trembling and tears starting to form in his eyes he jabbed the key unsuccessfully at the ignition until he threw them at the dashboard in utter frustration and anger. He popped open the glove compartment, hoping he had stashed some cigarettes there to help calm his nerves. He was reminded of the movie Airplane and thought to himself, he sure had picked the wrong day to quick drinking and smoking. He slammed the door shut and groped around for his keys. Then he saw it, the white corner of the photograph. He didn't even need to take it down from its spot above the visor to know he wasn't going to the liquor store. He wasn't going home.

His first test of faith in himself and he had almost failed.

Almost.

A memory came to him from the night before, which until now had been a blank. It was vivid and real, like he was reliving it. Gina had taken him home after he drank too much at dinner and probably embarrassed the heck out of her again. Sometime between her helping him get settled in his apartment and her leaving, she had asked him a question.

"Where are you, darling?" She spoke to him as if he wasn't in the room. Like she was talking to herself. "I'll be here when you get back," she promised. "Don't give up on me."

She wasn't worried he'd let her go, but that he'd lose himself further into his self-induced walking coma, or worse, kill himself with neglect and self-loathing.

He was lost, lost in his own mind for the last year. Trapped in a maze of guilt and denial and most of all fear. But Gina was at the end. There couldn't be that many more wrong turns to make before he was out.

Still his body wanted a drink despite his mind's determination to the contrary. He had been here dozens of times before and knew that one drink wasn't all he would have. The effects of the alcohol and nicotine withdrawal were coming to light. The last vestiges of both drugs were leaving his system and without them his body would be in confusion for a while. He could fight it. He really only had one thing to concentrate on. Sign Andrew Patterson. After that he could go home or even better, stop off at some greasy diner and celebrate with a cheeseburger and chocolate milkshake and fries. Nothing like eating to take you're mind of smoking.

No, he would call Gina and tell her what he had done and apologize and mean it. He wanted her here now. Just the sight of her would bolster his resolve. He would have to settle for a mental image of her. Not only how she looked, but the sound of her voice, the scent of her hair, the taste of her lips, the touch of her skin. If he went and had that drink now, all of that would be gone and he wouldn't blame her one bit.

He saw the keys near an empty Burger King bag on the floor of the passenger side. He scooped them up and pulled himself out of the car again, this time with more ease. Then he reached back in and pulled the photograph from the visor, tucking it into the breast pocket on his shirt without looking at it. With both Gina and Brad as his guardian angels, he could do this. He had to. Karen was good but Jake still remembered what it took to be good at this job. It was a job he loved and he needed it as much as Gina to bring him back to life, or rather, bring life back to him.

He noted Karen Blakely disappearing into the clubhouse. Her yellow suit was easy to pick out from a distance. Where was Patterson, he wondered? Someone like him would stand out louder than Karen Blakely. Well he had that jump on her. He knew what to look for. He was sure that Karen would be able to spot Patterson from a general description.

He locked the car and started to jog back to the clubhouse. That was a bad idea. Within fifty yards he was walking again and now panting on top of that. What had he done to himself the last year?

He spotted Eric Peters lounging with some other caddies. "Eric," he puffed, "have you seen Patterson?"

"Naw. Don't expect to for a while. He isn't planning on starting his warm up for another half hour or so."

"Where might he be?"

"Your guess is as good as mine," speculated the young man. "When he disappears like this I just relax and wait." Some of the other caddies chuckled as if they had heard this story before.

"Where will he warm up, then?"

"Over by the driving range," Eric indicated with a sweep of his right arm.

"Listen, if some woman comes asking for him, send her off somewhere to give me some time to talk to him."

"Gee, I don't know, mister," said Eric, less than subtly. Once again his comment evoked a chuckle from the caddies.

Jake pulled out his wallet and found a twenty wedged among some singles and a five. He handed it to Eric. "I'd really appreciate it."

Eric turned the bill over in his hand and pocketed it. "I'll see what I can do," he offered.

"Thanks," said Jake, relieved to have an ally. He walked back to the scoreboard leaving the caddies to their sweet smelling cigarettes and stories.

As soon as he was out of ear shot one of the caddies asked Eric, "Hey, Peters, how much did the lady give you to send that guy chasing gooses."

"A hundred," he answered.

They all broke out in laughter again.

23

Gina let the phone ring. She counted four rings then listened to hear the voice on the answering machine. She suspected it would be Jake, but she thought it might be too early for him. The glowing numbers on the clock read eight forty-five AM.

"Uh, hi," started the voice tentatively, as if he was deciding whether or not to leave a message, "this is Jonathon Jones from Frasier and Frakes."

Gina laughed to herself. She had met Jonathan perhaps a dozen times and even been to his house for dinner but he still acted like he needed to introduce himself.

"I think I may have messed up a deal with Jake and I was hoping you might give me a call and see if we can make sure I didn't make things worse. I'll be in my office..."

Gina didn't wait for him to finish and grabbed up the phone, "Jonathan," she said sleepily, "I'm here."

"Oh, great. I need to talk to you."

"I heard. Something about Jake?"

"I gave him a job today, a decent commission on the back end and a chance to maybe get back into things but I think – I know – my boss sent a backup in case he messed up. It's an important account and they think Jake will, well, you know."

"I know," muttered Gina. She sat up and rubbed her face, letting her hand brush back through her long auburn hair. She could still smell smoke in it and knew she wouldn't be able to fall asleep again until she washed it. Last night she was too tired and too frustrated with Jake to notice. "He was pretty cooked last night. When he gets going I seem to lose whatever progress I've made bringing him back. How did he sound to you?"

"He sounded up for it, like he was ready to take a step forward," commented Jonathan.

"That's good I guess."

"Well, that was until I talked to him a few minutes ago at the golf course."

"Golf course?"

"There's an regional amateur golf tournament and the winner gets to play in the next Pro-Am invitational. There's a fellow, Andrew Patterson, who is a shoe in for it and if Jake can sign him, it's a guaranteed contract with Callaway."

"The golf people, Callaway?" Gina asked, mirroring the question Jake had asked earlier that morning. She was no more of a golf enthusiast than Jake but was a sports fan and would stop to watch if she saw a golfer she was familiar with playing on TV.

"Right," answered Jonathan. "Anyway, Karen Blakely was sent out too and now it's going to be a competition to see who will get him. Jake saw her, called me, and it didn't sound good when he hung up."

"Where is the tournament?"

"A place called George Dunne National Golf Course. It's in Oak Forest. I wish he had a cell phone."

"Tell me about it," laughed Gina.

"Do you have one?"

"Yes." Gina read off the number to Jonathan. "Do you want me to go check on him?" she asked.

"If you don't think he'd get mad at me for calling you."

"I'll tell him I called you and you told me where he was."

"Great," said Jonathan. "I'll be in my office all day." He read her his number. "We've been watching the Chicago Marathon here. Have you caught any of it?"

"I'm afraid you woke me up. We were out attempting to celebrate my birthday last night."

"Happy Birthday. Anyway, some kid has a quarter mile lead on the Kenyans, on pace to set some sort of record. If things fall through with Patterson maybe Jake can get up there and see if he can sign the kid. I'm sure we can use him for something."

"I'll mention it if I find him. Oak Forest you said?"

"Yeah, it's a little south of 159th street off of Central Avenue. It should be pretty easy to find on a map."

"I'll call you later." She hung up the phone and pulled the covers off her legs. Despite physical therapy the muscle of her left leg were atrophied and compared to her right leg it looked like flesh-covered bones. She had injured the leg in a car accident as a child. The bones had been crushed and the nerves damaged. Since then she had lived with a leg brace and a crutch. She had convinced herself that the injury had made her less than a whole woman.

She was otherwise attractive. Long dark hair and chocolate brown eyes with a figure that always got her second looks. It was the third looks at her useless leg that turned guys off. She really couldn't blame them. When she met Jake, however, he seemed to glance over the presence of the brace and crutch. He had never made an issue of it and never patronized her by being overly helpful.

They had only been dating a few weeks when a mugger attacked her as she left work late one night. Jake had been at the hospital after she awoke from three days of unconsciousness. The nurses said he never left her side. Her bad leg had prevented her from being able to escape her attacker and it made her recovery difficult as well. Jake was there with encouragement and provided her a reason to get better. She never forgot that.

She had asked one time if her leg bothered him. If it was something he could live with. He had told her that if she could live with it, he certainly had no problem. She was scared that if she lost Jake, he was her last chance to find someone who could look past her imperfection. Jake was showing his imperfection as a human being and coming to terms with what happened to Brad Finley was something no one could deal with overnight. She hoped that today would see him put things back on track. Maybe Andrew Patterson was the key to him finding his way back to her.

She stood, grabbed her crutch and hobbled to the bathroom.

She showered washing her hair three times until she was sure the smoky smell was washed out or so thoroughly masked by the Herbal Essences shampoo it would be undetectable. She fitted her brace onto her weakened leg, dressed and did her face hurriedly. She figured it would take her about half an hour to forty-five minutes to get to Oak Forest from her condo in Elmhurst.

"Jake, baby, hang in. I'll be there," she told him in a prayer.

24

"Hanover's leading?" asked Carl Bateman from his golf cart with the poster board sign taped on the side designating it as an official tournament cart. He was talking to the old man in the yellow outfit who had just finished updating the scores. Carl was a large man. He had never walked eighteen holes in his life, although he did walk nine once. Once. He wore a dark red blazer with the NIAGA logo over the left breast pocket. A cell phone and walkie-talkie sat on the dashboard of the cart. Every few minutes the walkie-talkie would crackle with updated hole-by-hole scores.

"The best guys still haven't gone off," answered the man. "But he's had a good round so far.

"Any chance he'll stay in it?" asked Bateman.

"I doubt it. He's bound to run in to a double or triple bogey and sink down to the bottom."

"Too bad. Without Caulkin, Patterson will just run away with this."

"What's wrong with Patterson?" asked the scorekeeper.

Carl rolled his eyes and the old man chuckled and answered his own question. "He is a little strange." He nodded off to the parking lot. "Did you notice the USA Sports truck here?" he asked.

"Yes," answered Carl with a little excitement. "A little blurb on the nine o'clock report especially with the tie-in to the Pro-Am invitation can't hurt."

"Well, they're not going to send out a crew for nothing."

"I'll take any publicity we can get. Our membership is down for the last three years running. This is a chance for some great exposure. I just hope the tournament's not as boring as it looks like it might be."

"Well, it's a long day. I heard there is a sports agent around looking for Patterson."

"I know. His name is Jake Fischer. I set up his credentials."

"I heard it was a woman," retorted the scorekeeper.

"A woman?"

"Yeah."

"Two agents at an amateur tournament. Maybe they know something we don't. Is she looking to sign someone or just looking?"

"Word is she has an offer for Patterson even before he hits a ball. He must have been noticed by someone."

"Interesting," mused Carl. "Well, I need to check on the starter. We're two minutes behind with the tee off times. We need to keep this moving."

"By all means," agreed the scorekeeper sarcastically, "get those lazy bones to it."

CHAPTER 6 – FOURTH HOLE

25

The path to the fourth tee followed an asphalt cart path through a copse of trees. The sun was just starting to warm things up a bit and Scott reminded himself to take a drink from his water bottle. He handed it back to Paul who also squirted a slug down the back of his throat and tucked it back in the golf bag.

The joy of his last birdie was almost enough to remove the anxiety that was creeping in again. He stopped as he emerged from the trees and looked to his left, another water hole. This time the water ran along the left side of the fairway of a medium length par four hole. It was a dogleg to the left, meaning that the fairway took a bend about halfway to the hole requiring the first shot to be placed pretty well to be in good position to make the green in two shots. To make things worse, a series of sand traps lined the middle of the fairway on the right side at the bend of the dogleg. A tee shot hit too far it would be on the "beach" as opposed to the water. But a sand trap was always preferable to the water since you usually had a chance to hit the ball back into play again. This fairway would certainly be a challenge to Scott.

What he was most worried about was his tendency to slice the ball. Good golfers could control their tee shots to some degree and have the ball go straight, curve left or right at will. Scott was not one of those golfers. If anything his balls either sliced, like it had on the second tee, or pulled a little to the right. Neither of which would help him on this hole.

Paul handed Scott his three wood. Wood was definitely a misnomer since all of Scott's clubs were metal. When he first started out with his flea market clubs he had used actual woods. The club heads were a solid chunk of carved wood attached to a steel shaft with a metal plate screwed onto the face. They had served him well for many years.

For his thirtieth birthday Scott had treated himself to a decent set of clubs with metal woods and had instantly liked the control and distance the modern clubs gave him. Scott never saw wooden clubs sold anymore but he remembered reading about a club maker in Arizona or New Mexico who still made wooden clubs for a few clients who preferred them.

Scott looked at the club. If anything his three wood sliced more than his driver. "Are you sure?"

"You don't want to get in those sand traps, Scott," answered Paul.

"It'll leave me a long shot to the green."

"Trust me," answered Paul. Scott decided to take Scott's advice this time. Paul had been playing longer than Scott and had played enough golf with him to know what he was capable of. On this he would take his caddy's advice.

"Mr. Hanover still has honors," announced the red-jacketed official. Despite the coolness of the day, the overweight man seemed to be uncomfortably warm in the jacket. A little sweat wetting the side burns on either side of his balding head.

Scott placed his ball and tee in the ground, this time setting the ball just a little bit above the ground. He was used to hitting his three wood off the fairway and if he teed it up like he would with his driver, chances were he'd hit under the ball, sending it farther up than out.

He lined up with a spot he figured was halfway to the green. The ball would roll diagonally across the green and hopefully stop short of the sand trap.

He lined up and waited. Nothing. Not a sound. He turned to look at Paul but instead caught the lens of the camerawoman's camera staring at him. Everyone was waiting for him to hit. He felt stupid but he figured it worked on the last hole. It might help now. But no one seemed to get it.

"Anyone want to say anything?" he asked. A confused expression seemed to multiply over the faces of the onlookers. Ellie let her camera fall and her face brightened with a smile.

"Are you sure?" asked Ellie.

"What are you doing, Mr. Hanover?" inquired the official with no small amount of annoyance.

"Hey, every golfer had his quirks. In my case my quirk is more of a quack."

"What?" demanded the official?

Ellie stood straight, smiled and looked Scott square in the face. "Quack," she exclaimed.

Scott laughed. "Thank you." He looked over to Paul who shrugged sheepishly.

"Sorry, Scott," said Paul. He gave a quiet apologetic "quack" and Scott felt the tension melt into fun. That was why he was here anyway, wasn't it?

"Ahh," muttered the official, his annoyance now full blown disgust.

Scott took his practice swings, getting the feel of the slightly shorter shaft and weight of the club compared to his driver. He stepped closer and whacked the ball with the satisfying plink that a metal wood made when hit perfectly.

The ball soared left of where he aimed but then turned slightly to the right. It landed in the middle of the fairway bounced towards the sand traps on the far side. It rolled to a stop in the rough between two of the sand traps. He was farther from the hole than he wanted but he wasn't wet and he wasn't on the beach. Not too bad considering.

Jerry Spaulding took the tee next. He had his driver and was likely a golfer who could give his shot that needed hook and send it curving left along the dogleg to the hundred and fifty yard marker.

With his customary speed he pulled the club back and whacked it as hard as Scott had seen anyone whack a ball. He had aimed further to the left than Scott would have dared and the ball curved further to the left than Jerry had intended. Spaulding knew the result of his drive without having to see the ball splash in the far end of the water hazard.

Unlike the last hole, his temper showed and he smacked the club onto the tee.

The red-jacketed man raised his eyebrows at the display and announced with a satisfied tone, "Mr. Spaulding is now hitting three."

Once again he had received a penalty for hitting into a water hazard. He would have to count a stroke for his drive and one to get the ball back on the tee to try and hit again. He placed another ball and tee in the ground. Paul noticed the ball was slightly higher than before. He looked at Spaulding's caddy. He seemed oblivious to the mistake. Paul shrugged his shoulders and watched the angry golfer wind up again.

This time the ball not only went straight, but it went high, like a pop fly to center field, except it wasn't a tobacco chewing center-fielder in pinstripes and baseball cap with a glove waiting for the easy catch but one of the sand traps. A puff of sand erupted around the ball and Jerry's temper erupted again as well. Another dent was added to the ground and he stomped off to his caddy. He quietly growled at the frightened kid, obviously assigning him the blame for not noticing Jerry had mis-teed the ball.

Pete Baldwin approached the tee box with calm. He set his ball. Scott noticed he had an iron, probably a four or five. He hit the ball with a little draw to the left and it landed in the middle of the fairway where Scott had hoped his would be. "Nice shot," Scott complimented.

"Thanks," answered Pete. He handed his club to his caddy who had come up behind him leading the group to the fairway.

"I wouldn't mind being there with you."

"I wouldn't mind having your score right now," answered Pete. Scott nodded. He really had nothing to complain about at this point.

Scott would shoot first as he was still the furthest from the hole. As they walked out to his ball he and Paul whispered to each other.

"Boy, that Spaulding guy doesn't seem to be having any fun," said Scott.

"He should have noticed how high his ball was," said Paul. "Can't blame the caddy for everything."

"Does that mean I can blame you for some things?" asked Scott.

"I'll let you know," answered Paul.

"What am I hitting here?" asked Scott

"Well, with this tall grass you should probably stick with an iron. You'll probably be short of the green but with a good chip you can possibly make par, definitely bogey."

"Bogey would be fine. I'm already two under par, I can afford a few shots here and there," said Scott. He truly would be happy with a five on this hole. Any score under eighty-one today would be a great achievement in his mind. He had once shot a seventy-six but on that day he hadn't started out nearly as well as he had today.

Paul eyed the distance to the hole and handed Scott the four iron. "Your three iron will be too low. Better to get up and on to the fairway and be short."

"No problem," answered Scott.

The ball was sitting in a four-yard area of tall cut grass, or rough, between two sand traps on the right side of the fairway. Jerry's ball was in the trap closer to the hole and sitting pretty deep in the sand.

Scott swung a few times in the tall grass, getting the feel for the way it would grab his club head as he hit the ball. Closer to the hole, he thought, just hit it closer to the hole.

There were rare occasions when a shot took him further away. Like when he missed a downhill putt and the ball rolled twice as far away from the hole than he started or if he hit the ball with the edge of the club on a chip shot sending it sailing to the opposite side of the green. Once he had seen Paul send a ball rolling up the trunk of a tree he was trying to shoot around. It shot straight up into the air and ended up two yards behind him.

Scott had about two hundred and fifty yards to the hole and the best he could hit a four iron was maybe two hundred and ten yards when he got a good shot off the fairway. If he got a hundred and ninety out of this grass leaving only a medium chip to the green, he'd be grateful.

He lined up his club and took a deep breath. He tried not to think about the whole swing, just where he wanted the club to be on his back swing, and where he wanted to be after he hit the ball. He would be facing the green and watching the ball sail in the air. He imagined it landing in front of the green. He didn't need to think about everything in between. His muscles and bones had been through enough golf shots to have that part memorized. He would let them do their work. Nine times out of ten, they would do just fine. Well, eight times out of ten. Seven?

He brought the club back with a relaxed ease and fixed his eyes on a spot in front of the ball. The club swooshed through the grass and picked the ball up and into the air, leaving a little shaved patch of sod. It soared and headed to the right. It was closer to the hole, maybe fifty or sixty yards away but not on the fairway. He hoped he was in a good position to have a decent chip shot to get near the hole, at least onto the green.

Paul patted his should as he took the club. "Excellent shot, Scott," he said.

"Thanks," answered Scott halfheartedly.

"No, really," added Paul. You got it up and out and..."

They both finished the sentence, "closer to the hole!"

"It could have been on the fairway," said Scott.

"Fairway, shmairway. It could have been in the trees," retorted Paul. "Glass half full, my friend, glass half full."

Scott smiled and they stepped onto the fairway while Jerry Spaulding took his club into the sand trap.

The sand traps on George Dunne had steep edges cut into the turf and were slightly lower than the surround grass at the edge. Too low a shot and Jerry would run his ball straight into the dirt and it would likely roll right back where he started. The problem was his ball was sitting halfway down into the sand. He would need a sand wedge or a high iron if he hoped to get it out. A sand wedge wouldn't hit the ball as far, but its leading edge was designed to blast through the sand and get the club under the ball.

Jerry was already lying three after his first tee shot went into the water. It would be nice to get it close to the green, but if he was smart he'd just work on getting it out of the trap and then to the green and hope to make up the lost shots on later holes.

He grabbed what appeared to be a seven iron from his bag, ignoring the sand wedge held by the caddy. He was not playing smart. The seven iron might get him a few more yards but it would have a tough time getting the ball out of the pit it was in.

Jerry let the club hover above the sand. Touching the club to the sand while addressing the ball was an automatic penalty. He pulled it back in a full back swing and blasted it into the trap. A spray of sand shot from the club head as he brought it down into the trap and Scott and Paul were not all that surprised when the ball popped up and moved about one foot forward. The sand had gone much farther than that. Before he could stop himself, Jerry's temper flared one more time and he smashed his club into the sand – and froze. His shoulders slumped and he slowly turned to look over his right shoulder to the red-jacketed man behind him.

He held up two fingers of his right hand. Jerry had just been assessed a two stroke penalty for letting his club touch the sand when not hitting the ball. Not only was Jerry still in the trap, he had now used a total of six strokes.

Still, he was a little closer to the hole, thought Scott.

Humbled and disappointed at his position, he walked out of the trap and exchanged his seven iron for the sand wedge. The ball was now at least lying on top of the sand. He easily hit it out into the fairway. He walked out of the trap shaking his head, angry at himself at potentially blowing a good round. He would have about a hundred and seventy-five yards to the hole. The best he was looking at was a nine, maybe an eight for this hole, a score not unfamiliar to Scott and Paul.

The group walked up to Pete's ball. He hit a beautiful shot that landed him on the front of the green, a challenging one putt but an easy two putts from the hole.

Jerry was next to shoot again. He whispered with his caddy and took an iron from him. With more slowness than before he addressed the ball lying on the fairway. He took no practice swings, but seemed to be in less of a hurry than before. He swung the club and the ball took off, a small divot airborne after it. He made it to the green, but then rolled off the back, up hill from the hole and twelve or thirteen yards out. He had taken eight total strokes and was still not on the green. Scott felt sorry for him. He had been there many times. He hoped his ball would make the green.

Scott and Paul found the ball with the yellow duck emblazoned on it off the right side of the fairway. The grass was a little shorter here than on his last shot, but longer than the fairway. The chip shot required a partial back swing as it was well inside the distance he usually hit his pitching wedge. He figured a half back swing would do it and practiced it three times to get the rhythm. It felt right, but as he often found, his practice swing and the real swing at the ball didn't always match up. Paul had often suggested he use his practice swing to hit the all. Scott pointed out that then it wouldn't be his practice swing.

He moved his feet six inches closer to the ball then pulled the club back to where he judged halfway to be and easily swung it at his ball. It lifted out of the grass but headed more to the left than he had aimed. A break in the green helped it roll towards the hole and he ended up less than a yard away.

"Doable," muttered Paul excitedly.

"Doable," echoed Scott.

A speckle of applause acknowledged the shot. As Scott looked around he thought that maybe the crowd following them had grown. Why people would want to come see them golf was beyond his comprehension, unless they were just killing time until the good players started later in the morning.

Jerry was still off the green so he hit next. With even more caution he actually took a few practice swings. Despite the disaster this hole was turning into for him, he was determined to finish it with minimal embarrassment. Jerry stepped up to his ball. Scott noticed the buzz from a small airplane growing louder overhead. He would have stepped back and waited for it to pass rather than have the noise interfere with his concentration. More often than not, little distractions like that tended to affect his shots more than he thought they should.

Jerry seemed unaffected. A grim expression of determination twisted his face and he took a little back swing and pulled the club under the ball. What happened next had happened to Scott more than once in the past but for Jerry it was more icing on the cake. His pitching wedge slid under the ball on the slick grass. The ball popped up and a little forward and landed on the club face again to finally bounce onto the green. Jerry stood frozen, he eyes closed, a glimmer of wetness in the corners. Each time the ball hit the club it was counted as a stroke. What's more, he received one more penalty stroke for hitting the ball twice with one swing. He was lying eleven, ten yards from the hole.

If there was ever a time to smash his club into the ground or throw it up into a tree or into the water, this was it. Not a single person gathered around the hole would blame him now. He held his temper this time and slowly shook his head. Then a strange thing happened. He started to laugh. It was a light chuckle at first, like when you saw a funny bumper sticker.

Then it grew. He was starting make some noise with his chuckle and the staccato laugh seemed to grow stronger with every breath. His caddy, who had been trying to hold in his own amusement for fear of wrath from his boss, started chuckling as well. The contagious mirth swept through the group and soon everyone around the green was laughing with Jerry. It was a hole he certainly would remember and a story that would be told by everyone witnessing it for years to come.

He took his wedge to his caddy. The caddy pulled out Jerry's driver. He laughed more and eventually the caddy pulled out the putter.

The laughter had died and the mood lightened significantly. "In the hole," shouted one of the spectators as he lined up his putt.

"Quiet, please," said the Red-jacketed official whose own face now matched his jacket as he wiped at a few tears on his cheeks left from his own laughter at Jerry's expense.

Jerry hit the putt lightly, letting the downhill slope of the green do most of the work. The ball moved at a slow even pace and twisted along the slight, almost imperceptible undulations of the green as it he had planned the perfect shot. It head straight for the hole but decided at the last second to veer a little to the right, rim around the cup and end up four inches away from the hole towards Jerry. He was shaking his head, not at all surprised at the last bit of defiance the small white orb showed him. He popped it into the hole and to a small bit of token applause, pulled it out, stared at it, and with a sudden burst threw it into the water hazard where it plopped neatly to join his first shot. He handed his putter to his caddy, put an arm around the boy's shoulder and they walked off the green to enthusiastic applause.

Pete replaced his ball marker with his ball and carefully lined up his putt. It ended up six inches short and little to the left, but he parred the hole with little effort and little fanfare. It was hard to gloat when one of your playing partners just finished with a thirteen.

Scott placed his ball down and picked up his tiny Cayman Islands penny. It was copper with a picture of queen Elizabeth on one side and one cent written on the other. It was perhaps half the size of an American penny and just the perfect size for a ball marker.

He stepped back and carefully looked at the lay of the green. It should go straight in.

"Straight in," said Paul behind him as if he was reading his mind.

He stood up and took his practice swings, gauging the right speed. He didn't let his eyes fix on the hole itself. That was too big a target. Instead he looked at a little blade of grass that was poking up a few millimeters at the edge of the hole right in the middle of where he wanted it to go in. He stepped up, let his eyes trace the path a few times and popped the ball. It went straight and fell into the cup, rolling right over that blade of grass. He let out his breath. He tried to remember how many times he had shot a thirteen when first starting out. Plenty. Even nowadays a nine or ten wasn't out of the question on a pretty bad hole. Today, it looked like he was going to have mostly good holes.

26

Jake was confused. He had looked everywhere. Not only couldn't he find Patterson, but Karen Blakely had disappeared as well. Could she have found him first? Where were they?

He stopped in front of the scoreboard just as the scorekeeper was posting the latest results. There were about eighteen golfers with holes played so far and the old man in the yellow shirt and slacks was being kept very busy with reports on his walkie-talkie every few minutes. Hanover still held a lead but by only one stroke and there were half a dozen players right behind him. One player had required a special card, a three with a one drawn in front of it with magic marker. A thirteen. He was probably out of it for sure. His running total showed him shooting ten over par for the first four holes, a big deficit to overcome.

In Jake's inside jacket pocket he felt the crinkle of the contract paper, a one-year term with exclusive rights to the athlete for Frasier and Frakes. He had found a copy in his desk in his apartment buried beneath a stack of mail and magazines that were not bills but hadn't been important enough to demand his attention. Once he had a signature on it Jonathan would take over and negotiate the Callaway deal.

He had asked twenty people if they had seen Patterson and no one had for the last half hour. He kicked himself for not running after him when he saw the golfer earlier in the morning. He had hoped that any information he had gotten from Eric Peters would help him accomplish that goal. In reality it seemed to give Patterson a chance to give Jake the slip.

Now it was a race. Karen Blakely would say and promise anything to get Patterson to sign with her, even if she couldn't deliver it. It was her style. It was then up to the other people like April Weinstein to deal with the complaints later from the athlete and try and get them to forget previous promises with actual deals, usually not as big as promised. It was a body game for Karen. She wanted sign as many as possible and take her commissions. The more athletes she signed, the better chance that one of them might strike it big someday and take Karen with them. Jake preferred to find someone to fit a niche and insure a good fit with his or her sponsor.

He found himself back in the dining area of the clubhouse and considered his situation. He hadn't really been thinking clearly since he'd seen Karen earlier and needed to work out his options at this point. What if she had signed Patterson? What could Jake do then?

He stopped by a television and noted that it was tuned to the coverage of some race, probably a marathon since it was taking place on city streets; Chicago city streets. Of course, he realized, today was the Chicago Marathon. Usually all the top runners at those events were signed with someone and appeared in print ads in running magazines with the feet adorned with logo shoes. Jason Bernard was standing beneath the screen as well, shaking his head, sipping at a coffee cup that had stopped steaming.

"Kenyans?" asked Jake.

"No, some high school kid with an early lead. Now that's a kid who'll need an agent," he suggested.

Jake realized that Jason was right. Who would have thought that a no name would take an early lead in one of the top marathon events in the country? He briefly considered getting in his car, driving as close to the finish line as possible and trying to be the first to shove contract and pen under the kid's face. Then a thought occurred to him.

"High school, you said?"

"Yeah, a junior out of Morton High School in Berwyn, his first marathon race. The kids a natural, it'll top the news if he makes a good showing."

"You don't think he'll win?"

"Not unless he has nitrous tanks in his calves. He can't keep that pace. His inexperience will take its toll after the halfway point. When he hits the wall around twenty miles, he's going to hit it hard."

The wall was the place in the race runners came to where they felt like they couldn't take another step. It was part physical, part mental, and only the toughest and best trained could keep going once they reached it. You had to push yourself beyond what you thought you were possible of doing, and then push some more. The interesting thing about the kid being in high school was that he wouldn't be able to sign a contract for another year, until he was eighteen. His parents would have to be the ones to agree to representation. If Jake could find them before someone else...

Then a particularly devious thought hit him. Was it worth a shot?

He grabbed some change from his pocket and headed back to the phone outside the clubhouse. He dropped two quarters in and called Jonathan once again.

"Jake, where are you?" Jonathan asked with slight apprehension.

"At the course, of course" Jake heard Jonathan sigh with relief.

"Have you signed Patterson?"

"Can't find him."

"Jake, you have to. You need this."

"Hey, I know that. If you don't think I can..."

"No, no," interrupted Jonathan. "I know you can do it. But why are you calling?"

"If you'd let me get a word in, I'll tell you."

"Alright, I'm listening."

"Have you been following the marathon?"

"There's half a dozen of us watching in on the television in the conference room," answered Jonathan.

"Is April Weinstein there?"

"Yeah, why?"

"Who's out there trying to get him?"

"Hey, that's more than I can swing for you buddy."

"Not me. Listen, he's a minor, right?"

"I hadn't thought of that."

"Probably no one has. He can't even sign a contract to hammer a nail, right?"

"Right."

"Well, if April Weinstein thinks there's an advantage by sending someone to meet the kids parents, rather than the kid, they can sign him long before the race is finished."

"I'm not getting it."

"Who would she send?"

"Well, normally, Karen, but she's out there with..."

"Are you getting it?"

"If Karen smells a bigger fish, she'll leave Patterson to you."

"Bingo."

"You're a genius, Jake."

"Thank, you. Once she's gone, that'll leave Patterson wide open for me."

"I'll do my best." Jonathan was silent for a moment. "I called Gina," he said. "I was worried."

"I probably gave you reason to be worried. I was angry."

"And you had every right to be, but she's on her way there."

It was Jake's turn to be silent. "What did she say?"

"She'd come out to make sure you were okay and let you borrow her cell phone."

Jake laughed at the remark. "Well, to tell you the truth, a few minutes ago I was wishing she was here. Do you think my plan might work?"

"I'll put the bug in Weinstein's ear. Call me later."

"Okay." The recorded operator interrupted asking for more money but Jake just hung up. Now he'd wait.

27

Karen Blakely listened intently on her cell phone as April Weinstein outlined the situation. Two clients in one day, it was going to be a very good day for her. She pressed the END button and slipped the slim phone back into her purse.

"Who was that," asked her companion.

"Oh, my boss. Just calling to make sure the best amateur player in Chicago was on our team."

"I must say, Miss Blakely, I am somewhat flattered that you came out here to sign me." His pipe had gone out long before but he still held it.

When he had heard her coming along the path from the clubhouse he was at first angry that his solitude had been disturbed, but her offer and the papers she produced did a lot to move her to his good side.

"Of course this contract obligates you to representation by myself and my boss April Weinstein."

"Of course," answered Andrew.

"I will leave you be," she said, "but I'll be right here when you win to make sure we get you some face time on the evening news. USA Sports is covering it, you know."

"Yes, I heard."

She smiled and turned and walked back towards the clubhouse. He was totally a geek and his outfit looked like something Rodney Dangerfield would piece together but she had him. Jake Fischer could choke on her dust. She checked her watch. She had an hour to make it downtown. It could be done. April was emailing her a picture of the kid's parents to her phone. These things were marvelous inventions, she thought as she lightly tapped her purse appreciatively. She loved having every edge she could, but when it came to Fischer, it was no competition at all.

28

The crib was now reassembled in the baby's room. The second time had gone much faster and Sarah decided her initial mistake would never reach Scott's ears.

There were other things to do in here, like setting up the closed circuit camera they had bought and putting outlet protectors in the plugs. She knew the latter wouldn't be a necessity for a year or so, but being prepared wasn't a motto reserved just for the Boy Scouts.

A month earlier, she and her sister had painted the room. The ceiling was a sky blue with puffy cotton ball clouds swirling around like a warm summer day, the wall a series of murals depicting scenes from the A. A.

Milne's hundred acre woods. Perhaps someday the kid would want it painted over with racing cars or space ship if it was a boy, or ponies or flowers if it was a girl, or maybe something not so stereotypical like an underwater scene or a beach with palm trees.

A ringing phone interrupted her thoughts and she went back to the living room and picked up the portable phone from the living room coffee table.

"Hello," she answered.

"Hi, it's me," said her sister.

"Hi, Anna. What's up?"

"It may already be too late to get anything, but that huge rummage sale at in Northfield is today. Interested in going?"

"That's today?" asked Sarah with disappointment. She had been to the huge sale before with Anna and knew that there were veteran sale hunters camped out for hours before the doors opened to make sure they were the first to get in.

"Yeah, with getting Linus off to camp and Dale driving me crazy while he tried to get his presentation in order, it slipped my mind. Even if we're too late for anything good, I could use a trip out of the house," she said.

"Well, I'm kind of in the mood for a little celebrating myself. I just finished putting the baby's crib together," she answered proudly.

"I thought Scott was going to do that."

"He was, but he's out golfing and I just did it. It wasn't that hard," she confided, leaving out the part about having to do it twice. Maybe she'd tell her later.

"Him and his golfing. Why do you let him do that?"

"Well, partly because it's nice to have him gone for a few hours once a week and partly to build up a little guilt so I can get him to do other things for me."

"Like put the crib together?" commented Anna sarcastically.

"No, like mowing the lawn and fixing the fence gate and cleaning the gutters. After a round of golf he feels more obligated to do some work around the house than if I just nag him."

"I guess I can see your point," agreed Anna. "Anyway, I'll be there in ten minutes. We'll go out for lunch at that new Chinese place on Main afterward. I haven't been able to get Dale to take me there yet and I've been begging for two months."

"Sounds good. I'll clear out the trunk of the car and we'll be set."

"Oh, I'm so glad I called," said her sister excitedly.

"Me too. See ya." She pressed the talk button to hang up the phone. She turned off the CD player and for fun flipped the television back on. They were still covering the marathon and now it appeared other stations had picked up the coverage. She listened as the announcers marveled at the young kids ability to keep up an unprecedented pace. They were beginning to believe his inexperience was paying off. A group of veteran racers were now a quarter mile behind him and he seemed to be widening the gap every few minutes.

They were quick to point out that the race was far from over, but it would certainly be a day that many people in Chicago would remember for a long time to come.

They weren't far from the truth.

Another spasm of muscle contractions hit Sarah's abdomen. She took a few deep breaths and it passed quickly. She was quite sure it wasn't labor but still considered calling Anna to cancel their outing just in case. As she considered it further she figured she might as well go. The baby still had a few more weeks to cook and if something did happen, she wouldn't be alone.

29

Ted Lange was enjoying his morning at the tournament. A back injury prevented him from swinging his clubs competitively anymore, but he did like to teach others the game that had consumed six decades of his life.

He had first sneaked his dad's clubs out of the garage to the empty lot across the street when he was twelve. He had lost every single one of the balls his dad had in the bag in the tall grass. Most of his shots went wild but maybe one out of ten he sent soaring.

His father didn't find out about Ted's unauthorized usage until he went to play golf that weekend and noted all the balls were gone. Instead of getting angry, he bought his son a second hand set of clubs and a bag of used balls from the pro shop at the country club and presented them to his son. He had many great memories of golf outings with his dad who instead of getting irate at losing five dollars worth of balls, recognized Ted's love for the game and fostered it into a pro career. His dad had died of heart attack at thirty-nine and had never seen Ted play professionally, but he was always on Ted's mind when he did play, offering silent suggestions as Ted played and bringing unprovoked smiles to his face.

Ted loved to watch amateur tournaments and when the Northern Illinois Golf Association asked him to help at this event, he was excited to be able to meet a lot of the golfers as they warmed up. He had enjoyed watching a couple of the local qualifying tournaments and felt lucky to still be involved with the game after his injury.

He glanced at his watch. He had another ten minutes of his break before heading back to the driving range but he was interested in seeing how the field was coming so far and had wandered up by the clubhouse. He found Joe Caulkin, a former student studying the scoreboard as it was being constantly updated.

"Joe, sorry to hear about your wrist, tough break," he joked.

"I haven't heard that one a hundred times," answered Joe.

"Can't wait until the I'm finished at the driving range and I can get out on the course and watch. Where is the action?"

"I'd say the fifth hole."

"The fifth hole?"

Ted pointed to the Top Ten player section and the name and score at the top. Hanover, S –2 4

"The fellow who took your place, eh?"

"That's the one," answered Joe.

"He's having a good morning?" asked Ted.

"Great so far. He's ranked last you know."

"I know. I got to meet him this morning."

"You didn't do your old shoelace thing, did you?" inquired Joe.

"You know me too well," answered Ted. "He's got a good game somewhere in him," said Ted.

"Well, it looks like it's oozing out today," agreed Joe.

"Is that what I think it is?" asked Ted pointing at the altered number three card on the board?"

"Yep, a nontuple bogey I believe," he laughed.

"Well, there are really bad holes in all of us, my friend. I can't remember the last time I had a thirteen, but if I play long enough, I'll see it again."

"We'll have to see if Hanover can hold the lead, especially once the top twelve rated guys get out there."

"Patterson is suppose to have the game to take it," commented Ted.

"I'm betting not today," said Joe.

Ted turned to look at him. "You bet against Andrew Patterson?"

"Worse," he continued, "I bet against Andrew Patterson with Andrew Patterson!"

"Ay," cried Ted. "Well, maybe young Mr. Hanover can dig you out of that one. Patterson will probably shoot in the high sixties."

"Oh wait, here comes Hanover's group's scores for five." The yellow shirted scorekeeper pulled a green card from his stack and laid on the hook next to Scott Hanover's name under the column for the fifth hole.

30

Karen Blakely was walking quickly for the parking lot. She couldn't go too fast due to her too high heels and too tight skirt, but she seemed in a definite hurry.

Jake couldn't tell where she had come from. She reached her car and held out a key fob. She disarmed the car alarm with a beep and opened the driver side door. His plan had worked. He half hoped Karen would find the kid's parents. He was feeling a slight bit of guilt at his subterfuge, but he knew that she was capable of far trickier things than he could think of.

He noticed a caddy standing in the line waiting to tee off lighting a cigarette. He walked over to the young man. "Can I bum one off you, I quit this morning," he joked.

The kid gave a chuckle. "Me too." He should out a slim white cigarette and Jake took it.

"Thanks."

"Need a light?" he asked.

Jake twirled the perfectly packed cylinder of tobacco in his fingers and inhaled deeply imagining the smoke warming the back of his throat. He slipped it into his shirt pocket and nodded. "Not now, I'll save it for later."

"Suit yourself," said the caddy as he took another long pull on his own butt.

I won't smoke it until I sign Patterson, he promised himself, if only he could find him!

CHAPTER 7 – FIFTH HOLE

31

Scott was up first once again and once again there was water on the hole. It was like playing in the everglades. He remembered back to a course he played in Florida that had alligators hanging around the water hazards. At one hole his cousin Tom was no more than five yards from one of the reptiles that was at least ten feet from nose to tail. Tom was unphased by the presence of the creature and Scott had pulled out his camera to snap of shot of Tom hitting the ball with alligator right behind him. The photo hung in his office above his drafting table. Tom had offered to take a similar posed shot of Scott in front of the alligator but Scott passed. That would be putting too much temptation in front of fate. He didn't remember how he shot that day, but he did lose a lot of balls.

The water on this hole was on the left side again, but the fairway was straight four hundred and fifteen yards to the hole. The water wouldn't come into play unless he hit it short and hooked it.

Paul handed him his driver and looking over at the group by the tee he nodded his head.

"QUACK," they all shouted. Scott joined them in laughter. The joke had spread and Scott was pleased to see that even Jerry had joined in on the effort. The red-jacketed official seemed a little disturbed at the outburst. "Quiet on the tee," he insisted.

"It's okay," said Scott.

The red-jacketed man huffed and Scott placed his ball. He was careful to have the yellow duck logo facing the pin on the green. He wanted the ball to know where it was going.

A REALLY GOOD DAY

It was an average length par four but had the advantage of being downhill from the tee and he hoped he'd get to the green in two this time. It was always easier to rely on a having two putts to make par, than to try and sink one putts all the time. There was some sand up near the green, but that wouldn't come into play until the second shot. The green itself was very long from front to back and the pin was placed up near the front four yards from one of the traps. They weren't making it very easy for the players today, but why should they?

On his first practice swing he pulled the club back further than usual and pulled the club around as fast as he could. The club head missed the patch of grass he was aiming at and he nearly fell over. Paul walked up to him. "What are you doing?" whispered Paul.

"Wanted to see if I could get some more meat on the ball. If I can get two hundred and eighty yards on this one, I'll be just a pitching wedge away," he whispered back.

Paul motion for him to step off the tee and he held up a T with his hands in a time-out signal intended for the official, something you don't normally see during a golf tournament. Paul was so used to doing it from coaching little league and soccer he gave it no second thought. The red-jacketed man returned a confused expression and Paul turned to talk to Scott.

"You're going to put it in the water back on the fourth hole with a swing like that," he said softly.

"I've got the swing in me. I'm not even thinking about it. I just need a little more speed."

"Scott, it's not the speed but how the club face hits the ball. You know that. Just take an easy swing and hit it right in the middle."

"I know, but..."

"Trust me. I played baseball and I know the harder you swing the more you strike out. It's not time to try something new. Use your regular swing. You'll get it out there. It's wide open after the water and it's a big green."

Scott thought and breathed deeply. "I know you're right. I'm starting to think maybe I can finish in the top half today but I'm not sure my usual game will do it."

"Scott, you haven't played your 'usual game' all morning. Keep the same swing and stay in the zone. You'll do fine. Don't forget we're just here to have fun and get in eighteen holes on a great course."

"Okay."

Paul smiled and patted Scott's back.

"Is everything alright?" asked the official?"

"Just fine," answered Paul, "play ball."

Ellie laughed and quickly stopped when the red-jacketed man looked in her direction. She got her camera ready and started taping.

Scott took two more practice swings, this time remembering to just take an easy swing, not trying to kill the ball at all. The club swung straight and he felt the flow that came with practiced stroke. No thinking, just motion, fluid and smooth. All components of the swing coming together in perfect timing making it look effortless and beautiful.

He stepped up the six inches to put his club head behind his ball. He didn't want to kill it. All he saw was the yellow duck for a moment and then it was gone, the green tee leaning slightly forward and his head followed his upper body to track the ball. He didn't even remember taking the back swing or hearing the ping of the club face striking the ball. He felt like he was out of his body for a few seconds but a smattering of applause brought him back as the ball dropped neatly in the middle of the fairway and rolled up near the hundred and fifty yard marker.

Once again he found himself holding his breath and he let it out, taking a few quick breaths to replace the stale air in his lungs. He seemed to stare out at the ball for a long time and smiled. Wow, he thought. That was a great shot.

He knew it wasn't a three hundred and twenty–five yard drive you might see a pro do, but for him, it was really good.

Pete managed to put his drive to the right of the fairway in amongst some squat trees that lined the ridge marking the far side of the fourth fairway. Just down the other side were the sand traps that had nearly caught Scott on his last drive.

Jerry stood on the tee and threw a ball into the water before even starting. "There," he commented, "that's out of the way." They all laughed.

His tee shot ended up about five yards past Scott's and he beamed coming off the tee. "Great drive," commented Scott.

Jerry nodded in agreement. "Thanks, you too." He patted Scott's shoulder and they walked down the fairway together.

Pete was furthest from the green and shot first, chipping the ball left onto the fairway to avoid the low hanging branches of the trees. He was still behind Scott and Pete and walked up to his ball for his third shot. "My turn for a bad hole," he commented.

"It is closer to the hole," Scott pointed out. Pete was slightly confused by the statement, partially because it was obvious, but also he had no idea why Scott had said it. He shrugged it off and pulled out his seven iron.

With the power that all self-fulfilling prophecies carried he plopped the ball pin high into the sand trap to the right of the green. With the hole so close to the sand trap, it would be hard to pop it out and land it close to the pin. He was maybe looking at a six for the hole and wasn't happy at all with the shot.

"Closer to the hole," teased Jerry and he earned a rotten snarl from Pete. Scott tried not to laugh out loud.

Scott took out his nine iron and carefully lined himself up to land a yard or two to the left of the pin, hopefully safely away from any beach up there. With just one practice wing he stepped up to the ball and found himself staring straight at the duck, which was pointed directly at the pin again. What were the odds, he thought.

While he was thinking about that his body swung the club and the ball disappeared once again. He found it high in the sky, just to the left of the pin as he planned. As it came down it seemed to slide a little to the right and with an audible thud, left a black impression on the green and hopped to within two feet of the hole. Once again he seemed to stare at the ball on the green for minutes. The silence around him was a stunned silence. No one had expected him to hit the ball that well, despite his great playing so far. No one played this well in an amateur tournament – usually.

"Nice shot," said Jerry. "Five bucks says I can get it closer."

"Deal," answered Scott without thinking.

Jerry walked up to his ball with a pitching a wedge. He laid his club behind it and took his stance, lightly cradling the club in his gloved left hand. He wrapped his right hand around the shaft of the club, covering the thumb of his left hand. With his customary quick back swing he popped the ball even higher in the air than Scott had. It landed slightly to the right of the pin and behind it, but suddenly started a little roll backwards coming within a yard of the pin. From where they stood, they couldn't tell who was closer at this point, but both were in birdie range for sure.

"Double or nothing I sink the putt?"

"No way," Scott answered just as quickly as before.

Pete was already walking ahead of them with his caddy, headed for the sand trap. As they approached, Pete had a confused look on his face. There was no ball visible in the trap.

"I saw it go in," said his caddy. "I'm sure it didn't bounce out."

Nonetheless they searched the tall rough around the trap and nothing turned up.

"What do I do?" he asked the official.

"If you can't see it, you can look for it. It's a ball lost in a hazard. You can take a drop in the trap no more than two clubs lengths from where it entered."

"No penalty?"

"No penalty," confirmed the red-jacketed man.

Pete's caddy handed him another ball and Peter dropped it. He took his sand wedge and with an experienced swing popped it out nicely, the ball rolling within four inches of the hole but continued until it was three yards past and uphill of the hole.

He shook his head but realized that was as best as he could hope for in the situation. Scott and Jerry picked up their balls, marking their positions. Pete swapped the sand wedge for a putter and walked to the other side of the green to read the lay of the turf. He didn't seem like what he saw and was taking his time. He stood and lined up his putt tapping it down the gentle slope. The ball passed the hole on the same side as his sand shot did and rolled two yards past the hole.

"Don't say it," whispered Paul, reading Scott's mind again. Scott wanted to say "closer to the hole," but Paul's advice kept his mouth shut.

With more deliberation, Pete lined up his sixth shot and sank the putt with practiced ease.

It was obvious that Jerry's ball was a few inches closer than Scott's but Scott would wait until they finished the hole to pay off. He eyed his putt and it looked like it should go straight in. He was careful when he replaced his ball marker with the ball to line up the duck so it was facing the hole once again. He kept the backstroke on his practice putts sharp and short then stepped up to the ball and watched the duck. Once again it seemed as though his club moved without his knowledge and the duck was gone again. The beautiful sound of the ball hitting the bottom of the cup caused him to turn his head. Paul was grinning like an idiot, his fist punching the air in delight. Scott had sunk his third birdie in five holes. He couldn't remember the last time he had three birdies in nine holes let alone three birdies and two pars.

"Nice putt," complimented Jerry. "Should have taken the bet," he teased.

Jerry studied his putt carefully. It would take a miracle for him to have a chance at making a showing in the tournament after his thirteen, but he was determined to do his best nonetheless, an attitude that Scott admired. He sank his putt with ease and Scott grinned with him. "Nice bird."

"Nine to go," added Jerry with a chuckle. Jerry's caddy replaced the flagstick and as they walked off the green, the man with the walkie-talkie made his report. The boy with the leader board was already pulling numbers off, waiting for the report of the second and third place golfers to come in. The person at first place would stay there, at least a little while longer.

32

While the others in the growing crowd following the three golfers to the sixth tee, Ellie hung back and pulled out her cell phone and pressed the speed dial for Jason Bernard's Phone.

"It's me," she greeted him.

"Do you know what's happening at the marathon?" he thundered. She pulled the ear away from her ear to ease the pain somewhat.

"No, but..."

"Some high school kid is running away with it and the story of the year and I'm stuck here."

"Well, I think..."

He cut her off again, "and where the heck are you. I want to get our tape of Patterson and get out of here as soon as we can. This day is a disaster."

Ellie counted to three and breathed deeply. Usually people assumed her read hair came with a matching temper, but this Bernard fellow was more than mad enough for both of them. She was glad she wasn't at the clubhouse. "This guy I told you about before. He started with a couple of lucky shots, but now he's holding up. He's on track to smash some tournament records here."

"What? I thought the worst golfers went off first."

"They do, but that doesn't mean they're not good. Listen, I've got his every shot on tape and there's some really good stuff here."

"They didn't send us out to get tape on the sixtieth ranked player, they want the guy whose going to play in the pro tournament in a couple of weeks," insisted Jason.

"Are you that stupid?" she almost shouted, but kept her voice in the inaudible range to those getting ready on the next tee.

"Are you calling me stupid?"

"You just were complaining about how you were missing a story about some nobody high school runner coming out of nowhere and we have practically the same thing going on under our noses. Just because you don't think golf is a real sport, doesn't mean that fifty million Americans agree with you."

Jason was quiet on the other end for a moment or two. "Alright. You keep taping him. You'll be back for Patterson?"

"We should finish up the front nine just before he tees off," she assured him. "If he flubs up a couple of holes I'll probably come in sooner, but I don't think that's going to happen. He's having a great day."

"I'm glad someone is," answered Jason and he hung up.

She made one more call and placed her cell phone back in its belt holster. She checked the tape counter and the battery levels. She was set for the next four holes

Ellie smiled and jogged to catch up to the others. She glanced at her scorecard. Once more a water hazard would play a role in the hole and she wanted to be in on the quack.

33

Andrew Patterson watched as Karen walked quickly back towards the clubhouse. Dressed as she was it was difficult for her to move very fast and he could tell she wanted to. He folded his copy of the contract and slipped it into the breast pocket of his golf shirt under his sweater.

He hadn't even swung a club yet today and things were looking mighty nice. He had been miffed that she had found him during his meditative pre-game ritual. Karen Blakely said the scorekeeper for the big board had seen Andrew heading off this way and that was how she found him. After she calmed him down and explained her presence there he had become quite excited. He was going to do a commercial for Callaway golf. He was already a fan of the Callaway Tour Golf Balls and Karen seemed very excited to know he had some of their products in his bag.

A raucous noise erupted from the area by the clubhouse. People were cheering and hollering about something. How far away would he have to get for some quiet? If that happened while he was on the tee he would definitely have a word with the tournament officials.

Andrew had been a little confused to hear about this Jake Fischer fellow, another agent, apparently, who wanted to sign Andrew. Well, he had missed his chance, hadn't he? Besides he had quickly decided he rather liked this Karen Blakely. She seemed to know what she was talking about. Karen was very excited about the possibilities that would present themselves once he won the tournament. She appeared to be the kind of person who understood Andrew and his passions and predilections and eccentricities. She assured him they were all assets in the marketing world. Andrew could only agree.

34

Joe Caulkin slapped Ted on the back as the scorekeeper let the large white three slip into place under the fifth hole score for Scott Hanover. "I'm going out there. I don't want to miss any of this. I'm beginning to think I didn't make such a stupid bet after all."

"Three birdies in five holes. He's playing like a pro."

"Well, we've all had good runs," suggested Joe.

Ted nodded in agreement. "Well, I have to get back to the driving range," he announced as he checked his watch. He pulled a walkie-talkie off of its belt clip. "The tournament gave me this to help follow the scores on the course. I'd turn this thing on but I'm afraid it would disturb the golfers practicing," he said.

"Didn't they give you an ear plug?" asked Joe.

"I don't know? I don't think so," said Ted. He looked over the walkie-talkie. Joe took it from him and found the earphone receptacle. He handed back the walkie-talkie and fished in his pocket for his iPod and held it with his left hand while he unwrapped the headphones with his right. He handed them to Ted. "These should fit just fine."

Ted took them and plugged them into the socket. He placed them over his head and turned on the black box. A smile lit his face. "Thanks, Joe. I'll catch you later." He ambled back to the driving range, at one point his left hand coming up absently to rub a spot on his lower back.

Joe watched him and absently reached into the cast to try and reach an itch on his left wrist. Boy, would he be glad to get this thing off. He considered the situation. Two injured golfers were enjoying a vicarious thrill following a low ranked amateur. It felt good. It was fun and exciting and who knew how it would end. If only Hanover could beat Patterson. That would be exciting.

If only.

35

Patterson's caddy, Eric Peters, was still standing with the other caddies halfway between the clubhouse and the driving range. Their position gave them a perfect view of the ninth green. Golfers would soon be coming down the ninth hole ready to make the turn onto the back nine. Jake had been watching the caddy surreptitiously. Patterson would have to meet up with him before heading to the practice range. Jake would make his move then. He glanced at the start time listed for Patterson and then his watch. If Patterson was going to get in a decent warm up, Jake shouldn't have to wait very long.

The morning was beginning to get a little warmer and Jake took off his jacket and slung it over his left shoulder, loosened his tie and brushed absently at a stain on his shirt. He decided to walk to the driving range sitting to the north of the parking lot and wait there. Eric had said the golfer would warm up there. Twenty golfers were lined up striking balls with various clubs, some had their caddies teeing up the next ball, others just rolled the ball into place with their club head and swung leisurely at the striped orbs.

A sudden rumbling startled him as he watched. A caddy stood over the ball machine holding a dark green plastic basket that was being filled with balls from a large white box set next to a one-story brick building. The caddy took the balls over to a golfer who was doing some stretches at one of the teeing areas.

"Waiting for a spot?" asked an elderly gentleman in a NIAGA windbreaker.

"What, me?" asked Jake. "Naw, just killing some time."

"You here to watch?" asked the man.

"Here to watch one of the players at any rate," answered Jake. He extended his right hand. "Jake Fischer."

"Ted Lange."

"You work for the tournament?" asked Jake.

"Yep. Just here to help the golfers with any last minute adjustments and pointers. Most of the guys here now are the serious amateurs. Statistically, one of them has a pretty good chance of winning. They all have handicaps in the single digits."

"I never really understood the handicap deal," muttered Jake, not thinking about what he was saying.

Ted raised an eyebrow. "You're not a golfer?"

"I'm a sports fan. I know a little about most sports but mostly I know what makes a good sportsman."

"Interesting," commented Ted. He waited a moment. "And what is that?"

"What's what?" asked Jake, lost in his surveillance of the golfers practicing.

"What makes a good sportsman? Or should I say athlete."

Jake turned his attention to Ted. "No, sportsman. There's a difference," said Jake. Ted looked at him inquisitively. Jake often found his theory of the sportsman to bore many people and had learned not to expound on it if left to his own direction but he sensed Ted was genuinely interested.

"An athlete is someone who is very good at the game. They've mastered the techniques and the rules and the strategies and can play at the top of the field with no worry of embarrassing themselves – most of the time," he added. Ted Chuckled at the qualifier and so did Jake.

"So Tiger Woods is a good athlete."

"Well, yes. But that's not to say he's not a good sportsman as well, but at times, I think he slips more towards trying to be a better athlete and he loses something."

"So how do you define a good sportsman?"

"A sportsman loves his sport. He knows what is needed to be a very good player but he doesn't necessarily have to have all the skills. He plays because it's fun. He's not out to beat his opponent, although that is nice. He wants to improve his game and do a little better than the time before."

"I think I'd have to agree with you on that," said Ted. "There are a lot of athlete's here, but unfortunately not many sportsmen. They don't seem to make it to this level very often."

"Well, I think at this level, you do see mostly athletes. The ones that are both are the ones that take it to the top."

"Can't a sportsman whose not a great athlete make it?"

"Not for long. They may have a few good days here and there and some great shots periodically, but you have to put them together consistently to win."

"That's true," agreed Ted. "But I have seen my share of Pro golfers have rotten days."

"No one's perfect," pointed out Jake.

"But I also think an average player will have one or two really great rounds in them, statistically that is. I mean a golfer with a handicap of eighteen will shoot most of his holes one over par, some more, some less."

"So the handicap is how much a golfer is expected to shoot over par?"

"Simplistically, yes. It also takes into account the difficulty of the course."

"So your eighteen handicap is bound to shoot even par as much as he is thirty-six strokes over par."

"Again, to put it simply, yes. And if you extrapolate further, he should be able to shoot eighteen strokes under par as often as his shoots fifty-four over par."

"How often does a golfer shoot eighteen under par?"

"Never been done, at least not at the competitive level. I did see a golfer by the name of Al Geiberger shoot a fifty-nine or thirteen under par in the second round of the Memphis classic in 1977. That was before golf equipment was at the level it is now and you had to really play the course effectively to do that well. He ended up winning the tournament.

"Wow," commented Jake.

"For a pro golfer to shoot four rounds in a row under seventy is a pretty difficult accomplishment."

"So is fifty-nine the record?" asked Jake.

"Yep. Chris Beck tied it in 1991 in Las Vegas but he didn't win that one. David Duval did it in 1999 at the Bob Hope tournament in the last round to pull out the win. Pretty exciting. I expect the winner today will have a round around sixty-seven or sixty-eight. Four or five under par."

"But there's always a chance," added Jake.

"That's what I always say. No one thought Duval had a chance. But by the time he hit the fifth hole you could see it in his eyes. He was in a place few golfers ever find and he put together eighteen great holes. A year later he's hitting a quintuple bogey on the seventeenth hole at St. Andrews. Let a sand trap get the better of him. It all balances out."

"What about this Hanover guy. Last I checked he was two under par after four holes."

"Three under after five holes," corrected Ted tapping his walkie-talkie.

"Wow," commented Jake, "but odds are he'll be over par by the end and finish up near the bottom where he started."

"Odds are," repeated Ted. "But the funny thing about odds is even a million to one shot comes in once every million times or so."

"I guess so. I mean I could be struck by a meteorite right now," said Jake as an example. With out thinking he looked up into the sky and they both laughed.

"What do you do, Mr. Fischer?"

"It's Jake, and you could say I find sportsmen and sportswomen. I'm a sports agent."

"Oh, you represent anyone I'd know?"

"Currently I don't represent anyone. My last client..." Jake trailed off. He had started to go down too painful a road and needed to stop.

"Your last client what?" prompted Ted.

"I'd rather not talk about it."

"They dumped you or something?"

Jake looked at the older man. He had confused inquisitive expression and Jake felt his emotions begin to flood back. What a shot of tequila could do now. Something to numb the pain, to drive back the memories.

What was he doing? For the third time today Jake was tempting his ability to stay sober. He couldn't keep thinking about it like this. He had to keep his brain focused.

"Hey," apologized Ted, "I didn't mean to offend you."

"It's okay," said Jake. "A kid was injured because I let him attempt a stunt that was too dangerous. I paid for it with my career and my sanity and my sobriety." He couldn't believe he was telling this stranger this. He didn't care about Jake's problems.

"Brad Finley?" asked Ted.

The sound of Brad's name shocked Jake. How did Ted know about Brad? Had Jake mentioned the name? He asked, "How did you?..."

"My grandson roller blades. He mentioned the story to me last Christmas. I didn't know Brad Finley was your client, the name just popped into my head. But as I recall it was an accident."

"I should have known it was too much for him."

"Those skateboarders take lots of risks."

"He and his parents were counting on me to make sure they were acceptable and they sure didn't think he'd end up paralyzed at the end of the day."

"So you drank?"

"Yeah," answered Jake. As he looked at Ted the old man smiled and shook his head. His expression held sympathy but empathy as well.

"I wrecked my back five years ago. Drank for four years after that. I told myself if I couldn't golf, what was the point."

"You don't drink now?"

"One day at a time."

"Well for me I need to get through the one day part."

"Jake. Remember what I said about odds? What do you think the odds were that Brad Finley was going to get hurt doing that stunt? Looking back as objectively as you can."

"I guess it's in that one-in-a-million range."

"He could have been struck by a meteor. Would that have been your fault?"

"No, but I have no control over that. I do have control over where the commercial is shot and whether or not I think my client is in condition to attempt it."

"Then you must have thought it was safe or he wouldn't have attempted it, right?"

"I should have watched out for him. He was just a kid, a fifteen year old boy, Ted."

"The odds are funny, Jake. Like I said, even the one in a million come in every once in a while."

"Then I should be due for a one in a million in my favor. Maybe I should go out and get some lottery tickets."

"Maybe, but if you go back to doing what you did best, there's always a chance you'll come out a winner."

"Yeah, I think my girlfriend believes that to."

"I bet a lot of people have faith in you, Jake. Give them a chance to be right."

Jake stood silent for a moment. The plink of golf balls reentered his awareness and a murmur of voices crept into the world that seemed to be lost during his conversation.

"Maybe Andrew Patterson will come through for me."

"Patterson?" laughed Ted.

"What's wrong?"

"Jake, he's not your sportsman. Yes he's a good golfer but he'll never take the risks it takes to break out of the statistical bell curve."

"Well, he's all I got today."

"Keep looking up," suggested Ted. Jake was confused for a moment then remembered his reference to being struck to a meteorite and chuckled. "I will."

"And, Jake, with regards to one day at a time, call me if you feel the days is getting a little too tough." Ted pulled out his wallet, extracted a business card and wrote a number on the back. "That's my home number. If I'm not there my wife will know where I am. It'll be another lifeline for you."

"Ted," said Jake taking the card and extending his right hand again. "It's been a pleasure meeting you."

"I'll see you around, Jake. When I'm done here I plan on walking the course a little."

"Thanks for the information and the advice," said Jake and they shook. What were the odds he'd meet someone like Ted Lange today, here? It boggled the mind.

Jake started walking toward the clubhouse, scanning the area for a violent combination of colors and fashions that might be the start to something better.

CHAPTER 8 – SIXTH HOLE

36

The sixth hole seemed to stretch on for a mile. It was actually about a third of a mile, the longest hole on the course and perhaps the most difficult one to par let alone birdie. With three strokes in the bank he was well aware he could afford a bogey or even a double and still have a great round of golf, but boy wouldn't it be great to par this one.

"Mr. Hanover still has honors," announced the official. It was an unnecessary announcement but it gave the red-jacketed man something to do. "There will also be silence at the tee from the spectators," he added.

To the right and at the distance of a decent drive, a water hazard teased the edge of the fairway. It in fact was an extension of the same pond Scott had escaped on the third hole and he didn't want to give a ball to it on this one. "Oh, it doesn't bother me, if they quack," said Scott.

"Nonetheless, it bothers me," drawled the official, his voice falling down in pitch, the emphasis on "me."

Paul covered his mouth and coughed an inaudible insult to the man, but everyone knew what he said and managed to stifle their chuckles. "There will be no more talking while players are getting ready to hit or hitting," added the official.

Scott shrugged his shoulder. He glanced at the camerawoman and she gave a consolatory smile. She mouthed a quack and Scott smiled. It wasn't the same but he didn't need to be on the official's bad side.

He set up his ball and pulled his cap down a little to reduce the glare coming from the sun which they were now facing. It would continue to be in his eyes for the next three holes as they made their way back to the clubhouse. He took a couple practice swings, concentrating on keeping the swing controlled and steady.

The water pulled at his eyes and something felt wrong. He looked at his feet. He scrunched his face and without thinking about how amateurish it might look, he laid his club on the ground so that the head was at his left toe and the handle at his right toe. He then stepped back and looked to where the shaft of the club was pointed. It was aimed straight for the water hazard to the right. He looked at Paul.

"I wanted to say something but I didn't want you to get penalized by Hitler there," he muttered.

"It's okay," said Scott. "I knew it didn't feel right."

He left the club on the ground but redirected it so it now pointed down the left side of the fairway. He then realigned his toes along the shaft before picking up the club. It was a tricked he had learned when he first started golfing. The line your toes made always pointed to where the ball would go if you hit it well and with his tendency to add a little slice to his drives he felt confident that he'd keep it in the fairway now.

"Are you ready?" Mr. Hanover, growled the official.

Scott glared at him. "I would appreciate it," he said, directing his stare into the red-jacketed man's eyes, "if there was no talking right now."

The man gasped and sputtered and realized he had just broken his own rule. He tried to return Scott's glare but just nodded and averted his eyes from Scott's with a degree of unease that made Scott smile. A smile that was not unappreciated by others around the tee.

He retook a couple of practice swings, more to irk the official than out of need and stepped up to the ball once more. He eyed his imaginary target in the fairway and drew the club back, his wrists cocked. He seemed to hold the back swing longer than usual but it couldn't have been that long and he brought it around with a sensation of perfection. He twisted his body in the follow through and found himself staring straight into the sun with no idea where the ball was. He tilted his head down but his vision was covered with blue-white globs forming an amoeba pattern in front of his eyes. He gazed at the fairway looking to see a ball come down but saw nothing but white patches surrounded by darkness. His ball could have gone anywhere – left, right, into the water – he had no idea. He turned behind him and was able to make out Paul squinting into the sunlight. Paul's right hand came up and he pointed out into the fairway.

"Wow," he said. "That was up a long time."

"Where is it?" asked Scott.

"Right in the middle. You really got a hold of it."

"In the middle?" Scott asked incredulously.

"You'll see it. Just walk straight out."

Jerry shook his head. He had missed the shot in the sun as well and took Paul's word that Scott had nailed a decent drive. He stepped up to the tee with his own driver to take his turn at the hole.

Scott was able to follow Jerry's shot and watched it dribble along the right side of the fairway, stopping even with the inmost edge of the water hazard but still on the nicely cut fairway. "Nice shot," he commented. Jerry smiled and Pete took his place at the tee.

Pete was a little hesitant as he set his ball and squinted out into the sun. He lined himself up, an expression of trepidation on his face. As Pete swung Scott could tell the previous hole had gotten to Pete. His swing was off and the shot hooked far to the left. It landed past a line of trees, hopefully in a decent position where he might have a shot out of the rough. His frustration was not expressed by pounding the ground with his club, as Jerry had resorted to earlier, but with his palm placed over his brow and eyes, rubbing with deliberation. He seemed to be trying to figure out what he had done wrong, not realizing it wasn't his swing that was off, but his mind-set that had changed. He needed to get over the last hole before he could get his regular game back.

Scott continued to blink away the retinal burns and as they walked along the fairway, Pete and his caddy broke off to the left and Jerry and his to the right. "See it?" asked Paul, pointing again.

Scott shook his head. There were too many pieces of debris that looked like balls.

"You're going to like it," said Paul.

Pete's caddy found his ball and it was perhaps one-yard from the tree line that gave way to a fence along a hundred and 159th Street to the north. He wouldn't have a full swing so his only hope was to lay it up back on to the fairway and hope for a good third shot. Pete didn't look too happy with the results of his drive. He looked at Scott and Paul far up in the middle of the fairway and shook his head, muttering something neither could hear. Scott was still straining to see his ball and was concerned Paul hadn't really gotten a good look at it coming off the tee. Maybe Paul had imagined his ball in the fairway. For all Scott knew it had landed in the woods or the pond. He looked back over at Pete.

Pete tested how far he could take a back swing before receiving interference from the tall weeds and shrubs at the edge of the trees. It wasn't much. He punched at the ball and got it out, but it only rolled about five or six yards and was still in the rough. "Closer to the hole," muttered Paul and Scott. Pete did not appear to be looking at the glass half full at this time. He walked to the new ball position, ready to kill it if necessary.

He hacked at it with the same over effort that had landed his drive in a bad spot and the ball soared straight across the fairway to land in the rough on the opposite side, perhaps a hundred and ninety yards from the green.

Once again, Pete's anger showed. He swung again at where his ball had been as if not sure what had gone wrong.

Jerry had watched the whole show from the other side of the fairway and shrugged it off. He'd had his terror hole and could remember the feeling of frustration, but also the relief as he let it go and started to have fun. He swung and the sound of the well-hit ball echoed along the fairway. The ball stayed fairly low, but rolled quite a distance before stopping about even with Pete's but nicely in the middle of the fairway instead of buried in the rough.

"Let's go, urged Paul and Scott blindly followed him still not certain where his drive had landed. They were practically on top of the ball before Scott saw it. He turned to look back at the tee and then to the hole. He had to be a little better than halfway along the longest hole in the course. "I put it at about three hundred yards. I told you you'd like it," Paul continued. He pulled an iron from the bag and handed it to Scott.

"I hit that drive three hundred yards?" Scott said in disbelief. He bent closer to the ball and could make out part of the yellow duck logo stamped over the dimpled ball.

"Right in the middle of the club," said Paul. It was perfect.

"Wow."

"Wow," echoed Paul.

Scott looked at the club Paul had handed him. "My nine iron?" he questioned?"

"Well, I know your fairway woods aren't going two hundred and seventy yards and there are sand traps all along the front of the green. Get it about hundred and twenty-five yards from the hole and then you can put it in the middle of the green with your pitching wedge. It's smart course management," added Paul.

Scott thought about it. "But I could knock it up two hundred yards with my five wood and then have just a seventy yard chip to get it on."

"You're better off using a full swing club to get on the green, Scott, trust me. Your low irons hit very straight and there are traps on the back of the green too, remember?"

"Yeah."

"Trust me, Scott," he said once again.

Scott took the club and smiled. "Okay," he agreed. He carefully lined up his shot and stood still over the ball for a moment. This was usually the time he tried not to think. His usual pattern after having a great drive was to flub the next shot or two and end up bogeying or double bogeying the hole. He knew he could afford a bogey or two on the front nine but if only he could turn this great drive into something.

Paul noticed Scott's apprehension. "Scott. Hit the ball. It goes where it goes."

That's true, thought Scott. Who was he to think he could control the tiny object? There were a million different outcomes from every swing, some of them good, some bad. You took what you got. If this shot were bad, he'd still have one more chance to get on the green. If not then he could still be on in four and with a good put, par the hole.

He breathed out and let the club sit on the ground behind the ball, the grip hung loosely in his left hand. He gripped it and wrapped his right hand below the left on the shaft. What about a practice swing? No, not this time, he told himself. Not this swing.

The club glided back smoothly along the short cut fairway and his left shoulder dipped under his chin as his club lifted over his head, his arms stopped moving but his hands twisted a little more back, cocking the wrists. With surety and determination he swung for the spot in front of the ball, his body unwinding like a watch spring popped free. There was no divot like one saw when a pro golfer took a swing, but a bare patch of dirt with short stumps of grass appeared in front of where the ball was. Scott once again lost sight of the ball to the glare of the sun. He turned his attention towards the hoe and waited for it to drop. After what seemed like too long a time it fell a hundred and fifty yards directly in front of him and bounced once.

"There you go," said Paul, as if he had no doubt whatsoever.

Pete Baldwin was shaking his head and Jerry Spaulding nodding his. Scott just smiled.

Pete walked to his ball and it was evident from his stance he was still frustrated with how he was playing the hole, especially after his last hole. Scott wouldn't be surprised if Pete flubbed the next shot – and he did. The ball landed smack dab in the middle of the sand trap on the right side in front of the green. With more anger than common sense he tossed his club back over his shoulder before realizing the pond on the left side of the fairway was nearly directly behind him. The club splashed in the water three or four yards from the edge of the pond.

His caddy was trying to keep from laughing until Pete walked up to him and spoke an order into his ear. The caddy shook his head violently at first. Pete spoke to him some more. Scott could tell the caddy had closed his eyes and was considering what his boss had just told him to do. After contemplating his options he removed his socks and shoes and rolled up his pants almost to his groin. Scott and Paul watched as the caddy stepped into the pond and waded out, feeling with his foot on the slimy bottom. The look on his face was pure disgust. Within a few seconds, however, it turned to triumph and he lifted a club up with his foot and pulled it up out of the water. Then, for some reason, the smile faded as he tossed the club on the fairway and kept searching.

"It was the wrong club," laughed Paul.

"Oh, my God, do you think Pete's played here before?" asked Scott. Paul lost it and his laughs earned a glare from Pete across the fairway. Paul immediately tried to stifle it but the chuckles turned to tears on his face and his upper body convulsed with swallowed mirth.

Within another twenty seconds, Pete's caddy's foot had found another golf club in the murk and this time it was Pete's. He waded to shore, and climbed out, wiping mud from his feet and checking for leeches as he shivered in the cold air.

Jerry had been enjoying the show as well and after the club had been successfully recovered, he set up his shot. He went for the green and from where Scott and Paul stood, probably made it. It was impossible to see the green as mounds of grass covered earth in front of the sand trap allowed only the top of the flagstick to be visible. Jerry looked over to the pair and shrugged. Their guess was as good as his.

The majority of the observers shadowing the threesome were a few yards behind Scott and followed as he walked up to his ball. He passed the white hundred and fifty yard marker and could see the red hundred-yard marker flush in the ground ahead of him. He was dead in the middle of the two. Perfect for his pitching wedge as Paul had promised.

"Course management, eh?" commented Scott.

"Course management," said Paul.

"Is there some course for that?" joked Scott.

"Yeah, but you have to take divot repair as a prerequisite."

"Gotcha."

This time Scott did take one practice swing, adjusting to the slightly shorter shaft of the club. He just needed to land the ball on or near the green and stay out of the sand and he could par this one. He still couldn't see the green clearly but Paul assured him all he had to do was aim at the flagstick, which he did.

He didn't hold back, but he didn't put any extra effort into the swing either. He just hoped it would go straight. For the third time he found himself staring into the blinding sun. He looked for and found the flagstick poking up and hoped his ball would fall somewhere in that vicinity.

For a moment he was sure the ball had shanked to the left or right because nothing was coming down where he hoped and then there was an almost audible whistle, like a bomb falling from the sky and a thump as he saw his ball come down just to the right of the stick. How far forward or back, he couldn't tell. He almost didn't want to go up and look. The watchers behind him started passing him and he walked up slowly, excited but afraid. He had lost his depth perception in the blinding rays of the sun. It was possible what he heard was the ball landing in sand on the opposite side of the green. With the distance he was getting off his clubs today, that was entirely possible.

Ellie, the camerawoman was the first one to crest one of the mounds in front of the green and she turned to face Scott. She was smiling and she held a thumb up. Then she held her two hands about a foot apart in front of her face. Scott stopped and shook his head. She vehemently nodded hers and her smile grew. Pete had also reached a mound and his reaction confirmed Ellie's report. He stood there shaking his head from side to side, muttering something under his breath. He walked back down and took his sand wedge to his ball in the trap. He punched it out neatly thanks to his practice on the last hole and walked off while his caddy smoothed the trap.

Scott reached the mound and looked at the situation below him. The flagstick was pretty much in the middle of the green, which had a downhill slant from the left front corner to the back right. One ball was about a foot to the right of the hole and Scott assumed that was his. Jerry's ball was just off the green on the fringe, seven yards from the hole but putt-able. Pete's was five yards from the hole in front of the pin.

Scott's eyes returned to where his ball sat. Don't miss this one, he told himself. Don't miss it. He had missed one-foot putts before and he wasn't going to take this one for granted.

He walked down and placed his tiny penny behind his ball and picked it up. He realized it was the same ball he had started with six holes earlier. How often did that happen with this much water on a course? Never, was the answer.

Pete marked his ball with a quarter and Jerry set up his putt. He hit it straight and for a moment it looked like it would make it but it died a few inches from the hole. He walked up and knocked in an easy par and pulled his ball out. Applause rippled from the onlookers and Paul and Scott joined them.

Pete took his time reading the green. His caddy stood back, obviously angry with Pete for making him wade through the muck and not about to offer any advice on the putt.

JAMES HOSEK

Pete's putt missed the left side of the hole and ended up a foot away. He walked up, took a second to aim and knocked his seventh shot in the hole, a double bogey. A courteous round of applause accompanied the effort, which Pete ignored.

Scott placed his ball back on the ground and picked up his penny. He slid it into his pocket and rubbed its rough surface between his fingers, remembering how it came to be his ball marker.

37

Sarah and he had taken a vacation to the Cayman Islands for their second anniversary. Sarah had strictly forbidden him from taking his clubs with and was determined they would have a romantic getaway. Unfortunately, their second day there, the previous night's dinner of jerk chicken decided to play havoc with Sarah's stomach and she ended up confined to bed with occasional trips to the bathroom. Scott tried his best to make her more comfortable but she quickly grew frustrated and annoyed with his well-intended attention. With a sigh and great reluctance she suggested he go out and play some golf. He asked if she was sure and she shooed him out of the room before she could change her mind.

Scott had the concierge in the hotel book him a tee time at a local course and arrange for a club rental. When he reached the golf course he bought a couple sleeves of balls, some tees, and a Titleist glove putting the whole tab on his credit card. He found himself grouped with a very nice Canadian couple who played the course several times a week and assured Scott he would find it challenging and fun.

It wasn't until the first green that he realized his regular ball marker was back in his own golf bag in Chicago. One of the Canadians gave him a tiny, bright, coppery, Cayman Islands, one-cent piece to use. He ended up shooting pretty poorly but did have fun. When he returned to their hotel room that evening Sarah was sleeping. He quietly emptied his pockets on the nightstand, placing his two remaining golf balls on top of the slightly used golf glove to keep them from rolling off and his penny on the table. He slipped into bed next to Sarah.

The next day Sarah was feeling normal again. She noticed the penny on the table and Scott explained how it had come to be ball marker. "If that's all you have to show for your afternoon, it seems like it turned out to be a pretty expensive penny," she commented.

Scott chuckled. "I didn't look at it that way. I should hold onto it then."

"I would expect so," she joked.

From then on, that coin had been in the pocket of his golf bag. Now as he let the tiny coin slip from his fingers in his pocket, he remembered that vacation. How Sarah had not made Scott suffer along with her that

110

afternoon. How she had lifted her ban on golf during what was supposed to be their romantic getaway even though Scott would have gladly stayed with her.

Somehow he knew that wouldn't be happening after the baby came.

38

Scott crouched down behind the ball to verify it was a straight shot to the hole then took his stance. He adjusted his putter so the lines on the back pointed along the path he wanted the ball to take. Just don't leave it short, he prayed. It an easy shot. A gimme as many casual golfers would play it. They would just pick up the ball assuming it would go in with one shot. Yet Scott had missed his share of one-footers and he'd even seen pros miss them too.

Scott never liked to take a gimme, even when playing just for fun. He believed there were no gimmes in life. You had to follow through on every task you started. What's more he loved the sound of the ball falling into the plastic cup. It was music to his ears, even after a particularly bad hole.

He pulled the club three inches back then pushed it into the ball. The duck emblazoned ball rolled for the hole and dropped straight in, the clunking sound confirming he had done it again. Another birdie, he was now four strokes under par. It was unbelievable. The applause was more than courteous this time and Scott pulled the ball out and clenched it in his fist. What a day.

What a day.

39

Jason stared at the television screen with disbelief. Eric Gunther, the high school runner who had been leading the Chicago Marathon for over half its length, was dying. His pace had dropped precipitously and many were speculating he was injured. The group of Kenyans and other top runners were about to pass him and several did as he slowed to a walk.

Well, thought Jason, that'll certainly make for an interesting story. He had envisioned hours of coverage for the teenager if he actually won, but as a fader or worse, a non-finisher, he might make a few seconds of mention in the commentary of the race. Perhaps his little golf tournament might make a report after all. He had mixed feelings regarding this. It meant having to actually edit the tape they'd shoot, and it sounded like Ellie was getting plenty, but it might not be the punishment he thought it had been.

He glanced out at the scoreboard. Hanover had hit a four on his last hole, a par five. What did that make him, three or four under par? Four said the scoreboard. He had three holes to finish for the front half of the course.

No one was close at this time. There were a few one under pars but most of the early players were shooting several strokes over par.

He realized that the good golfers would tee off last and so he wondered if Hanover's score would hold up. If it did and he pulled off an upset from dead last, it would be the Eric Gunther story but with a happier ending. Of course, he could also fade on the back half of the course and he'd have nothing - but maybe.

Well, it wasn't worth getting excited over at this point. He'd relax here in the clubhouse and may be get one of those donuts he'd seen at the courtesy breakfast table for players, officials and guests. He was a guest, wasn't he?

The chirp of his cell phone interrupted his thought and drew a few stares from other. He'd have to switch it to silent mode. The caller ID display read "Number Not Available." It couldn't be the camerawoman again. Her extension showed up last time. His wife didn't have this number. It had to be someone from the affiliate office.

"Bernard here," he answered.

"Bernard, what's with this Hanover? He going to make a run at it?" Jason was startled to hear the voice on the other end. It was Harold Frisk, head of the Chicago affiliate office of USA Sports. He started to answer but Frisk cut him off. "You heard about the marathon, eh? Heck, you're probably watching it at the clubhouse right now with some coffee and donuts."

"Yes, sir, I mean, he's doing well, but he's ranked last so he could just be having a good run right now and fade later."

"Your camerawoman thinks he's doing well and can keep it up."

Jason fumed. That girl had gone behind his back. Frisk probably golfed three or four times a week, thought Jason. "I was planning on meeting up with her after the first nine and seeing if we have anything to use. But the best golfers haven't teed off yet."

"I don't care about the best golfers," interrupted Frisk. "I lost my high school kid, now they're saying he was taking some sort of performance enhancing drug and may have had some cardiac problem. I need my story for tonight. With the Bulls and the Bears off, no baseball teams in the playoffs, I need a big local story. Heck, if he does pull it off, we may take it national. You would take it national, Bernard."

"Yes, sir."

"Call when he finishes the front nine."

"What about Andrew Patterson?"

"What?"

"He's the favorite, top amateur in the area."

"Eh, never bet the favorite my boy. Can't make money betting the favorites. But get some tape just in case. You know, him playing, what does he think of Hanover."

"Right. Hanover."

"Just get it Bernard."

Jason waited to make sure the connection was discontinued and hung up. He remembered to turn on the vibrate mode and slipped it into his pocket. The word national kept going through his mind. If the story was picked up nationally it would be a huge break. Maybe this golf thing wasn't so bad after all. He turned his attention to the scoreboard and looked at the information for the seventh hole. It was a par three.

Jason Bernard found himself a little excited now. Was he actually beginning to get interested in a golf event? If someone had told him that this morning he'd have laughed.

40

Andrew Patterson slipped his unlit and cold, empty pipe into his trouser pocket. He was walking back slowly to the clubhouse, then he'd find Eric Peters, hit a few dozen balls and get ready for his tee off. He patted the breast pocket under his sweater where the contract was tucked. Recognition and fame lay ahead. He needed it not to get to him. He still had a round of golf to play.

There was a crowd at the scoreboard. Soon enough his name would be at the top of the leader board, a scene that might appear in a television commercial someday soon.

Andrew sensed the morning warming up. Some light clouds to the west were breaking up as the burning sun in the east rose higher in the bright blue sky. In a few more weeks the leaves would fall from the trees and begin to litter the fairways with additional hiding places for errant shots, but that was not a worry today. Today was Andrew Patterson Day and in a few hours everyone here would know it.

As he made his way past the line of parked golf carts Andrew shuddered. The noisy infernal machines had always annoyed him. More than once he had found his concentration destroyed by their engines sputtering as their lazy occupants raced to the next shot. Carts, he thought, ruined the game and defeated the whole purpose of it being a sport. Why play golf if you didn't want to get any exercise? What was everyone in such a hurry for anyway? And who drove these carts? Most often the older men with pot bellies who could barely lift their overstuffed gigantic golf bags into the back of the cart, let alone carry them on the course.

Andrew often carried his own bag when he played practice rounds. He used a caddy when he needed one but he enjoyed the invigorating feel of

113

walking four or more miles along the crisply cut fairways and greens, along the sparkling ponds and streams, and through the sprawling, unforgiving trees.

Today Eric Peters would carry his bag. If he performed well he'd take him to the Pro-Am contest in a couple of weeks. Maybe he'd even get to be in Andrew's commercials, but more likely the ad agency would insist on an actor or perhaps actress to play the supporting role.

"Hi," interrupted and artificially upbeat and insincerely cheery voice. "I've heard a lot about you Mr. Patterson." The man extended a soft, plump, nicotine stained hand to Andrew.

Andrew looked at the hand and smiled. "All good, I hope," he joked. The hand fell away in the embarrassment of rejection.

"They say you're the man to beat, and I'm willing to bet they're right."

Something about the man's demeanor and approach was vaguely familiar. Had he met this man before? Certainly he'd have remembered such a shabbily clad character in any incarnation.

"Can I help you?" prompted Andrew.

"Well, it's more like I can help you," pitched the man. "My name is Jake Fischer and I'm an agent with Frasier and Frakes." Jake had replaced his coat and tie and even combed down a few stray hairs with his palm in preparation of meeting Patterson.

Ah, realized Andrew. The man Karen had spoke of. His manner was similar to hers. The patronizing words and fake smile, nice to see, but transparent to their real motives. These agents were out for money. If they wanted to make Andrew a few bucks along the way so be it. Andrew was beginning to feel a little flattered that so many people were after his attention but after evaluating his first impression of this Fischer fellow, he was happy that Miss Blakely had found him first.

"How interesting," commented Andrew, "it seems that I am very popular among your ilk today."

"My ilk?" asked Jake Fischer, very confused. He was pulling a folded stack of papers from his jacket pocket, a set that looked very familiar to Andrew, as they seemed identical to those Karen had in her purse for him to sign.

"Yes. You wouldn't happen to know a Miss Karen Blakely, would you?"

"Yes," answered Jake cautiously, not willing to admit that somehow he was too late after all. But he knew what was coming before Andrew Patterson said it and his mind was melting into confusion. He had sent Karen to the marathon, he thought.

"She's already signed me. She has big plans for me you know. Well, I'd say it was a pleasure to meet you but it wouldn't be true," blathered Andrew inconsiderately, "good day to you."

As he started past the agent, Jake inexplicably began to laugh. Andrew stopped and turned. "Did I say something funny, Mr. Fischer?"

"Funny?" asked Jake.

"You're laughing," pointed out Andrew.

"Oh, it's not you personally, although..." started Jake letting his eyes roam up and down Patterson as he toned his laugh into a chuckle.

"I see," grumbled Patterson.

"Mr. Patterson, you don't know me. You don't know where I am or where I've been but I know you. To tell you the truth, this is actually a bit of a relief. Believe me when I wish you luck in your endeavors with Miss Blakely."

"Well, better luck next time," Andrew said with no conviction as he started off in search of Eric Peters.

"That's that," said Jake out loud after Patterson was out if earshot. He had tried but Karen had somehow found Patterson before him and now, thanks to Jake, she was on her way to the marathon and possible a second big contract. He knew Jonathan and Gina would understand. But how was he going to take this failure and turn it into something good?

A sudden silence then murmur spread through the crowd at the scoreboard. Jake walked over and noticed the man in the yellow slacks and shirt was hanging scorecards for the first group at the seventh hole. He still couldn't see the score from where he was and walked closer, pushing politely through the crowd.

41

Anna and Sarah politely pushed through the crowd. Even this late in the morning the rummage sale was still a mad house. Anna was looking for a sofa to replace the torn and sagging one that crept into her life after she was married. Her husband, Dale, would not be pleased by a change, he claimed the cushions conformed ideally to his body shape and insured maximum comfort while watching television.

Sarah hoped to find a glider rocker. She imagined herself nursing her new baby, listening to a CD while the tender infant snuggled in for a meal, the chair softly carrying them into a peaceful relaxation.

A jolt from a tweed-coated woman woke Sarah from her daydream and the woman bustled off with out an apology. "How rude," commented Sarah.

"It's definitely a Darwinian sale, Sarah," commented her sister, "the most aggressive shoppers will get the merchandise and the weak left holding a pink flamingo lawn ornament when it's all said and done."

"Glider rocker," affirmed Sarah and they pushed to the middle of the basement where the woman at the door said living room furniture could be found.

Within a few minutes they reached the narrow rows of furniture, more than half of them adorned with bright orange SOLD signs, to be picked up over the next few days when the moving of such large objects would be possible. She would send Scott and Perhaps Dale to pick up their purchase.

There were three glider rockers unclaimed. One was particularly well worn but comfortable, one didn't glide but claimed to need only minor repairs that any handyman (or handywoman, thought Sarah, fresh from her crib assembly) could tackle, and one that – that seemed just right.

It was oak with large, overstuffed cushions on the seat and back and was accompanied by a large rocking footstool as well. She ran her hands over its surface, feeling the glossy finish to the wood and the soft inviting feel of the cushion.

"Sit in it," encouraged Anna.

Sarah did so and immediately found herself gliding in the comfortable chair, rocking softly, lulled into her daydream with more vividness than before.

"It's a bargain at two hundred and fifty dollars," said a rummage sale volunteer with "Cecily" written boldly on her nametag. "I've seen the same chair in the department stores for eight hundred with the stool," she added.

"It's nice," answered Sarah, noncommittally. "I'm really just looking."

"Suit yourself," retorted Cecily who huffed off to assist another interested buyer, a young man looking at a leather recliner.

"It's a little high," commented Anna.

"But it's so nice. But you're right, Scott would kill me if I bought it."

"Hey, he's out golfing, right?"

"Well, maybe they'll mark it down a little. Perhaps I should get that woman back and see if they'll bargain a little." Before she could get up another woman with a "Sally" nametag approached.

"Interested in the chair?" she asked.

"Possibly," interrupted Anna, knowing Sarah's answer would give her desire for the chair at any cost away. "But it does seem rather expensive for a rummage sale. I know it's for charity, but..."

Sally looked at the tag and shook her head, "Cecily must have changed this," she said, "no wonder someone else hasn't taken it yet." She pulled a thick black magic marker from her pocket and crossed out the two in the price.

"Are you serious?" asked Sarah?

"It's great for nursing," she answered, nodding at Sarah's distended abdomen, "so I'm told. You seem to like it. It's yours for fifty."

"Sold," agreed Sarah. She pulled herself up out of the rocker. "The stool too?"

"Absolutely," smiled Sally.

Sarah smiled back. Within five minutes she had made a purchase even her penny-pinching husband would be proud of.

"Is there anything else I can help you with?"

"I'm looking for a sofa," answered Anna.

"Let's look around," suggested Sally. "There are a few nice ones left." As they worked their way down the aisle Sarah was surprised to see the young man handing Cecily two hundred dollar bills for the recliner. It wasn't in great shape but it was obvious that it wasn't the recliner's shape he was interested in. "She has her uses," whispered Sally as they passed. Anna and Sarah smiled at the remark.

A row of televisions were all tuned to the local USA Sports Network affiliate as the coverage of the Chicago Marathon played over the screen. Sarah thought she heard something about a kid using performance enhancing drugs and nearly dying halfway through the race. A clock in the upper corner of the screen marked off the time elapsed for the lead runner, a very dark, tall thin man apparently from Kenya. As he ran he grabbed water cups, drank some and dowsed himself with others. His thin frame seemed like it didn't have the endurance to run over twenty-six miles but it was probably his light weight that contributed to his bodies ability to accomplish such a grueling task with ease.

At times the camera showed other runners, none in competition with anyone but themselves, trying to finish a race they may only run once in their lives, just to be able to say they did it. Many had a leisurely jogging pace, some were even speed walking while other were draped over supporters arms, weeping at the cruelty of an unexpected injury or a cramp or the realization that today would not be the day they completed a marathon.

Sarah thought that maybe there were such things as marathon widows and perhaps widowers to go along with golf widows. There were people who loved to run more than anything else in the world and when they ran they were in a different world.

Was that how it was for Scott? She had never thought of it that way. She had at times been grateful to get rid of him for a while but she never really thought about what his golfing did for him.

She hoped he was having fun and not doing too badly. She knew he would be happy just not to be the last place finisher among the field and Paul was there to keep him from getting too serious.

She was happy with her chair and was sure Scott would be excited for her too. First the crib, now the glider rocker, what a great day it was turning out to be.

She turned and saw that Anna and Sally were quite a bit ahead of her a she had been distracted by the televisions. As she started after them, another contraction grabbed her attention. She had been having mild ones every ten or fifteen minutes all morning. They had become a simple annoyance as she got used to them. Her doctor had told her to expect them from time to time as her uterus exercised in preparation for the big day. This one, however, caused her to stop. She breathed in slowly and let the tightness gradually fade away. Did it mean anything that this contraction was stronger than the previous ones?

When she and Anna left the rummage sale she would call her doctor. It didn't hurt to ask, she thought. And it would put her mind at ease if the doctor told her it was nothing to worry about. She was glad she had accomplished two major tasks today. Now if Anna could get a new sofa that would be icing on the cake.

CHAPTER 9 – SEVENTH HOLE

42

Another par three but no sign of water on this hole. It didn't need it. The green was surrounded by sand traps and the front was pushed in giving it a kidney shape. Scott and Paul looked down and Scott cringed at the pin placement. It was near the right front of the green. At a hundred and ninety yards it would be difficult to land a shot to close to the pin. Too short and you were in the sand. If you hit it to the left and short, you had to hit over the indentation of the green. Most likely the shots would be toward the middle or back of the green. Few would likely birdie this one today.

Paul checked the wind and handed Scott his five iron. Scott nodded in agreement.

"Mr. Hanover still has honors," droned the official, as if tired of the phrase.

"Straight for the pin?" asked Scott.

"A little left," answered Paul, "you've been fading your low irons a little." He stepped back off the teeing area and the crowd assumed an eerie silence.

Scott stood for a moment, looking at the green below him. Apart from the thirteenth hole in the back nine, also a par three, this was one of the easier holes on the course. But the way they placed the pin had made it much more challenging than some of the longer holes. If he could be sure to make it past the sand trap he'd definitely get par. Heck, just hitting the green would make him happy here.

He had once heard a golf pro trying to explain to a commentator the difficulty of hitting on the green. He compared it to basketball. A golfer who was able to get his ball on the green in the regulation number of strokes was similar to a basketball player hitting a free throw from the half court line. To get it within six feet of the pin, generally considered a doable one-putt distance, was like sinking the free throw without the ball touching the rim.

"What about a hole-in-one?" joked the commentator.

The pro laughed. Well, he contemplated, instead of half court, stand behind the opposite goal, throw it with your opposite hand, while hopping on one foot blind-folded and still miss the rim. That's your chance of making a hole in one.

Scott had never had a hole-in-one or even seen one in person. He'd seen a few on highlight tapes from golf tournaments and had chipped some in from fifteen or twenty yards, but never for the elusive eagle, a score two under par, much more difficult to obtain that two over par, he mused.

He placed his ball on a tee and pushed the tee almost completely flush with the ground then lined up the duck so it was pointing a little to the left of the pin. He then drew his imaginary line behind the ball and stepped to the left side and lined up his feet parallel to that line. He turned his head and watched the flag barely rustle in the light breeze.

He took his two practice swings and stepped up. The sudden, distinctive rumble of a Harley Davidson motorcycle roared along 159th street to his left and he stepped back. He knew better than to swing when all he could think about was how he wouldn't let some noise bother him. Usually it bothered him much more than he knew and it was better to step back and start over.

"Whenever you're ready," urged the official, impatiently.

Scott ignored him but did see Ellie and her camera, poised to capture his seventh tee shot. He took two more practice swing, the club barely brushing the grass. He moved his shoes forward and set them into the ground. If there were other sounds from the road, he didn't hear them. There was no roar of planes or putter of golf carts. He didn't even hear anyone breathing.

He pulled back the club and let his wrists bend as it cocked in position to unload. He seemed to wait a fraction of a second longer than usual but once his downswing started there was no stopping it. The club hit the ball squarely and a wooden thwack resounded from the trees.

The ball soared high and straight, just to the left of the pin, but drifting closer as it neared. It was definitely not in danger of hitting the sand traps in front of the pin, but some extra power had seeped into his stroke and it looked like it might land behind the pin and perhaps roll off the back of the green, maybe into another sand trap.

Scott sagged, disappointed in the shot, but knowing no matter what it would still be a good round. The ball drifted closer to the pin but it was obvious now to everyone that it would sail past it.

"Stick," Scott heard someone say, encouraging the ball in flight to stay on the green. Scott knew his shot lacked the backwards spin pros could impart on their ball to have it roll back up the green towards the pin. He hoped it might stay on the green and he could...

Tunk

The sound reached them a fraction of a second after the ball struck the flagstick dead on. It almost seemed to stick to the fiberglass pole for a moment before proceeding to drop straight to the ground, disappearing – into the hole! It must have been trapped between the pole and side of the hole because with the speed it had it should have popped right out.

"Oh my god," muttered Scott. He blinked. And started breathing in short heavy breathes.

"It's in the hole," shouted Paul, breaking the silence. "It's in the hole!" He stepped up to Scott, yelling and yelling the same thing over and over. "It's in the hole! IT'S IN THE HOLE!"

The crowd around the hole was cheering and screaming and jumping and hugging each other and Ellie was getting it all on tape. She was starting to cry with happiness for Scott Hanover but managed to keep the camera rolling. Nothing else she would see this day would match what she had just seen. It was pure luck the ball didn't fly past the flagstick and race off the back of the green into a sand trap, pure, unadulterated luck. Even though she wasn't the one who hit the ball, she felt a wave of adrenalin race through her body. She didn't know this guy from Adam but she was so happy for him she couldn't believe it. He was having the best round of golf she had ever seen. He had parred two holes, birdied four and now had an eagle. A hole-in-one. He was six under par after only seven holes. She doubted Patterson would be doing that well after eighteen holes. This was the guy to beat today and pretty soon the people at the scoreboard would know it. Jason Bernard would know it and she had been there.

Jerry and Pete took their turns congratulating Scott, both sincerely in awe of his amazing luck.

"That's not normally the way you get a hole-in-one," commented Jerry.

"I'll take it anyway I can," answered Scott.

Jerry and Pete played the hole in the shadow of "the shot." Both ended up with bogeys after landing in different sand traps. Scott was convinced he'd be with them or worse if that ball hadn't hit the stick just right.

Amazing, thought Scott. Amazing. He could walk off the course now and be thrilled with his score but as he watched the score update show him move to five strokes ahead of the nearest competitor a realization came over him. It was his tournament to lose now, and he was quite capable of fulfilling that prophecy. He glanced around the crowd that had continued to grow all morning. He wondered if any of them had come to the same realization. Right now all they were thinking about was the fact that they were here to witness his amazing hole-in-one on seven.

It was pretty amazing he told himself.

One in a million.

43

Eric Peters was waiting by the ball machine at the driving range. His boss, Andrew Patterson, was walking down the sidewalk from the clubhouse, on his way to warm up. Eric checked his watch. Patterson was up in twenty minutes. He had given Eric instructions about his warm up ahead of time so that he could perform his routine uninterrupted. Eric unzipped a side pocket on the golf bag and pulled out the expensive designer golf shoes in their plastic bag. He set them in front of a bench, laces untied and ready to put on. Patterson was a fairly easy man to caddy for once you got used to his eccentricities. He never asked advice and really only needed a person to carry his bag and hand him the next club.

A roar erupted from the crowd by the scoreboard. People were jumping up and down and Andrew Patterson turned his head disgustedly, as if they were commenting on his walking away from them. But they weren't, observed Eric. They were excited about something on the scoreboard.

Andrew reached the practice range area and wordlessly started to put on his soft spike Pierre Cardins. As Patterson stood up he noticed one of the other caddies racing down to the driving range area, looking like he was going to burst. Ignoring the over-excited youth, Andrew took his five iron from Eric's hand and started his stretching routine at the tee box. Eric had made sure the adjacent practice areas were empty and was worried that the caddy racing toward him was going to interrupt the boss's routine.

He quickly reached them but was too out of breath to speak.

"Keep it quiet," cautioned Eric, "Mr. Patterson needs a few minutes to get ready." He rolled his eyes in Patterson's direction.

The caddy's breath started coming back to him and between huffs he whispered to Eric, "he...got...a...hole...in...one..."

Eric whispered back to confirm what he had heard, "a hole-in-one?"

"Hanover. Seventh hole. Hit the pin and dropped straight in."

"Holy bajeezus," gasped Eric.

"Eric," came a stern voice from the tee box. Eric walked over and lined up five balls, three inches apart along the AstroTurf matt and stepped back as Patterson did his practice drill. Eric stepped back to ask another question, "What's he shooting so far?"

The caddy was now recovering from his all out sprint and answered quietly, "six under."

"Omigosh," muttered Eric. "That's amazing."

"They said they might have to change the pairings. He's like five strokes ahead of the rest of the field so far."

"Eric," prompted Patterson once again. Eric resumed his duties.

"I'll catch you later," he dismissed the caddy. The boy walked along the practice area divulging the news to the other whom responded with gasps and utterances of amazement and awe.

"What was that about?" asked Patterson. The question was out of character Eric noted. He was slightly hesitant to reveal the news but figured Patterson would hear about it soon enough. "A guy got a hole-in-one on the seventh hole."

"Lucky shot," concluded Andrew.

"Aren't all eagles?" commented Eric.

"Precisely. No room for luck in my game. Skill and planning win golf matches. After eighteen holes, it'll catch up one way or another."

"What are you planning to shoot today?"

"Six under, why? What's that fellow have now?"

"Bobby said he's at six under after seven holes."

Andrew stopped in mid-swing. He didn't turn to face Eric, but started his swing over. If this fellow was on the seventh hole he had started earlier this morning and was one of the poorer players by handicap to enter the tournament. Still, handicaps rarely lied. This fellow would have his bad holes too and end up being a footnote at the end of the day.

Andrew had never hit a hole-in-one in his two years of the game but had come within several inches of the cup a few times. His ace would come someday, perhaps more than one, but only with practice and attention to the details of the game. Luck was in the details, he thought. And luck worked both ways as well.

44

Gina Beck swung her braced left leg with practiced ease out of her white Honda Civic and then pulled herself out. Once standing, her practiced gait would give little away her disability. She took a look around. There was Jake's Geo Metro. He was still here. "Thank, God," she sighed with relief. Her worst fear was allayed. She noticed a crowd gathered in front of the clubhouse and figured that would be as good a place as any to start looking for Jake.

She didn't fail to notice what a wonderful fall day it was turning out to be and hoped she and Jake would get a chance to see some of the golfers. More than anything though, she hoped he'd been able to get the player Jonathan had sent him for. She also hoped he would be happy to see her.

She walked toward the clubhouse. A man at a table labeled "Check In" asked if he could help her but she smiled and walked on. Her smile had almost super powers and one of them was getting men to let her do what she wanted – most of the time. He shrugged and let her go, assuming she must know what she was doing.

It was difficult to see if Jake was in the crowd. A mass of people were gathered Near a large series of scoreboards watching as an elderly man busily hung numbers under the various holes for each player as they were reported to him. In a moment she saw what everyone had been murmuring about. Posted under the seventh hole along the line of scores for Hanover, S was a green card with the number one printed on it. A golfer had hit a hole-in-one. That would have been neat to see. The other two golfers on the hole had turned in fours and she was duly impressed by Hanover's six under total score. She thought it was unusual such a good golfer would be among the first groups teeing off but who knew what the tournament officials were thinking.

"Forgive me," said a familiar voice in her left ear. Gina turned. It was Jake. She smiled and gave him a hug and a kiss.

"Forgive you for what?"

"For everything."

She took in the look in his eyes. They were deeper than they had been in a year, clear and almost bright. Shiny with early tears. Hopeful and apologetic.

"Are you okay?" she asked tentatively.

"I am now."

"Did you get to that golfer?"

"Jonathan called you?"

Gina nodded.

Jake stepped back and sighed. "I found him, but Karen Blakely got there first."

"Oh, sweetie," she consoled.

"He's a jerk anyway not the kind of athlete I can handle well. I think it's for the best."

"Let's go. I'll buy you breakfast and we can talk about it."

"You can buy me breakfast, but I'm not leaving."

"Why not," asked Gina, intrigued by his response.

"Look at this guy, Hanover. He's on fire. I have a feeling he's going to be more of the type that Callaway wants."

"What does Jonathan say?"

"I haven't run it by him. I want to see how it plays out some more. Even if Callaway doesn't want him, maybe I can work a small deal with Second Swing or Nevada Bob's," he suggested, naming a few smaller golf chains that might not afford the budget of a golf giant like Callaway but would want to reach the weekend golfers with one of their own.

Gina looked over Jake, leaned in and took a little sniff at him.

"I'm okay," he assured Gina.

"Oh, I know you haven't been drinking. You haven't talked like this since before London. But that jacket really needs a cleaning," she said, wrinkling her nose in disgust.

Jake smiled. He shrugged off the jacket and pulled off his tie. "This isn't me anyway. I was trying to be a little upscale for this Patterson fellow but who can complete with Karen Blakely in a tight dress and heels?"

"Ahem," interjected Gina.

"Present company excluded, of course," corrected Jake.

"Jake," interrupted an excited voice, "help me out here. You know sports pretty well." Jake turned and found himself looking at the sportscaster, Jason Bernard, he had met earlier in the dining area.

"Pretty well," agreed Jake, hesitantly. Jason was standing on the other side of Gina half staring at the scoreboard, "A hole-in-one is pretty rare, right?"

"Pretty rare," he parroted.

"They make the news, usually, don't they?"

"You bet."

"I got to find my camerawoman." He glanced at his watch. "Shoot, that Patterson guy is up soon." He fished out a cell phone.

"Who's that?" whispered Gina, apparently not offended that the excited man had totally ignored her..

"A sportscaster who hates golf, well maybe I should say hated golf. I guess he sees a chance to upstage the marathon coverage."

"If this Hanover can win, it'll likely upstage the whole sportscast."

"Very likely," agreed Jake. "If he wins."

Gina grabbed Jake's arm and snuggled up close. "You're really okay?"

"It was shaky a few times, I won't lie to you."

"I haven't seen you like this for a long time, Jake. It's good."

"I met a guy who's been here, Gina."

"Really?"

"Yeah. I know just wanting to go doesn't mean much because I've promised you a lot in the last year and let you down every time."

"Go where?" asked Gina.

"After this is over I'm going to find a meeting. Tonight."

"A meeting?" asked Gina, not sure, but hopeful she knew what he meant.

"AA, Gina. I'm going."

"Brad would be proud," she reminded him.

"I know," choked, Jake. He hugged Gina and they stood there for a while, silent. The crowd started to melt away, the moment of excitement fading, and life got a little better.

45

Karen Blakely banged at the dashboard of her Mercedes convertible. Not only was she stuck in traffic, but April had ended up sending her on a wild goose chase. The radio was reporting that Eric Gunther had dropped out of the race and preliminary tests were showing an adverse reaction to performance enhancing medication, namely phenylephrine. Phenylephrine was found in common cold medications and as one gymnast found out in the Sidney Olympics, it was enough to disqualify her from competition even though she just wanted to get rid of a stuffy nose. Gunther must have practically overdosed on the stuff and his body couldn't handle the strain. If he lived, he'd probably not be allowed to race competitively again.

Karen looked for an exit but at the rate traffic was moving on the Dan Ryan, she'd be half an hour going four blocks. The marathon was tying up several overpasses and people were trying to get on and off the expressway to get a look at some family member or friend jogging themselves into early arthritis and several days of sore muscles.

She glanced at her watch. Patterson would tee off in twenty minutes. It would take him four and half hours to play his round to she'd definitely be back for him getting his trophy, but she wanted him to see her on the course, observing him. Let him know that she was there for him. She also hoped to insure he'd get footage on the sportscasts tonight and that he was wearing a Callaway cap instead of that ridiculous tam she caught him in earlier.

She could see an exit a hundred yards ahead. The cars were barely moving. This was ridiculous. She checked her mirror and the shoulder was empty. With a heavy foot, she slid out of her lane onto the shoulder and raced past the line of cars to the off ramp. The flash of lights made her heart sink. Not a ticket, she thought. She slowed a little and a short burst from the cruisers siren encouraged her to stop.

No problem, she thought. A sexy smile and a promise not to do it again had worked before. The officer in the state trooper car was typing on a little keyboard, running her plate. How ridiculous. The door opened and out stepped – a woman. Karen's forehead hit the steering wheel. It was just not turning out to be her day.

46

Ellie's cell phone buzzed in her pocket. She glanced at the display. It was Jason Bernard. The group following Scott Hanover was on their way to the eighth tee. She answered the phone.

"Did you get it?" asked an excited voice.

"Mr. Bernard?" she asked. She hadn't been expecting excitement from him, not today. Then she remembered her talk with her uncle Harry.

"The hole-in-one. Tell me you got tape," pleaded Jason.

"It's in the can," she confirmed.

"What happened?"

"His shot hit the flagstick and just dropped in. A one in a million shot."

"Holy cow. When will you be in?"

"Two more holes, maybe half an hour, forty minutes."

"Patterson will be teeing off before then."

"Forget Patterson," she said, "this is the story."

"He could fade. We have to have Patterson."

"The hole-in-one is at least a story."

"Absolutely," agreed Jason, "but if he doesn't win the tournament, he's not the one the people are going to focus on. Could he lose it?"

Ellie thought. Half the great shots she'd seen Hanover make, including this one were pure luck. The second hole was a total disaster until he chipped it in. The fourth was not far from the same. Not to mention the other two golfers turning in embarrassing holes to drop them out of contention. "Yeah," she agreed reluctantly, "he could lose it."

"Then we get some Patterson and still follow him if Hanover doesn't bungle the last two holes in the front half."

"Front nine," corrected Ellie.

"Whatever. Listen, I'd like to do a quick edit when you get it so we can get the hole-in-one on the air. I think they'll run it before the nine o'clock report. We have everything we need in the truck, right?"

"Right."

"Great. Keep taping," he instructed her and hung up. Like she needed that bit of advice. She raced ahead to catch the golfers. Hanover was going to tee off again. There was water on the next hole. If only that stupid official would let up.

47

"Are we sure about this?" asked Lucy Penndel.

"Ninety percent," said her cameraman, Alf Redding. Alf usually worked with Jason Bernard and was surprised when he found out that Jason would not be on the Marathon and he would be working with Lucy. Lucy was okay, but not a great sportscaster. But more and more women were breaking into the field and experience was the best teacher. She was actually interested in listening to his tips and suggestions.

"How could this happen? All that footage with the family and coaches – unusable," she fumed.

"It happens," said Alf. They had spent nearly an hour tracking down Eric Gunther's family and friends in the crowd, getting reactions and commentary on how Eric was doing and his dream of just running a whole marathon before his seventeenth birthday. Now the miserable kid was on his way to the hospital with a drug overdose.

Lucy was doomed to interviews with foreign speaking African runners who had dominated the American marathons for years. She'd be lucky to get ten seconds of usable video from them. The Gunther story would play, but if only he had won...

The race, as far as the major competitors were concerned would be over in an hour. She now dreaded having to cover the Gunther story. Nobody liked a cheater, even if it was news. Most people would be angry with the kid for what he pulled, not sympathetic. Lucy wanted no part of the whole situation.

"Let's get some shots of people who are walking, you know, why are you doing this, what do you hope to prove, sort of stuff."

"Gotcha, chief," agreed Alf, amiably. He hoped Jason was having more fun than he was. He doubted it.

CHAPTER 10 – EIGHTH HOLE

48

Scott stared at the listing of the top golfers that was displayed by the kid who had been following them from the start. There was Hanover, S at the top, now six under par after seven holes. He never thought he'd see such a thing and now it seemed too bizarre. Right now he just wanted to get that videotape and replay his moment of glory over and over until everyone around him was sick of it.

He had never had a hole-in-one before and he was beginning to think Ted Lange was right. He'd be able to pull off a great game, but his inner golf voice warned him of double and triple bogeys yet to come, perhaps even today. But to be the leader at this moment filled him with pride.

"Mr. Hanover is teeing off," intoned the red-jacketed man.

"Paul, I need the quack," whispered Scott as he stared at the fairway. The hole curved in a dogleg to the right and along most of the right side was a giant water hazard. He'd been lucky so far. He was on his second ball of the day, the ball from his hole-in-one safely tucked away to be mounted on a plaque to further commemorate his achievement. Sarah would likely make him hang it in the basement, but he'd have one made nonetheless.

"Can't do it. He'd probably assess you a penalty on the spot."

"Can he do that?"

"Probably."

"Just a little one."

"It's not the same," warned Paul.

"I need something."

"Hit the ball, Scott. The water's not there."

Scott laughed. "What water?" he asked.

Paul smiled. "I don't see no water," he added to the joke.

Scott teed up his brand new Duck logo ball and mouthed a duck prayer to himself with a silent quack. What water, he told himself. What water?

He took his practice swings, feeling confident in his swing and delighted how the round was turning out.

What water? What water?

He pulled back the club and swung. The ball rose up and out and started a little fade. A little was okay. The water was all the way to the right. Once it hit the ground the ball would come to rest dry.

The fade turned into a pull, a little closer to the water, but still not in danger. Maybe off the fairway in the rough, but that would be fine too.

The pull turned into a full-blown slice and the memory of his tee shot on the second hole returned, except this time he didn't have the relative safety of some tall grass.

The ball, which had started out aimed down the middle of the fairway, bounced on the rough three yards from the water, and landed with a splash in the hazard. Scott let out an "aarrggh" from the tee. He shook his head and turned to find Paul and hand him his driver. The Duck was back. Oh boy, was he back.

Paul said nothing, knowing Scott knew the situation. Since it was a lateral water hazard he'd be allowed to take a drop near where the ball went in but one penalty stroke would be added to his score. Hopefully he'd be on or near the green with the next shot and get it in the hole with two more strokes for a total of five, a bogey. It wouldn't kill him. Paul and Scott both bogeyed their share of holes every time out but today had been a good streak while it lasted.

"On in three," Scott droned, voicing the words of encouragement that Paul had held back. He didn't mean it, but he really couldn't be that disappointed. He'd missed water on four holes already. Twenty percent wetness was a good thing, at least on the deodorant commercials."

Ellie Burke tried to force a smile. Jason was maybe right. This guy had a good run, but now it wasn't looking good. There were still eleven holes to play. One or two bad holes would erase his negative score and put him in the bottom half of finishers in no time.

Ellie was angry as well. Angry at the tournament official that had banned Scott's pre-drive quack. It was a silly thing but it was part of the superstition of golf. Players had little routines or things they said or did to prepare for their shots and an annoyed, fat, greasy, ignorant, self-important official had denied him his. She pointed her camera and took some footage of the red-jacketed man, mentally composing the commentary she would suggest to Jason if ever this footage made the air. He would turn out to be the bad guy, for sure.

Jerry Spaulding teed up next after giving Scott a supportive pat on the back. "Tough luck," he commented, knowing exactly what the fellow golfer was feeling. Jerry knew Scott wasn't a great golfer but he had been rooting for him ever since the fifth hole and this was a blow to his rhythm and momentum. One bad shot usually lead to another and another and the more frustrated you got the more bad shots you made until you had a thirteen! "You'll get it on," he said and then placed his own ball on the tee.

His shot also showed a little fade but it managed to stay on the fairway just near the turn in the dogleg, perfect position to be on the green in two.

Pete Baldwin followed. He made no comment to Scott but he too had been secretly rooting for the underdog golfer. Pete knew he had no chance of winning an opportunity to play with the pro's, but he was vicariously hoping that maybe Hanover might at least give the hot shots a run for their money.

Scott was still way ahead of the rest of the pack and there was still time to pick up any strokes he might lose here, but he knew the psychological damage that a shot like that played with an amateur golfer's mind. The brain would take over from the muscles and once one begin to over analyze what went wrong, it only got worse.

Pete's shot went straight and a little to the left. His drive was perhaps as long as Jerry's, but he was thirty yards further from the hole thanks to the dogleg in the course.

The crowd, which was still growing like a bacterial culture on a Petri dish, followed the three and their caddies down the fairway. Scott would shoot next. They reached the spot were his ball splashed into the water. Paul handed him a new ball and Scott carefully rolled it in his hand, rubbing his thumb lightly over the imprinted yellow duck. "You don't see any water, do you?" he asked. He held the ball to his ear and smiled. "He said, 'what water?' Paul."

Paul laughed.

"What did I do wrong on my drive?" he asked.

"You want the technical explanation or the psychological?"

"What's the difference?"

"The technical you ain't going to fix. The psychological is pretty easy to fix."

"Then lets make it the psychological explanation."

"Okay, Scott. Why are you here?"

"To win this tournament."

Paul made a nasal buzzing tone. "Wrong answer."

"To shoot my best round ever?"

Another buzz.

"To not finish last?"

A third strike sounded. "You are here to play golf, my friend, nothing more, nothing less. Enjoy the day, the course and even the view over this pond, but don't think you're here for anything other than to play."

"I'm so stupid."

"When you play in the tournament or against other players, you have unneeded pressure on you. When you play golf, it's just you. No one else is here. You can hit it in the water or in the trees or in the hole. As long as you're hitting the ball, you're in the game. Do you get it?"

"I wasn't playing golf, was I?"

"No, you were shooting for another eagle. Sorry to say, it ain't going to happen."

Scott chuckled. He looked across the pond at the green. There was sand behind the green to the left and some in front. Someone who saw the water and who had just hit a ball into it might chip further up the fairway to avoid it, but not a golfer. Not this golfer. "Seven iron?"

"Seven iron," agreed Paul.

Scott held out his hand with the ball in his palm, glanced at the red-jacketed official to make sure his drop was in the proper area, and let the ball tumble from his fingers. It landed on the thick tall grass like it was set up on a tee. He took the club from Paul.

For some reason he thought of Sarah. He loved his golf and he loved her and he hoped there was room for both of them in his life, but he would put the clubs away for a while and spend the time with his new family. If this was going to be his last game for a while, he'd have fun.

He'd been having fun. It always seems fun when you have a good game or a good hole or a good shot. It only took one shot, was the saying, to bring you back again. He'd be back again, perhaps with a son or daughter in tow to share the peacefulness and tranquility he found out here.

He lined up the shot and took his practice swings. He hit the ball square and it sailed over the water (what water) and thumped on the green rolling to four feet away from the pin.

"Playing golf," said Paul. Scott wondered what his caddying bill was going to be for today. Whatever it was, Paul had earned it.

Jerry raised his brow at the shot. Scott was sitting on the green in three strokes and potentially a one putt away from par after plopping one in the pond. It was a pretty good comeback. He had a feeling he'd sink it.

Jerry's shot rolled off the back of the green on a little fringe of grass that separated the green and the sand trap.

Pete shanked his eight iron and the ball ended up in the water five yard short of the green. He moved up and dropped a ball and chipped it into the back sand trap and almost threw another club into the water.

His next shot out of the sand rolled well past the pin, almost off the green and Pete looked about ready to give up. He was still away and would shoot again, this time his sixth stroke.

He putted with little concentration, or so it appeared to Scott, and his putt showed it. It ended up six feet short of the hole. Two more putts put him in the hole with an eight.

Jerry knocked his ball to within inches of the hole with his first putt and sank the next one with a lazy one-handed knock in.

Silence greeted Scott as he replaced his tiny penny with his ball. The green seemed surrounded with people and more were up at the next tee. The camera was aimed at him and despite all this pressure he knew he would make the shot. He had seen the ball go in the hole in a déjà vu like trance. He would par the hole and stay six strokes under par. He was playing golf. He was having fun.

49

The cheers were heard all the way up at the scoreboard. Scott Hanover's drive into the water had many observers on edge. Was this hole going to be the start of his downfall? The cheers could mean only one thing. The scorekeeper listened to the report from the eighth hole and pulled a square number card from his stack, holding it close to his chest until he could hang it on the paired brass hooks. It was a four. Hanover had parred eight. He was still six under and leading his closest competitor by five strokes. It was unlikely that many of the best players just teeing off or about to would equal that score for the entire round. A few people started moving, then more joined them as they realized that the threesome would be teeing off at the top of the hill just five hundred yards away. Some walked and others jogged over to the ninth green. Many hoped to catch a glimpse of a golfer having a tremendous round, others hoped they would be witnessing the start of his demise. In any case, few wanted to miss it.

As they settled in around the green their attention turned to the top of the hill in the distance. Observers who had been watching the action on the eighth tee from the elevated vantage point were now parting to either side. Before long a man walked into the empty space. He wasn't wearing tights and a cape. He wasn't glowing with a heavenly aura. He was just a golfer. A golfer having a really good day.

50

"Shall we take a little walk?" suggested Jake.

"Sure," answered Gina. She continued to hug his arm as they followed the crowd to the ninth green.

"Are you going to sign him?"

"Why not?"

"You know if he wins, Karen Blakely is going to be really pissed off."

"I know," smiled Jake.

"If he loses, what have you lost?"

"Exactly."

"Aren't these guys suppose to be amateurs?" she asked.

"Yes."

"Then how can they sign up to do anything?"

"Well, technically they are limited to receiving five hundred dollars per appearance or sponsor and can't accept any cash for a tournament, but physical prizes are okay. But there are always ways to work around it. Delayed payouts until he loses his amateur status, compensation as a consultant or something like that."

"Sound like you know your stuff," teased Gina.

"It's coming back," added Jake. "Hey, do you have a cell phone?"

"You know I do." She detached herself and rummaged through her purse and pulled out the tiny black box. "Here," she offered.

Jake dialed in Jonathan's phone number.

"What's going on?" begged Jonathan. April Weinstein says that Karen Blakely signed Andrew Patterson."

"Yep," answered Jake.

"Jake, I thought you'd get it. I really did."

"Nope."

"Is Gina there?"

"Yep."

"Is your next answer going to be nope?"

Jake had to think about it. It wasn't going to be but he had to say it, "nope."

Jonathan laughed. "Are you okay?"

"I think I may have a real Cinderella for you. Forget Patterson."

"Forget Patterson?"

"Forget Patterson. He's the favorite. Everyone expects him to win. Think Hanover."

"Think Hanover?"

"What Eric Gunther didn't pull off, this guy might."

"What, some kind of upset?"

"He's finished eight holes and is six under par and shows no sign of dropping away. If he stays there he's probably going to win."

"Probably?"

"It's still a long shot."

"But if he pulls it off, he'll be a much bigger story than Patterson and a better play for Callaway."

"That's what I'm thinking."

"Is Blakely there?"

"She left a while ago. No sign of her coming back."

"Sign him before she thinks to."

"It wouldn't look good if she were representing Patterson and Hanover."

"When has that ever stopped her?"

"Never I guess."

"It sounds like you're back."

"I'm on my way Jonathan. Thanks for sending me here."

"Hey, I almost screwed it up!"

"I think I needed to screw up and realize that the world wasn't going to end. That nobody was going to die. I'm not the guy to represent Patterson anyway. After talking to his caddy and him, I don't think I'd have the stomach for it. But, Hanover, he's the sportsman, you know?"

"Yeah, I know," agreed Jonathan. "Good luck."

"Thanks." Jake pressed the END button and handed the phone back to Gina.

"I think he's getting ready to shoot," she observed. They watched as the golfer on the tee stared at the green.

51

"Your registration is out of date," observed the officer standing next to Karen's convertible. "That's three violations."

"Three?" whined Karen before realizing that arguing the matter wasn't going to help.

"Improper use of the shoulder, lack of proper vehicle registration and failure to use a turn signal." The cop stared at her through the mirrored sunglasses. "Thought I'd missed that, eh?"

Karen slumped further into her seat.

"Three violations on one stop can allow me to impound your vehicle and book you in at the barracks and have you post five hundred dollar bond. Then it's another seven hundred and fifty to get your car out of impound and one hundred twenty five towing fee."

"But you don't have to?" squeaked Karen, hopefully.

"It's a busy day. I'll just write your citations. Consider yourself lucky," she warned.

"Thank you," said Karen meekly. As the office walked away she muttered an inappropriate description of the female cop under her breath. The policewoman stopped in her tracks. Karen slumped yet further again, but the officer continued on.

Karen looked at her watch. Patterson would be teeing off any second. The only thing that made her smile now would be Jake's expression when he found out she had gotten to Patterson first. If only she hadn't been sent on the Gunther goose...

Fischer she muttered. Could he have been behind getting her out of there. Well, it didn't matter. Patterson and the Callaway account were hers. Only a disaster could ruin things now.

52

"We're going to make a change in the back nine pairing," said Carl Bateman. He was sweating despite the cool day. Three other officials were gathered with him at the registration table. Carl added another listing. He pulled Scott Hanover out of the first threesome, and pulled put a question mark by the three players in the last threesome.

"Hanover will go out last in a twosome with whomever is closest after the last group makes the turn."

"That'll be Patterson," remarked one of the other red-jacketed men.

"It could be anybody," warned Carl. "No one thought Hanover would be doing this well. He's already holding the tournament record for nine holes. Heck it might even be a state record for all I know. Someone find out." Another red-jacket nodded.

"Does anyone know where the USA Sports guy is?"

"I saw him at the scoreboard ten minutes ago."

"I think his cameraman had been following Hanover all morning. Let's try and make sure he has all the information he needs to get this on the air. Gentlemen, the only thing that could assure us a better chance at air time on the sports tonight would be if Tiger Woods showed up." All the men looked around hopefully for a second or two.

"We should do an equipment check," recommended one of the men.

"Didn't someone already do it?"

"Not on the first ten threesomes. Heck, nobody thought it would matter with them."

"That's all we need in too many clubs, an illegal driver or an illegal ball. We'd have to disqualify the guy," observed Bateman. "Alright, we'll pull his caddy aside and do it discretely after the ninth hole," ordered Bateman pointing to the third red-jacket. "Call me immediately if there are any problems. And make sure he's filling in his scorecard correctly too. That's all we need is for him to get disqualified," he worried again.

53

"The final threesome of the day is on tee," announced the starter. "Mr. Frederick Martin will be first, followed by Cary Newman and Andrew Patterson. Mr. Martin, whenever you are ready."

Andrew stood confident. The other two golfers he was with were good but neither had the ability and self-confidence that Andrew had. He had played with Martin before and knew his weaknesses. Newman was an unknown but was rated below himself and Martin. It was Andrew's to take.

A roar erupted from the scoreboard area just as Fred Martin was about to swing. He waited for the murmur to die down then hit his first drive. Long and straight down the middle.

Eric Peters whispered into Patterson's ear, "Hanover just saved par on the eighth. He's still at six under."

Andrew's expression did not waiver. He knew that Hanover must have made some lucky shots in addition to his hole-in-one. But he wasn't going to allow some twenty-handicap golfer's lucky shots destroy his concentration. There was a reason why he had a high handicap and Andrew knew the bad holes would catch up. While it wasn't unexpected to occasionally shoot one under par, he knew that many amateur golfers tended to explore the upper limits of how far over par they could shoot. Two, three or even four strokes over were not uncommon.

Newman stepped up and cloned Martin's drive with a very full swing. He looked young, perhaps even late teens. Not enough maturity and experience to compete at this level, concluded Andrew.

"If he keeps it up he'll set some records," observed Eric quietly.

"If you keep it up I'll have that kid over there carry my bags," responded Andrew. He hated advice from caddies in general and absolutely despised talk about anything else. Why were people so excited about a golfer having a few good holes? The round was eighteen holes. Consistency and concentration would win the tournament, not lucky shots.

Andrew stepped up to take his turn at the tee box. He slid a tee and a brand new ball from his pocket. Leaning lightly on his driver he inserted the tee with ball atop it into the ground. He grasped the club as he always did, set the club head two inches behind the ball, drew back and swung in a beautiful, precise fluid motion that seemed to negate some of the odd appearance of his golf attire. Despite his eccentric appearance, most of those observing saw he had the skill to back up that eccentricity. His ball also sailed straight but landed a good ten yards past the other drives in the middle of the fairway.

Andrew had attempted many sports in his life but none pleased him more than golf. It's many variables and slow speed allowed him to plan for a wide variety of possibilities and when a shot went as planned, as it did over ninety percent of the time, it excited him. Putts were the most thrilling part, the more difficult the shot the better. Sometimes he found himself aiming for difficult positions to try out putts that had several different breaks along their length that required precise knowledge of how the ball would roll and turn. Too much speed and it would miss, too little the same. Nine times out of ten, he hit just right.

As he and Eric headed down the fairway he noticed the large crowd gathered around the ninth green. The first group would be coming in now off the back nine. In two hours, Hanover would have likely finished his round and be well above par and Andrew would be three under, Perhaps four if he got a good roll on the ninth tee shot. Then the attention would be on him. It was only natural they lock onto this Hanover fellow now, after all, what was there to do until Andrew teed off?

54

"Well, Joe, are you glad you made that bet with Patterson now?" asked Ted.

"If only he can keep it up. The other guys with Hanover have had at least one disaster hole each, if he can just limit his bogey holes on the back nine, he might pull it off," answered Joe. The two men were standing by the ninth tee as Scott Hanover sank his putt on eight. They had witnessed a ball bouncing into the water and figured it was Hanover's since he would still have honors. Scott's recovery and ability to save par surprised them both. Most golfers would have bogeyed or double bogeyed a hole starting like that. But Scott was able to let it slide right off and now he was standing on the ninth tee, staring down to the green tucked over to the left of the four hundred and forty yard fairway. Joe had seen Scott is frequent consultation with his caddy and assumed he was playing a big role in keeping the amateur on track. A good caddy could make a big difference, Joe had found, if you let him.

"I hope he does win," commented Ted Lange. "Hanover winning will do more for the amateur end of the sport than Patterson could."

"Even if he finished second, it'll be the best match I've seen."

"They're having a meeting about pulling Hanover out of the order and letting him pair with the next top golfer after everyone finishes nine," whispered Ted.

"You mean he could go head-to-head with Patterson?"

"If Patterson can come close to six under."

"That might be too much pressure for Scott. Here he's playing with guys a little better than him. Once he sees a few of Patterson's arrow straight drives he'll fall apart."

"If he was going to fall apart it would have been after he put one in the water," argued Ted.

"True," mused Joe.

"On the other hand, think of the pressure it might put on Patterson?" suggested Ted.

Joe shook his head in disagreement. "He's got ice water in his veins. Nothing fazes him. He's got the mental part of the game under control."

"How often has he played against someone who was beating him?" pointed out Ted.

Joe thought it over. "Never, I guess. Do you think it might put some stress on him?"

"He might try to get more aggressive if he needs one or two more strokes under than he was planning on."

"It will be interesting to see. Would Patterson make any changes to his carefully planned game if things weren't going as he planned? He'd have to depend on some lucky shots, which isn't his style. He knows which greens to two putt and which to go for it."

"But despite all his golfing ability," pointed out Ted, "he can't capture that spirit of the game that Scott Hanover has. Patterson likes golf because he's good at it and he can excel. Scott loves golf because it's more fun than frustration. And that, I think, gives him an edge today."

"Just today?"

"Especially today. He has nothing to lose and can walk away happy shooting par. He knows he can have bad holes and expects them. Patterson doesn't even allow for a bad hole. If he had a bogey today, it would devastate him."

"Did you ever have a day like Hanover is having?" asked Joe.

Ted smiled. "Every day for the last year," he answered enigmatically.

The hushed conversations around the tee quieted down and Ted and Joe watched as Scott Hanover got ready to hit his drive on the ninth hole.

CHAPTER 11 – NINTH HOLE

55

Scott looked down the ninth fairway. It was the longest par four on the front nine at four hundred and forty yards. What's more, the fairway was wide open to either side and stretched out straight downhill. He could hit the ball almost anywhere and still have a decent shot to the green with his second shot. The green itself was large and the flag placed nearly dead center. Anywhere he landed on the green he would have an easy two putt in. If he could end up the first nine holes still six under par he'd be very happy. It certainly wasn't impossible. But he was starting to think too much. What if he did this, what if he did that? Paul was right in telling him that his game was affected more by psychology than mechanics.

Still his last drive haunted him. He needed to get a nice straight drive. He needed to know he still had those shots in him. To his left he could see the driving range. It was deserted now; all the golfers were currently on the course, twenty groups of three. Sixty golfers. The sixtieth rated player was now leading.

He remembered his lesson on the driving range earlier that morning and had an idea. He handed his driver to Paul and knelt down on the grass and untied his left shoelace, the crowd around him observed in confusion. He then cinched the shoelace and tied it down as tight as he could. Paul handed him back the driver. He remembered Scott telling him about Ted Lange's little trick and he figured at this point, it couldn't hurt. Scott placed his ball on a tee and placed the club head directly behind it. No practice swings this time.

Scott was no longer on the ninth tee. He was at the driving range and a strange old man had just had him tie his shoelace too tight and it was hurting him. Suddenly, in his mind, the image of a ball sailing straight out from the practice tee and rolling up against the fence two hundred and seventy five yards away filled his mind. It happened in slow motion. He looked down and a ball was on the tee.

Something was wrong with his left foot but he didn't remember what it was. Muscles in his back and shoulders and legs started moving his body. His eyes remained focused on the ball. There was no duck just a red stripe marking it as a range ball, for practice only. The club head disappeared from view but he sensed it hovering over his left shoulder and like a sledge hammer hurtling down on a rock, he felt his body uncoil and the ball was gone.

His head looked out and there was no practice range. No field of balls littering the grass, no large block numbers labeling the distance the ball had traveled, but a tiny white flag waved in the distance. There were people surrounding the green stunned into awed silence.

Ow, my foot, Scott thought, but his eyes stayed glued to the ball. The ball sailed out and continued to rise and rise and then seemed to hang in the air. The ball was still flying away, getting smaller with each passing moment until it came down to the ground and rolled and rolled, taking full advantage of the hill's slope. It was still rolling when applause erupted from around the tee echoed by the spectators around the green. Still the ball refused to stop until it had eked out every inch of distance it could.

"Where did that come from?" asked Paul.

"I don't know," answered Scott honestly. It had to be the longest drive he had ever hit in his life. A set of white stakes marked the distance one hundred and fifty yards from the center of the green and his ball was twenty-five yards past them. He had just slammed it out three hundred and fifteen yards.

For sure it wasn't a world's record and there were undoubtedly others here that could match the feat, but to Scott it was his best shot of the day. Better than the hole-in-one that was luck, better than his long putt for birdie, better than his chip shot on two for par. He had hit the ball perfectly and had gotten every bit of distance his body and club and ball could offer.

With a stinging reminder from his left foot he bent down, untied and loosened the lace retying it normally. He walked with a slight limp from the tee and smiled to Jerry Spaulding as he stepped up to follow Scott's incredible drive. "Is that how it's done?" he asked.

Scott smiled deeper. "It's all downhill," he commented.

56

Joe Caulkin observed Scott Hanover retying his shoe on the tee. Ted Lange smiled as he watched Scott repeat the exercise he had used before to get him to balance his brain for his swing. "Watch this," he prompted Joe.

They watched as the amateur golfer robotically swung as perfect a swing as either of them had ever seen and for a moment as the ball flew through the air, it looked as though it might land at their feet. The ground was hard enough and the ball hit with just the right angle that it rolled for nearly fifty yards before coming to a stop.

"Wow," said Joe.

"Wow," agreed Ted.

57

Jerry's drive veered to the left and was off the fairway but safely away from the trees and perhaps two hundred yards from the green. Pete's sliced to the right and rolled between some short pine trees, leaving him no clear shot to the green.

As the group moved off the tee, a massive crowd of people followed them. There were perhaps fifty people there and another fifty around the green. Word was spreading. Hanover had just nailed a monster drive on the ninth hole and was coming in. Everyone who didn't have to be somewhere else to be was migrating over to watch him play the rest of the hole. The area in front of the scoreboard, until now their only way to keep track of Hanover's progress, was quickly deserted.

Pete decided to play it safe and hit his ball back to the fairway instead of trying to find a direct route through the trees to the green. His ball landed about five yards behind Scott's.

Jerry had a good line to the green but was two hundred yards away. His second shot took him on and off the back of the green, but only a good chip and putt away from par.

Pete Baldwin placed his third shot on the green but five yards from the pin. He was on in three.

Scott was ready for his second shot. Paul handed him his pitching wedge and Scott once again resumed his normal routine of lining up the shot and taking two practice swings. He swung at the ball and someone in the crowd yelled, "It's in the hole," for luck.

It soared up heading for the pin, landing three yards in front of it, rolling past the hole two inches from the edge of the cup and stopping three feet behind it. Scott shook his head in disbelief. As long as his drive was, this shot was straight. Two inches to the left and it might have gone in. Applause had erupted again. Scott felt strangely not affected by the cheers and attention. Two putts, he thought. Two putts. Just get par and stay six under and you'll have the best nine holes you ever shot in your life.

142

Scott's only competition had always been with himself. Even when he and Paul played, he didn't care if Paul always won, if he could just have a little better score than the last time he played, that would be a great accomplishment. He didn't track his handicap after every game; he just looked at his total score and tried to take every hole one stroke at a time.

He walked on the green, placed his small penny on the grass behind his ball and picked it up, handing it to Paul to be checked for damage and to clean off any debris that might interfere with it rolling straight.

Jerry chipped his ball onto the green and was still two yards away from the cup when it stopped rolling. But definitely doable, thought Scott.

Pete putted to within a foot of the hole and quickly tapped his ball in to get off in five. Better than the last hole but adding one stroke to the plus side in his total score.

Jerry putted his ball and it followed Pete's into the cup, completing his second par in a row. Jerry was still ten strokes over par, nine of them from one hole. Even without that hole, he would be far behind Hanover.

Scott walked up by his marker, put his ball in the same position he had picked it up from earlier and pocketed the penny.

He looked at the green carefully. He looked at Paul who shrugged, obviously content to stick to metaphysical advice, rather than practical. But Scott could here his words nonetheless. "Put it in the hole."

He lined up his feet, swung the putter like a pendulum to set his speed, and with cool, deliberate precision he did just that. He put the ball in the hole.

Another birdie.

Scott Hanover was now seven strokes under par.

Seven!

It took him a while to notice that the crowd had once again erupted in cheers and even Jerry and Pete were clapping at the accomplishment.

Scott walked two steps over to the hole and pulled out the ball. He held it up like he had seen the pros do on television and waved it around and smiled - and cried.

What a wonderful, beautiful day.

And it was only half over.

58

"Tell me you have it all," begged Jason. He was a different man from the one Ellie had met in the parking garage this morning.

She nodded.

"We need to get some footage of Patterson in case things go bad."

"He's already teed off," pointed out Ellie. "Let me edit out the hole-in-one and satellite it in then I can catch up with Patterson down the course."

143

Jason considered her idea and nodded in agreement. "Okay, I should probably get some words from Hanover."

Ellie told him about some of the events on the course and Jason smiled at her stories. This guy was going to make this story shine. Screw the marathon.

Ellie looked around and saw Scott Hanover and his caddy, Paul, going over his scorecard. She waved and Scott noticed her. She motioned him over and he walked over to the camerawoman.

"This is Jason Bernard," she introduced, "Scott Hanover."

"Great to meet you," said Jason as he shook Scott's hand firmly. "Great round so far, eh?"

"Yeah."

"Listen, we want to get some tape of you before you head off again. For the sports report."

"Terrific," said Scott.

Jason looked at Ellie. "Is here okay?"

She motioned Jason to his left to get a better angle to the sun and hefted the camera to her shoulder, "Ready."

Jason began an impromptu introduction and his professional skills and presence took over. Ellie was impressed how easily he flowed into his "on camera" personality.

"We're here at George Dunne National Golf Course in Oak Forest, Illinois for the Northern Illinois Amateur Regional Golf Tournament. The winner today will get a slot in the next PGA Pro-Am tournament. A dream that most amateurs will never realize but golfer Scott Hanover is giving a lot of duffers a vicarious thrill with his incredible round today and an amazing shot on the seventh hole which we'll show you in a moment."

He turned to Scott, "You're now seven strokes under par. An incredible accomplishment for a professional golfer let alone an amateur. Scott, did you ever think you'd be doing this well after the first nine holes?"

Scott looked at the camera and took a breath. "No way," he answered honestly. "I've had a bunch of lucky shots."

"Do you think it'll hold up?"

"I don't know, but even if it doesn't today will be a day I will always remember."

"On the seventh hole," Jason glanced down at a scorecard he had grabbed from the clubhouse earlier, "A hundred and ninety yard par three, you did something most golfers only dream of. What did it feel like?"

"Like you said, most golfers only dream of getting a hole-in-one. I've come close a bunch of times but when I hit the ball I was sure it was going to zoom off the green."

"What happened?"

"It hit the flagstick head on and just dropped in. Like I said, a lucky shot."

"Well, luck or not, it's the same score," pointed out Jason.

"Yeah."

"How long have you been golfing?"

"About twenty years. Since college."

"Were you on your college team?"

Scott Laughed. "Not likely."

"Looking forward to maybe playing with the pros?"

"Well, it'd be nice to win, but I'm afraid today will be my last game for a while."

Jason looked confused.

Scott continued, "My wife, Sarah, is expecting our first child in a couple of weeks and my time is going to be taken up with my family."

"I'm sure you're wife would understand," suggested Jason.

"You don't know my wife. Besides I promised and I intend to keep that promise. A round like today is not how I usually play and I would be way out of my league in a professional tournament."

"Perhaps when your son or daughter is older?"

"Perhaps," smiled Scott.

"Do you want to tell us a little about the quacking?"

Scott laughed. "Well, it started as a private joke with my caddy, Paul Bauer. When we first started golfing years ago I guess I had a tendency to hit balls into the water whenever we found some on the course. He called me the duck and made sure to give me a reminder quack whenever water was in play. Some of the observers today picked up on it and it helped me shed some of the nerves I was getting, well, until the official put a stop to it?"

"He wouldn't let the people quack?"

"Well, I think it was starting to annoy him a little, to tell the truth."

"Does Paul have a nickname?"

Scott laughed again. "Paul has always been 'Zorro.' He uses a black glove and green tees, which he has loaned me today. Oh, he also had some special balls made for today."

"Special?"

Scott pulled out a duck logo ball and held it up. Ellie zoomed in and held the shot for a moment."

"Very nice," commented Jason. Jason looked back into the camera. "Well, Duck, let's take a look at that amazing hole-in-one earlier today." He paused a moment. "Cut. Okay, now we'll do a throw back and head for the truck. "This is Jason Bernard reporting from George Dunne National Golf Course." Another pause. "Okay, Scott. Thanks. We'll see you at the tenth hole."

"Can I get a copy of all this?"

"You'll get everything I have," answered Ellie.

Jason shook Scott's hand once more and Ellie shook it as well. They headed off to the parking lot and the USA Sports truck parked there.

Paul came up behind Scott. "You're going to be on TV," he said.

"My fifteen minutes," added Scott.

"Maybe more than that," suggested Paul.

59

"Mr. Hanover," called an urgent voice. Scott turned and a large man wearing a red jacket with a white plastic name badge pinned to the lapel. "Terrific round so far."

Scott didn't know what to say. "I guess," he muttered. The man seemed a little hesitant, like he was there to more than just compliment Scott on his golf game. He had some news and Scott had no idea if it was good or bad.

"Usually," he continued, "we try to group golfers to allow the better golfers to finish last, you know, have some head to head competition. Makes for a better tournament."

"Makes sense," agreed Scott.

"You were rated last among all the golfers today yet you're way ahead of the rest so far."

"I still am rated last, last I checked," pointed out Scott.

"Yes. One of the officials will need to check your equipment."

"Excuse me?" asked Scott.

"Just to make sure it falls within the USGA regulations. I'd hate to see you disqualified."

"Disqualified? Shouldn't that have been checked out earlier?"

"Technically, there's no time limit to when a violation can be discovered. But we just want to make sure."

"You think I'm cheating?" asked Scott angrily.

"No. No. But we need to make sure that if any accusations are made we can say you are well within the USGA rules."

"Check away."

Carl Bateman motioned another red-jacketed man to check the bag Paul was standing next to. "There is one other thing," added Bateman, "provided everything checks out okay. We'd like to pull you out of your current threesome to play in a final twosome with whomever has the next highest score, provided, of course, you're still in the running after everyone has come in from the front nine."

146

"But, that could be two hours or more," realized Scott. "I'll lose my momentum." The statement sounded stupid the moment Scott said it. Momentum? He could scarcely call his performance on the course anything that he had planned or had control over.

"Well, yes, and normally, we don't want to destroyed the rhythm a golfer may have developed, but if you don't mind."

"What if I do mind?" asked Scott, wondering what might happen if he fought the officials ruling.

"Technically, we can disqualify you. We do have the ability to change grouping and order in the middle of the match."

"I'm sure you do, but how would that look," pointed out Scott. "The USA Sports people just went to put some stuff together about me already. If you pulled me out, well, a lot of people might be starting to thing that you want one of the favorites to win rather than a nobody."

"Not at all, not at all," Bateman backpedaled, "we want the people who came out here today to see the best match ups we can provide. It makes for a more dramatic finish if the best scorers round out the tournament."

"I suppose it makes sense from your point of view," agreed Scott.

"Who knows, maybe having some stiffer competition will help your game."

Scott laughed. "I can't see doing any better than I already have."

"Yes, well, you're probably right about that," muttered Bateman.

"Well," considered Scott, "it seems like I really don't have much of a choice anyway. Do what you got to do."

"Thank you, Mr. Hanover. Grab some lunch. Relax. We'll find you when we need you," Carl instructed. He walked about twenty feet to a golf cart and drove off.

"What was that?" wondered Paul.

"I guess we'll take a break."

"You know you can't really do anything. You can't practice putting at the putting green or hit balls at the driving range."

"Really?"

"I think you can chip around the tenth tee, but that's while you're waiting to tee off."

"Well, then, let me buy you lunch, Paul."

"Excellent idea."

60

Sarah and Anna made arrangements to pick up their furniture the next week. Sarah's contractions were still persisting but were once again tolerable.

"Same thing happened to me," said Anna when Sarah asked her about it. "It was a false labor. I dragged Dale to the hospital and they sent me back home. I didn't have Linus for another ten days."

"Sounds reassuring," said Sarah.

"You'll be fine," added Anna. "When I did go into labor it lasted twenty-two hours. You'll have plenty of time when it does happen. Trust me."

They browsed for a while longer among the pickings left by the earliest shoppers. Anna ended up buying some children's books and Sarah found a few more stuffed animals to add to the collection that had built up in the nursery thanks to a baby shower, hand me downs, and favorites Sarah had saved from her childhood. This kid was in definite danger of being buried for days under a fake fur avalanche if the trend continued.

"What's going on over there?" asked Anna.

Sarah looked as Anna pointed to the rows of televisions they had passed previously. A group of people, mostly men were mesmerized by the television show multiplied like the reflection in a fly's compound eye dozens of times. A man was walking toward them and shaking his head. He noticed their interest in the group gathered to watch the TVs.

"Some guy hit a hole-in-one," he mentioned, assuming they would be interested in the explanation.

"Too bad Scott's missing that," commented Sarah. "What, like Tiger Woods or someone?"

"Naw, some guy playing in an amateur tournament. He's walking away with it after nine holes. Winner gets a chance to play in a pro tournament," he added and walked on.

"Hey that sounds like the one Scott is playing in. Oh, dear, I hope he's not doing too badly. It sounds like there are some really good guys playing. I wonder If Scott got to see it when he was there?" said Sarah.

"Bleh," gagged Anna. "He's probably sitting in the clubhouse watching it on TV with Paul."

"Let's see if they show Scott playing or in the background or something."

Anna looked at her watch. "We really should be going, Sarah."

"It'll just take a minute," she argued. "Let's hurry before they move onto another story." She pulled Anna by the hand and led her through the thinning crowd.

"...and apparently," a neatly groomed, well-dressed, anchorman commented as Sarah got close enough to see one of the screens, "his caddy had nicknamed him 'The Duck' because of his propensity to hit the ball into any water on the course."

"And he did fulfill that prophecy on the eighth hole," added a too bouncy blonde anchor whose painted red lips pulled out to a perfect smile over her bright, white teeth.

"But still managed to pull off a par, despite the penalty stroke," added the first sportscaster.

"That's funny," Sarah mentioned to Anna, "Paul calls Scott 'The Duck' too." She paused a moment. "They can't be talking..."

"I thought you said Scott was out of his league with these guys?"

Suddenly Scott's picture filled half the screen next to a man holding a microphone with the USA Sports logo prominently displayed.

"...I've had a bunch of lucky shots," said Scott to the television audience.

The camera cut away and Scott was standing at a tee getting ready to swing. He hit the ball and the camera followed it jerkily until it focused on the flag on the green. The ball hit the flag and dropped in the hole, the camera zooming in until it was clear the ball had indeed gone in.

"There it is, once again," commented the first anchor, "Scott Hanover's amazing hole-in-one. As he said himself, one heck of a 'lucky shot.'"

Sarah's jaw dropped. "Oh my god," she muttered. "Did you see that?"

"Everybody's seen it, lady," commented a man standing near her.

"That was my husband," she said. "He's on TV."

He turned to her, "No kidding? Wow, what a day he's having, seven under par for nine holes. If he keep that up he'll break the professional golf record for eighteen holes."

"Record?" asked Sarah.

"Yeah. Apparently he was in the first group to tee off but they're making him wait to finish so they can put him head-to-head with a golfer doing as well, or at least close to him. USA Sports says they're going to come back in a couple of hours to show stroke by stroke coverage of the back nine."

Sarah looked at Anna. "I have to go there," she announced, resolute and firm. "I have to be there."

Anna smiled and chuckled. "I though you hated golf?"

"I do, Anna, but I love Scott. I think it would mean a lot to him if I were there, he promised this would be his last round of golf for a long time. He's on TV, Anna," she added, trying to convince her sister.

"Sarah, I have to get home and start getting ready for my dinner party tonight."

"That's okay, I'll go myself," said Sarah.

"You can't go by yourself, what about your contractions?"

"You said yourself they're nothing to worry about."

"Did I hear you say that was your husband?" asked a familiar voice. It was Sally, the extraordinarily nice salesperson who had helped them earlier.

"Yes," grinned Sarah proudly.

"That guy interviewing him, Jason Bernard, He's my husband," she explained, almost as proudly as Sarah. "Why don't I take you to the tournament. I'm sure Jason could get you out with the golfers, especially since he's covering the story."

"Do you think it would be hard to get on the course?"

She nodded her head. "Every amateur golfer in the area is going to be rushing down there to see your husband finish his round. It's really turning out to be a huge story. And Jason was worried he got stuck with this golf tournament as a punishment," she added. "Besides, I have another reason for going."

What's that?" quizzed Sarah.

"That women who was working with me, Cecily..."

Sarah thought a moment then remembered the first woman who had offered help when she was looking at rockers. She shook as she recalled her rudeness and stuffy demeanor.

"...her fiancé is playing in that tournament too. If your husband can beat him, I'll do whatever I can to see that moment."

Sarah laughed and turned to Anna. "Anna, go on home, I'll get a lift from Sally."

61

"Two hot dogs," ordered Paul, "and a large Pepsi."

"The same here," added Scott. The young, teenage girl working the lunch counter smiled and rang the orders up on her cash register then turned to get them ready. The hot dogs were twirling between a set of rollers on the counter behind her. She pulled four buns from the steamer and placed them on separate sheets of waxed paper. She then loaded the hot dogs from the warmer with a set of tongs, laying them in the warm buns. She wrapped each dog and placed them all on a tray near the cash register. She then pulled two large Styrofoam cups from a stack, dragged them through a bin of ice and set them under the soda dispenser until the foam dripped over the sides.

"Eleven dollars," she said with her continuing smile.

Scott reached into his wallet and pulled out a ten and a single and handed them to the girl. He slipped another two singles into a pickle jar labeled "tips."

"Thanks," she said. "Um, you're that guy, right? The one on TV?"

150

Scott turned around and noted the thirty-five inch television in the corner turned to USA Sports. A report on the Chicago Marathon was currently playing but a crawl on the bottom of the screen promised shot by shot coverage of the Northern Illinois Amateur Regional Golf Tournament later in the day. "I guess I am."

She pulled a scorecard from under the counter and pen from next to the cash register. "Can I get your autograph?" she asked shyly. "Who knows, it might be worth something someday."

Paul laughed. "I'm sorry," he apologized. "It just struck me as funny."

Scott cautioned him with a look and took the offered pen, "What's your name?" he asked.

"Cassie," she replied.

He wrote, "To Cassie: Thanks for the dogs, Best Wishes, Scott Hanover."

"There," he said, "thanks for asking."

Cassie looked pleased at the scorecard. "Good luck the rest of the round," she said.

"I'll take all I can get," he answered.

When they were out of earshot Paul teased, "she likes you, Scott."

"Shut up," said Scott. They stepped over to the condiment table and Scott pumped some mustard onto his dogs and slathered them with relish and onions.

"I'm just saying," continued Paul, adding a layer of ketchup over his tube steaks.

"Eat your hot dogs," instructed Scott as they sat down a table. No sooner had they sat down when another man slipped himself into one of the two empty chairs around the table.

"Better get used to that," he warned.

Scott seemed puzzled.

"The autographs. Could be someday you'll be tired of signing them."

"I doubt it," laughed Scott.

"I'm Jake Fischer," He held out his hand and Scott wiped some mustard from his before shaking.

"Scott Hanover. This is my caddy Paul Bauer." Paul's handshake left a little ketchup on Jake's hand but Jake seemed to politely ignore it.

"I know. You've had an amazing round so far."

"Amazing is the word," agreed Scott. "Are you playing?" he asked.

"No, just watching. I'm a sports agent."

"Like Jerry Maguire," piped in Paul.

Jake chuckled. "Not quite."

"Show me the money," grunted Paul, continuing his parody.

"Well." Started Jake, "I'd like to talk to you about some sort of agreement."

Scott stopped in mid bite and put down his hot dog. "You want to represent me?" he asked.

"Yes."

"Why?" asked Scott incredulously.

"You're the kind of sportsman I look for."

"Lucky?" asked Paul jokingly.

"Genuine," answered Jake. "You play because you love the game. You're already a hero to the thousands of golfers this morning and that number will grow before you hit the tenth tee. USA Sports is going to play this up to draw attention from the Marathon scandal and you have won a place in today's events, whether you win or not?"

"Marathon Scandal?" asked Paul.

"Some kid took an early lead then almost died from a drug overdose," explained Jake.

"I'm not going to win," pointed out Scott.

"You don't have to win, just have fun. Callaway wants a real weekend golfer that people can associate with. I think that's you. Other people think it may be someone else out her today, but I have an eye for these things."

The golf guys Callaway?" interrupted Paul.

"That's the Callaway," answered Jake.

Paul let out a low, long whistle. Scott seemed impressed too but explained further. "Well, even if I do win, I can't play the Pro-Am. I'll be on labor watch."

"Labor watch?" asked Jake.

Paul explained, "Scott and his wife Sarah are expecting their first kid in a few weeks. Scott promised there'd be no more golf for a while. He gave in too easily though, if you ask me."

"Nobody asked you," jibed Scott.

"Congratulations, Scott," said Jake, "that's great. Listen. I can't promise you'll get rich from this; you can't because you're an amateur. There are alternate ways to compensate you, perhaps a college fund for your kid, but we can talk about that later. No one's going to care if you play in the Pro-Am after what you've done today. You're a Cinderella, an unknown, showing up at the ball with a carriage drawn by ducks. You're the kind of guy Callaway needs. Take a ride with me and I promise you'll have some fun along the way."

"I really don't think anyone would be interested in me," argued Scott.

"Let me take care of that part." Jake pulled a stack of papers folded into thirds from his pocket. "Sign a letter of exclusivity with me. It won't commit you to any endorsements or sign over your life, it just means I have first right of refusal to represent you if any offers come along."

"It can't hurt," pointed out Paul. "I'd do it."

"It can't hurt," agreed Jake.

For the second time in less than ten minutes, Scott gave his autograph.

62

Andrew Patterson's tee shot on the second hole landed in the middle of the fairway. He knew he could par this hole with a perfect approach shot. Without words, his caddy handed him his eight iron. Andrew didn't even check if it was the right club. He didn't need to line up the shot. He had a natural sense of where to put his feet. It was like his body was programmed to play golf. If only he had found this sport earlier. But there was still time to make his mark. And it would start today.

He popped the ball up neatly on the green and a slight backspin pulled it within a yard of the hole. This put was simple for him. A light tap and it was in. There were a few people crowded around him with more coming now that Hanover had finished and they wanted to see what Patterson would do in the face of Scott's seven strokes under par score.

Andrew knew that a score like that was due entirely to luck, especially from such a low rated player. Luck had a habit of turning. He would finish the front nine three or four, possibly five under par if he had some luck of his own on a chip shot or two, but his steady, consistent style would bring him to the win, as it always had.

CHAPTER 12 – THE TURN

63

When playing a weekend round of golf, "the turn" is a very important part of the game. It is the break at halfway through the round where you've finished the front nine and are getting ready to start the back nine. There usually are refreshments available and if your not playing on a forest preserve course, alcohol may be involved.

During this break the score for the first nine holes is tallied and entered on the scorecard. At this point you can have several outlooks on the rest of the game, the most common being "time for a fresh start." This position is adopted as a result of making stupid mistakes on the first half of the course. A six should have been a five. A twelve-inch putt shouldn't have been missed. None of those mistakes will happen on the back nine, you'll tell yourself.

Less often, you're playing well. A few strokes behind your best score but since you always do better on the back nine there's hope for the entire round.

Today, Scott was stuck. He couldn't hope to do better than he already had been doing. Even a bad back nine would be his best round ever. He could bogey every hole and still have his best round ever. If he could keep making pars, maybe a few more birdies he might even come close to a sixty.

He looked at the clock above the lunch counter and stared at his empty plate. Two hours to wait.

Jerry and Pete had already started the rest of their round and were continuing to put up pars and bogeys on the giant scoreboard. The last few threesomes out were keeping to the expectations of an excellent round, the leader among them, Andrew Patterson with a two under par after three holes. A score that matched Scott's at that point.

As Scott looked around the clubhouse it became apparent that the place was getting pretty crowded. A glance at the parking lot revealed cars parking along drives and even out on to Central Avenue as the lot filled up. He suddenly realized they were there because of him. His piece on USA Sports had garnered attention and many people were not going to be content with watching the conclusion to his round on a twenty-five inch television. They would want to say they were there when.

"What should we do?" asked Paul. "Another hot dog?"

"Maybe later," answered Scott. "Let's get some air."

"Dig it," answered Paul.

Scott pulled his cap down over his eyes. He didn't want to be recognized from his television appearance and felt a little foolish thinking he might, but the girl who sold him his lunch knew him. God, what would Sarah think of that?

"Where should we go?" asked Paul as they exited the dining area to the outside.

"Let's go check out eighteen. No one will be there yet," suggested Scott.

They walked through the crowd. Most people congregating around the scoreboard, some commenting that scores for Hanover's last couple of holes weren't up. Others passing along the news that he was going to go off with the second place golfer after everyone finished nine.

Assuming I stay in first place, Scott thought silently.

The asphalt path was dry and crunchy with loose stones. They entered a green cave formed by the overhanging tree limbs. The leaves were touched with a few hints of early fall color. They emerged into a secluded semicircle of trees surrounding the eighteenth green. Across the closely mowed grass a dark, black, eerily still, pond taunted Scott. Directly across the massive water hazard were the gold championship tees of the eighteenth hole.

"Peaceful isn't it," interrupted a voice to their left. Ted Lange emerged from the shadow. "Getting crowded here," he commented.

"Just killing time," said Scott.

"Yeah, I heard you'll have to wait for Patterson to finish."

"You think he'll be leading everyone else?" asked Paul.

"Yep, but he won't top Scott's score. Very few golfers have for nine holes. I think you've used up this corner of the universe's luck for the day."

"That's what I've been telling him," agreed Paul. Scott punched Paul's arms and then raised his eyebrows, warning Paul not to return the punch. Don't want to damage the prizefighter before the tenth round.

"I guess your idea about having a great game once every blue moon or so seems to be coming true for me."

"Your game today has nothing to do with me," pointed out Ted.

Scott looked confused. He remembered the tight shoelace and the philosophical discussion at the driving range. "Then who?"

"You."

The confusion persisted. "What? I just decided that today that not only would I have par or better on every hole but get my first hole-in-one as well?"

"Not exactly, but you're letting it happen. A lot of golfers when they start doing well, try to over analyze it. Try to concentrate on the things they're doing differently that allow them to get a little bit longer drive and that more accurate putt. You're not good enough to let that happen."

"You got that right," said Paul, pulling back in anticipation of a second well-deserved punch in the arm.

Scott just settled for an angry glare and turned back to Ted. "I guess you're right," he said after considering it for a moment."

"You're playing golf, Scott. You're a good golfer some of the time and average most of the time and lousy occasionally."

"You got that..." started Paul until he stopped himself and laughed. "Well it's true," he said.

Ted continued, "Don't let the game play you. Don't think about what you've done in the past. Every hole, heck, every shot is different from any shot you've ever played before. You can't play any better by looking at what you've done. You need to see what you have to do. Then do it."

"What If I can't do it?"

"Did you think that ball would go in the hole at seven?"

"No."

"You'll always be surprised at what you can do when you don't approach it with the attitude that you can't do it. Don't let your past dictate what you're limits are. There's always a little more room on the end of the bell curve, Scott. The probability will never hit zero, no matter how far out you go. It's an amazing quirk of statistics. Some things are statistically unlikely, but never, never impossible."

Ted looked out over the lake. "I'll let you boys alone. I'll see you at ten. I'm kind of excited to see what happens myself."

"I hope I won't disappoint you," offered Scott.

"Just remember. You're not playing against Andrew Patterson or the tournament record. You're playing against what you're capable of. Play golf and you'll do fine and not have a single regret."

Scott shook his hand. "Thanks for the pep talk."

Ted smiled and shuffled off, clicking on a walkie-talkie hanging from his waist, slipping a set of Walkman headphones over his ears.

"Nice guy," commented Paul.

"Yeah," agreed Scott absently. What a strange coincidence that Ted Lange was here when he and Paul arrived. It was even odder that Ted not only had been at Scott's qualifying tournament, but also was here to help out at the driving range. It was like he was some sort of guardian angel, a Clarence keeping Scott on track. He found Ted's presence reassuring and left it at that. He turned back to look over the small lake. Just eight more holes and he'd be standing over there looking this way.

Not is his wildest imagination would Scott have been able to foresee what lied ahead for him then. He hadn't a clue.

<h2 style="text-align:center">64</h2>

Sally squinted as she exited the Speedway gas station. She was folding a Chicago area map back into it's neat compact form and smiled broadly as she crossed the pump island back to her car. Sarah had remained in the front seat at Sally's insistence. Sally was concerned the gas fumes might affect Sarah's unborn child. Sarah fiddled with the radio, unsure where on the dial the sports stations were. She knew there were a couple in Chicago but all she found was Spanish language music stations and talk radio on the AM side and rock, oldies, alternative, rap and one classical station on the FM side.

Sally pulled open the driver's side door. "I've got it. We're about twenty minutes away. Straight down Lagrange Road for another five miles then east on 159th street. You find anything about the tournament on the radio?"

"I'm sure Scott would have been able to tune in the sports station in a minute, but if they happened to be playing a commercial for hair regrowth formula or a tooth whitening service when I scanned it, I probably missed any sports stations."

"Well, I'm sure we'll get there before it's all over. I can try and call Jason's office and get a message to him."

"That's okay," said Sarah. "Let's just get there."

"Good idea." Sally pulled out of the station and out onto four lane road. She glanced at Sarah who had turned off the radio in frustration and was absently making small circles on her stomach with her hands. "I'm trying to convince Jason we need one of those soon," said Sally.

"What?" muttered Sarah as she was brought out of her daydream.

"A baby."

"Doesn't he want kids?"

"He says he does but doesn't think the time is right."

"You can always find some excuse to put it off," added Sarah, "but you need to bite the bullet and do it. Once it becomes a reality your whole outlook changes. It's no longer, 'will be make good parents?' but 'I can't believe we're going to be parents.'"

"I'm afraid to push too hard but if we wait too long, it may not be an option."

Sarah smiled consolingly then her face grimaced with pain. "Yeow," she remarked as he hands instinctively reached out to grab the edge of the dashboard.

"What is it? Is it the baby? Is it coming?" asked Sally in a panic.

Sarah waited to answer, Breathing deeply, letting the cramping sensation in her belly dissipate before answering.

"Just a contraction. I've been having little ones all morning. That one was out of the blue. Whew."

"Should we go to the hospital?" asked Sally.

"No. It's probably just false labor. Anna had the same thing with her kid. I'll be fine."

"Are you sure?"

Sarah started her absent massage of her belly once again. The painful expression that had torn across her face was replaced by a glowing smile just as quickly. Sally was jealous but excited for Sarah.

"Is being pregnant as wonderful as they say?" she asked

"Other than the back aches and peeing all the time it's the most amazing thing I've ever experienced. I feel the baby twisting and turning and kicking and punching. It's hard to believe that at some point in the near future it'll be out here with me, rather than inside. It boggles my mind sometimes."

"Do you have some names picked out?"

"Don't get me started," she fumed. "Scott seems to have a predilection to the strangest names possible and is adamant that we agree rather than leaving it to me. How would you like a boy name Iggy or Izzy or Monty? Or a Girl named Amber or Bunny or Cassandra?"

Sally laughed. "I'm sure you'll come up with something soon."

"Well, once this golf tournament is over, we'll have to sit down and think about it seriously."

"He sounds like an interesting man, your husband," said Sally.

"Interesting, strange, bizarre at times, but ultimately lovable and hopelessly addictive," Sarah listed.

"That's a strange description."

"I suppose. But it fits him."

"I can't wait to meet him," said Sally.

"What's Jason like?" asked Sarah.

"He's driven, like most people in his profession. But he's honest and ethical. Two traits that perhaps don't help many people in his line of work to succeed."

"They sound like the kind of traits you'd want in a father though."

"Yeah," agreed Sally with a sigh. "Plus he's as cute as a bug."

"I wasn't going to say anything," agreed Sarah.

"That's okay, covet my husband why don't you," joked Sally.

"I'm sure it's mostly the makeup and special camera lenses."

"Sarah, I live with him. It ain't no special camera lens lady." They both laughed and Sally pulled over to the left turn lane at the stoplight. The green sign with white lettering said 159th street. The traffic going east seemed a little heavier than that going west and a mile down the road they were bumper to bumper crawling.

"You don't think this has anything to do with the tournament," asked Sarah.

"It must be an accident," commented Sally.

As they crept along for another mile the flashing lights of a Cook County Sheriff's police car reflected off the hoods and roofs of the cars ahead. Traffic eventually stopped moving altogether. Sally noticed a uniformed sheriff's deputy approaching the car and rolled down her window.

He bent over to speak to her, "We're diverting traffic around the area, ladies, too many people trying to get to the golf course up ahead. Some guy is shooting a heck of a game and everyone wants to see it. They had to close it off and there's a huge gridlock of people trying to turn around to get out."

"You mean we're not going to make it?" asked Sarah.

"You're heading to the golf course?" asked the cop.

"We were hoping to."

"Golf fans?"

"No, not really."

"Well, no one is getting there now. We'll probably have to let some television crews through but I don't see that happening for at least an hour until we can get things cleared."

"Scott is going to be disappointed I couldn't make it," said Sarah.

"Scott?" asked the officer.

"My husband," explained Sarah, "he's playing today."

"Scott Hanover?" he asked.

"Yes," answered Sarah in surprise. "You know him?"

"They've been talking about it for the last hour on The Score."

"The Score?" asked Sally.

"You know, the sports station on the radio." He thought a moment. "Do you have some ID ma'am?" he asked Sarah.

Sarah pulled out her wallet and slipped out her driver's license.

"Just wanted to make sure you weren't pulling a fast one on me."

"My husband in covering the tournament for USA Sports," explained Sally.

"Jason Bernard?" queried the officer, his voice somewhat elevated in pitch. Sally produced her ID and the officer stood up and gazed at the situation. He grasped the shoulder mike to his radio. "Hank, I got a couple of ladies that need to get into George. Can we do it?"

"Why?"

"Hanover's wife," the officer explained.

"Done," came the answer. "Come on up. We'll use a snow plow if we have to."

"Ladies, I'll pull my cruiser up and turn it around in the median here. You can then pull out and follow me. Stay close." He turned and headed back down the line of cars to the police car.

"Nice service," commented Sally.

"Scott will get a kick out of this."

"He'll get a bigger kick with you there."

"I hope so. What if he's mad? What if I make him nervous or ruin his concentration?"

"I don't think that will happen," Sally assured her.

"I hope not."

65

Karen Blakely rubbed at the back of her heel and nearly fell over. She had been hiking down the shoulder of 159th street and thought maybe a tiny piece of gravel had worked its way into her shoe. She couldn't imagine what was holding up the traffic and quickly realized she was going to have to walk if she was going to get back to the golf course at all. She watched as a police car several blocks ahead turned onto Central Avenue escorting a station wagon south. Her own car was three blocks back, parked in a Target parking lot. The map showed she had a mile and half walk to the golf course and there were no sidewalks along the busy street. The grass edging the shoulders sloped steeply into a damp drainage ditch.

Trying to walk there had proved to be even more of a challenge than the gravel shoulder.

She cursed as she watched the car disappear towards the golf course. How did they rate an escort past all this mess? She was grumpy and tired. She had four hundred and fifty dollars worth of traffic tickets in her purse and was worried she'd miss her chance to get her new client some airtime on USA Sports. She had not been able to follow the tournament for the last couple of hours. Between the traffic, crabby state troopers, a dead cell phone battery and the seventeen blisters forming on her feet, the great start to her day was deteriorating rapidly. She couldn't imagine it getting worse.

She checked her watch and smirked as a couple of guys in a pickup whistled at her. "Want me to carry you, baby?" one had shouted.

The thought that kept her going was the look that must have been on Jake Fischer's face when he finally caught up to Patterson.

In took her another couple of blocks to realize the traffic wasn't due to construction or an accident but a tangle of cars trying to turn onto Central Avenue and get to the golf tournament and even more trying to get out as they were apparently turned away.

A policeman worked his way among the stopped cars. "Can I help you ma'am?" he asked.

"I'm just trying to get to the tournament," she said. "What's with all this traffic?"

'Haven't you heard? Some guy is setting a record or something. Had a hole-in-one, I believe."

"Patterson? Is his name Patterson?"

"I don't think so."

"Andrew Patterson. He's the favorite to take it away today."

"Andrew," muttered the officer, "doesn't sound right."

"Well, he's my client. I'm an agent. I have my credentials right here," she said, tapping the lapel of her jacket. Her hands touched rough fabric, not the smooth cool plastic of her credential pass. Karen's eyes rolled up into her head as she remembered putting the pass in the glove compartment of her car as she left the parking lot earlier that morning. It was still locked in there. "Uh, I'm sure they can issue me a new pass when I get there. Please?" she begged. She was on more stable ground with a male cop than the woman who had stopped her before. He was already letting his eyes stray to he chest, rather than her face. She pulled her Registered Sports Agent credentials from her wallet and showed them with a smile. "I am who I say I am. I need to get there."

"Well, you'll still have to walk," he said.

"No problem." She slipped off her heels and massaged what was left of the soles of her feet. "A little dirt never scared me."

"Well, good luck to you and Mr. Patterson," the officer offered.

Karen took a few steps and the gravel added another layer of discomfort to her blistered feet. She moved over to the grassy part of the shoulder and felt a little relief in the cool grass despite the uneven and bumpy ground. It was going to be worth it, a big contract with Callaway, a nice cut for her and a stepping-stone to the pro golf tour. With her smile and looks it wouldn't take long to find those golfers unhappy with their current representation, looking for a fresh, vivacious, hungry, new agent.

A sharp pain stung her left leg. A stick from a stray bush had grabbed at her pantyhose and drew a thin line of blood across her skin. She dabbed at it with a Kleenex and cursed the golf fans that made this trek necessary. Next time, she thought, I'm getting a helicopter.

66

Ellie took her tray of three hot dogs, a bag of chips and the largest Pepsi they had to an empty table. She was glad to be rid of the camera equipment for a while and to get some calories into her system. It was shaping up to be a long day. A few more camera crews were on the way and coverage would be pretty good, considering they were only planning on covering Hanover and whoever he was golfing with the last nine holes. The equipment in the truck was transmitting all she had taped so far and the producers back at the studio would have the fun of putting together the wrap up show.

"This seat taken?" asked a woman's voice.

Ellie looked up to see the woman's half smile. "No. Please. Sit down." She watched as the woman slid onto the seat, careful to watch her left leg that had a metal brace wrapped around the foot and presumably continued all the way to her hip.

Gina sat with practiced elegance on the plastic seated chair setting her own tray down with an apple and banana on it. The healthiest food she could find here. "I'm Gina Beck," she said.

"Ellie Burke." The two shook hands.

"I wish I could eat like that," commented Gina.

Ellie laughed. "I'm sure it will catch up to me someday, probably after I have my first kid. I'll blow up to two hundred pounds and stay there."

"Maybe. I'm only a few steps behind that," commented Gina, patting her slightly bulging stomach.

"Naw. I should eat better anyways. Starting tomorrow." They laughed again.

"Is your husband playing?" asked Gina.

"Oh, I'm not married," answered Ellie, holding up the fingers of her left hand. "I'm here covering the tournament for USA Sports."

"Oh, you're a sportscaster?"

"Naw, behind the scenes. I'm a camera operator. I do some editing in the field too, but I like catching great moments on tape. It can be fun."

"Are you the one who got Scott Hanover's hole-in-one?"

"That's me."

"So you'll be covering his back nine. It should be exciting that they're going to have him wait to play with one of the better golfers."

"It'll be Andrew Patterson," said Ellie. "They don't think anyone else will be close. If it wasn't for Scott Hanover, they say Andrew Patterson would walk away with the tournament since his only serious competition Joe Caulkin broke his wrist."

"I heard about that," said Gina. "Do you know him?"

"Met him this morning," answered Ellie. "Did you hear about the bet?"

"Bet?"

"Patterson bet Caulkin five thousand dollars against the whole field he would win."

"Men and their egos."

"Well, it will be an interesting final nine. Why don't you tag along with me, Gina? It'll be nice to have some female company in this testosterone fest."

"That would be nice. I'm actually here with my boyfriend. He's an agent."

"Sports agent?"

"Yes."

"Don't tell me, he's representing Andrew Patterson."

"He was going to but another agent beat Jake to him."

"Sorry to hear that," said Ellie.

"It's okay, he has his eye on someone else now."

"Hanover?" asked Ellie.

"Well, yes."

"Wow. I'd like to meet your boy friend," she said.

"Finish your lunch, then we'll take a walk."

"I'll need to do an update with Mr. Bernard soon," Ellie explained.

"Then between updates," said Gina.

"Who knows, maybe Jason could do a little sidebar piece with your boyfriend?"

"I'm sure Jake wouldn't be opposed to that at all."

67

The scorekeeper updated Andrew Patterson's score to three under after the fifth hole. The next closest golfer was two under. Scott Hanover's score was the same at the fifth hole and it looked like it was shaping up to be a duel between the favorite and the long shot. USA Sports was showing updates after every hole with Jason Bernard standing near the scoreboard and Ellie transmitting the feed live with three hundred yards of cable linked to the microwave transmitter antennae atop the van roof in the parking lot. Despite the course now being closed, hundreds of cars still jammed 159th street and Central Avenue. Some had portable TVs and just decided to camp out in the traffic jam and catch the action indirectly. Others walked to and lined the chain link fences surrounding the golf course. A few braved the barbed tops of the ten-foot fences but county cops pulled down most and others fell back bleeding.

A few made it over. Some of them were escorted out by some of the larger red-jacketed officials from the tournament but most blended in with the crowds of on lookers inside. A helicopter brought the second and third camera crews from USA Sports along with more equipment. The golf course arranged for them to use the starters booth at the clubhouse to set up a control center. It was cramped but would serve their needs. The engineers even set up monitors for the people out by the scoreboard to watch.

Ellie and Jason went over the course map picking camera locations on each hole and giving the cameramen and technician teams their series of locations. It would be tight, but if everyone followed the plan, it would work out. Ellie took the other two cameramen to the ninth hole and they practiced following the inch and half diameter white ball as if flew from tee to fairway and fairway to green then were putted into the hole. None of them had covered a golf tournament before and both were excited as Ellie to be a part of it.

"Where is Hanover," Jason asked Ellie.

"Don't know. Haven't seen him for a while," she realized.

"I hope he didn't run off, scared with all this publicity."

"I doubt it. But I'm sure he's doing his best to avoid the crowds and autograph seekers. He doesn't need all that right now."

"Ellie, my dear," greeted a stocky, tall, well-dressed man clenching a cigar with his teeth.

"Uncle Harry," greeted Ellie with a hug.

"Mr. Bernard," grunted the old man. He put out a paw and Jason tried not to wince from the strength of the grip. "We spoke earlier. My Ellie here says you're the best man for this job. With what I've seen so far, I'd agree. That whole Marathon turned into a nothing story and we were the only sports or news outlet to have the foresight to have a crew out here. The officials have given us exclusive broadcast rights and the other guys will have to live off the highlights we feed them. Good job, son," he said, clapping Jason hard on the back.

Jason looked at Ellie. Her eyes said it all. Harold Frisk was her uncle.

Ellie smiled and winked. "He's the best, Uncle Harry. Let me introduce you to some other friends."

"Listen, Bernard," Frisk said as Ellie began to drag him away, "Next weekend, we'll have to put in eighteen ourselves, eh?" He disappeared behind a bobbing red ponytail.

Jason rubbed his hand and shrugged his shoulder to loosen up the effects of his first personal meeting with USA Sports executive. Golf? With Frisk? How was he going to get out of that? Well, hopefully Frisk would forget the invitation by Monday.

Frisk's comments and confidence left Jason feeling a lot less upset about missing out on the Marathon assignment. He was surprised that Ellie had presented him in such a good light despite his comments to her earlier that the morning.

He pulled out his cell phone and called home. No answer. The sale, he remembered. He called Sally's cell phone and listened to it ring. At the same time Sally's phone rang in his ear, he heard another phone ringing behind him. RING-ring. RING-ring went the echoing rings.

"Hi sweetheart," her voice muttered into his free ear and she kissed it. "I've got a surprise for you."

Jason turned to see Sally and smiled and hugged her. "How did you get here?" he asked.

"I have a very influential friend," she explained. Jason watched as Sarah stepped into sight, very pregnant and smiling.

"I don't get it."

"This is Sarah Hanover," Sally introduced, "Scott's wife."

"You're kidding," he said then corrected himself. "You're not kidding," he realized. "Mrs. Hanover, how very nice to meet you," he said, shaking her outstretched hand. "Of course, Scott mentioned you were expecting a baby, I should have put two and two together. What a reporter I am."

"Is he around?" asked Sally.

"No one has seen him for a while, probably for the best. He's up for some pressure in an hour or so."

"Well, I ran into Sarah at the rummage sale. She saw your report on television and decided she needed to be here."

"From what I've gathered about your husband talking to him, I think he'd be extremely pleased to have you here."

"We're going to look around," said Sally. "Call me on my cell if you find him first."

"Roger," said Jason. Jason watched the two women disappeared into the crowd. He immediately thought that hanging around Sarah Hanover all day was going to put the baby bug in her bonnet and he was in for another round of "let's have a baby" talk tonight.

Jason looked at the scoreboard. Patterson had parred number six. Still in a dead heat with Hanover but number seven was up. He had Ellie send one of the new cameramen to cover the hole just in case. They could also catch the eight and ninth as well. It wouldn't hurt to have some extra footage on Patterson.

"Your lucky day," said a high, too familiar voice. Jason turned and stared at Lucy Penndel.

"Well, it depends on how you look at it, Lucy. If this Hanover hadn't come out of nowhere, I'd have maybe a ninety second spot tonight instead of three hours of weekend afternoon coverage. It's more of opportunity rather than luck, I'd say."

"Well, I'm sure you'll be helpful in the background coverage," suggested Penndel. "I'm sure Keith is going to want his best face on this event," she said. Her confidence oozed like toothpaste and seemed just as gritty.

"Actually," interrupted Harold Frisk who had returned without his niece. "Bernard here is going to do the commentary today."

Lucy muttered and stammered a bit. "Mr. Frisk," she managed to say after swallowing a big ball of conceit.

"It's Jason's show," reiterated the top man. "Ellie convinced me of that. Jason, you just tell Ms. Penndel whatever you would like her to do, and I'm sure she'll do it."

"Yes, sir," said Jason smiling.

Frisk took another puff on his cigar and the blue-gray smoke seemed to bond to Lucy's hair, possibly due to some reaction with her hair spray. "I'm going to check out the control booth they set up. Looks pretty good. The top official here, Bateman is the fellow, he's going to take me out on his cart once the real competition gets going later. Jason, let's have a good show. Good things coming up boy. And don't let me forget that golf game next week."

Jason turned to Lucy. "I think a nice side-bar piece on Patterson's putter might be nice. I here it's jade or something. Want to work on that?"

Lucy turned on her heel, cell phone already speed dialing Keith Kelly. If he did answer, thought Jason, he'd likely give her the same orders. He wouldn't go against Frisk.

68

"His equipment checks out okay but his balls may be a problem," said Kenny Chase. He was in the trailer that was acting as Carl Bateman's temporary office and headquarters for the tournament. He rolled a golf ball over the desk. "You can get these printed up from a half a dozen firms out of the back of any golf magazine."

Bateman picked up the duck logo ball and turned it over in his hand. "Is it regulation?"

"Right size. It performs well on the bounce test but it doesn't have a brand logo. If I had to guess I'd say it was a Top Flite but without cutting one open, it's impossible to tell if there might not be a problem."

"Well, we'll get his permission to check one."

"Two problems. First of all I don't have the equipment here to do an internal check of a ball, and second, if he happens to run out of balls while on the course and we destroyed one, it could be trouble. He has to finish the course with just the balls currently in his bag."

"Then we will have to let him play it. Hopefully no one is going to make a big deal," said Bateman.

"They will if he sets a record."

"Then what do we do? Check it out quietly after he finishes?"

"There is another option," explained Chase. He picked the ball back off Bateman's desk. "Hanover lost a ball on number eight. It's in the water hazard. We could get a diver to look for it."

"What? Now?"

"The clubhouse has equipment. One of the greens keepers likes to go ball hunting in his spare time."

"What are the odds he'll find the ball?"

"Well, we know about where it went in from the news coverage."

"I thought you didn't have the equipment to check it out."

"I think I may be able to get access to the equipment I need nearby. It would certainly save a little time and possibly embarrassment later on. Look what happened with that kid in the Marathon. Their saying now he swallowed a bunch of the Ephedra capsules. Nearly killed himself in the process."

Carl Bateman considered the idea and found no flaws. It certainly wouldn't hurt to protect themselves in this situation. "Let's do it. But keep it quiet; we don't need any bad publicity at this point. I'm going to be driving Harold Frisk around for the last nine, for God's sakes. He'll freak if this turns out to be something like the marathon."

"I'll do my best," said the other man wondering how he would keep a scuba diver splashing in a water hazard quiet.

Bateman looked Kenny Chase in the eye. "No illegal clubs, no extra clubs, no distance measuring devices?" he asked.

"No, sir. Just the balls."

"Check it out, Kenny. Check it out."

69

Karen Blakely was ready to punch the red-jacketed man at the card table in the face. "I'm not walking back to my car for my credentials," she shouted for the third time. "Here is my ID. You have my name on that list. Just give me another badge, you moron."

As soon as she had uttered the word she knew she was in trouble. "I'm sorry," she apologized. "I've had a bad morning. I was stuck in traffic earlier, got three tickets from a woman cop, had to park a mile and half away to get here and have blisters bigger than my big toes on the bottom of my feet. I represent Andrew Patterson and I need to be here."

"I'll vouch for her."

Karen turned and was confused to see Jake Fisher's cheerful face. "Uh, Fischer. Uh, thanks, I guess."

Jake handed his credential pass to the man. "We work together, I'll make sure she doesn't cause any trouble."

"I really shouldn't do it," said the man at the table.

Jake smiled, "I'd consider it a favor. Give me your address and I'll get you a couple of court side seats for the next Bulls game from our agency."

"Really?"

"Yep."

"If you vouch for her, I guess. She is on the list."

"Exactly," agreed Jake. "No harm in bending the rules a little."

The man scribbled on a blank pass and handed to Karen. "Hold onto this one," he warned.

Karen held back a snarl and forced a smile. She was more confused by the source of her aid. "Looks like you've had a tough morning," said Jake with some concern. He then added, "Any luck with Eric Gunther's family?"

She froze in mid stride, brushing away some debris from her dress. "You knew I was going to the Marathon?" She thought a moment. "No," she muttered mostly to herself, "you couldn't have. Did you get?..." She thought some more. "Why did April get that sudden revelation to send me out after that high school kid's family? It was you..." At that point she was pretty sure the wild goose chase had been initiated by Jake Fischer and Jonathon Jones and was ready to burst into anger when she realized the last laugh was hers. "But I had already signed Patterson when April called. I'm sure you must have found that out already. You wasted your time, Fischer.

You're not needed here now. Why not go crawl back in the bottle you got out of this morning and leave this business to those of us still sharp enough to make things happen." She continued to stomp up toward the scoreboard.

"I could do that," agreed Jake, "but I'd like to see how things turn out here. You've missed quite a bit while you were gone."

"What are you talking about, Fischer? Didn't Patterson get a hole-in-one or something?"

"Not Patterson, Hanover. Scott Hanover."

"Big deal, so some hacker gets a lucky shot."

"He's had twenty-nine lucky shots, well, maybe ten or twelve were truly lucky, the rest just didn't hurt him."

"What are you talking about?"

"Better call April," said Jake.

"I will." They reached the scoreboard. "There you go," she pointed out. Patterson is still in the lead, well at least tied," she said as she compared the running list of scores under the sixth hole. Just then an old man started laying in tiles for the seventh hole. Patterson had bogeyed it. He was not alone in posting a four on that hole, more than half the golfers had a four or worse. But among the threes, fours and fives, there was a single solitary one; Hanover, S.

Patterson was now solidly in second place, three strokes behind Hanover.

"Well," pointed out Karen. "I'm sure Patterson's skill will let him catch up. Skill will always win over luck, Fischer. Why do you care about Hanover anyway?" she asked. Then turning slowly she answered her own question. "You signed him, didn't you? You stupid drunk. Who is going to want to hire a hacker with a hole-in-one? You're a fool."

Jake smiled as Karen blasted her blather over him. He didn't care now that he didn't sign Patterson. Patterson was going to get what he deserved. "Well, we'll see how the shoot-out goes," he said.

"Shoot-out?"

"That's what USA Sports is calling it. Hanover and Patterson, as long as Patterson keeps second place over the last two holes, are going head-to-head to finish off the tournament. It's going to be televised. Heck, they've already been showing highlights from Hanover's round already."

"Highlights? How?"

"Some bored camerawoman followed his first nine and caught every shot. Pissed off her reporter until he realized he was sitting on the hot story of the week, maybe the year. Unknown last ranked golfer makes run for shot at pro-tour."

"It'll never happen," said Karen. "That hacker will blow three strokes on one hole once he's up against Patterson. There's no telling the damage nine holes will do. And all that television time for my client. How kind of USA Sports."

"Good luck," said Jake as he left Karen to clean the clods of wet grass and mud from under her shoes. He smiled. This might turn out to be a good day after all. He had expected maybe Patterson would par the hole, but a bogey, something must have gone wrong.

70

Eric Peters knew he had said the wrong thing almost as he was saying it. "This is the hole Patterson eagled," he announced as his boss took the outstretched club.

"What did you say?" asked Patterson.

Eric swallowed hard and bit his lower lip.

"Perhaps I should rephrase that, Eric. Why are you talking?"

"Sorry, sir," apologized Eric.

Andrew's shot landed pin high but to the left. Had the caddy distracted him? There was an indentation in the green between his ball and the hole and a series of undulations that would test his green reading abilities. He had planned on parring this hole but he had also planned on landing on the right side of the green near the back, down hill from the hole.

He didn't look at Eric as he held out the club almost behind him. The other two golfers with him landed their shots in precisely the area Andrew had envisioned for himself. It wasn't the wind. He knew that. How had Hanover aced this one? It was impossible with the pin placement. He glanced at the boy with the leaders board held high and realized that even if he eked out a par, he would be two strokes behind Hanover. Two strokes! What was going on? The next closest golfer was two strokes behind Andrew. When Andrew had an unexpected birdie on six he had felt buoyed and relieved. There was no way he could lose now.

Andrew walked to the green and he thought. He thought about how golfers always played to their ability. An eagle on one hole would always be balanced out by a double bogey with an eighteen-handicap golfer, which was what Hanover was. Andrew would just keep playing his game and Hanover would melt and fall.

Hanover's score hadn't changed since he had finished the ninth hole, which was strange. He must be halfway through the back nine by now.

He putted first and the ball skipped over the rough fringe, rimmed the hole and rolled down the hill to lie by the other two markers. Andrew couldn't believe it. He had been robbed of a second straight birdie, although he wasn't shooting for a birdie. He just wanted to be within two

170

feet of the hole. Had he not rimmed the hole, he would have. As it was, the ball made it to the down slope of the green and just kept rolling. That was why he didn't try to make these miracle shots. They more often turned into disasters than miracles. Except for Hanover, he thought.

His next putt stopped three inches past the hole and little to the right. He sank the next one for the bogey. He was now back to three under par. That was where he had planned on being in his game plan. Okay, an unplanned birdie was counteracted by an unplanned bogey. He'd par the last two and by then Hanover would have dropped a couple of strokes and he could get on with it.

As they made their way to the eighth tee he overheard one of the red-jacketed officials mention that Hanover had been pulled from the course. His group had gone on without him. Disqualified, thought Andrew? No, they would have taken his name down. Wouldn't they?

At the eighth tee he studied the fairway, a severe dogleg right with a lateral water hazard under the crook of the knee. To the right of the tee, near some trees, a golf cart with an attached trailer was waiting. One man sitting there was wearing what appeared to be a black rubber suit. "How odd," thought Andrew. The other two golfers in his group teed off first, both having parred the last hole. The second one drove his tee shot into the water.

Now it was Andrew's turn again. Eric silently handed Andrew his five wood. Andrew knew there was no need to kill it on this hole when he planned his game. He looked at his caddy whose head was down. Eric seemed to be trying to be as invisible as possible. Perhaps he had been too hard on Peters. Andrew didn't believe he was susceptible to the psychological pressures other golfers felt. He played his game. He counted on his consistency and skill. In the end, that was what would win it for him today. Why should this tournament be any different?

71

Joe Caulkin smiled to himself as he looked at the scoreboard. Hanover was three strokes ahead of Patterson after seven holes and had a birdie on nine as well. He wiggled his fingers sticking out the end of his cast. How he wished he were out there battling Patterson for this tournament. When he injured his arm the first thought he had was that Patterson had won. He barely heard the doctors giving him instructions as they wrapped his wrist first with a thin, compressed cotton bandage, and then some light gauze, followed by the moistened fiberglass cast material. He had felt the warmth of the cast through the bandages as it set and was surprised by how light it ended up being. He wore the sling because in the process of breaking his wrist he also sprained his shoulder. He had tested it this morning and the pain was better but still there. Four ibuprofens later it was gone, but he knew better than to push his body faster than it could handle.

He thought back to two weeks earlier when he had watched Scott Hanover finish a distant third in the qualifying tournament. Hanover had been ecstatic with his finishing putt. He had jumped around like a kid, whooping and hollering and smiling. The smile had lasted until Hanover had seen Joe's wife hugging him as he received his first prize trophy. Scott Hanover had no one there to share the day with and Joe had felt sorry for him.

"Mr. Caulkin?" interrupted a woman's voice. "Hi, remember me from this morning?" asked a perky redhead.

"Ellie," he smiled.

"This is Jake Fischer and Gina Beck. Jake is now Scott Hanover's agent and we were wondering if you'd seen him?"

"No," answered Joe. Then he said, "agent?" He was beginning to feel a little less sorry for Hanover now.

"Well, if he needs one, I have the first right of refusal," corrected Jake. "If he pulls this off though, it'll be a bigger deal than Patterson winning. I understand you're the reason Scott Hanover is playing today."

"Guilty," answered Joe, lifting his casted arm slightly. "Are you serious? Someone would want to use Scott Hanover as a spokesman? Does Patterson have an agent too?"

"Yeah, a woman named Karen Blakely."

"Wow. Makes me mad I broke my arm."

"Callaway is looking for a Cinderella," explained Jake. "Someone not expected to move up to a pro tournament without a fairy grandmother or something."

"Callaway?" asked Joe.

"They want Patterson," said Gina. "At least they did this morning. Once the rest of the tournament gets played out on television this afternoon, who knows?"

"And Callaway isn't the only sponsor looking for a new face to sell products. Think about it, Mr. Caulkin," continued Jake, "who wants to buy a ball that Tiger woods can hit three hundred an fifty yards when you can buy the ball that Scott Hanover used to get his hole-in-one and set a tournament record for nine holes."

"Well, the guy has earned whatever does come to him," agreed Joe. "He's having a heck of a day and I can't wait to see the rest of it."

"If you see Scott, please let me know," said Ellie. She wrote her cell phone number down and handed it to Joe who tucked in into his sling.

"Will do."

CHAPTER 13 – EIGHTH HOLE (AGAIN)

72

With a precision stroke, Andrew chipped his ball onto the eight green and watched it land with a satisfying thud ten feet from the hole, precisely in the area he had planned. From there he had a decent uphill putt with little if any break. Of the other two golfers with him, Frederick Martin had landed in a far sand trap, Cary Newman landed on the green but twenty-five feet from the hole, far from making a birdie.

Martin hit a nice shot out of the sand but the ball rolled past the pin until it stopped fifteen feet past the hole. The green sloped down to the water hazard and it was the best he could do from that position.

Newman analyzed his lie and approached his ball with confidence. However, it was apparent to Andrew that the golfer was aiming too far to the left. Couldn't the idiot read a simple green? It wasn't that difficult. If it sloped to the left, you aimed to the right. He watched as the man clubbed the ball and as predicted it rolled a foot left of the hole then continued until it stopped four feet from the cup.

Frederick Martin seemed to have a good read on his shot but seemed afraid to hit the ball hard enough, perhaps because his last shot had rolled too far past the hole and he was now hitting uphill. Anything short of a confident putt would leave him still far from the hole. Martin hit the ball and as Andrew foresaw, it lost steam and stopped still a good six feet from the hole. Martin angrily smacked his putter head on the green, leaving a dent that his caddy quickly repaired.

Andrew snorted at the burst of anger the man had shown. Even when his putt on seven rimmed the hole, he knew that getting emotional wouldn't help him get the ball in the hole.

It was his turn to putt. He laid down his ball and picked up his golden dollar that he used for a marker. It was large but the rules said nothing about what size a ball marker could be but did say a coin was acceptable. The coin glinted in the sun. Before every tournament he would go to the bank and get a roll of the dollar coins and crack it open to find the shiniest and least scratched one available.

He squatted to reexamine the lie. If anything he wanted the ball to end up on the right, to the left would leave him a downhill putt and he avoided those at all costs, even at the price of missing a birdie. He took two practice swings to set the speed of his stroke and then stepped up. With robotic accuracy, he putted the ball. It headed straight for the hole but broke slightly to the right leaving a six-inch tap in for par, exactly the score he had planned for this hole. He carefully lined up the short putt and tapped it in. Polite applause ringed the green and he pulled out his ball handing it and his putter to Eric.

Eric knew better than to say anything, like good par or nice hole. Andrew Patterson already knew he had a good par or nice hole and hated being told them by people who presumed to know better. Eric slid the putter carefully into its felt case then slid the club gently into Patterson's bag. He placed the ball into the sleeve along the side of the golf bag. He had once placed a ball in his pocket and Patterson had demanded it from him and threw it into the trees. Apparently he didn't like to think of his balls mingling with whatever Eric had in his pocket or perhaps being damaged by Eric's divot repair tool or car keys.

Martin lined up his next putt and once again it was short, but this time only by inches. He knocked the ball in carelessly and picked it up, striding quickly from the green, having bogeyed the hole after parring seven.

Newman had the downhill lie that Andrew deftly avoided. As practiced his putt, Andrew, standing across the green, noted the speed of his swing and quietly shook his head. Cary Newman's putt sent the ball speeding from the club face and it actually bumped right over the hole. That was why Andrew never left a downhill lie. Even if you hit the ball straight on, the extra speed it gained could still deny you the hole.

Newman lined up his next two-foot putt and managed to get that one in. Andrew smiled. He was back to having honors, a position he enjoyed. He knew his drives could make even a confident golfer a little nervous. He wanted these guys to see him nail the next one. Neither of them had a chance of taking the tournament from him, but they would know he was the best.

He glanced at the scorecard. Hanover's score still remained stubbornly at seven under. Maybe he had been pulled form the tournament. He decided to find out and approached the boy holding the leader board.

"Why haven't you updated Hanover's score?" he asked.

"He's not been playing."

"Was he disqualified?"

"Disqualified? No, sir, they're putting him in the last group."

"In this group?"

"I guess," answered the boy.

"What? He's just sitting around, waiting?"

"I suppose."

Well, it explained why his score hadn't been creeping up. They were going to put Hanover in with Andrew, presumably to build a little suspense into the tournament. The more Andrew thought about it the more he liked the idea. There was nothing better to put the fear of God into someone than to have him golf with God. At least it would seem like that for Hanover. He walked to a red-jacketed official. "Is it true that there will be an addition to this threesome?" he asked.

"Addition? No. Top two guys after nine go head to head. Televised and everything."

"Televised?"

The red-jacketed man pointed to the man carrying the television camera with the USA Sports logo that Andrew had long ago let slip out of his awareness. The red-jacketed man glanced at the leader board. "Looks like it'll be you and Scott Hanover," he commented.

"Looks like," agreed Andrew.

73

There was a crowd watching the golfers teeing off at the tenth hole. As Scott and Paul headed back to the clubhouse one of the onlookers happened to glance in their direction and gave a double take. He seemed confused why someone was walking away from the eighteenth hole so early but quickly returned his attention to the golfers heading out on the back nine.

The two friends passed the rows of parked golf carts and neatly lined up handcarts that were used in an ordinary golfing day. Today, they sat unused.

"Ready?" asked Paul.

"Ready as I'll ever be, I guess," answered Scott.

They were amazed at how many people were now crowding around the clubhouse area, many watching the scoreboard as it was updated, others gathered around the ninth green applauding the golfers like it was a major tournament. Small groups were wandering around the edge of the tenth fairway, making their way to more distant holes to watch the game play out.

Suddenly the man who had seen them earlier from the tenth tee turned around again, finding the two once more as they walked along the cart path, he confirmed the suspicion that had been growing in his head. "It's him, from TV. It's Hanover," he shouted. Dozens of heads turned and looked to where the man pointed at Paul and Scott. A sea of people closed in on them. Most wanted to shake Scott's hand, others wanted autographs. It was unreal to say the least.

After a few minutes four red-jacketed men started pushing aside the curious and escorted Scott and Paul through the throng. As they reached the clubhouse, Jake Fischer managed to get near Scott. "Where have you been?" he asked. "Everyone's looking for you."

"Apparently," commented Paul.

"Just checking out a few of the last holes, staying loose," he answered. They had walked around the near side of the pond that formed a boundary for not only the eighteenth hole, but the seventeenth as well and checked out the pin placement on the sixteenth green. The quiet they had just left was a stark contrast to the mayhem they found themselves in now.

"I was afraid you'd miss your tee off," said Jake. "You weren't thinking of taking off, were you?"

"No," said Scott. "Just killing time." A woman next to Jake coughed and pulled on Fisher's arm.

"Oh, excuse me," started Jake, "I'd like you to meet my friend, Gina Beck. She's a huge golf fan," he teased.

"Actually, I do follow golf a little, enough to be very impressed with your accomplishment this morning," she said. She held out her hand and Scott shook it.

"Nice to meet you, Miss Beck."

"Gina," she corrected.

"Mr. Hanover." It was Bateman, the tournament official. "Everything checked out – so far that is?"

"There's a problem?" asked Paul.

"Probably not, we'll let you know. It looks like you'll be in the last group. You're still three strokes ahead of the next closest player."

"Wonderful," said Scott with all the enthusiasm he could muster. Nervousness flooded him and he tried to remember what Ted had talked about earlier. He was here to play golf, not get sidetracked by all the excitement or agendas of the other people here. Play golf.

"Mr. Hanover," shouted a woman. Scott caught sight of a redhead bobbing a short distance away in the crowd.

"It's okay," he instructed his guards.

Ellie worked her way up. "Just a quick question," she said. "If you could have anything you wanted right now, what would it be?"

"Are you taping this?" asked Scott.

"No, just curious," she said.

Scott thought a moment but before he could answer, Paul did. "A beer," he said. Laughter rippled through the crowd.

"A beer?" questioned a voice from behind Ellie. "A beer?"

Ellie stood aside, grinning as Sarah appeared before them.

"You're here," said Scott.

"I'm here," she agreed.

"How? Why?" he muttered shaking his head.

"Will I do instead of the beer?" she asked.

Scott laughed and kissed her and hugged her as well as her distended belly would allow. A few camera clicks could be heard from the crowd.

"I saw you on TV," Sarah explained. "At the rummage sale. Sally here gave me a ride." She indicated a blonde woman dressed casually standing next to her. She extended her hand.

"I'm Sally Bernard, I believe you already met my husband, Jason."

Scott's look of astonishment increased Sally's smile. "Small world, isn't it," she said.

"Very small," Scott agreed. His arm was draped over Sarah's shoulders and his escorts opened the clubhouse doors. The crowd inside was asked to leave the small dining area. Scott pulled out a chair for Sarah and the seven of them sat around a large round table.

"Who's this?" asked Sarah, indicating Jake and Gina, the only people she hadn't met already.

"Oh, this is Jake Fischer, a sports agent and his friend, Gina Beck."

Sarah's eyes widened. "An agent?" she asked. Her surprise turned to suspicion. "He does know you're done with golf for a while after this."

"I've mentioned it but he insisted he still wanted my soul. Either that or our first born and I had to toss a coin."

She punched his arm – hard! "Good thing I wasn't on the table. We'll have to talk about this later," she said.

"Busted," commented Paul.

"Shut up," said Scott and passed the arm punch to his caddy. Paul turned and punched Jake. Jake just rubbed his arm, a little confused.

"They're just kids," pointed out Sarah. "They're like that all the time," she explained. She turned her attention back to Scott. "Anna and I just happened to pass some televisions at the rummage sale and they mentioned something about 'The Duck' and there you were, talking to a reporter."

"Did Anna come?" Scott asked.

"What do you think?" asked Sarah.

"Right. But you're here. You came."

She grabbed his shoulder. "I'm sorry I missed the hole-in-one, Scott." She started to tear up.

"We've got it one tape," Scott assured her but he knew what she meant. He remembered he had been thinking about her when the ball went in.

"It wasn't easy getting here, you have created a small sensation. Everyone is talking about the guy who shot a twenty-nine. Even the cop on 159th street knew about you."

"Cop?" asked Scott.

"We were stuck in traffic and he got us right in. There must be hundreds of cars trying to get into this place."

"Wow."

"Oh, I put the crib together," she mentioned leaving out the fact that she had to do it twice. He didn't need to know that.

Scott showed the appropriate look of surprise and awe. "You what?"

"Yep. You're not the only one with hidden talents."

The girl from the snack bar brought a tray of drinks with a couple of baskets of nacho chips, dripping with cheese. "On the house," she announced.

"Thanks, Cassie," said Scott and they all dug in.

Sarah cast a wary eye in Scott's direction, "Cassie?" she asked.

"I gave her an autograph earlier," he explained.

"Wow, at lot has happened since this morning," she stated. As she reached for a tortilla chip she felt a contraction come on and stopped herself to concentrate on her breathing.

"Are you okay?" asked Scott. His jovial mood had flashed into concern at the apparent agony on his wife's face.

"Just...a...little...practice...contraction," she stammered. She took a few more breaths. "I've been having them all day. Anna says it's probably false labor."

"What did the doctor say?"

"Well, I haven't called him yet. I figured if they were still happening after the tournament I'd call and see if I needed to do anything."

Scott eyed her suspiciously. "You're sure it's not the baby coming?"

"Honey, If I was in labor, I wouldn't be sitting here and neither would you." She placed her hand on his. "Don't worry about it. I'm fine. You go have fun."

Scott kissed her and looked in her eyes. Everything seemed fine. Besides, the kid wasn't due for two more weeks.

"By the way," started Ellie between bites of cheese covered chips, "They're going to use three camera crews to cover you and Patterson. That won't make you nervous, will it?"

"Not as nervous as a crowd of onlookers. They better keep them back," Scott warned.

"Way back," added Paul. They all laughed. Paul stood up. "I'm going to track down your clubs. I'll meet you at the tenth tee."

"I'll be there," Scott assured him.

"We'll all be there," added Sarah.

"Wouldn't miss it," said Sally. Scott was still three strokes ahead. There was a chance that Andrew would lose. She liked these people and really wanted Scott and Sarah to have this day end up with a win, but she knew that from this point on everything was icing on the cake for them, win or lose. She tried not to let her gaze at Sarah's belly linger too long.

She wanted some cake too.

74

The crowds had moved on. The two men in the cart rode along the right side of the eighth fairway until they had reached the area that Kenny Chase had marked on the map. Somewhere in the cold, dark, mucky water was a ball that Chase wanted. There were likely hundreds if not thousands of balls in that water. It had been nearly three months since the ball retrieval company had swept the hazards to reclaim and recycle the errant shots of the everyday golfers.

Few had landed in the water today but that few included Scott Hanover. The ball he was looking for was supposed to have a yellow duck imprinted on it, "like a rubber ducky," Chase had said.

"This is the spot," said the driver. "Looks like fun," he commented.

The man in the wetsuit hopped out and swung the tarp off the equipment in the wagon behind the cart. He set up the tank on the edge of the wagon, turned the valve and checked the pressure gauge and slipped his arms into the vest. He grabbed his mask and snorkel, slipping the mask snugly over his face and placed the mouthpiece from the tank into his mouth. He sucked a dry mouthful of the canned air content that the gas was flowing properly. He wouldn't need fins. They would just stir up the mud anyway. The water was only three of four feet deep. The weight of the tank would be enough to keep him near the bottom.

The diver walked to the edge of the water and sat on the grass, then dangled his feet in. If he reached with his toes he could touch the soft bottom. It was strange that as a kid he waded through far more disgusting waters than these and had delighted in salting any leeches that had attached themselves to him during his explorations. Years of diving in the warm, clear waters of the Caribbean Sea had spoiled him.

The best case he figured was that he'd spend twenty or thirty minutes looking and report back to Chase that the ball was unfindable unless they dragged the whole pond and sorted out the contents. If it weren't for the hundred bucks Chase had slipped him he wouldn't be doing it all.

The diver slid off the bank and shivered as a thin layer of water flowed under the suit next to his skin. It would take a few minutes to warm up but then it would provide a layer of insulation, but that first shock was a killer. A dry suit might be better suited for the conditions, but he'd make due.

He bit down on the mouthpiece and lowered his face into the water. The part of his face not covered by rubber was almost instantly numbed. The water was murky and he could see maybe three feet. As he sank in the pond the bottom became clearer and white and gray domes sticking up from the silt began to appear.

This was going to be impossible. He tried picking up a ball but the silt he stirred up obscured his view of balls for a one-foot radius. He waited for the debris to settle then using his fingertips, slowly moved over the bottom, sweeping his eyes from side to side, looking for the yellow duck design that had been described to him. He went out perhaps three yards then turned to his right. He would sweep a ten-yard by three-yard box. If he didn't find it he'd start picking up all the balls he could find and sort through them on the bank. Maybe he'd get lucky.

Another three yards of slow progress and he was back at the edge of the pond. Carefully he turned left. His previous path had left wake of cloudy water despite his careful movements under which nothing visible. He turned his head from side to side; scanning as much an area as possible as he swam back out. A glint of yellow caught his eye. He slowly brought his right hand to the area and picked up the ball. A cloud of silt came up with it, obscuring it. He brought it closer to his mask and once it was six inches away a smiling yellow duck looked at him through the glass.

This was it. At least it was close enough. He stood up and let the water drip off his back. All around him mud was stirring and if this wasn't the ball they wouldn't find it today without dragging the entire bottom. He let the regulator fall out of his mouth and he pushed up his mask. He looked at the ball in his right hand again and smiled.

"You got it?" asked the driver. He had been sure this was a wild duck chase as well.

"Got it," answered the diver.

"Gotta be a miracle."

"The diver tossed the ball to the driver and started to climb up. As he got out on the bank he noticed the crowd disappearing over the hill that held the ninth tee. Everyone except a cameraman who had his lens trained on the two. He waved and smiled at the cameraman. The cameraman waved back, let his camera drop and turned to follow the rest of the tournament people.

"Hey, I'm going to be on TV," said the diver.

"Congratulations," said the driver. "Let's go."

"Yeah, I want to get dry, fast."

"Coffee's on me."

"You bet it is."

75

Karen fumbled four quarters out of her purse. The payphone required two for the first two minutes. Any more calls than this and she'd have to get more change or call collect. It had taken her five minutes to even get to the pay phone through the hoards of people threading their way through each other around the clubhouse.

She dialed April Weinstein's extension. It rang for four, then five times. "Come on," muttered Karen. "Pick up already."

After the sixth ring a familiar voice said "Hello?" It was familiar but not April's voice. It was Jonathan Jones'.

"Where's April?" she asked.

"Karen? Is that you?" asked Jones.

"You know it's me Jonathan, I need to talk to April. I'm on a payphone and I can't waste time chatting."

"I thing she went to the restroom," he answered, delighted in her situation. "Cell phone dead?" he asked.

Karen didn't answer him but scrunched up her face as she recalled her wild goose chase earlier this morning. "Had a little fun with April and me today, Haven't you Jonathan?"

"How's that?" Jonathan asked, enjoying the position he had.

"You knew I couldn't resist trying to get the kid signed up too, well your plan didn't work. I got to Patterson first. I don't know about this Hanover fellow, but Callaway wants Patterson and I've got Patterson."

"Callaway is going to want a winner," answered Jonathan. A distant voice cut in over the line.

"What are you doing in here?" asked April Weinstein.

"Heard the phone ringing," answered Jonathon, his voice muted by his hand over the mouthpiece.

"Give me that," insisted April, closer still.

"Karen?" she asked.

181

"Please deposit fifty cents for the next two minutes," interrupted the automated recording.

"Shoot," muttered Karen as she dropped one of the quarters. She popped in the first one.

"Please deposit twenty five cents," urged the voice again.

"I'm, trying, I'm trying," answered Karen. The quarter had rolled under a bush. She got on her knees and reached into the brush to get the coin. She smiled as she pulled it out and stood up staring at the quarter. The bump on the back of her head from the shelf of the pay phone almost knocked her on the ground. Her exclamation was a little more serious this time. She picked up the handset and slipped the second quarter into the slot. Five quick beeps signaled the phone had successful consumed the coin and granted her credit for two more minutes.

"Are you all right?" she heard over the phone.

"Fine. Listen, April. I need a new phone but most importantly we need to get someone from Callaway here. With this thing being televised it will be a great time for them to announce their newest spokesman, Andrew Patterson on USA Sports Network."

"That sounds like a good idea. I'll see if Tim Carousel is in town. In any case I'm coming down there too."

"You have thirty seconds," interrupted the voice.

"You better get yourself a helicopter, unless things have changed dramatically the roads are a mess. Heck, I'm a mess."

"Hold it together Karen."

"I am holding it together. And bring me some sneakers, these shoes are killing me," she added.

"I'll try."

"Just do it," she added.

"Please deposit fifty cents for the next two minutes," asked the operator's recording.

Karen slammed the handset onto the payphone and leaned against the wall exasperated. What a day this was turning out to be.

CHAPTER 14 – NINTH HOLE (AGAIN)

76

Andrew Patterson waited patiently as Eric Peters pulled his driver from the bag and slipped off the club cover. Eric placed the grip in Andrew's palm like he was a surgeon awaiting the next instrument for a complicated procedure. He dropped the ball into his other hand. Andrew wouldn't tolerate the ball being placed in his hand. Then he handed Andrew a tee.

Andrew placed his ball on the tee and eyed the spot he wanted his drive to go. He needed to stay on the left side of the fairway to minimize the risk of any of the sand traps guarding the green. Other than that he was free to give it a good hit. A long drive wasn't necessary to par this hole and he wasn't about to risk the short pines trees separating the driving range from the hole by being too aggressive.

Andrew's style of play was referred to as "course management." It required discipline and many players didn't have the patience to put it to use. It meant playing safe shots rather than going for the killer drive and trying to make the green in regulation rather than going for every birdie and eagle possibility. Most of the time Andrew could count on par. There were the rare bogies, usually due to factors beyond his control such as hitting a sprinkler head or a twig, or being forced to putt through someone's ball mark.

On the other side, and more frequently, were the birdies that came his way. Usually he could count on three to six per eighteen holes with his style of play, more than enough to win every tournament. The fact that Hanover had five birdies and one eagle on the front nine indicated his style was very aggressive and would catch up with him eventually. It always did. Andrew enjoyed watching other amateur golfers self-destruct. Pulling out too much club when the shot called for a four or five iron. It gave him an advantage and confidence.

This hole was four hundred and forty yards. Andrew could safely hit his drive and leave the ball about one hundred and eighty yards from the pin. A perfect distance for his six iron. He could pretty much two putt from anywhere on the green and one putt if he was near enough for a short chip. The one-putts were occasionally there, but on this hole he wouldn't count on it unless his second shot was perfect.

He placed his tee in the ground and then set his ball on it gently, the letters "Callaway" lined up straight where he wanted to hit the ball. He lined up his club and set his stance. The setup was key. He strove to be consistent. There was no need to be the longest driver on the course to win, but if he could hit the fairway nine-five percent of the time, he was way ahead of the rest of the pack.

He drew back the club and his perfectly trained muscles coiled and unwound bringing the head of the driver to meet the ball with a satisfying plink. The ball sailed straight out, bounced behind the two hundred yard marker and rolled another twenty-five yards. It was just where he wanted the ball to land. He let a slight smile cross his lips as the applause from the crowd acknowledged the shot.

Frederick Martin, the player who had hit into the sand next to the green on the previous hole was next on the tee. Andrew noticed he had one of the severely oversized drivers that were a favorite of amateur golfers. They hit the ball a long way if you hit the right, but most players didn't have the skill to control it.

Mike slipped his tee with the ball atop into the soft ground. He stepped back and leaned toward the tee a little. Slice, thought Andrew as he watched Martin line up.

Fred took a practice swing, the club whipping through the air with an audible whoosh and his body almost contorting into a pretzel with the follow through. He left his feet where they were and slid the club head forward to just behind the ball. The elongated stance forced him into an almost baseball swing and he swung at the ball like it was a grenade about to go off.

The ball had a great sound off the club and sailed out far, but the spin carried it to the right, first a little, then more then almost at a sixty-degree angle to his intended line. It rolled into some pine trees that where also bordered the first fairway. His reaction was not polite but what would one expect from a player like that.

Cary Newman set up next. He also seemed determined to kill the ball. His drive, however went straight, and rolled nearly fifty yards past

Andrew's shot, a three hundred and ten yard drive. The crowd erupted with applause at the monster drive. Even though Andrew was beating Newman by three strokes at this time, everyone seemed to appreciate the showoffs more than those with a consistent game.

The three started moving down the fairway. The golf cart and trailer that had been parked by the water hazard at the eighth hole took the opportunity to speed along the right side of the fairway and beeped through the crowd before the players had to take their second shots.

Martin was up first. The crowd along the fairway had spread where he had entered the woods and his bright red shirt could barely be seen between the boughs of the thin white pines. It seemed he was going to hit out. Andrew remained well back of the wayward golfer. He couldn't remember the last time he had ended up in the trees.

There was a crack from the woods and a white ball sailed out and rolled very well along the fairway, taking several good hops and fatefully ending up in a sand trap at the right front corner of the green.

"Am I on?" asked a hopeful voice from the trees.

Andrew chuckled to himself. This guy knew nothing about course management. He was a moron for trying for the green from such a lie, even for getting into a lie like that in the first place.

A few onlookers kindly shouted, "On the beach, Fred," and the sand prone golfer emerged from the woods, shaking his head looking very much like he wanted to pound his club in the ground.

Andrew was next. He was aiming for the green as well, but had a much better chance. The pin placement was excellent for a birdie attempt. It was near the middle of the green. As long as Andrew stayed below the pin, which was a little downhill, he'd have a good shot.

Eric handed him the seven iron. Andrew placed the club behind the ball, letting it tell him where to stand and how to grip it. He made minor adjustments until it felt like the club was an extension of his arms, a part of his body. Even the ball felt a part of him.

His clubs were custom made by an old Pro in Tinley Park, not too far from here, thought Andrew. The old man had him swing a series of bamboo poles with weights and he eyed Andrew's swing with each stick, offering suggestions occasionally but mostly muttered to himself and nodded occasionally. Andrew must have swung fifty of the canes before the old man was satisfied. The club maker had been highly recommended by Andrew's golf instructor and when he went to pick up the clubs four weeks later, he was amazed at the difference from the clubs he had started with.

The weight was different, the grips, the balance. He swung a few in the old man's garage and knew he had gotten his money's worth. As he swung the seven iron now he watched as the ball sailed to a point a little right and short of the pin, sticking in the soft green with a thunk. A divot had flown up behind the ball. Eric ran up to get it. Andrew hated when players left the courses in awful shape. As the caddy gently stamped the strip of turf back into place, Andrew handed him the club. Eric sprayed it with a water bottle, brushed off the dirt, and then dried it with a clean part of towel he had looped under his belt before placing it back in the bag.

There was applause. Andrew was two yards from the hole and felt sure he would drop another stroke on this hole and end up four under par. One better than he had planned on. He had underestimated his skill and ability to play this course. A problem he could easily live with.

Cary Newman approached his fairway shot with more assurance than the last hole. There was no water to worry about and the pin placement was generous. He talked the shot over with his caddy for a half a minute. They seemed to be arguing about which club to use. Andrew heard a little of the discussion. What kind of golfer was this? What kind of caddy was this! He shook his own head in disgust. Didn't this guy know what his clubs could do? Didn't he spend any time at a driving range checking his distance or any time reading the course? Of course not. Andrew had seen him make stupid mistakes all morning. He was sure Newman would make another now.

It appeared that Cary won the argument with his caddy. Newman's caddy reluctantly gave Cary the club and stepped back, looking down and shaking his head. Cary swung and the ball sailed over the flagstick, bounced off the back of the green, and then rolled onto a slope of rough cut grass. A simple shot and he had over clubbed it. It was sad, thought Andrew, when your caddy knew how well you could hit a club better than you did.

Frederick Martin led the three golfers as they and their caddies walked up to the green. His ball had rolled a foot or so into the trap. There was perhaps four yards of sand before the green and a six-inch lip to hop over. It was a simple chip out since the green sloped up from there and all he had to do was whack the ball out and up, thought Andrew. Two putts should get him in with a bogey thought Andrew. Martin took his sand wedge to the trap and set himself up, his right foot on the grass, the left foot lower, in the sand. Andrew cringed as he looked at Martin's setup and waited. As he was, tilted to the left, Martin's right knee needed to be bent more. Frederick took a half swing and chopped into the sand behind the ball. The ball flew nearly four yards and caught the edge of grass just before the green. It plopped back into the sand, right next to the small ledge. A simple adjustment in his stance could have avoided this.

Andrew chuckled to himself at Martin's performance. These were the two best players he was going to face today. If they were making such simple mistakes then Hanover would undoubtedly follow suit, especially once he was matched up one-on-one with Andrew on the back nine.

Martin took his second shot out of the sand and the ball plopped up and even cleared the fringe to make it to the green but a good ten yards from the hole.

Newman walked around the back of the green and chipped his ball skillfully on, stopping just a foot short of the hole. A little more swing and it might on hit the pin and dropped in. Just the sort of lucky shot Andrew imagined must have besieged Hanover in the front nine.

Cary Newman marked his ball and Andrew picked his up as well. Frederick Martin putted a little long and sank his second putt for a double bogey, two over par. The last two holes had been brutal to his score and he stormed off, not acknowledging the scant applause. Newman sank his putt easily and was rewarded with a more enthusiastic greeting. It was only a par but he had been able to make it an up and down. The crowd apparently liked to see someone come back from adversity. Andrew preferred never to be in such a position.

Patterson placed his ball on the green. He had a two-foot putt, his favorite distance. He could sink two-foot putts all day. Even with sloping greens and chewed up grass, the odds of missing from this distance were very low for a player of Andrew's ability.

He looked the green over, confident it was a straight shot. This would be a perfect place to pick up an unexpected birdie, a little insurance against Hanover's luck. Eric handed Andrew the jade-headed putter. It was a simple design, just a flat, three quarter inch thick blade with a line scored across the middle of the top, inlayed with mother-of-pearl. Other players favored putters with special materials inset into the face and a flat tail with a series of lines or circles to help them line up the putt. Andrew's was similar to the generic putters that one obtained from a miniature golf course, simple, but elegant. The putter had been commissioned from a sculptor. The artist had been intrigued by Andrew's request and had adamantly pointed out that he had no skill in designing or building golf clubs. Andrew just asked that the club balance at a point six inches up the shaft from the head and have a perfectly flat hitting surface. The sculptor exceeded Andrew's expectations.

The jade was dark and richly grained. The mother of pearl inset was iridescent and a perfect addition. The handle was gold plated. Solid gold would have been too heavy and would ruin the functionality of the club.

When he first took it to the practice green he dropped a ball twenty yards from a hole. He lined up the mother-of pearl sight line with the hole and hit the ball. It rolled the sixty feet and dropped right in the hole. Perhaps Andrew could have done that shot with any putter he happened to pick up, but he was very pleased with the craftsmanship of this work of art and promptly sent the artist a bonus check of one thousand dollars to show his appreciation.

Patterson stepped up to his ball. He could hear some of the whispers from people in the crowd as they perhaps were getting their first glimpses of his unusual club. He drew back about three inches then hit the ball and watched it roll squarely in to the hole. He allowed himself a smile. The applause started thin, but then people were starting to realize they had just witnessed a birdie. It would be Andrew Patterson and Scott Hanover playing head-to-head in the final nine holes. Andrew pulled his ball out and handed the club to Eric who wiped the club with a cloth before slipping it back into its case. Martin and Newman waited at the edge of the green to shake Andrew's hand. They had already found out that they would be finishing the tournament without him in their group. They congratulated him in a sportsmanlike fashion and Andrew graciously accepted their best wishes. Perhaps each thought they still had a chance but as long as Andrew stuck to his plan, he was unbeatable. Un-beatable!

77

"Congratulations, Mr. Patterson," greeted Carl Bateman. He had just wedged himself out of his golf cart. Another large man, smoking a cigar, remained in the cart, seemingly not impressed with Andrew's presence. "I just wanted to let you know we'll be pairing you with another golfer for the final nine holes."

"So I've heard," answered Andrew.

"Ah, yes. Well, Mr. Hanover seems to have created some sensation, Mr. Patterson, and the Northern Illinois Amateur Golf Association and the tournament will greatly benefit from the coverage the USA Sports Channel will be providing." Bateman nodded at Harold Frisk sitting in the golf Cart. "We're planning on teeing off in about twenty minutes."

"Hmm," muttered Andrew. "Hardly seems fair. I mean Hanover has had two hours to rest and relax and I'm suppose to be ready to compete in twenty minutes?"

"Well, Uh, that's just the way it worked out. Nothing to be done about it really. No rules against it."

"That's okay," said Andrew, happy to get the official into a worrisome froth, "I'll be fine. I'm loose and warmed up. Twenty minutes will be fine."

"Wonderful, wonderful. We'll see you on the tee." Carl returned to his cart and beeped the horn as he sped back the hundred yards or so to the clubhouse.

"That's Patterson?" growled Harold Frisk. "What a colorful character. Where did he get those clothes?"

"Yes, quite interesting," agreed Carl. "I'd think that would tend to draw more interest."

"If the viewers take him seriously."

"I assure you, Mr. Patterson is a serious and quite accomplished golfer."

"You think he can beat Hanover then?"

"Based on skill alone, no doubt. Patterson's had a good morning. His play is very consistent, I'm sure he'll continue at this level," Bateman mused out loud.

"Well, hopefully it'll come down to the last hole. Best sports events always come down to sudden death. The Bull's fifth world Championship the winning shot went in with the buzzer. Wonderful game. Had a court side seat for that one. Never forgot it."

"Well, I'm sure no matter what happens, this even will thrill the viewers."

"Well, Let's not get too carried away, Mr. Bateman. It is 'golf' after all."

"Right, right," agreed Carl. He pulled up to the makeshift USA Sports control room. "I'll meet you here in fifteen minutes," said Carl as Frisk swung his legs to the ground and pulled himself out. Frisk grunted and puffed out a cloud of cigar smoke.

"We got it," said a voice from Bateman's left.

"What?" he uttered. The man standing next to the cart caught him by surprise. He was wearing a black rubber suit, dripping water onto the ground. He held up a white golf ball with a yellow duck on it for the large red-jacketed man to see.

"That's Hanover's ball?"

"Yep," answered the greens keeper slash scuba diver.

"I didn't think you'd find it," commented Bateman.

"Almost didn't. What do you want with it?"

"Get it to Kenny Chase. He'll need to analyze it."

Carl breathed a sigh of relief. Chase would check the ball out and any possibility of scandal would be quietly put to rest with no one the wiser.

He hated to think what Frisk would think if he knew that the tournament hadn't checked out Hanover's balls before he started. Well, no worries about that. He hit the gas pedal and drove off to the tenth tee.

78

Ellie pulled the batteries out of the quick chargers and loaded them into her bag. Her tape camera was replaced with a live transmission camera that would have its images passed through the control room and then to the studios downtown then fed to the network affiliates to any station interested in picking it up. Several markets had already shown interest according to Uncle Harold and Ellie hoped more would. A boring Saturday was turning into an exciting day and she was helping to make it possible.

"What's up Ellie?" asked a squeaky voice.

Ellie clenched her teeth in apprehension. "Hi Lewis," she answered without turning around.

"I got some tape to send up. Getting your camera ready?" he asked.

Of course she was, couldn't he see that?

"I was out taping Andrew Patterson. The guy is going to be hard to beat. He's got the game down."

"That's why he's ranked number one," agreed Ellie.

"Something weird though, on eight."

"Something weird?"

"There was a diver out there looking for a balls I guess. Kind of strange, don't you think? That water must be freezing. Guy must be nuts."

"Probably," said Ellie. She was carefully adjusting and readjusting her equipment, waiting for Lewis Filtry to finish setting the tape up for transmission. So far so good. If she could just...

"So what you doing after the tournament?" asked Lewis.

Too late.

Lewis Filtry was the kind of guy who just didn't get the message. He'd asked Ellie out maybe two dozen times and even though she'd made excuses every time, he just didn't get it.

It's not that Lewis wasn't a nice guy, he was very sweet and considerate. He just wasn't Ellie's type. She liked to think she wasn't that shallow when it came to looks, but she had to have some standards. Those mutton chop side burns and thick black plastic eyeglass frames were just too much for her. She started to make another excuse then stopped herself. Maybe there was another way to handle Lewis.

"I'll probably go home and wash my hair," she said. Lewis shrugged and went about his work. "Maybe..." she continued, her voice shifting into a sultry tone, "you'd like to help?"

"Excuse me?" gulped Lewis.

"You can wash it over and over and over. Wouldn't that be nice?"

I...I...I suppose, Ellie," he stammered.

"Then you can wash my feet, between my toes. Maybe even help pick the junk from under the nails.

"What?" asked Lewis. His surprised excitement was turning to confusion.

"Then you could swab my ears. I get so much of that sticky wax in there. You would be careful, wouldn't you?" she asked playfully.

"You're not suppose to put Q-tips in your ears Ellie."

"I trust you, Lewis, they just get so dirty."

The cameraman's expression was taking on an air of disgust. "Um, I was thinking a bite to eat," he said.

"Oh, I could never enjoy a nice meal with such dirty toes and ears," she answered.

"Uh, too bad, I guess," said a relieved Lewis. "I'll catch you on the course," he added as he trotted off to the control room at the clubhouse.

Ellie smiled. Maybe that would cure him. It might also get her a strange reputation at the station. Oh well, it was fun.

She carefully taped up the box containing her tapes from this morning. She would transfer them to DVD for Scott Hanover along with the coverage this afternoon. It would make a wonderful keepsake no matter how it would turn out.

Jason Bernard had assigned Ellie to be on Hanover and Patterson. She would be filming their swings and shots, mostly from behind. The third cameraman, Alf Redding, Jason's regular partner would be situated to capture the ball coming toward the green and the third man, Lewis Filtry was available to float around to get various shots of the course and zoom in on the balls as they landed in the fairways or hazards as the case might be. He also would help Lucy Penndel to capture immediate reactions from the golfers of their own and their opponent's shots.

Jason Bernard would be doing on air commentary from the control booth, warm and dry and full of hot coffee. Ellie smiled as she thought about their meeting earlier that morning. His attitude had nearly turned a hundred and eighty degrees. Perhaps some of the change had been due to the fact that she had her Uncle Harold urge him to jump on the story, but she felt that Mr. Bernard had also recognized that Scott Hanover's amazing round so far was a major sport story. She knew Jason wasn't going to become a golf fan, but his professionalism as a reporter and now commentator pushed his apathy for golf aside. He would do a good job, not only because this was an exciting sports event in its own right, but also because he realized it was good for his career.

Ellie adjusted the small mirror inside the van that the reporters used to check their appearance before going on camera. Her freckled face and fiery red hair were not the type of appearance that got one on camera but her interest didn't lie in that end of television. She hoped to be a producer, Like Keith Pendell some day and treated her experience as a camerawoman as invaluable. She had started out interning in the editing room and doing research for the producers. She knew if she asked Uncle Harold to get her a producing job, he would pull the right strings, but she wanted to earn it in her own mind. There would always be those who thought she had gotten any advancement because of her relationship to Harold Frisk, but as long as she knew she earned it, she could put up with that.

She let loose her ponytail, brushed out her hair a little and gathered back up all the hairs that had fallen loose during the morning. She rarely wore makeup and there was certainly no reason to do it today. She popped out a fresh stick of Doublemint gum and slipped it into her mouth. She closed her eyes and enjoyed the burst of flavor that last only for a minute before it was chewed out of existence.

She checked her watch and quickly snapped out of her relaxed state. There was only ten minutes until the scheduled tee off of the final pair. She slipped the battery bag over her left shoulder and lifted the camera onto her right. If nothing else, this job made her feel less guilty about not exercising regularly. She slid the van door shut and punched in the code to set the alarm into the keypad by the handle then raced for the clubhouse. Her heart was pounding with anticipation. She hoped Scott Hanover could pull it off. A three-stroke lead was not all that great in an amateur tournament, especially against a player like Patterson. Ellie had heard about Patterson's skill and consistency and knew that Hanover had been playing on luck and a prayer. She hoped it would hold and added her own prayer for him to hang in.

She remembered Hanover's shot into the water on eight. Did the scuba diver Lewis mentioned have anything to do with that? Maybe just a souvenir hunter hoping to get one of Scott's soon to be famous duck logo balls.

79

Jason Bernard slipped the headphones on. "Can you hear me?" asked a voice from inside them.

He adjusted the microphone to sit at the corner of his mouth. "Loud and clear," he answered.

"Okay, Mr. Bernard. I'm Freddy King. I'll be feeding you statistics and information you may want to use on the air. I'll probably be telling you stuff that you can't use or don't think is appropriate so just ignore me if you want to. Won't bother me."

"Do you have all this stuff memorized?"

The voice laughed. "A little. Mostly I'm doing research in the archive and the Internet. There are a few other people here who may want to contribute but I'll filter out the bad stuff."

"I wish I could say I knew a lot about golf."

"You play?" asked Freddy.

"A couple times in college. Never got the bug I guess."

"Well, you know the basics. I'll fill you in on any special or obscure rules that may come into play. This is your first time in the commentator chair?"

"Yeah. You always think that you'll jump right up to the NFL or NBA."

"Well, golf isn't that bad. It might be a little slow since we're only covering two players but it's been done before with great success. Challenge matches, like when Sergio played Tiger in the dessert," pointed out Freddy.

"Right," said Jason. He had no idea what Freddy was talking about but he didn't want Freddy to know it.

"Listen, if you have any questions, just flip off the live switch on your mike. I'll still be able to hear you here."

"Terrific," said Jason.

"You'll be fine. They got a camera on you?"

"Yes."

"Cool. I'll be able to see you but you won't be able to see me."

"I better watch what I do with my fingers," assessed Jason.

"Gross," said Freddy.

"Don't worry, it'll mostly be voice over shots. Occasionally we'll have a reported on the course add a little live reaction from the players and observers."

"Excellent. This is going to be smooth as butter, Mr. Bernard."

"Please call me Jason."

"Yes, sir, Jason. I'll be back in five."

Jason leaned back in his chair. He had five monitors in front of him. One was tuned to the Chicago USA Sports Live feed. One showed him sitting at the small table, an aerial map of the golf course taped up behind him. The other three were blue screens and would display the feeds from the three roving cameras on the course. One of them came alive. A distorted view of a girls face appeared. The camera was pointing up at her chin and she smiled into the lens.

"You guys getting a picture?" asked Ellie's familiar voice.

The director answered her. "More like a horror picture," he joked.

"Yeah, right," she answered. The view changed as she picked up the camera. The screen showed a crowd of people around the tenth tee. She started to turn and Jason was amazed to see the right side of the fairway lined with onlookers. The left side was all trees and off limits. Halfway down the fairway was a sand trap on the right and more sand traps guarded the green. Just behind the green a narrow break in the trees showed the path to the eleventh tee as Ellie zoomed in on the green. A pole topped with a red flag sat in the hole to the left side of the green. "Pretty easy par four," commented Ellie."

"Why is it easy?" asked Jason.

"Oh, Mr. Bernard," said Ellie, "Didn't realize you were set up yet."

"Ready and waiting."

"Excited?" she asked.

"Busting at the seams." His voice was sarcastic in tone but Ellie knew he was excited to be given this chance, even if it was just a golf tournament. "But I really would like to know why this is considered an easy par four."

"Well, it's a long hole but straight. No doglegs. The fairway is wide open and the flag is on a relatively flat area of the green. A good second shot would allow a seasoned golfer to maybe birdie."

"And what would you shoot?" asked Jason.

"Me. A six. See that sand?" She zoomed in to the sand trap on the right. That's where my first shot from the ladies' tee would end up. I have an uncanny ability to find and land in every sand trap on the course."

"Sounds like you at least have fun," commented the director.

"Every swing," laughed Ellie. "Let me know when we're ready to go on. I think the golfers are starting to head this way." She clicked off her mike. From here on out the banter would be limited to professional comments and directions. Even though she didn't plan on staying a camerawoman all her life, she took her job seriously and wanted to do the best job she could.

"Getting settled in?" growled a voice from behind Jason. A heavy large hand settled on his right shoulder, followed closely by a blue cloud of cigar smoke.

"Mr. Frisk. Yes, absolutely."

"You'll do fine. I've got an eye for talent and you've got it. Caught your interview with Hanover. Good work. Keep it up."

"Yes, sir," answered Jason.

"I'm going to be out following the golfers. I'll be out of your hair. Let Bob, the director, do his job. Listen to Freddy. He's a smart kid. He knows what people like to hear. He'll make you look good, if you let him. And don't let Penndel try to steal the show. Ran into Keith Kelly. He was begging me to switch you two. Technically it's his decision since he's producing but I overrode him. What's the point in being head honcho if you don't flex your muscle every once in a while." His bear claw grip on Jason's shoulder tightened and he shook him in his chair. Another puff of smoke filled the small room. Jason knew smoking wasn't allowed around the electronic equipment but if no one else was going to point it out to Harold Frisk, he wasn't either.

"Now where is that Bateman fellow?" wondered Frisk out loud as he stepped out.

"How's the shoulder?" asked Bob after the big man left.

"Don't ask me to go bowling tonight," answered Jason.

Bob laughed. The other two cameras came on line and the director made sure they were in place. The second monitor showed Lucy, standing slumped by the tee. She was nodding her head and sighing. This was definitely worth it, thought Jason. To see Lucy Penndel working the sidelines while he had the booth was too good to be true.

"You think you pulled something off, Bernard?" questioned a voice from behind him. He swiveled around in his chair. It was Keith Kelly. "You think that sending Lucy to the sidelines like a rookie is going to get you ahead? Not if I have anything to do with it."

"Hey, it wasn't my decision," answered Jason.

"I bet. You just had Frisk's niece do your dirty work. Almost as good as doing the boss's daughter," she added.

Jason held his anger. "I hope you're not implying there is anything going on between me and Ellie."

"People can draw their own conclusions," answered Keith.

"Hey, I didn't want to be here today but the story broke and I was on the scene. It's only fair I get to reap the rewards."

"Don't screw up," he warned and left the control room.

"You don't want to mess with him," commented Bob.

"Yeah, I know," agreed Jason. "But I can't let him spread rumors like that."

"Hey, no one would believe them, Jason," pointed out Bob.

"Thanks, Bob," said Jason.

"No problem."

80

"Five minutes," announced a red-jacketed woman poking her head into the dining area of the clubhouse. Scott, Paul, Sarah, Sally, Jake and Gina were still gathered around the table. They had been laughing at some of Jake's stories and acted like old friends now.

"Well," started Jake, "I don't suppose you need it but good luck anyway, Scott."

"Hey, I'll take all I can get."

Paul was staring out the window. "What is that?" he asked.

Jake turned around to follow his gaze. "Oh. You guys haven't met your opponent yet, have you? That colorful, eccentric and dare I say, strange man, is Andrew Patterson."

"He must be good if he can get away with dressing like that," said Paul. The rest laughed. "Don't stare to long at him, Scott, that outfit could induce a seizure."

"Well, to each his own, I guess," said Scott.

"Sarah, Gina, you two are with me," insisted Sally. "I've arranged for a tournament official escort for Sarah and me and I'm sure it would be no problem to add Gina. We'll be able to make our way easily through the crowds and follow the boys on their quest."

"You make it sound like they're hunting a dragon," commented Jake.

"More like birdie hunting," she joked. "We'd better be off," she insisted. Scott helped Sarah out of her chair.

"I better hit the bathroom again," she said. She kissed Scott and stroked his cheek. "Good luck, my love. Have fun."

"I'll try," answered Scott. He hugged her and she, Gina, and Sally headed to the bathroom. He turned to Jake. "Where will you be?"

"I'll be around. Karen Blakely, my colleague, will likely be trying to get the best exposure for Patterson she can. I need to make sure you're accomplishments get played up too."

"Listen, Jake," said Scott, "I appreciate your faith in me and all, but I'm not all that sure about being a spokesman for anybody. Sarah's right. I'll going to be really busy in a few weeks and I can't make any promises."

"Fair enough, Scott. I came here today to try and restart a career that has been dragging; no, sinking, during the last year. I was sure that if I could sign Patterson and get him a decent contract, then I'd get my confidence back and be able to pick up where I left off. What I discovered is that I'm not the kind of agent that gets Pattersons. I'm a little guy and I have a little life that up until a little while ago I thought was worthless.

"Scott, you've got a terrific wife, coming all this way to see you play. You've got a great friend in Paul to caddy for you. You've built up a mild fervor in the amateur golfing world of guys who are thinking; hey I can do that too. Companies want people like that. Win or lose, there will be something for you. It may not be an national campaign with Callaway, but something."

"Gina seems pretty nice," observed Scott, changing the subject. "She's just a friend?"

"Well, more than a friend. If I can get my act together, maybe a lot more."

"Well, I'll see you, Jake."

"Break a leg," offered Jake. He shook Scott's hand. Paul offered his as well.

"If you ask me it's a blessing you're not Patterson's agent. What if he wanted you to dress like him?"

Jake laughed and patted Paul on the shoulder. "Take care of our boy there."

"Hey, how do you think he got this far," Paul answered, smiling.

81

The only bad part to this arrangement was that Hanover would get to tee off first, realized Andrew. If Andrew went first, Hanover would have the pressure to equal or better Andrew's first shot. He hoped the crowds and the television coverage, which didn't accompany Hanover to such an extent on the first nine, would provide a distraction to the golfer.

Andrew finished brushing out his spikes and Eric Peters followed him to the tee. Eric was careful to remain behind and to Patterson's right. He was watchful for Patterson to put his right hand out. Upon that signal, Eric was to hand him the next club that Patterson had listed on his course plan. Eric was always amazed at how Patterson could predict how he would play a course. It was eerie at times. He always made his shots and sometimes got lucky, although it really wasn't luck. Eric knew Patterson didn't believe in luck. It was fortuitousness. A long putt might roll into the hole instead of a foot from it. A chip from the fairway might land close enough to the hole for a birdie attempt. He'd never seen Patterson get a hole-in-one or an eagle, but those were rare, even for the professionals.

Hanover and his caddy walked up to the tee, side by side. Compared to Andrew's outfit, Scott Hanover was severely underdressed for the occasion.

"Ready for the shoot out?" asked a woman wearing a green blazer emboldened with a USA Sports logo and the same logo on the microphone Andrew found sticking in his face. He looked up and a man was pointing a camera at him.

"Shoot out?" he asked.

"Yes. Show down, perhaps is a better term."

"I will play my game, and Mr. Hanover will play his as we've been doing all along. I am confident that I will, in the end, win."

"Why are you so confident? Scott Hanover is on pace to set a PGA record."

Andrew laughed. "Mr. Hanover has been lucky, but to sustain such a pace is like sprinting the first mile of a Marathon and expecting to keep it up the whole race. It simply can't be done."

"Well, we'll see," answered Lucy.

"Mr. Patterson, Just wanted to introduce myself and wish you good luck," said Scott.

Andrew took his hand. "Good luck to you Mr. Hanover."

"Oh, make it Scott."

"Andrew," reciprocated Patterson.

"And so begins the battle for the road to the PGA," said Lucy Penndel.

From the control room Jason winced as he watched Lucy's image replaced with an animated, spinning USA Sports logo as they went to a commercial break. "...battle for the road...?" he muttered in disbelief. Even for Lucy that was pretty bad.

"Didn't even know we were at war," commented Bob.

82

Ted Lange had found a spot fifty yards down on the right side of the tenth fairway. Joe Caulkin stood next to him. Curious onlookers crowded the fairway and red-jacketed men tried to keep them well back of the line between close cut fairway and the taller rough cut grass, allowing the golfers a little leeway for bad shots. It was obvious they weren't prepared for so many onlookers, many having arrived in the last hour. There were even reports of people scaling the fences surrounding the course and staking out spots along some of the later holes.

Ted had been to enough tournaments to know that by the time these two reached the seventeenth and eighteenth holes it could be a logistical nightmare. He had urged the tournament officials to get some more security in and had been advised that some forest preserve officers and Cook County Sheriff Deputies were on the way. Ted saw a few uniforms throughout the crowd, but suspected they were here just as spectators at the moment.

"Well, Ted, I never imagined Patterson would find himself in a position to have to catch up when this tournament started. He did make than one mistake on seven though but he also made a couple shots I don't think he was counting on," commented Joe.

"Hmm," mused Ted. "You do have to give him credit, he is technically a good golfer."

"Oh, yes. But no risk taking at all, no guts when it comes to maybe trying to cut off a few strokes," answered Joe. "Scott could easily lose that three stroke lead in two or three holes. Maybe even one if he has a disaster."

"Anything is possible, Joe, and that goes both ways. Its just statistics, every gambler will tell you that when a hot streak comes along you got to play it for all its worth and when the cold streaks are there, you just kind of hunker down and wait it out."

"I suppose. I've seen golfers have great rounds before, nothing like seven under for nine holes but I guess there have been some who have topped that."

"A few. But they always balanced out the record setting nine holes with an average back or front nine to keep the whole round out of the books.

"You think that'll happen with Scott?"

"Joe, I have no idea what will happen, in terms of the final score and who will win this tournament or not. But I do know it will be one of the more interesting rounds of golf I've ever seen."

"I'll go along with that."

"Looks like they're getting ready to tee off," noted Ted.

83

"The final two players this afternoon will be teeing off at the tenth hole now. First up is Scott Hanover of Chicago, Illinois. Currently at a course and tournament record of seven under par for nine holes and leading by three strokes." The announcement caught Karen Blakely by surprise. They were teeing off already? She looked at her watch and held it to her ear. The stupid thing had stopped. What were they making batteries out of nowadays? First her phone, now her watch. What else could go wrong today?

It could take April an hour or more to get here. Hopefully she'd be able to find the Callaway rep she mentioned. Karen had emptied her purse twice more in search of change for a phone call. She could always make a collect call, she supposed, but if April was on her way, then Jonathan might pick up again. It was all turning into a big mess.

The crowd had grown in the last fifteen minutes and most had migrated to the tenth hole. There was a slight hill between the first fairway and the tenth and that seemed to be good spot for most people to see what was happening. She started to work her way through the people, ignoring the catcalls and hoots from several middle-aged men who seemed to have had a few too many despite the forest preserves ban on alcohol.

As she squeezed by the scoreboard she heard a rip in fabric and a tug on her right side. A large nail had snagged her blouse and a rip ran along the right side. She cursed the nail and unhooked herself from its rusty clutches. It just kept piling on.

She pushed through the people with out even asking to be excused anymore and the comments she received were more rude suggestions than suggestive comments. A red-jacketed man stopped her as she tried to get to the inner circle of people on the tee. She reached to show him her badge and – it was gone. She stood still and let out a deep breath and started to laugh. The laughter built until a few people around her started to stare. It was growing out of control and she wondered if this was what it was like to have a nervous breakdown. She thought of the unkempt, poorly shaven image of Jake Fischer and figured she wasn't too far from his place on the totem pole.

"She's with me," said Jake's voice. She turned her laughter into a chuckle as she turned to see Jake Fischer standing behind her. He was flashing his credentials to the official who gave a wary look at her the shrugged as if to say, better your problem than mine, and stepped aside to let them pass.

"Lost you badge again?" asked Jake.

"You probably took it so you could come to my rescue again," she said.

"I swear I didn't."

"Don't think I'm letting you in on Patterson," she warned.

"I wouldn't dare," said Jake.

"Why are you helping me?"

"Let's say I'm keeping an eye on you," he answered.

"You don't think I'm interested in trying to snag Hanover from you, do you?" she asked.

"No. Scott Hanover would see right through you. I'm just interested how you're going to handle things when Patterson loses this tournament."

"Loses? Not likely. The guy is a robot. All it will take is for Hanover to start playing his usual game and the tables will turn very quickly."

"Well just remember, Hanover is getting just as much coverage as Patterson is. You never know what those fickle executives at Callaway are going to do. Maybe they'll like the idea of an underdog that came close rather than a favorite who just played his usual game." Jake nodded towards the tee, "Hanover's getting ready to hit."

"Quiet please," announced a large red-jacketed official standing off on the right side of the tee.

CHAPTER 15 – TENTH HOLE

84

Scott was nervous now. It seemed like the whole thing hit him at once. He hadn't felt it when he shook Patterson's hand or was briefly interviewed by Lucy Penndel. He hadn't felt it as he as Paul joked about ending up ten under par for the round. It was the sudden silence that had spread in a wave through the crowd. It started around the tee but then sounds that were more distant faded out and there wasn't even a murmur from the clubhouse where people where huddled around the television monitors the USA Sports crew had setup. Even though Scott couldn't see it, they all showed an image of him standing over his ball, his gaze searching the distance – for something.

When he saw Sarah and Sally and Gina standing about twenty-five yards away he knew what he had been looking for. Sarah blew him a kiss. He blew it back. In the control room, Bob had the second cameraman zoom in on the woman he had exchanged the kisses with.

Jason immediately recognized Sarah, "Scott Hanover just got a good luck kiss from his wife, Sarah. Interesting story how she got her," he said. "More interesting is their expecting their first child in a couple of weeks. Okay," he commented, "he's getting ready for his tee shot."

"Using his driver," Freddy added in his ear.

Jason continued, "He'll be using his driver on this par four, four hundred and forty yard hole straight to the green, some trees to the left but nice and open on the right. With the fairway playing downhill we should get some long drives." The words from Ellie replayed in his head as he made his comments. He'd be sure to ask her for some more advice as the play continued.

The nervousness drained from Scott like a heavy bathrobe slipping off his shoulders to the ground. He blew out a deep breath and shuddered with a warm wave. He took his practice swings and stepped up closer to the ball. His eyes focused on the duck and it seemed like all he could see was the ball, like it had enlarged to fill his entire field of view. With almost supernatural force his body took over from his mind and the club pulled back straight from the ball and hovered above his head for a brief instant before slicing through the air on the way down. The whoosh seemed to echo in his ears and the plink of the metal club head hitting the ball chimed in his head.

The ball rose as it flew, faded a little to the right and landed about two hundred and forty yards down the fairway about two yards from the edge of the rough and five yards from the feet of the crowd.

The applause was polite and short. It wasn't an amazing shot but to Scott it was terrific. On a normal day, a two hundred and forty yard drive in the fairway was great cause for celebration. Paul clapped his shoulder as Scott stepped out of the tee box. He gazed at Sarah and she was clapping and shouting and smiling bigger than he had seen in a while. His smile matched hers. He could walk off the course now and be a happy guy.

"Now teeing off," announced the voice from the clubhouse speakers, "Mr. Andrew Patterson of Wilmette, Illinois, at four under par after nine holes."

The red-jacketed man nodded at Andrew to take his place in the tee box. Andrew let Eric place his driver in his hand and he stepped up. He placed a new tee into the ground, adjust the height carefully and then Eric handed him the ball.

85

Jason absorbed the information Freddy was feeding him from the studio in his headphones. He raised his eyebrows as he learned more about the eclectic golfer now standing on the tee. "Andrew Patterson, although three strokes behind at this time, is the favorite to win today. His major competition, Joe Caulkin had to bow out due to a broken wrist he suffered last week. Oddly enough, his replacement, Scott Hanover, is actually ranked last of the golfers playing today. A strange turn of events and one I'm sure Mr. Caulkin is watching with great interest.

"Andrew Patterson is undefeated in his amateur tournament play and has only been playing golf for the last two years!" He turned off his mike feed and asked Freddy, "Is that right?"

"You bet," answered Freddy.

Jason remained silent while Patterson readied himself to tee off.

86

Andrew placed the ball on the tee and stood up. He glanced down the fairway and almost imperceptibly shook his head as his gaze landed on Hanover's ball to the right. He was in a bad position for approaching the green. There was a bunker directly between him and the pin, which would require the "amateur" to stick a two hundred yard shot. Andrew was aiming for the left side and knew he would be about twenty yards further than Hanover with a good roll. He was hoping for a slight draw to pull the ball to the left and stay out of the rough.

He lined up his driver behind his ball. His trajectory was lower to start than Scott's but rose and drew to the left. It landed even with Hanover then rolled a little to the left of center, twenty yards past the first golfer's ball.

"Perfect," he thought. The applause was greater than Hanover had received. Andrew thought perhaps it was due to the extra distance he had obtained but it was far shorter than he was capable of if he wanted to give up some of his accuracy.

The golfers and their caddies started walking over the tee box down the fairway. The crowd surged behind them but kept a fifteen-yard buffer zone without the need for tournament officials to control their movement.

Ellie followed them with her camera and Lucy Penndel was keeping up along the side of the fairway, listening intently to instructions over her headphones from the director. Ellie couldn't hear them but soon her own headphones crackled to life followed by a question from Jason Bernard. She had been following his commentary so far and thought it was pretty good. She knew someone had been feeding him information but she seemed pretty confident that his analysis of the hole was straight from her.

"Ellie, are you there?" asked Jason.

She clicked her transmit button, "Right here," she answered.

"Any more comments on this hole?"

"Just that Patterson has a better approach to the green from the left side. Scott Hanover is going to have to contend with the sand trap on the right side."

"Do you think Patterson planned it that way?" asked Jason.

"Absolutely. He hits it where he wants and manages the course better than anyone I've ever seen."

"But not Hanover?"

"No. He's been very lucky today but I don't think he'll make the green in two. That'll make it tough to get par. On the other hand, Patterson could birdie if he gets close enough to the pin."

"Thanks, Ellie. Can I bug you later?"

"Sure thing, boss," she answered. She clicked off her mike and smiled. By the time these nine holes were over, Jason Bernard would have a reputation as a pretty good golf commentator. She wished she were producing this event. She had dozens of ideas bubbling.

Andrew stopped about ten yards behind Scott's ball. The crowd had fallen further behind and spread out over the whole fairway. If other golfers had to follow behind them, they couldn't. He took in the lie that Hanover found himself with and smiled. Andrew was confident that his superior drive would take one stroke off Hanover's lead. There was no chance for Hanover to birdie and pretty good chance he would bogey this one, especially if he landed in the sand. Andrew's smile reflected more than his own excellent tee shot, it relished in the predicament that Hanover had gotten himself into.

Scott and Paul looked at their position. "Well, Scott," started Paul, "that sand is a problem. If you try to hit over it from here you'll roll off the back and probably end up in that tree line. You could hit it short and chip on in three."

"Think I could roll right through the sand?" asked Scott.

"Not with that lip on the trap. I'd hit your seven iron then chip the twenty five yards over the sand."

Scott turned back to look at Patterson then turned back to Paul. "He's smiling."

"He knows he's picked up at least a stroke on you already. He's good, Scott. But remember, you're not here to beat him."

"I'm not? Oh, yeah, I'm just playing golf."

"Trying to beat this guy is the surest way to lose. Play it smart and get a good chip. If you bogey, you bogey."

"Okay," agreed Scott. "The seven it is."

Paul pulled out the club and handed it to Scott. Scott looked for Sarah and found her halfway to the green and smiled at her. It was strange having her here. Now he was beginning to think he might do better if she weren't here. But the more he considered it, the more he felt her presence helped. It gave him a focus and hoped she might become more understanding of his passion for the game.

He chopped a couple of practice swings, lining up to the left of the sand trap in case the ball rolled further than anticipated.

Ellie whispered into her mike for Jason, "He's using a seven iron. He's going to play it safe and hit it short," she added. She listened to her headphones as Jason seamlessly incorporated her comments into his commentary. As Scott readied to swing, a quick "thanks" from Jason came in through her headphones.

Scott hit the ball less than perfect. It sailed more to the right than to the left. He had turned his club open a little as he swung. The ball landed five yards behind the sand trap's right edge. It was safe, but he had the whole length of the sand trap to clear to get it on the green. The applause was sparse and weak. He shook his head a little and handed his club to Paul.

"Hey," commented Paul, "It's not in the sand."

"Not in the sand," echoed Scott.

Patterson and his caddy tromped past them, neither of them looking back. Eric handed Patterson his seven iron and Patterson walked up to the ball. He stopped a moment to check the wind on his face. It shouldn't be a factor, he thought. He let his club sit on the grass an inch behind the ball and as the sole rested on the ground, he let his left arm hang loose letting the club tell him where it wanted to be. He gripped the handle and rocked his feet a little, adjusting his balance. He took another glance at the flag hanging limp on the pole. He looked at the ball then swung the club. A strip of grass in front of the ball followed the ball into the air. The ball was high and straight and landed on the front edge of the green, rolling another four yards. He was two yards from the hole in perfect position. Easy par was his plan but a birdie sat in the back of his mind.

The applause was more vigorous and he sensed the crowd possibly turning allegiance. Most of these people had come to see Hanover try to duplicate his first nine holes. Andrew was confident they would still get a good show, just not the one they expected and they seemed to appreciate his skill.

"Wow," muttered Scott. "That was pretty good."

"From where he was hitting, he had a great approach to the green."

"You'll have to help me do that," said Scott.

"Hey, I'm happy every time you hit the fairway."

"Touché," agreed Scott.

They walked to Scott's ball. Sarah was in the crowd nearest to where his ball landed. "Nice shot, Scott," she yelled.

"He did land a good one," joked Scott.

"Not him, you. But you missed the sand pit. Isn't that extra points?" she asked.

"I don't want extra points."

"Oh," pretended Sarah as she chuckled at her joke.

Paul handed Scott his pitching wedge. "A lob wedge would come in handy here," he pointed out.

"If I knew how to hit one."

"A minor point," added Paul, "then again, you don't know how to hit any of your clubs."

Scott laughed and nodded. He looked at his ball. The grass was tall and thick and helped to support the ball slightly above the ground. He swung his club through the grass a couple of times to get a feel for the drag on his swing. He measured out a back swing he figured would land the ball just past the sand and let the ball roll to the pin. He lined up his feet with the pin and stood ready to hit his third shot. In the hole, he told himself.

He pulled back two feet and chopped the club under the ball, clipped the grass along the path of the club in the process. The ball lifted free and bounced too close the lip of the sand trap for comfort, but then in landed on the green and rolled straight up to the pin. An unseen bump in the path of the ball caused it to break an inch to the left. It was enough of a deflection to deny Scott another birdie. The ball passed over the rim of the hole and stopped four inches from the cup.

The applause was almost deafening.

"I don't believe it," said Lucy Penndel from behind Scott. She walked up to the Scott, listened to a voice in her headphones then pointed Scott's eyes to the camera across the green. "Terrific shot, that should have been in," said Lucy.

"I'll take a par any day," answered Scott.

"Good answer," muttered Paul.

"Well, Andrew Patterson has got to feel a little pressure on his putt after that chip," continued Lucy.

Scott thought about it for a moment and answered, "You know, some how I doubt it."

Lucy raised her eyebrows in surprise. She looked back to the camera in the distance, "Back to you, Jason."

She lowered her microphone and was slowly nodding her head as she looked at Patterson's cool posture and relaxed appearance. "I kind of doubt it too," she muttered.

Scott took his putter and Paul left the golf bag on the side of the green. Andrew nodded his approval for Scott to finish the hole out of turn. Paul pulled the flag and Scott tapped in his ball for par. Paul handed the flag to Eric Peters and the pair stepped off the green.

"Think he'll make it?" whispered Scott.

"What par? Or the birdie?"

"Birdie."

"I don't know. I don't think he's counting on it. I'm pretty sure he wasn't counting on you parring the hole."

Andrew stepped up and squatted to examine the ground between his ball and the hole. It was pretty much a straight shot. He concentrated on just one thing. He didn't want to the leave the ball short. If he hit it too light and it stopped inches from the hole, then he would have wasted a birdie chance. It was better to hit for a little bit beyond the hole but not too much. If he missed the birdie then he'd have an easy par putt.

He stood and took his putter from Eric. This was the first time most of the people watching had a chance to see Andrew's special club. He heard a murmur of comments and ohs and ahs that were hushed by the officials around the green. He lined up his putter and drew it back four inches then hit the ball. It rolled straight to the hole and dropped in, bouncing off the back of the cup before hitting bottom.

The response to Andrew's putt exceeded that for Hanover's chip shot. He smiled as he took his ball from the hole. As he walked to where Eric stood by the hole, he resisted the urge to hold the ball up in acknowledgment. He handed him his the putter and continued, not waiting for his servant. Officials held back the crowd as the camera crews, and golfers made their way through the narrow path in the trees. The scorecard holder was quickly updated the scores. Patterson was now two strokes back with eight holes left to play.

87

Harold Frisk puffed at his cigar and nodded, so far, so good. The tenth hole had a bit of excitement and now the play was closer than before. Ideal elements to keep the viewers viewing and consequently watching those commercials. He figured they could fit in two or three spots before the golfers had to tee off again. He had been watching the feed on an iPad the control room technician had given to him. An earpiece let him follow the commentary and communications with the control room.

Carl Bateman had more than once looked over Frisk's shoulder to see what was happening but gave up after it became apparent that Frisk didn't want to share his toy. Bernard had been doing a good job with his commentary and Frisk had been surprised to hear Ellie giving her analysis of the course as well over the earpiece, something Freddy wasn't equipped to do and Ellie seemed to have a knack for. Fortunately Bernard had the good sense to make use of it.

Bateman's golf cart had been the first through the path in the trees and he parked on the right side of the tee about ten yards down the fairway. Even without the iPad, Carl wasn't going to miss anything.

88

"That was an incredible chip," said Sally as Gina and she helped Sarah along as they followed the silent woman in the red jacket.

"I thought it was going in," said Sarah. "My jaw must have been hanging to the floor. If I knew he was this good I would have skipped that rummage sale this morning to see him play the first nine holes, although I still don't understand everything about this game."

"I'm pretty good at understanding most sports," said Gina, "comes from dating a sports agent. What questions do you have?"

"Well, this may sound stupid, but why are they using those big fat-headed clubs to tee off but then use the flat ones on the fairway?"

"You really don't have much understanding," realized Gina.

"Well, I know they have to hit it in the hole and that par is the number of strokes it should take, but the different clubs seem confusing."

"Basically," began Gina, "there are three kinds of clubs. The woods, which have the big fat heads, the irons, which have the flat heads, and the putter."

"Putters I know from miniature golf," said Sarah.

"Basically the same thing here," said Gina. "The woods will hit the ball further than an iron but generally have less control. Most golfers have three or four woods in their bag. The one that Scott used to tee off is called the driver but is also considered a one wood. As the number increased, the loft of the club increases and the distance it can hit, shortens."

"I guess that makes sense."

"Usually they'll have a three and five wood in addition to the drive."

"What happened to two and four?" asked Sarah.

"That, I couldn't tell you," laughed Gina.

"In the irons, they also start at one and usually go through nine, nine being the shortest distance. But then there are various wedges too."

"Wedges?"

"They are basically irons that have even more loft. Scott used a pitching wedge to hit onto the green. There are also sand wedges and loft wedges depending on the conditions. Usually most players don't have a one or two iron, but some do."

"That's just too confusing."

"It can be. But to answer your question, they pick a club that will allow them to hit the distance they need to get where they want. Most of the time they'll want a long tee shot, then use an appropriate iron or wedge to get onto the green."

"Scott took three shots to get on the green. Is that bad?"

"If you don't hit it four inches from hole it can be. If he had two putted it would have been a bogey."

"Right, bogey. And a birdie is...?"

"A birdie is one under par, which is what Andrew Patterson scored."

"Now Scott is only winning by two strokes?"

"Right."

"Why don't they just list their total score? Why all this under par stuff?"

"I guess it lets other golfers figure out how far ahead or behind they are no matter where they are on the course."

"Don't worry, Sarah," added Sally, "You'll pick it up."

"I'm just glad to be here. I think it really means a lot to him."

"I know it does," added Gina.

Gina and Sally stopped as they realized Sarah had stopped a step earlier. She was holding her belly and her face twisted into a wide grin. She blew out some air, stretched her neck a bit then smiled. "That was invigorating," she said. The two women looked at each other, slightly confused.

"Are you okay?" asked Gina.

"Fine." Sarah was moving again and the two women quickly found themselves jogging a couple of steps to catch up.

"She's fine," echoed Sally.

"Couldn't be better," added Gina as they caught up.

89

"Is it true you've only been playing golf for two years?" asked Lucy Penndel. She had managed to pull Andrew Patterson aside before he could make his way to the eleventh tee.

"Yes," answered Andrew without expounding.

Lucy paused a moment, waiting for more but Patterson just smiled. "What made you decide to play?"

"I like to set challenges for myself. In my business life and my personal life. My goal was to play in a PGA tournament within four years. After today, I will have reached that goal in half the time I set aside."

"If you win," added Lucy. Her comment was met with an unusual look. As if any sane person doubted that Andrew Patterson would emerge victorious from the tournament. Lucy continued. "Would you consider yourself a natural golfer?"

"Do you mean I have a natural ability at this game?"

"Yes,"

"No. I have studied golf and the techniques and methods needed. I've obtained the best equipment available and I know my potential and my limitations. I don't rely on luck and I don't take chances."

"Seems like a sensible way to approach the game."

"I think so. The results are self-evident."

"Well, you are two strokes behind."

"Actually, considering where I expected to be at this point in my game, I'm two strokes ahead. Mr. Hanover will have a tough time maintaining his streak. As you saw, he has no course management and has to rely on lucky shots."

"It only takes one lucky shot a hole," pointed out Lucy.

Andrew smiled. "I must get ready, I'm due to tee off."

Lucy looked at the camera Lewis Filtry held, "And there is Andrew Patterson. Confident and apparently possessing the skill and precision to back it up."

Karen Blakely had managed to work her way through the crowd to where Andrew Patterson was being interviewed. Andrew seemed to be handling himself well. As he finished she waved at Patterson and smiled. He nodded in acknowledgment. Good, Andrew knew she was there and now she could make sure that her interests were being promoted.

A sudden bump from behind her nearly knocked her to the ground. She steadied herself and turned around. It was the cameraman who had just finished shooting the interview. "Sorry," he apologized.

"You nearly knocked me into the ground," she protested.

"My fault entirely," agreed Lewis Filtry. He eyed Karen. She was a mess but was also pretty hot. "You've been watching the tournament?" he asked.

She responded with a look that pointed out what a stupid question that was. She was here, wasn't she?

"A lot of water on this hole," observed the cameraman.

Karen remained silent.

The crowd was forced to settle in down the fairway as the gold tee was set back in a little cove of trees which provided little space for anyone other than the golfer, caddies and the plump, no-necked, red-jacketed official who was acting as referee. The fairway of the long par five twisted around two water hazards, the first on the left, and the second on the right.

"Betcha Hanover knocks another one into the water."

"Another one?" asked Karen. How had he gone seven under par hitting balls into the water?

"Yeah, nailed the water hazard on eight. He still ended up parring the hole. I wasn't here when it happened but I got tape of the guys getting the ball."

"Somebody went in to get Scott Hanover's ball?" she asked. "Didn't the officials try to stop them?"

"What officials?" asked Lewis.

"When he was golfing. There must have been somewhere there to keep onlookers out of the water."

"Oh, they didn't get it then, it was after Patterson and his group finished the hole. They had scuba equipment and everything."

"Scuba equipment? How do you know they were going after Hanover's ball?" she asked. Something didn't sound right here. Who would bring scuba equipment to a golf tournament?

"Why else would they be there? They only pulled out one ball."

"That is strange."

90

Jake let the people file past him. It didn't take long for the tenth hole to become as deserted as the ninth already was. Some litter reminded him of the throngs of onlookers who had flowed like an alien creature from a horror movie. He looked at his own scorecard and saw that he was about three hundred yards from the fourteenth tee. He then looked at his watch. Maybe forty-five minutes to an hour before the golfers would work through the next three holes. He decided to wander back to the control room and watch the action on some of the monitors set up for public view. He thought about getting a cold drink, a soft drink. He patted his pockets, searching for his wallet and found the tubular object in his shirt pocket.

He pulled out the cigarette. It had been slightly flattened and the end was ragged and starting to crumble. He held it in his right hand and looked at it. For fifteen years he had smoked them, and now, for that last six hours, the thought had rarely crossed his mind. There was something else in the pocket, flat and smooth. He didn't have to take it out to remember it was the picture of he and Brad.

He remembered why he kept the cigarette. It was to celebrate signing Andrew Patterson. He suddenly realized that at the time he made the deal with himself, Karen Blakely had probably already done the deed.

He rolled the paper tube to restore its cylindrical shape and put the filter end into his mouth. Absently he searched his pockets for a match or a lighter. After a few seconds he stopped himself, closed his eyes and exhaled deeply. Was he ready to make such huge changes in his life? He had messed up getting Patterson and Hanover wasn't very excited about a career as a golf spokesman.

He pulled the cigarette from his mouth and walked towards the clubhouse. Near the tenth tee was a wire garbage can. He crumbled the cigarette over the container. He hadn't earned it and it would only take one puff for him to go buy a pack at the liquor store on Central, and then, why not a six-pack as well. By six o'clock he'd be sitting in a bar watching the sports report and Karen Blakely standing in the background behind Andrew Patterson.

Alternatively, he could buy Scott and Sarah and Paul and Gina dinner at a nice restaurant and get back on track for a normal life. Brad Finley was in the past. Maybe it was time to do something else with his life. What else could he do? As long as Gina stayed with him, he didn't care what he did.

CHAPTER 16 – ELEVENTH HOLE

91

Andrew obtained his driver from Eric Peters and stepped up to the tee. Water to the left. Sand traps lined the fairway to the right with some low hills beyond them. It was a fairly long hole and a good drive would still leave him two strokes from the green but with the hazards edging the fairway, this was not the time to try for a three hundred yard drive. A slight fade to the left would be appropriate.

"Whenever you are ready, Mr. Patterson," announced the red-jacketed official. Another official next to him raised his hand to ask for quiet from the crowd. Soon they were silent.

Now was the time to play a little psychological warfare. Scott Hanover had ended up in the water on the last water hole he had played. Andrew hoped he could either draw him into the water on this hole, or push him into the sand on the other side. He grinned as he thought of what was going through Hanover's head. He placed his ball down and then looked right at Hanover. The young man was smiling, apparently happy with is lucky par on the last hole. Watch this, thought Andrew.

He whacked the ball and followed it into the air. It soared over the edge of the water hazard before finding the middle of the fairway and bounced slightly to the left, rolling to a stop two hundred and thirty yards down the fairway. Excellent, thought Andrew. He walked towards Hanover and met his eyes.

"Good drive," said Scott. Andrew simply nodded and took his place down from where Scott was standing.

"Nice guy," whispered Paul.

"I can hit it farther than that," answered Scott.

"Yeah, that's what he wants."

"What?"

"He's playing you, Scott. He wants you to make a mistake. He needs you to make mistakes for him to win," Paul continued quietly. "Just keep it to the right. Stay away from the water."

"Yeah. I sure could use a good quack."

Paul nodded in agreement and handed Scott his driver. As Scott walked to the tee box, Paul headed for the golf cart parked ten yard down the fairway. He glanced at the starter as he passed him. It was the same annoyed official who had quashed the quacking on the eighth hole. Whether or not the lack of a quack was the reason Scott ended up in the water he didn't know for sure, but if there was something he could do about it, he would.

"Mr. Bateman?" he asked. He remembered the Tournament chairman from their earlier meeting after the ninth hole.

Carl Bateman turned to face him. "Yes?" he answered. His tone was gruff and he seemed slightly annoyed to be bothered at this moment, as if he was the one approaching the tee.

"Um, Scott and I have a little tradition on water holes and the official there seems to be bothered by it but I really don't think it's that big a deal."

"Bothered by what?"

"Well, I usually will quack whenever Scott has to tee off near water. Back on the eighth hole he stopped us from doing it, I guess because it annoyed him."

"Well, I don't think it's appropriate..." started Bateman.

"Let the boy quack, Bateman," urged the other man in the cart.

"What?" responded Carl.

"He's the duck, for goodness sakes," he growled. "It'll be good for the television coverage."

Carl thought for a moment then yelled, "Henderson."

The red-jacketed man standing near the tee turned to sound of Bateman's voice. Bateman beckoned him with a finger. Henderson seemed startled to be called by the head of the tournament association. "Wait here," he said to Scott who was just starting his practice swings. He jogged as quickly as his large frame would let him. Despite the cool weather, he found himself sweating, either from the extra exertion or a sense of apprehension.

David Henderson was soon standing next to Carl Bateman in his cart. "Yes, sir?" he asked.

"This fellows says you banned him from quacking on the tee."

"It was disturbing the other golfers," he answered.

"It was not," said Paul. He angered quickly at the official's lie. "They were quacking with me halfway through the front nine. Heck, even the camerawoman from USA Sports was doing it and most of the onlookers. It only bothered him." He pointed at the logo emblazoned on the left breast pocket of the man's red jacket.

"It was a very distracting practice," Henderson defended himself.

"Certainly not against the rules," pointed out Bateman. "He can quack," he ordered.

"Yes, sir," muttered Henderson. He walked back to his position this time, wiping his face with a handkerchief he had pulled from a rear pocket of his slacks.

Paul searched for Ellie and found her. She looked confused. He simply mouthed "quack" and she smiled in acknowledgment. He turned to find Sarah and her friends. He walked over and quickly explained what they should do.

Scott was standing on the tee confused.

"On three," shouted Paul. "One, two, three..."

Scott smiled with realization and appreciation at what Paul had just done.

"Quack," bleated out Paul, Ellie, Sarah and the girls and about a dozen other people who had caught onto what was happening.

Ellie listened in her headphones as Jason explained what had just happened. "And there is why he is called the duck. Apparently he's never seen a water hazard he hasn't liked. Let's see if his little good luck ritual can help him negotiate the water he will find on both sides of the hole."

Andrew Patterson stood slack-jawed at the display. He had never seen anything like it in any tournament he had ever played. This was insane. A quack? What was going on?

"They call him the duck," whispered Eric in clarification.

Scott stepped up confidently to the ball. He looked at Andrew's ball sitting on the course and then hit his own. It sailed up and over the water; almost a perfect duplication on Andrew's shot, but it rolled another twenty yard's past the first golfers drive.

The crowd erupted in applause and quacks at Hanover's accomplishment. Andrew was amazed at the shot and the reaction. How did a noisy, distracting quack, allow Hanover to hit a shot like that? He was even in a good position for his second shot. This wasn't right. The guy did have some luck and it was a factor that Andrew was finding difficult to deal with.

"That was amazing," commented Joe Caulkin to Ted Lange. "I think Patterson was pretty surprised by that shot."

"I think he's in for some more surprises," added Ted.

The golfers led the crowd down the fairway. Paul leaned over to Scott, "I thought you used up your quota of amazing shots."

"Apparently not," answered Scott. He looked at his friend. "Thanks," he added.

"What...oh. Well, it really wasn't fair so I thought I'd try. Think it made a difference?"

Scott just pointed ahead of them to the white ball lying in the fairway.

"Right," agreed Paul.

Andrew found himself in position to hit ahead of Hanover again. At least there was that. There was no way this guy would get a second shot off like that. Andrew was three hundred and ten yards from the green. He wanted to be about a hundred and twenty for his third shot and Eric wordlessly handed him the seven iron again. He'd once again be playing the left side of the fairway. The flag was on the right side of the green but approaching from the left gave him more area to play with.

We walked up to his ball. It lay next to a leaf. He picked it up and the ball rocked away, and then fell back. He breathed with relief. Had the ball not returned to its original position, he would have had to take a penalty. He had never taken a penalty for something like that. Why was he so careless? He knew it wasn't Hanover putting pressure on him. That was ridiculous. Perhaps it was that distraction of the brief interview with that reporter, Lucy Penndel. In any case he made a mental note to be more careful. All he needed at this point was to make a stupid mistake.

He lined up his shot and once again the ball sailed high, landing and rolling a short distance to the exact spot he had aimed. He smiled. Nothing less than perfection, he noted.

"He sure can hit it straight," commented Paul.

"Well, assuming I don't, where do I go?"

"Water to the right. Stay left, like Patterson. You have two hundred and ninety yards to the green."

"Three wood?" asked Scott.

"That would leave you a nice chip. Your chipping has been excellent today. Can you keep it straight?"

"Well, considering I usually slice a little with club, if I aim left I'll be okay."

"Then go for it." Paul pulled the club out of the bag, removing the stuffed elephant cover from the wood.

Scott drew his imaginary line from the left side of the fairway to the ball, and then placed the head of the club about a yard behind the ball in that line. He stepped around the club to place his feet parallel to that line.

Andrew chuckled at Hanover's little dance with the club. The guy couldn't even line up a shot.

Scott set the club short of the ball and took two practice swings, both cutting a swath of grass from the ground. He stepped up and took his back swing. As he brought it down he saw the twisting of the club head as it struck the ball. It soared up from its lie on the grass and for a hundred and fifty yards sailed straight, then spin overtook airspeed and it began to turn. It bounced near the middle of the fairway but it had picked up considerable motion to the right. It landed halfway to the water and rolled, disappearing in the tall grass next to the water hazard about seventy yards from the hole.

"Rats," commented Scott. "Do you think it went in?"

"Probably," answered Paul.

"Well. On in four and one putt, eh?"

"Good plan," agreed Paul.

Ellie's camera lost the ball in the tall grass. She listened to see if another camera angle had caught it. Jason's voice once again crackled to life. "Difficult to tell from this angle where that ball ended up," he said. "A penalty here could narrow Hanover's lead by another stroke or eliminate it all together." Bob's voice cut in on her headset and instructed her to work her way along the right side of the fairway to see if she could spot the ball. In the meantime, Alf Redding followed Patterson to his position on the fairway.

Andrew could barely contain his glee. This was going to be easier than he thought. How could someone with that little control of his swing have gotten this far? He had seen the golfer line up to hit near his ball and watched as he dropped his shoulder to soon, causing the club head to twist. And what was he doing hitting a three wood from two hundred and ninety yards? He was asking for trouble, especially on such a narrow fairway.

The crowd was following Andrew to his ball. Eric handed him the pitching wedge and he looked towards the green, easy par and perhaps another chance at birdie. He line up and whacked the ball. It soared up straight at the pin, then landed with a thunk and rolled back a few inches. It ended up three yards from the hole, pretty much in the center of the green. This particular green was flat and he nodded his head with approval.

To his right, Hanover and his caddy were walking slowly to the water hazard lining that side of the fairway. Nearby was a camerawoman scanning the ground with her camera as well. There were no onlookers on that side due to the presence of the water and a murmur could be heard circulating through the crowd like a secret being passed in a classroom.

Paul and Scott approached the edge of the water. In the dark water, several balls could be seen. "I don't see one with a duck," commented Paul.

"It must have gone in right around here," added Scott.

"Hey," called Ellie a couple of feet away, "I think I got it," she announced.

"You see it?" asked Scott. He walked over to the edge of the water where the camerawoman was standing.

"Not in the water," she said, "There." She pointed with her left hand to a clump of tall grass at the edge of the water. Hanging over the pond and nestled in the blades of the long grass was a tiny yellow duck sitting on a white ball.

"Wow," said Paul. "That's hard to do."

Jason Bernard stared at the image on the monitor. "That is either incredibly lucky, or incredibly unlucky, depending how you look at it. He didn't lose the ball in the water, but how he's going to hit it from there is going to be quite a trick."

Alf raced up to where Hanover, his caddy, and Ellie were standing. He looked at the ball nestled in its precarious perch. He whistled low and long. "Lotsa luck," he murmured.

Andrew seemed confused by what was going on by the bank. Wasn't Hanover going to take a drop and get on with it? A red-jacketed official jogged over to the site. He paused, looking at the edge of the water and slowly nodded his head.

Eric leaned over and whispered, "They're saying he found the ball but it's perched on some sort of grass ledge."

Andrew smiled, even better. Hanover would try to hit it and then knock it in the water. He might take the lead on this hole if Hanover's stupidity held.

"Are you going to hit it?" asked Paul.

"You know me," answered Scott, "I've never seen a lie I couldn't hit."

"I know you can hit it, do you think it'll end up anywhere playable?"

"What are my options?"

"None, really," interjected the official. "You must play the ball as you find it."

"Technically it's over the edge of the water," said Paul. "He could take a drop."

"It has to be in the water," said the official, then he paused and added, "I think."

"Doesn't matter," said Scott, "I'll give it a try."

"I wouldn't risk a practice swing," said Paul. "You could knock it off that grass with a easy puff of air."

"That's what I figured," agreed Scott. "What do you think, my pitching wedge?"

"How do you feel about your sand wedge?" asked Paul.

"Not good."

"Pitching wedge it is," said Paul. He pulled the club from the bag and Scott took it carefully. The others stepped back and he gripped the club and wiggled the weighted shaft around, getting a feel for the club and trying to line it up in a path that would hit the ball. He aimed for the left side of the green, hopefully avoiding any water, but if he caught it on the toe, he was screwed. He was conscious to avoid twisting the club again like as he did on his last shot.

"You can do it, Scott," shouted a voice from across the fairway. Scott knew at once it was Sarah. He turned, shading his eyes to try and pick her out from the crowd. Her bulging stomach gave her away quickly. He smiled and waved and nodded his agreement.

"Go for it," shouted other voices in the crowd. "On the green." "In the hole." "Let her rip."

Officials started to quiet the crowd and Scott settled in to get ready again. He could do this. It was just hitting the ball with the right touch. Not too hard, not too soft. An easy partial back swing and just keep your eye on the ball, he told himself. He imagined Andrew Patterson smug with the knowledge that Scott's self-destruction had begun. He couldn't let that stand.

He pulled the club a little bit above parallel to the ground and whispered "please," as he aimed for the clump of grass. The air exploded into a puff of grass blades as he swung. The clutter distracted his eyes from the ball. "Where did it go?" he asked Paul.

"Straight up," he answered staring at the sky. "Wow," he commented once more.

Alf Redding was following the little speck and it seemed to be staying aloft for a very long time. "It might make the green," added Paul. The ball whistled down and with a splunk, plopped onto the longer cut fringe that surrounded the green. Scott let his breathe out. He still had five or six yards to the hole, but he was out of danger. What a shot.

"That was just amazing," commented Jason Bernard. "That ball seemed too scared to come down in the water, as if Hanover would never forgive it if it got even the slightest bit wet. But based on what we've seen from this young amateur so far today, it really isn't all that surprising at all."

The crown applauded with enthusiasm and Andrew turned and looked at the people around him thinking, "Why are they applauding?" Couldn't they see how lucky that shot was? There was no skill. He just whacked at the grass and got lucky. He could just have easily ended up in the pond. He shook his head and started walking to the green.

Scott looked down the bank. A few shattered stems remained where the ball had been a few seconds earlier. He shook his head in disbelief.

"If you can't be good, be lucky," said Paul, perhaps not the last time today.

Scott turned and waved at Sarah. She was jumping and clapping and hooting with the rest of the crowd. Boy was he glad she was here. He noticed that Ellie's camera was looking at him and he smiled at waved at her, punching the air with the satisfaction of a great shot. The image flashed over television screens all over Chicago and several other cities. None of the people knew or ever heard of Scott Hanover before. He was just an average guy, having an above average day and the excitement was enough to get people who didn't even golf to watch the television. Those who did golf were awed by his performance. He was turning sows' ears into silk purses left and right and giving Andrew Patterson, top Chicago Amateur, a run for money.

Andrew approached the green. Don't do anything stupid, he told himself. He knew there was a great tendency of golfers who were a little behind to take risks and push themselves to catch up. He reminded himself he had a game plan and Hanover didn't. He needed patience. Hanover couldn't keep up this show forever. The game was Andrew's to win.

Scott was up first as technically his ball wasn't even on the green yet. Paul handed him the putter and they looked over the lie. "You'll need to give it a little more than you think to get through this fringe," he cautioned.

"I figured. I just don't want to leave it short. I can smell a par."

"Patterson could be looking at birdie," said Paul.

"I'll still be ahead," added Scott and he lined up his feet for the putt. Putting on the fringe was not as exact a science as putting on the green. When you were on the green, you could usually count on a fairly consistent surface. It was easier to judge the speed of the ball and how hard to hit it.

On the fringe, the grass was cut a fraction of an inch higher. While it didn't look that much different, it could really slow the ball down to start. And then the transition from the somewhat taller grass to the closely cropped green could change the direction of your putt significantly.

Scott took a couple of practice putts, adding a little more force to the swing than he though necessary then stepped up to the ball. This time there was extreme silence as he stood ready to take his shot. He kept telling himself not to leave it short, especially not two or three yards short.

He drew back the club, mimicking the force of the practice swing and pushed the club head through the ball. He hit it hard enough that it jumped off the grass a little rather than just rolling. After a foot of the fringe it hit green and continued rolling. It wasn't headed straight for the hole but it would be close. For a minute it looked like maybe he had hit it way too hard and it would roll well past the hole. He hadn't noticed that the crowd was now cheering the ball on. One guy, perhaps the same on who had yelled it before, shouted, "It's in the hole."

As the ball drew nearer to the hole the cheers grew louder and then an amazing thing happened. The ball made a tiny break, a minute shift in its direction following an unseen contour in the ground that he had missed. Its change in bearing took it straight for the hole and even before it plopped into the black opening, the crowd erupted in wild cheers.

"Oh my god," said Scott to himself. He had another birdie, he was now eight strokes under par.

92

"An incredible putt," commented Jason Bernard. "I'm sure it surprised him as much as anyone else. The pressure in now on Andrew Patterson to make his putt so that Scott Hanover's lead does not get larger. At this pace, Hanover is set to tie the record for the best eighteen holes for the PGA." The last fact was courtesy of Freddy from the studio. "Actually, since Hanover was hitting from the fringe, that stroke won't count as a putt. So far he hasn't had anything higher than a one putt on any hole and three holes with no putts. He's averaging less than three quarters of a putt per hole." Jason was pretty impressed with that last statistic from Freddy. What was it going to take to stop this guy? Hopefully nothing. One screen held a close up of Patterson's face. Bob switched that to camera.

"Here of course is the most surprised person. I'm sure he was counting on picking up a stroke or two here, but Hanover's luck on the front nine seems to be spilling over to the back."

93

Joe Caulkin stood on the far side of the green. Hanover was making some incredible shots. Doing things he didn't think were possible. How Scott got the ball off that grass hanging over the water was a miracle in its own.

Ted Lange nodded slowly to himself. He mentally calculated and extrapolated Hanover's score if he kept up this pace. He had never seen anything like this before and wondered if his little talk with him this morning at the driving range had anything to do with it. Part of him knew the pendulum could swing at any moment. This could quite easily be the end of his incredible run. Even if it was, he was glad he was here to see this much.

Andrew Patterson took his putter and waited for the crowd to quiet down. He couldn't let the lucky putt get to him. He had to play his game. He would come out ahead. He would be happy with the par on this hole. That was what he planned on and that was what he was shooting for. There was no point in making a mistake now.

The last bit of cheers from around the hole quieted and he stepped up to his ball, eyeing the path he had imagined on the green, mentally calculating how hard to hit to hit the ball.

"In the hole, fancy pants," yelled a voice from the back of the green. A several people around the heckler shushed him. Andrew chuckled at the comment. That was a new one.

He lined up his club head again, tracing his imaginary line across the white inlay on the top of the putter head. He drew back and hit the ball. It rolled up to the rim, hesitated a split second, and then plopped into the cup. Cheers erupted again and quite unintentionally Andrew raised his putter in the air and yelled, "yeah!" He quickly regained his composure and took a deep breath.

There was no need to get excited. A birdie is possibility on every hole where one made the green in regulation. It wasn't something to count on and he didn't. Why wouldn't this guy implode already? Wasn't the crowd enough to give him nerves? Then he realized Hanover had messed up but a lucky shot had saved him. What were the odds the ball would find the only outcropping of grass to save it from falling in the water? Hanover's luck couldn't hold. It wouldn't. He reached in and pulled his ball out, handing both it and the putter to Eric who had just placed the pin back in the hole.

94

Jake Fischer shook his head in disbelief as the television replayed Scott Hanover's last two shots. This guy should be playing on the pro tour. Well, maybe not. He knew Scott's handicap was eighteen. He was having a good day. He hoped that he would let him parley it into some cash for a college fund for his upcoming child or maybe let him and Sarah fix up their house or take a nice vacation after the baby was born. It wouldn't hurt his pocket either.

For the last year Jake had burned his savings and was beginning to buildup a pretty sizable credit card debt. Gina had been forced to pay dinner tabs more than once and he hated putting her in that position.

A thwacking sound in the background suddenly got significantly louder and Jake watched a small helicopter landed a couple hundred yards away on the now empty driving range. The force from the blades was enough to send balls rolling away in a circular path around the base of the helicopter so when it landed the grass was clear. Two people got out, a man and a woman. The woman looked familiar. He squinted and his jaw dropped in disbelief. The two ducked under the spinning blades and jogged for the cover of the shack where golfers got range balls and were quickly out of view. April?

CHAPTER 17 – TWELFTH HOLE

95

Ellie had rushed to the twelfth tee by way of a shortcut. The golfers and officials had followed the cart path behind a small wooded hill. She cut around the east side and came up to the green from the other side. People who had already lined the fairway parted as they saw her camera. She pulled out her scorecard and clicked on her microphone to describe the hole to Jason.

"A slight dogleg to the left with a some water on the left side," she said. They'll need to stay in the middle and they'll have a good line to the green. The fairway rolls downhill like on ten so we might see some good long drives. There are a couple of sand traps around the green but a lot of space for errant shots. The right side of the fairway is very open. If Hanover slices another one, he'll still be in good shape." Jason thanked her for the info and repeated the information for the viewing audience.

As she lifted the camera to her shoulder, the golfers were coming into view, following Uncle Harold and the tournament official in their cart. Uncle Harold was smiling as he watched the USA Sports feed on his iPad. They were over half a mile from the clubhouse and he was still getting good reception.

96

The official on the tee announced, "Mr. Patterson still holds honors."

Andrew received his driver from Eric along with his ball. The tee he produced from his own pocket and he slipped it into the ground by the golden tee markers. It was basically the same shot he had on ten. This time his draw would help the ball follow the dogleg, rather than set him up for a decent approach to the green. He wanted to be close, this time. This was a hole he planned on birdying. It was relatively short for a part four on this course, only four hundred yards and a decent drive would let him place the ball very close to the pin with his pitching wedge.

The water was little to no concern, as he would stay primarily in the middle of the fairway. He lined up his shot as soon as the crowd quieted and quickly drew back the club and swung hard at the ball. It rose and started its draw after traveling two hundred yards. It followed the dogleg perfectly and landed and bounced and bounced and rolled until it was a yard or so left of the hundred-yard marker. A three hundred yard drive in the center of the fairway. He had a birdie in the hand, so to speak.

"He's not letting up," said Paul. "I guess your miracle shots on eleven didn't impress him too much."

"I'm not trying to impress him," answered Scott. "So what do I do, whack it out there?"

"Can you make it draw like Patterson's did?" asked Paul.

Scott looked at Paul with his best hound dog expression, slumping his shoulders forward.

"Just asking. Listen, the right side is wide open. Aim for Patterson's ball, if it slices, your still in good shape."

"And if it doesn't?"

"Try not to knock Patterson closer to the hole."

Scott laughed at the thought. He put his ball on the tee, and then looked around the crowd for Sarah. Behind him Paul held up both hands like a conductor. He lifted his hands in an upbeat then spread them out wide. The crowd received the cue as intended and a raucous "quack" echoed across the course followed by a quick flurry of laughter.

Scott shook his head. How did he forget that was coming? He saw Sarah and she gave him a thumbs up. She had been moving ahead of Scott and Paul and he hadn't had a chance to talk to her yet. He'd try and catch her at thirteen, the next par three hole.

Scott lined up his shot and took a couple practice swings before stepping up to the ball. He drew back the driver and his expression turned to a grimace as he swung at the ball. The plink sounded great and he felt like he had hit it solid. It rose and rose and turned and turned. Another slice. What was he doing wrong? It wasn't as bad as he three wood on the last hole and the ball bounced on the right side of the fairway and continued to roll until it had settle far into the rough on the right side. The applause was polite. Most people were waiting to see what he would do with this shot.

"I think you got over three hundred yards on that one," said Paul.

"Yeah, but I'm still farther away from the hole than Patterson."

"And that tree might be a problem." Paul pointed to an ash that was positioned on the right side of the fairway and looked to be in a direct path between Scott's ball and the green.

"I'll just hit over it."

"Yeah," said Paul, "good plan."

97

"Is that bad?" asked Sarah as the three started walking down the fairway.

"He certainly didn't hit it like Andrew Patterson," commented Sally. "But with his luck, he can turn any bad shot around."

"He'll have to hit out of the rough cut grass and over that tree," pointed out Gina.

"Why do they call it the rough? Why not tough? Like you said, it's a harder shot." The women giggled at her analysis.

"Well, Scott's still two shots ahead. Even if Patterson picks up one or two strokes Scott still has a chance."

"Oh, I don't care if he wins," said Sarah. The other two stopped and stared at Sarah who stopped a split second after them. "If you had heard him this morning. He was up at the crack of dawn, so nervous about today. So worried he would embarrass himself in front of the other golfers. He's got nothing to prove to anyone, now. He could have stopped after that hole-in-one and everyone would have remembered that guy who was on TV. He and Paul are having a blast. It's be nice if he could beat Patterson, but even second place is somewhere he never imagined he'd be."

"You're right," said Sally. "I guess I'm just so anxious to root against Andrew. Cecily Waterston will be unbearable if he wins. I won't hear the end of it."

98

"He's leading with his wrists too much," said Ted Lange.

"What?" asked Joe Caulkin.

"Hanover. Those slices. He's getting tired."

"Tell him," suggested Joe.

"That won't fix it," he answered.

"Why not?"

"Because then he'll be thinking about that. He needs something else."

"Well, think of something," encouraged Joe. "He may be running out of saves soon."

"I'll think about it," said Ted. Then quietly, almost to himself, "I'll think about it."

99

Karen had seen the helicopter coming in and pushed her way back through the crowd. After she got through most of the people she followed the eleventh fairway to the passage through the trees. A smartly dressed woman stood near the clubhouse, her hand shading her eyes as she scanned the area. In a moment she saw Karen standing on the tenth green and waved at her, a small paper bag in her hand. Karen smiled. April had come. Next to her was a tall man wearing khaki slacks, a knit golf shirt and sweater. He seemed a little bored. Karen walked as quickly as her shoes would let her. Things were looking up.

100

Scott and Paul found the ball pretty quickly. The taller grass made an effort to hide it, but not completely. The flag on top of the pin could be seen through the yellowing leaves of the ash tree that stood about thirty feet tall in front of him.

"About a hundred and twenty five yards to the pin that way," said Paul pointing at the tree."

"Up and over," said Scott.

"You hit a branch and you don't know where it's going. You hit the trunk it could end up right here at your feet."

"What's my alternative."

"Hit it low under the branches and roll it up on the green with a three iron."

"If I hit it too hard, I'm screwed. Too light, I'm screwed."

"You just need to get it on the green, then two putt in for the par."

"I'll take the pitching wedge," decided Scott. "I'm going over the top."

"Good choice," agreed Paul.

"I thought you wanted me to hit it low."

"Just and idea, Scott. That's what you're paying me for."

"I'm not paying you."

"And your getting your money's worth," he added. They laughed.

It would be hard to get under the ball in the tall grass but he had little choice. He took some practice swings, getting a feel for how the grass affected the club head as it passed through. If he only hit the ball with that swing he thought as he stepped up and laid the club on the grass behind the ball.

Andrew knew there was no way Hanover would get the ball up over that tree in that tall grass. He almost laughed as he watched the golfer take his practice swings. What a waste, he thought. He might as well hit it with his putter. The officials called for quiet and Hanover started his back swing. He started the swing and Andrew saw Hanover's head come up and back ever so slightly. As the club hit the ball it didn't loft into the air as

227

Hanover had intended. He had hit the leading edge of the club square on the ball and sent it rocketing low towards the tree. It hit a branch and deflected up and to the right. The errant ball went over the green toward more trees that bordered the water hazard behind the green. As the ball entered the trees a wooden crack echoed the fairway. After what seemed like seconds but couldn't have been more than an instant, the ball arced up and out of the trees back towards the green. It landed on the fringe and rolled until it was sitting an inch or two on the green, no more than ten yards from the hole. "Son of a..." muttered Andrew.

The crowd was silent in disbelief. Half of them didn't know what had happened, the ball had gone in so many directions. Scott had heard the second collision with a tree but the yellowing ash had blocked his view. He ran to his left to get a sight of the green. At that moment he saw something white float out of the trees on the opposite end of the green and fly back toward the pin. He blinked and craned his head forward. He shook his head vigorously. Paul was standing beside him. He turned and asked him, "Is that my ball?"

Paul nodded as applause rippled through the crowd. The astonishment of the amazing shot was wearing off. "Not exactly what I had in mind, but it'll do."

"Wow," said Scott and smiled. "It'll do for sure."

101

"What happened?" asked Sally. She had heard the sound of ball hitting wood and then the applause.

"My husband is the luckiest man alive," said Sarah.

"What? Apart from being married to you?" asked Sally.

"He was right to think he might embarrass himself today. But somebody is watching over him."

"The golf fairies," suggested Gina.

"Golf fairies," agreed Sarah.

102

"He pulled his head up on that one," said Ted Lange. If he hadn't hit that tree, Patterson might be looking at the lead right now."

"What can you do?"

"I don't want to risk getting him disqualified by giving him any advice how to play. But I have something in mind, Joe. I'll catch up to him after this hole."

Joe thought about writing out a five thousand dollar check to Andrew Patterson. He had the money and could afford to do it, but the loss would be more than financial to him. It would be something Patterson could hold over him. He knew he wouldn't be playing as well as Scott Hanover was up to this point, but if Hanover self-destructed now, it was Patterson's game to lose.

103

"That was just pure luck," said Jason Bernard as the shot replayed on the monitor. The live shot returned showing Scott Hanover's ball sitting calmly on the green, waiting to be hit in for perhaps an easy par. "I'm sure he didn't intend on hitting the ball that way and it could have just as easily ended up in the water rather than on the green. Once again, Andrew Patterson is feeling the pressure of Scott Hanover's run of luck, versus his skill and planning. At this point, it's a pretty even match for the two and half holes they've played together."

The monitor was switched to Patterson lining up his shot. He took a partial back swing and knocked the ball up in a beautiful arc. A strip of turf followed it, just like Jason had seen pros do. It landed on the green two yards beyond the pin, leaving a dark dent on the soft green. From there the backspin Patterson had expertly applied rolled the ball back towards the pin and it stopped eighteen inches away. The crowd cheered the superbly played shot and Patterson walked towards the green, absently handing his club to his caddy. "He's thinking, birdie," added Jason. "Unless we see a miracle putt from Hanover, this match is now down to a one stroke difference." He turned and saw Bob shaking his head slowly, blowing a deeply held breathe of air out between his lips. USA Sports Chicago was getting its money's worth today. A commercial flipped on and Bob got up and walked over to Jason. "We just picked up six more affiliates. I think we've got this showing live in twenty markets. This is getting big Jason. You're doing a great job."

"Yeah, I wish I knew what I was doing."

"Just listen to the voices in your head and put it in your own words. So far it's been very impressive."

"Thanks," said Jason.

"Coffee?" asked Bob.

"Sounds great."

"Just don't spill any."

104

"I'd be surprised if he missed that one," said Paul. They were on the far side of the green now and Andrew had just marked his ball with a giant gold coin. "He won't," agreed Scott. "I'll just have to get this one in."

"There's a little break to the right," said Paul.

"I see it," said Scott.

The crowd quieted as Scott lined up his shot. He swung the cub back for a couple of practice swings, and then stepped up. His head turned as his eyes followed the path his ball would travel. Back and forth, three times. He drew the club back and hit the ball. It rolled and as predicted followed the break but missed the hole by six inches to the left and behind and was still a yard away by the time it stopped.

"Closer to the hole," said Paul.

"Closer to the hole," agreed Scott. They walked up to the new position, trying not to look at Patterson to see if he was smiling. If Scott missed this putt the match would be tied and most likely that was it. He was riding his luck right now and it seemed to be stretching pretty thin if the last couple of holes were any indication.

He squatted and eyed the path to the hole. It appeared straight.

"Just hit it at the hole and mean it," advised Paul. "It wants to go in. You saw what it did before bouncing off those trees to avoid the water."

"That's true, I've never seen a ball try so hard to get on the green before."

"It's dedicated, I'll say that for it."

"So basically all I need to do is give it a nudge, it'll do the rest."

"Precisely," said Paul.

"Okay," agreed Scott and he stood and lined his feet parallel to the ball intended path. Two practice strokes and then he stepped forward three inches. He felt his hands gripping the putter like he was trying to strangle a goose. He breathed deeply and relaxed his grip. He hit the ball and it rolled straight, landing in the hole with a gratifying plunk.

He walked over and pulled the ball out. He looked down and saw that Patterson's coin marker was a golden US dollar. It gleamed in the sunlight and appeared in mint condition, unmarked or dulled by time. Patterson passed him as he left the green. He laid his ball down carefully in front of his marker and picked up the coin, sequestering it back into his pocket. He had planned on birdying this hole and his approach shot had guaranteed it. Hanover had just given him another stroke. He placed his putter behind the ball, adjusted his feet and twisted his head to look at the hole. He popped the ball in as easy as sitting in a chair. Everyone watching knew there was no other outcome. And they cheered for him once again. It was now a one-stroke game and there were still six holes to play.

105

"Darn," said Sally. "He got it in."

"Hard to miss from there," commented Gina.

"Oooh," added Sarah. The cry was one of surprise mixed with a sprinkle of pain and confusion. She started to take a few deep breaths, remembering what they had learned in their Lamaze class. She had to focus on breathing through the pain. This was the worst one today, nothing like any of the previous contractions. Did that happen in false labor? Was she pushing too hard walking around the course like this? The two women on either side of Sarah recognized her distress and grabbed her arms to help steady her. She gripped each one of them on their upper arms and Sally muffled a cry of pain as Sarah's hand squeezed her bicep like a talon.

"Contraction?" asked Gina.

Sarah paused long enough in her breathing to stammer, "oh, yeah."

"I'll go get Scott," offered Sally.

"No," gasped Sarah. Her breathing started to return to normal and the sharp pain in her abdomen dissipated more slowly than it had come. "I'll be fine in a minute."

"You need to get to the hospital," said Sally.

"Not until they are six minutes apart," said Sarah. "I can't be in labor. I'm not due for two weeks."

"I'm going to tell him," said Gina.

"He's got to finish this game," urged Sarah. "I want him to finish."

Sally glanced at her watch. "I'm timing you. If they get to six minutes apart we tell him," she said.

Sarah nodded. "I'll be fine." She released he grip and stood up. Let's go. I don't want to miss any of this."

106

Karen had reached the clubhouse and was a bit surprised to see the expression on April and her guest's faces. "What happened to you?" asked April. She handed the paper bag to Karen.

"What?" asked Karen. Then she realized what a mess she must be. Mud on her shoes and feet, a torn blouse, her hair unkempt and frazzled. "I've just been out watching the game." She opened the bag and breathed a sigh of relief to see her sneakers from the office and a cell phone.

"Tough game," commented the man.

"Karen Blakely, this is Tim Carousel, Callaway Golf. Mr. Carousel, Karen Blakely, our top agent."

Karen held out her hand and Carousel shook it. "This Patterson guy is losing," he commented, waving back at the scoreboard. Karen noted he had a British accent, along with an ugly set of teeth.

Karen looked at the updated score. Andrew had just picked up another stroke on Hanover. He was only behind by one. "There are still six holes to go," said Karen. "He's already picked up two strokes in three holes. He'll win it. No doubt about it."

He nodded to the monitor. "He's the colorfully dressed character there?" he asked.

"Yes," said Karen.

"Well, he's got something, if not style," pointed out Carousel.

"Exactly," agreed April, sucking up as best she could. She shot Karen a glare and handed her the new cell phone.

"Any place to get a drink around here?" he asked.

"It's a forest preserve," pointed out Karen.

"Meaning..."

"They don't allow alcohol in the forest preserves, Mr. Carousel."

"You've got to be kidding. It's a bloody golf course. There has to be alcohol," he insisted with his undeniable logic.

"I'm sorry," said Karen.

"Bloody useless," muttered Carousel.

"Let's watch the next couple of holes on the monitor and then we can cut to the sixteenth green to watch the last three live. It's a madhouse out there now, but I figured a short cut to get us there before the rest of the crowds.

"Sounds like a good plan," said April and she ushered Carousel back to the clubhouse. "How about a soft drink?" she offered.

"I don't suppose they have any tea?" he asked. April looked at Karen who scrunched up her face and shoulders in the wordless expression meaning, I don't know.

"We'll see," said April.

107

Jake watched as the three went into the clubhouse. He looked back at the scoreboard. Scott's three-stroke lead was down to one. It wasn't looking good. He glanced at the map on his scorecard and looked for the break in the trees midway on the left side of the tenth fairway that would get him to the thirteenth green and the fourteenth tee. He decided to head down and pick up the action there. Waiting here was going to destroy whatever nerves he had left.

Gina was still with Scott's wife, Sarah, and the USA Sports guy's wife, Sally. The fact that she felt confident enough to leave him alone gave him the confidence to know he would make it through this day. It was nice to have something important to worry about. It seemed like Scott Hanover was going to provide that something today.

108

"Scott," shouted Ted Lange. Scott Hanover turned to see the man he had met earlier waving from the crowd.

"Mr. Lange. Hey, how about this. I guess you were right about there being a great game in everyone. Today is my day, well, except for the last couple of holes. Had a couple of bad shots there. My slice keeps wanting to come in."

"You're doing great, Scott, and call me Ted."

"Any advice?"

"Wouldn't want to get you disqualified," he said. "Not very kosher to give or receive advice during a game."

"Right," realized Scott as he remembered reading something about that in the Rules of Golf book that sat in the top drawer of his desk at work. It was casual reading whenever he needed to get his mind off of the rat race.

"Just remember what I said, play golf, don't play against Patterson." He held out his left hand to shake.

Scott looked a little confused and extended his left hand for the reverse handshake. Lange gripped it and squeezed, seeming to almost crush the bones in his hand. "Good luck, son," he added and let go.

Scott quelled a grimace and flexed his hand a few times to get blood back into the tissues.

"Come on," called Paul and Scott turned to jog after his caddy and the rest of the crowd up a little hill to the thirteenth tee.

"What did you do?" asked Joe, noting the confused expression and pain on Hanover's face.

"Adjusted his swing a little. With his left hand hurting he'll grip tighter with the right, keep the club face from opening up."

"Are you serious?" asked Joe. "That'll really work?"

"I have no idea," answered Ted honestly, "but I couldn't let him keep swinging like he was."

"I suppose, but you must have bruised him pretty good."

"He'll be fine. I'm just an old man."

"We'll see, I guess," said Joe. It might work, he thought. He followed Ted and the rest of the crowd to the next tee.

CHAPTER 18 – THIRTEENTH HOLE

109

"Just an easy par three, a hundred and eighty-five yards," said Ellie into her microphone. "Sand to the left and right but the front and back of the green are unguarded. If they use the right club they should be on the green. Unless Patterson has a great tee shot, he'll have a tough time picking up a stroke on this hole. It's actually the easiest hole on the course."

"Thanks, Ellie," said Jason. He went on to give his commentary as Andrew Patterson put his ball in the tee area and stood up, looking straight at the hole. Ellie's camera had a side shot of the tee that showed him looking to the right of the television screen.

Ellie added, "I think he has a six iron."

Jason added the detail to his observations and thousands of heads across the nation nodded in agreement with the selection of the club.

110

Andrew could par this hole with his eyes closed. If he could put his tee shot within inches of the pin adding another birdie to the growing list was not out of the question. The way Hanover had been hitting lately, he'd likely end up on the fourteenth tee. Maybe, Andrew considered, he might even capture an eagle for himself. Why should a nobody like Hanover be able to score a hole-in-one and not him?

No, he told himself. He couldn't think that way. If he tried to hard he'd mess it up. He banished the thoughts of a hole-in–one from his mind and pictured the ball, visible on the green, inches from the pin. He looked down at the ball sitting on the tee he had sunk nearly flush with the grass. He let the weight of the club, his six iron, hang in his hands for a moment. With his robot-like precision he drew the club back and swung at the ball.

It rose gracefully and with precision headed straight for the pin. The applause started before the ball even landed and with a thunk audible from one hundred and eighty-five yards away, it stuck on the green, six inches from the hole.

"Way to go, fancy pants," yelled a familiar voice from behind him. He ignored the comment and basked in the moment. He imagined the television picture showing him frozen with his club hanging over his left shoulder, in a split screen with the ball sitting inches from the hole. He was ready. The Pro-Am was in the proverbial bag.

He lowered his club, dug out his tee and walked off the back of the tee to where Eric was standing. The boy's mouth was agape at the splendor of the shot as he absently took the club from Andrew.

111

Karen smiled as the shot was replayed on the television screens. She finished tying her shoes. She glanced at the ones she had been wearing and tossed them into a nearby garbage can. She wouldn't be sad to see them go.

Carousel seemed impressed by Andrew's tee shot on thirteen and asked, "What ball is he playing?"

"Why, Callaway, of course," she answered, relieved that Patterson really was using Callaway Tours.

"This boy may prove to be of interest after all. I'd still like to see him in the lead," he commented.

"He may be after this hole, definitely by the next one," April assured him. She leaned back and looked at Karen, raising her eyebrows, silently asking if that were possible. Karen nodded almost imperceptibly and April smiled and looked back at the screen. "Two more holes," she said.

"Excellent," said Carousel. "Where is that tea?"

112

Jake stood with other onlookers in the clearing behind the thirteenth green. From his vantage point it looked like Patterson's ball was going to hit near where he stood, but it seemed to lose speed rapidly and acted as though a magnet in the hole was pulling it down. The shot was sure to put a little pressure on Scott. Pressure Scott didn't need now that his lead was only one stroke. Even though Jake didn't have a golf club in his hand he was feeling the pressure too. He really had thought that if Scott could win this he could convince him and his wife to parley the experience into a decent payday.

Hang in there, the thought. He tried to push the assurance across the neatly mowed grass to where Scott now stood on the tee. You can do it.

113

Scott let out a breath that was almost a growl. Patterson wasn't making this easy. He looked around until he spotted Sarah and the other women. He waved and she waved back. She looked a little uncomfortable, but so would he if he was walking around over eight months pregnant. But he was so glad she was there.

He shook out his left hand a few more times, the sides of his palm still ached from Lange's gorilla grip. He hadn't thought the old man had it in him. What a goofy thing to do to a guy who was having a little trouble with his swing.

He set up his ball and laid his six iron on the grass slightly behind it. He grasped the grip with his left hand then his right laying his right pinky over the left forefinger a little lower on the shaft. God, his left hand hurt, was all he could think of. He gripped a little tighter with his right hand then took a practice swing. He surprised even himself with the swing. It felt perfect. He had been doing something wrong the last couple of holes but now he was back to the swing he had on the driving range.

He felt his brain settling into the balanced state he had imagined earlier, like two pools of liquid equally balanced in the two halves of his skull. He took a second practice swing, not letting himself think about things, but letting his body settle into the feel of the swing; the weight of the club, the rustle of his pants legs, the speed of his body. The club whooshed over the grass in a path that would take the ball straight to the pin.

He sighed and chuckled to himself. Lange had done the hand squeeze on purpose. Scott had not been playing golf. He had been swinging a club and swinging it poorly. He'd been feeling the pressure and started over-analyzing things, slipping into old bad habits. He'd been letting Patterson get to him. He'd been playing against the man when what Patterson did didn't matter. It was what Scott did that mattered. He knew he had the great shots in him. He'd seen a few every time he went out. Most of the time, they came when he least expected it. Today, he was starting to expect it all the time and was actually beginning to believe he was a better golfer than he was. Sure he had the best score of his life, but next week, or next year, or five years from now, when he picked up his clubs again, he would quite likely have the worst game of his life.

The pain in his hand was almost gone, but the lesson wasn't. Technically, this was an easy shot. It was an easy hole. Even on a bad day he should do well. He stepped up to the ball. Almost with surprise, his body started the back swing. He let it take over and for the split second the club hovered above his head, everything was perfect. The club arced down and the ball sailed out over the grass. It headed straight for the pin.

"It's in the hole," shouted someone in the crowd.

It'll be short, thought Scott, but not much. The ball didn't stick like Patterson's, but bounced forward and landed a yard shy of the hole.

"Way to go, Hanover," said Paul. His hand was on Scott's right shoulder and Scott realized he was still standing in his after swing pose, his club hanging over his left shoulder. "I bet Patterson thought he was getting another stroke on you this hole."

"He still may, that's no gimme."

"It's a piece of cake, piece of pie. Lemon meringue. With whipped cream."

"Make it cheesecake, strawberries on top," laughed Scott.

"Definitely doable" said Paul.

"Definitely not a gimme," countered Scott.

"Ah, come on, it's done. It's in the hole. The fact you can still see it is just a technicality."

"With your optimism, I'm surprised it just doesn't roll in right now."

"Give it a minute," said Paul. They laughed and Paul took the club, sliding it into the bag over his shoulder and the two walked down the slight hill towards the green. Scott found Sarah and waved. She waved back then held her hands a yard apart. She was really getting into this. Cool, thought Scott.

Andrew and Eric followed. Andrew was shaking his head almost imperceptibly with disbelief. Where did that come from? Hanover almost looked like he knew what he was doing.

114

Kenny Chase had been on the street nearly half an hour and had traveled about a mile before he saw what he was looking for. The blue signs with the white outlines of a cat and dog, sitting side by side, sat next to the large white letters proclaiming, "Oak Forest Animal Clinic." They'll have one, he thought.

He parked the red Blazer with the Northern Illinois Amateur Golf Association logo decal on the side of the door in front of the clinic. The little sign in the window indicated they were open and through the large plate glass windows that looked into the waiting room, he noted two dogs on leashes, and one woman trying to calm what he presumed was a cat in a pet carrier. He bustled through the door and walked up to the woman sitting behind the desk.

"Do you have an x-ray machine?" he asked.

She stared past him, confused at his lack of pet. "Is the animal in the car?" she asked with concern. Perhaps the pet was too injured to come in on its own power."

"Oh, no, miss. I don't have a pet." He thought a moment then added, "It is sort of animal related in a way."

She looked confused. "We have an x-ray machine. What do you need?"

"A favor," he said and pulled a white ball out of his pocket and placed it on the counter, yellow duck logo up. "I need an x-ray of this ball."

The woman looked even more confused and squinted at Kenny, concerned about his sanity. "We don't do that." Her answer was slow with some hesitation between the words. She had seen a lot of strange requests over the years, but this was the first golf ball x-ray she had been inquired about.

"It's very important. I'll pay whatever the normal charge is," he added.

"Connie, what's going on?" asked a woman in a white lab coat. She had walked up to the counter and laid a manila folder with colored tabs along the edge in front of the receptionist.

"The man here wants his pet golf ball x-rayed."

"Did it swallow a tee?" asked the doctor. She laughed at her joke and Connie laughed too.

"It's not my pet. I need an x-ray of this ball. I'll pay double your normal fee," said Kenny, hoping that Bateman would reimburse him the expense.

"What is this for?" asked the veterinarian. Her name tag identified her as Dr. Susan Galway.

"We need to make sure the ball is legal. It's for a tournament. It's on TV," he added.

"He's right," drawled one of the men waiting with his dog in the plastic chairs along the window. "Saw a bit of it before I had to bring Kaiser here in for his blood test. Guy hit a hole-in-one, he did."

"That's right," said Kenny. "Please, it'll take a few minutes and I'll be out of here."

"I don't mind waiting," replied Kaiser's owner. "Never seen an x-ray of a golf ball before."

"Teddy," yelled Dr. Galway to the back, "do you have time for an x-ray?"

A short, bespectacled man with a crew cut and animal print scrubs appeared. "Of what?"

Susan Galway picked up the ball, noticing the yellow duck printed on the side for the first time. "A duck," she answered.

Teddy's forehead wrinkled in confusion as she placed the ball in his palm. His eyes widened and the look on Dr. Galways's face told him she was serious. "I'll see what I can do," he answered.

115

"How's it going?" asked Sally.

238

"How's what going?" asked Sarah in return.

"The contractions."

"Oh, that. Nothing yet. I think it was just a one-time thing with that last one. Probably exerting myself a little too much."

"It has been over ten minutes," pointed out Gina.

"Let's go sit at that bench," said Sally. To the right of the green and near the sign labeling the next hole as the fourteenth was a wooden bench. A few people stood on it now, trying to get a look at the thirteenth green, but not wanting to give up their prime viewing spot for the tee shots on fourteen.

"After Scott putts," promised Sarah.

"Okay," agreed Sally, "but if another one comes, we head right there."

"I'll be right behind you," said Sarah.

116

Andrew marked his ball with the golden dollar and picked it up. He walked to the back of the green, paying no attention to Scott. Scott and Paul examined the green and both decided it was a straight shot. "Good luck, buddy," offered Paul.

"Thanks," said Scott. He lined up his feet and set the speed of his putt with three practice swings. He stepped up and pulled back the club when a bee landed on the ball. He stopped and stood up. He waited a minute but the bee remained stubbornly on the ball.

"Is there a problem?" asked the red-jacketed official who had given Scott a hard time on the front nine.

"There's a bee on my ball," said Scott loud enough for the crowd to hear. A chuckle bounced through the onlookers.

"Well, shoe it off and play."

"I don't want to get stung," said Scott. He looked back at the ball and watched. The bee seemed to be extremely interested in the yellow duck on the ball. "I think he thinks it's a flower." Another chuckle.

Then Henderson rolled his eyes back, stomped to where Scott's ball sat, bent over and waved his hand over the ball.

This apparently was the wrong thing to do. The bee took off but started to buzz at the logo on the man's jacket. He stumbled backwards, brushing at the insect but it persisted in hovering by his chest. He almost fell as he continued to walk backwards. He turned and ran into the crowd. Scott couldn't see if the bee was still following him but the crowd around the hole was now in stitches, Scott with them. He was almost crying with sight of the large, sweaty man battling the tiny bee when suddenly there was a yelp from deep inside the crowd.

"I guess he found a better flower," observed Scott to the delight of the crowd. With a big grin on his face he set up his shot again. Not trusting his memory, he set his putting speed with a few practice swings and then stepped up to the ball. The crowd noise died off quickly as they sensed his need for concentration.

He eyed the path he wanted the ball to take. Straight in, he told himself. He drew the club back and tapped the ball forward. It rolled toward the hole, inching to the right side, caught the rim, rolled nearly three hundred and sixty degrees around the opening, hesitated and dropped in.

The onlookers exploded into appreciate applause. "Show off," shouted one man.

"Cheesecake," said Paul from behind him. "Knew it was in the whole time."

"At least one of us did," said Scott.

"Hey buddy, that's what you hired me for."

"Hey, I'll never doubt you again," promised Scott

"Ah, wait until next hole," answered Paul.

117

This was ridiculous, thought Andrew, as he walked up to the hole. He placed his ball in front of the coin then picked the golden dollar up by its edges. As he stood up the coin twisted in his fingers and fell on the ball causing it to roll an inch to the left. Andrew froze in horror. What had he done? The ball had moved. Was that a penalty? He couldn't remember the rule. Why did he have to use such a huge, heavy coin? A little dime would have just bounced off.

He stood up, panicked. The eyes of the onlookers indicated he was not the only one who had seen the unintended motion of the ball. A red-jacketed official approached. It was a different one than had shooed the bee off Hanover's ball. If only it had been as simple as a bee on his ball, thought Andrew. What had he done?

The official had a tiny book in his hands and his was flipping pages one by one as he came up to Andrew. "Just need to be sure," he said as he stopped a foot away from the ball and incriminating coin lying on the green. He continued flipping pages.

118

Alf Redding had zoomed in on Patterson's face. Jason pushed the button to talk to Freddy. "What's the rule, Freddy?"

"I'm checking."

"Well let me know before the official announces it."

"I think it's no penalty," said Freddy.

"You think?"

"I'm pretty sure."

"I know I don't know this stuff, Freddy, but I don't want to sound like I don't know it."

"It could go either way," answered Freddy.

"What do you mean?"

"Here's the rule, see what you make."

Jason sighed and turned his mike live again, as he listened to Freddy relay the details to him. He in turn relayed them to the audience. "It's basically the official on the scene's call," he concluded. The red-jacketed man stopped his page flipping and he face lit up.

119

"Here it is." He announced. He read from the book, loud enough for the closest people to hear.

"'If a ball or ball-marker is accidentally moved in the process of lifting the ball or marking its position, the ball or ball-marker shall be replaced. There is no penalty provided the movement of the ball or the ball-marker is directly attributable to the specific act of marking the position of or lifting the ball.'

"I consider removing the ball marker part of the act of marking the ball. There will be no penalty," he announced.

A few boos issued from the crowd but Andrew closed his eyes in relief and let out the breath he found himself holding. He moved the ball to its original position, picked up the coin, palming it in his fist then pocketing it. He stepped into position. The official slipped his rulebook into his jacket pocket and stepped back. Andrew tapped in the putt.

The crowd applauded but not with great enthusiasm. The call, realized Andrew, was slightly controversial. If he had dropped the coin while starting to mark the ball there would be no question, but the call was made and he wasn't going to argue it. He pulled his ball out of the hole. Eric replaced the flag and took the gold handled putter, wiping the head before replacing it in its sleeve.

"It should have been a penalty stroke," whispered Paul.

"It could go either way," disagreed Scott.

"You were robbed."

"I can afford it," he answered.

"That bee was hilarious," Paul added, changing the subject.

"I thought that guy was going to land on his butt," said Scott. "Where do you think he stung him?"

"One can only hope."

120

Several red-jacketed men and women opened a corridor through the crowd. Bateman and Frisk led the party through in their golf cart and the golfers followed. There was no sign of the bee attack victim as Scott scanned the faces. There was no sign of Sarah either. She must have moved to the next fairway, he concluded.

121

"Oh, boy," gasped Sarah.

Sally and Gina took their positions and helped Sarah walk toward the bench. She tapped the leg of one of the men standing on it.

"Hey," he said, "I was here first, find some..." He looked down at Sally and his eyes caught the grimace on Sarah's face and bulge in her stomach. He elbowed the guy next to him. "Get off the bench, Eddie."

"What," said Eddie, trying to get a view of the golfers.

"Lady needs to sit down." He hopped off and dragged Eddie with him.

"Oh, yeah, be our guest," insisted Eddie once he had taken in the situation.

"Thank you," said Gina. She and Sally lowered Sarah to the seat and sat next to her. "Sixteen minutes," said Gina as Sarah puffed though the contraction.

"We're getting you out of here," concluded Sally.

Sarah's breathing began to return to normal. "Not as bad that time," she gasped.

"You're sweating like a pig," observed Sally.

"Even if this is real labor, not a false labor like my sister thought, it could be hours before anything significant starts to happen. My water hasn't even broken yet."

"I'm with Sally," said Gina.

"Well, I say I can make it," insisted Sarah. "I just need to rest a little. Sit down and take some pressure off everything and I'll be okay."

Sally gave her a questioning stare.

"I'm still timing them," said Gina.

Sarah nodded and took a few deep, cleansing breaths. "It'll be fine," she insisted. "My sister was in labor twenty-two hours with her first kid. My mom was twenty-eight. I have a genetically long labor programmed into me. I'm not going to drop a kid on the eighteenth tee," she joked. "I'll wait until Scott gets on the green." The others laughed with her.

122

"Looks like he found his game again," commented Joe Caulkin.

"He still has five holes to play," Ted reminded him.

"Isn't it just as likely Patterson will mess up?"

Ted thought a moment, "Yeah, I suppose you're right. But something doesn't feel right."

"What do you mean?"

"Something has to happen to stop Patterson."

"Something like what?"

"You tell me, you know more about the man than I do," said Ted.

"He never makes a mistake," said Joe.

"He did just now," Ted reminded him.

"What? The coin? That was an accident."

"Fortunately it was one that didn't cost him anything. But if things go just right, something may happen that he has no direct control over. His caution will end up doing him in," explained Ted.

"That would be nice," said Joe.

A new red-jacketed official had taken over the officiating on the tee. "Mr. Patterson is up," he announced. "Quiet on the tee."

"Here we go," said Ted.

CHAPTER 19 – FOURTEENTH HOLE

123

Another long par five awaited Andrew Patterson. This one was uphill. There was some water that came into play on the second shot, but this would be an easy par. There was plenty of room for Hanover to make a mistake and Andrew was beginning to wonder how long he would have to wait before he would take the lead. If he could birdie this one, he'd definitely at least tie the lucky jerk. Still, there were five holes to play. Andrew was playing better than he expected. If he could keep it up, he'd certainly have played his personal best. But beating his own score wasn't good enough. He needed to win. Waiting a year for his next chance was unacceptable with victory so close. Hanover had been ranked last of all the players and here he was, head to head with number one – and winning. Inconceivable.

Eric handed Andrew his driver and then stepped back behind the tee. Andrew set up his ball and eyed a spot in the middle of the fairway. No need to hold back but no need to go wild either. He set up and blasted the ball straight out. Both sides of the fairway were lined with people and they started applauding before the ball's first bounce on the fairway. It rolled up near the two hundred and fifty yard marker. Not bad for an uphill shot, thought Andrew. His drive had gone three hundred yards straight down the middle. Not bad at all.

He pulled up his tee and stepped back, handing the club to Eric. Hanover seemed in a good mood as he stepped up to the tee. He seemed amazed by the sea of people to each side. "I hope I don't hit anyone," he said to the amusement of those close by. He set up his ball and lined up his shot.

In reality, Scott hadn't been joking with his last comment. He wondered how the pros made the people disappear in their minds. He remembered one guy who got hit by one of Tiger Woods' rare errant shots. The fan was okay and even ended up with an autographed hat from the golfer. Scott didn't think anyone here would be happy with a signed cap.

He hoped for a par here. It was a little longer than the first hole he had played and uphill instead of down hill. He had always liked par fives. If you could have two so-so shots as long as you had one good one to get on the green. Even if you got on with four shots, a good putt could always save par. He remembered a par five he had played several years ago where his third shot had taken him four or five yards to the right of the green on the down slope of a hill. He then proceeded to chip the ball up over the hill and drained it right into the hole for a birdie.

Yep, he liked par fives. He stared at Patterson's drive in the middle of the fairway. The guy was consistent. And good. Scott realized that Patterson had a pretty good chance of beating him when all was said and done, but he didn't have to make it easy for him. One thing Patterson couldn't do, even if he ended with a lower score, was take away this day; Scott's hole-in-one, his never-ending series of miraculous shots, the bee on the last hole, his wife cheering him on.

He performed his pre-teeshot ritual complete with two practice swings then stepped up to the ball. The crowd observed a considerate silence.

Carl Bateman watched as Hanover started his back swing. Bateman squirmed in his seat, feeling a sudden sense of discomfort. As he did his foot hit the gas pedal of the cart. The gas engine throttled to life and the tan vehicle jumped forward a few feet before Carl could get his foot back on the brake. The distraction was too late for Hanover to change his swing.

Scott heard the noise but his body wanted to swing and he couldn't stop. The club head glanced over the top the ball, knocked it off the tee and sent it rolling five yards closer to the hole. He stared at the ball then slowly raised his head, his eyes finding the offending golf cart among the onlookers on the right side of the fairway near the tee.

People near Bateman's cart started backing up. Coming towards them was a very angry man with a golf club in one hand. Paul dropped Scott's bag with a clatter of clubs and caught up to Scott, grabbing him by the shoulders. Scott tried to shrug him off then stopped. Even from fifteen yards away he see the fright in Carl Bateman's eyes. The man was terrified and his jaw was working to either spew out an apology or a denial that it was his fault.

"Not worth it," muttered Paul.

"Let him hit it again," shouted a voice from the crowd. It was joined by a groundswell of support for the do-over. Scott turned around and started walking back. Andrew Patterson was talking to the official at the tee. Scott looked into the red-jacketed man's face. The official seemed sympathetic but the shaking of head confirmed to Scott that the shot would stand. Scott knew it would but God, it sure sucked.

"Can't let distractions get to you. Should have stopped that swing," said Patterson. Paul stepped quickly in front of Scott and stared into the other golfer's eyes. He spoke but directed his comments to the official while retaining his gaze on Patterson. "Isn't there a penalty for commenting on the other golfer's swing?" he asked.

Patterson's expression turned to terror and he turned to the official. "There is, but..." he considered, "Mr. Patterson's comment doesn't qualify."

Paul nodded in silent acceptance but he was confident that Patterson had gotten the message. You don't jump on another player's misfortune. Paul handed Scott his three wood and they walked up to his ball. Boos started to issue from the crowd, most directly at Carl Bateman, but some went Andrew's way.

124

Jason Bernard was stunned in his booth. He talked privately with Freddy. "Can't he take the shot over if someone distracts him like that?"

"No way. It's up to the golfer to stop his swing if something prevents him from keeping his concentration."

"So, what? He hits from where it landed?"

"That's it."

"I thought he was going to wrap that club around that idiot in the cart's neck."

"Me too."

"I got to get back on," said Jason. He switched over to the live feed. "That just goes to show how much concentration is required to compete in this game at this level. The man in the golf cart, Carl Bateman, must feel awful at this time. And Andrew Patterson can't be feeling that great either. If he does win by only one stroke, he's got to wonder if he came about that stroke fairly."

Jason continued, "Hanover is setting up for his second shot. He has five hundred and forty five yards left."

125

"That jerk," whispered Sarah.

"Calm down, it's done," whispered Sally back.

"He should get to do it over."

"Then golfers would be claiming all sorts of things distracted them," added Gina.

"But this was so obvious," complained Sarah.

"Just relax," warned Sally, "you don't want to speed things along, if you know what I mean."

"I will. I will," she promised. She took some deep breaths but shook her head slowly. It just wasn't fair.

126

"Foot slip?" asked Harold Frisk.

"What," answered Bateman, distracted from his current state of panic.

"I'd be up there apologizing after he takes this next swing."

"What? No. Best to leave it be."

"Perhaps, for you, but this is on television, eight million homes and growing by the minute. You could end up being the shlub of the year or a decent guy who made a mistake."

"He should have stopped his swing. No penalty for that."

"He's just an amateur. He doesn't have the discipline that Tiger Woods has. Once he starts, he's got to go. Apologize, you're making the tournament look bad."

"He wants to hurt me."

"He'll want to hurt you less after you prove to him it was an accident and not intentional."

"Alright, alright. I'll apologize. After he swings I'll drive over there."

"Bateman," said Frisk with the tone one would save for a dog that just peed on the carpet.

"Yes," whined Carl.

"Walk over there."

"Right," muttered Carl.

127

The silence that befell the crowd as Scott set up for his second shot was unnaturally quiet. There weren't even any stray coughs or sneezes. It's only one stroke, Scott told himself. You're on in four and a one putt for par.

He turned his head to look down the fairway. He could see Patterson's well-hit drive, teasing him from the middle of the fairway. Patterson could be on in two with a decent fairway shot. Scott had thought about using his driver off the grass to try and get some extra yardage but he knew he wasn't used to that sort of lie with the club and could quite easily top the ball again. He wouldn't get as many yards with the three wood, but in the end, he'd still get there.

He set up his club and started to take a practice swing when the quiet just got to him. He stopped. Looked back at the tee and nodded his head lightly. "Well, at least I can say one thing about that shot," he said loudly so even those in the back could hear, "it's closer to the hole."

The joke broke the tension like a two hundred pound kid doing a cannon ball into a swimming hole. The crowd laughed and Scott joined in. Carl Bateman remained silent but tried to smile, Scott noticed. After a moment, the crowd settled down into its normal murmurs and rustles. "That's better," said Scott. "It was just a little too quiet there for a minute." Another chuckle and he settled back to hit the ball. He skipped his practice swings, set his club and feet and swung at the patch of turf where the ball lay. It soared out. He was aimed a little to the right so that when the ball bounced and rolled it ended up two yards from the feet of the people two hundred and thirty yards down the fairway but it was a good shot. Three hundred and fifteen yards to go.

The applause was genuine and the people seemed grateful that he had been able to salvage a decent second shot.

"Mr. Hanover," said a quivery voice.

Scott turned to see Carl Bateman standing in front of him. He looked at the man and slowly lowered his golf club.

"I truly am sorry about what happened there. My foot slipped and knocked the accelerator. I was clumsy and feel awful about costing you a stroke."

Scott took in the man's words and measured their sincerity. He put himself in Bateman's place and tried to imagine how the man felt.

"Please let me know if there is anything I or the tournament can do for you. I wish I could make it up to you, but I don't think that's possible."

"No, Mr. Bateman, it isn't," answered Scott. He took the man's outstretched hand and shook it. "But I do accept your apology and I do realize that distractions are part of the game. I apologize for approaching your cart in less than a friendly manner. It was poor sportsmanship on my part."

Carl seemed taken aback by Scott's apology. He decided to leave the exchange at that. As he turned to leave he noted the camerawoman behind the tee who had been filming the exchange and then continued back to his cart.

"Very nice," commented Frisk. "Saw the whole thing on TV. Now get this thing down the fairway."

128

"Well that was a spot of bad luck," said Tim Carousel as he sipped his tea from a Styrofoam cup. He raised his eyebrows in surprise at the taste, pleasantly surprised at the quality.

"That should give Patterson at least a tie for the lead," added Karen.

"Yes, but he seemed rather a poor sport about the whole thing, even thought it wasn't his fault."

"He was stunned," suggested April. "Could have been him it happened to," she added.

"I suppose so," said Carousel. "I'm sure after another couple of holes the whole thing will be quite forgotten."

"Exactly," said Karen.

Carousel looked at his tea in one hand and the emptiness of his other and realized what was missing. "Any chance for a biscuit?"

129

Scott was still up as he was still furthest from the hole. Paul handed him the five wood this time. "Just knock it two hundred yards closer," he advised.

"No problem," said Scott. As he approached the ball he glanced at the people standing just a couple of yards away and stopped. His eyes widened and he walked up to two of the men. "Jerry, Pete. How'd you guys do?"

Pete raised his hand. "Last."

Jerry lifted his, "second to last."

"Well, I'm not done yet," said Scott. They all laughed.

"Don't let that fancy pants beat you," said Jerry.

"Yeah, if he wins, everybody's going to start dressing like him and I won't be able to stomach going to the golf course any more."

"Well, listen, catch up with me afterward, I'll buy you guys a drink."

"You're on," said Pete. "It's the least you can do. We're rooting for you."

"Thanks." He stepped back and eyed his ball and picked out the direction he wanted to aim. He took a couple of practice swings this time then stepped up to the ball. The back swing felt great and the ball sailed up off the grass. It ended up a little more left than he planned and he cringed as the line of onlookers flowed back from the edge of the fairway as his ball rolled a yard or so into the rough. He was maybe a hundred and twenty yards from the hole now.

The rough wouldn't be too bad. Prior to today he had had a lot of experience with the rough.

"Nice shot," said Paul. "You're on in four, buddy."

"Hopefully." Paul eyed him with misapprehension then Scott remembered his promise. "Right, on in four," he echoed. He handed the club to Paul and they walked up to near where Andrew would hit his second shot.

Andrew knew he was quite capable of putting the ball on the green from two hundred and fifty yards out, half the time. From two hundred yards out, that number became ninety-five percent of the time. With Hanover's topped shot on the tee, he was willing to go for it today. He'd lose some accuracy, but the thought of a birdie was exciting.

He handed the four iron that Eric had produced according to Andrew's club list back to the caddy and said, "two iron."

Eric checked the bag and sure enough, there was a two iron. He hadn't seen it before and quickly counted the clubs again to make sure Patterson hadn't played this far with an illegal club count. He had counted when they started and was sure they hadn't. Most golfers had a standard set of three woods, eight irons, sand wedge, putter and perhaps a loft wedge or maybe a seven wood. Eric looked in Patterson's bag and realized he wasn't carrying a sand wedge. He was confident if not cocky, thought Eric.

Patterson twirled the club head in front of his face for a moment. He rarely used the two iron and almost didn't put it in the bag this morning. It wasn't on his club list but he had room for one more and had the foresight to select this one. The two iron had its uses and this was one. He took a couple of easy swing with the club, grazing the top of the grass, getting used to the shaft length and weight compared to his other irons. With silence besetting the crowd, he stepped up to hit his ball. The sound it made was quite different than that of wood or even another iron. The virtual flatness of the face assured no spin and the ball rocketed low over the fairway, landing about one hundred yards from the hole but bouncing with such speed that it continued to roll until it was just short of the fringe on the green.

That, he thought, was good enough to get him a birdie.

Scott let out the breath he was holding. "That was a grass burner."

"Must have been a two iron," said Paul, "I used to have one."

"Oh yeah, what happened to it."

"You know that water hazard on twelve at Highland woods?"

"Yeah," said Scott. Then he realized what Paul was saying. "Oh."

"Yeah, oh," copied Paul.

The two continued their walk down the fairway.

"It is a great day to be golfing, Scott," said Paul.

Scott sniffed the air and stretched his neck to feel the breeze. "It's a really good day, Paul."

130

"Hanover is going down now," commented Lucy Penndel to herself. Lewis Filtry heard the comment.

"It only takes one really bad shot to ruin a players momentum," he added.

"The guys not playing on momentum, it's all dumb luck," added Lucy.

"Well if he loses, that ball probably won't be worth the trouble those guys went to get it."

Lucy turned and looked at the cameraman like he had just landed from another planet. "What are you talking about Filtry?"

"On eight. Some guys in scuba equipment went after Hanover's water ball. I think they found it. They certainly seemed happy."

"Guys with scuba equipment?"

"Yeah. I told Ellie Burke about it. Oh, and that woman who I bumped into at the eleventh tee. She seemed interested."

"You mean Patterson's agent?"

"Is that who she is?"

"She came up to me an insisted I get more one-on-one interviews with the guy."

"Well it was a pretty weird thing seeing them go to all that trouble for a ball. That water must be freezing."

"You think they were fans?" asked Lucy.

"Well, they could have been with the tournament, they had a golf cart and trailer," added Lewis.

Lucy digested this information. Something was going on. A fan wouldn't go through the trouble of getting scuba equipment, they'd just jump in the water, freezing or not. It must have been the tournament officials that wanted it, but why? She could think of only one reason that made sense. They suspected Hanover was using spiked balls.

Holy cow, if he was, this would blow this tournament wide open and turn Scott Hanover into another Eric Gunther. The best part would be if Lucy could break the story. Unfortunately, stuck here she was not in a position to track down who the scuba divers were and what they had found. She pulled out her cell phone and dialed.

"Keith?" she asked when the other line was answered.

"Lucy. Honey, I'm sorry, Frisk overruled me, the old windbag," answered Keith Kelly.

"Forget about that, I may have something else here."

"What?"

"The tournament officials may believe Hanover is using juiced up balls. It appears as if they've quietly retrieved one he hit into a water hazard earlier. I think they're having it analyzed."

"You think he's a cheat?"

"How else could he be doing so well?" asked Lucy.

"It makes sense," agreed Keith.

"I can't get away to check it out."

"It's okay, I'm here are the clubhouse. I'll ask some questions."

"Great," said Lucy. "Don't tell Jason."

"Mum's the word."

131

Kenny Chase carried the small white envelope containing the CD out with him to his Blazer. Step one was done. The technician had even taken the x-rays at several exposures. Kenny had looked at them on the computer screen of their digital system. It appeared to be a normal ball but to be sure he needed to get inside. Fortunately he only had do go west one stoplight before he found what he needed.

He pulled into the Dominick's grocery store lot. The store was sure to have a decent meat department, and if he was lucky, a butcher on the premises. The duck logo ball was in his pants pocket. His red jacket drew a few looks but he barreled through the aisles to get to the back of the store. He quickly found the open freezer case near the tank of live lobsters. A man wearing a blood-stained apron over white work clothes similarly stained was sliding a package of butterfly pork chops into the display area.

"Can I help you?" he asked. "Pork chops are excellent today."

"I have an unusual request," started Kenny.

"I've been doing this for twenty-two years," said the butcher, "I've pretty much seen it all. I've even had people walk out of here with a two liter bottle of blood."

Kenny pulled the golf ball from his pocket and asked, "Can you cut this in half for me?"

The butcher raised his eyebrows. "I take it back." He reached over and took the golf ball. "I'd ask you why but I really don't want to know." He looked at the lack of other customers at the counter and smiled, "I'll see what I can do."

The butcher pushed through the swinging door separating the meat preparation area form the display cases. Kenny could see him holding up the ball and discussing the problem with another butcher. Kenny assumed they would just band saw the ball in half. All butchers used the powerful saws to cut through frozen slabs of meat. Oddly, though, the second man pulled a large cleaver from a hook on the wall and hefted in his hands a few times. He placed the ball on a butcher-block table in the center of a piece of meat, which kept it from rolling off the table.

With all the drama of a circus performer, he waved the knife slowly in the air above the ball, eyeing the target with care and suddenly raised it high above his head and slammed the knife onto the ball. Kenny had expected the blade to hit the ball off center, sending it flying to one direction and the knife slipping to the other, perhaps hurting one of the men. By some miracle, the cleaver had found the exact center of the ball and the two halves were spread neatly on the top of the meat.

The first butcher gathered them up, rinsed them in a sink then dried them on his blood-stained apron as he walked back out to the front. He placed the two pieces on a small sheet of butcher paper, wrapped them up and taped it closed. He then handed the package to Kenny.

Kenny took the package, stunned at the display he had just witnessed. "How much?" he murmured.

"No charge," chuckled the butcher. Frankie loves a challenge and chance to show off.

"Thanks. Are you sure you don't want to know what it's for?"

The man shook his head, smiled and waved goodbye as he disappeared in to the back again. Kenny placed the small package in his pants and headed out of the store. He was tempted to open the package right now but decided to look at the ball more closely when he got back. He'd already taken some basic measurements. The orb was 1 11/16" in diameter. Its weight was 1.6 ounces on the scale at the veterinary clinic they reserved for weighing tiny animals. Kenny had seen many doped balls in the past. He knew what to look for and part of him hoped that Hanover was clean.

Kenny wondered if it even mattered now. For all he knew, Patterson was in the lead and Hanover had descended down the rankings out of contention. He debated calling in, but figured he'd find out how things were going when he got back. He hopped back into the Blazer and pulled out onto 159th street. He roared along the left turn lane passing the stopped cars to their irritated honks. The state cop who waved him down saw the NIAGA logo on the side and nodded Kenny through after checking in on his radio. Kenny again drove in the left lane. The police were slowly untangling the traffic mess, having cars turn around and head back out along Central Ave. They halted this process to let Kenny get back into the golf course parking lot.

After he pulled in he noted the place seemed dead quiet. The large mass of people by the clubhouse were silently watching the event play out on the television monitors scattered around. Even more strange was the helicopter parked on the driving range.

Kenny thought it was certainly turning out to be a day he would always remember.

132

Scott took his pitching wedge from Paul and used it to draw a line from the flagstick to his ball, and then set his feet parallel to that line in his usual routine. A few shouts of encouragement greeted him from the crowd. He looked at the people and saw Sarah standing about fifteen yards away, smiling and absently rubbing her bulging stomach in smooth circles. Baby must be kicking, he thought. The other two women flanked her. Both had expressions far too serious for the event.

He looked at the ball and took a moment to pray for a straight shot. On the few occasions he had skipped Sunday services to play golf with friends from out of town Scott had justified his playing hooky by pointing out to Sarah that he usually ended up praying much more on the golf course than he ever did in church. And what better place to worship God than in the setting of nature – carved into eighteen well-designed and manicured holes!

He took his two practice swings, confident the rhythm was right and stepped close to the ball. The crowd could have been singing the Halleluiah chorus and he wouldn't have been phased right then. He swung at the ball and it rose into the air as planned and landed just a few inches to the right of the pin, but unfortunately it kept rolling back until it was almost touching the back fringe of the green. No amazing back spin this time.

"Nice and straight," commented Paul.

"Just a little too much Wheaties this morning," added Scott.

"But you're on in four. You can sink that putt, buddy."

"You bet," agreed Scott and they walked up the course to the green. The crowd flowed in behind them. Despite the demands for the limited number of good viewing spots to watch the proceedings, Scott noticed that Carl Bateman and his passenger always had a place reserved as they moved to the next shot, and the red-jacketed woman who escorted Sarah and her new friends, made sure they always could see what was happening. He hadn't seen Jake Fischer for a while, but Ellie was there at almost every shot, usually inconspicuous, capturing the event for the television audience and for posterity.

Patterson's ball was slightly further from the hole than Scott's and he stopped behind it, eyeing the green, nodding in confirmation at times as he judged the path of his putt.

"Think he'll eagle?" asked Scott.

"No," answered Paul. Despite his skill, he's too conservative. He's too afraid to leave the ball short.

"I've noticed that."

Paul left unsaid the fact that even if Patterson birdied and Scott parred the two would be tied. If Scott bogeyed, Patterson would hold a one-stroke lead, all because of an idiot with a heavy foot.

Scott walked around to the back of the green and marked his ball and checked it over for any damage. He cleaned off a bit of mud and slipped it into his pocket and waited for Patterson to putt.

Andrew stood with his gold-platted, jade-headed putter ready to strike the ball. He refused to think the ball would go in. He wanted to be near the hole and get his birdie. His two iron gamble had paid off and now he wanted a safe shot to completely eliminated Hanover's lead and hopefully grab it for himself. He struck the putt and the ball rolled unerringly for the hole, and then broke a little to the left before stopping ten inches away.

The crowd commented with a collective awe and then applause. Andrew, smiling contently, walked over to mark his own ball while Scott went to take his first putt.

Scott and Paul eyed the green and decided to play it a little to the left. Scott set his stoke with three practice swings and stepped up to ball. How could Patterson just walk up and hit it? The guy must practice putting in his bedroom for an hour every night before he went to bed. He drew the putter back and hit the ball. It rolled a little to the left then broke back toward the hole and stopped about five inches short. Scott slumped in place and the crowd applauded his effort nonetheless.

"Two strokes," he muttered.

"You'll get them back," said Paul.

Scott chuckled. "He'll have to make a mistake at some point and I don't think he will."

"He can't control everything," added Paul.

"Maybe," said Scott. He looked at Patterson who nodded for Scott to finish the hole. Scott tapped in his ball and held it up to the cheers of the crowd. Andrew shook his head. The guy bogies and still the crowd thinks he's great. Andrew placed his ball in front of his coin, slid the golden dollar out and palmed it straight to his pocket. He smiled as his hit the ball with an almost nonchalant air. It rolled straight into the middle of the hole with no doubt as to him scoring the birdie. The crowd cheered him as well, perhaps with slightly more vigor than they had for Hanover. After all, Andrew was the better golfer.

133

"What a setback for Hanover," announced Jason Bernard. "After thirteen holes of nothing over par, he turns in his first bogey of the day, and all because of an unfortunate distraction from the crowd. He's got to be disappointed with that. Let's get some reaction from Lucy Penndel on the course."

134

Lewis flashed Lucy the thumbs up to let her know they were now on the air. Lucy's expression turned to a slight smile. Next to her stood Scott Hanover. "Tough break on that hole, Scott."

"It's part of the game," said Scott.

"Still, without the flubbed shot, at worst you would be tied with Patterson at this point."

"Well, Lucy, in this game, I never assume anything is going to happen. I came out here today hoping not to embarrass myself and I think I've succeeded. Andrew Patterson is statistically, and literally, the better golfer. I've had a great run of holes, the best in my life. If it's over, so be it. If he does win today, the better golfer will have claimed the title."

"That's a pretty generous and gracious attitude, Scott. And very sportsmanlike." Lucy decided to ask one more question. "There is a rumor that the tournament is investigating your equipment, specifically your balls. They think you may be using spiked balls to get some extra distance. Any comment?"

Confusion clouded Scott's face. What was she talking about? "The officials checked my equipment at the turn. Everything checked out okay."

"So you're denying that you're balls are juiced up?" Lucy asked. Suddenly an angry voice shouted in her earpiece.

"What are you doing, Penndel," shouted Jason Bernard from the control room. Lucy ignored the question.

"You saw me play that last hole," answered Scott. "Does it look like I was cheating?"

"Well, good luck. I'm sure it will turn out fine," added Lucy. She turned to face the camera directly. "We'll bring you the results of the official's tests on Scott Hanover's golf balls as soon as we have them. Back to you, Jason."

135

Jason gathered himself quickly as his own image appeared on the monitors. What was Lucy trying to pull? Was she still mad about Jason getting the commentary position? "I'm sure we'll find that Scott Hanover's equipment is within regulations," commented Jason. "That aside, what a terrific guy Scott Hanover has proven to be. He never had any idea he would be in contention in this tournament, let alone have a three stroke lead at one time and set a nine-hole record, but even if Patterson maintains his lead, Scott Hanover will leave today with something more valuable than a win or a spot in the Pro-Am tournament. He'll have the admiration and best wishes of all those watching this incredible match today. And let me point out that there has been no official word from the tournament that they think Scott is using spiked balls. Probably just a rumor from the crowd."

Bob signaled for the technicians to go to commercial. "Interesting turn of events, Jason," he said.

"I can't believe Lucy would throw that out to Scott like that. Have you heard anything about what she's talking about?"

"Not a word," answered Bob.

"I can't help but feel sorry for Hanover. It'll be almost impossible to regain the lead. Patterson is on a roll, five birdies in a row. Hanover never even came close to a streak like that."

"It's not over 'til it's over. We're picking up ten more affiliates after this next commercial break, by the way."

"Wow," said Jason.

136

Kenny Chase stared at the monitor that had just flashed to a Miller Lite commercial. How did that reporter find out they were checking out Hanover's golf balls? Bateman had wanted this kept quiet, now it had gone out to millions of viewers.

He pulled the paper wrapped ball halves from his pocket. He peeled off the short pieced of masking tape and hesitantly unfolded the paper. What if Scott Hanover was using a doped ball? He'd be pulled from the tournament and Patterson would finish the round alone and walk away with the prize.

Kenny didn't really care which one of them won, but he didn't want Patterson to win by default. He wrapped the ball up again without examining it. Patterson was winning. If he kept the lead it didn't matter what kind of balls Hanover was using. Better to wait and see how things played out. If Hanover lost, there was really no strong reason to check it out. If he were winning by seventeen, he'd check the ball out. Definitely better to wait.

137

"You know," said Joe Caulkin, "I wouldn't mind paying off my bet to Patterson if he won in a good match, but to take the lead because of that idiot in the cart."

Ted Lange nodded in agreement. "Still four holes, Joe, two long par fours, a medium four and that par three by the pond. Plenty of places for something to happen."

"I just wish Patterson had to sweat it out a little longer."

"It could work to your favor. Too much confidence can be a downfall as well."

"Let's hope you're right."

138

Sarah stood still while the crowd flowed around them.

"Breathe," Sally reminded her.

Sarah started her patterned breathing while Gina checked her watch. "eleven minutes, they're getting a little closer."

"Still too far apart," gasped Sarah as she stiffened against the pain, "plenty of time."

Sally looked for a bench but couldn't see one. Their escort asked if there was anything she could do. Sally shook her head. After another thirty seconds Sarah started to straighten and take a few deep breaths.

"Okay, I'm ready," she said.

"Are you sure?" asked Gina. Sarah's look answered her question and they walked through the trees to the next tee.

139

"Hanover is cheating?" asked April Weinstein as she took in Lucy Penndel's interview.

"A cameraman did tell me that a scuba diver had gone after a ball in the water hazard on the eighth hole. It must have been Hanover's," explained Karen.

"Well, unless Hanover gets the lead back it really doesn't matter," realized April.

"Hanover's not playing Callaway balls, is he?" asked Tim Carousel.

"I doubt it," answered Karen.

"Be a shame if he was," commented Carousel.

"We'd better start heading out to the course," said Karen.

"Yes," agreed April. She turned to Tim Carousel, "You can meet our boy and wish him luck on the last couple of holes, nothing like a little encouragement to send him along."

"I assume we'll drive," drawled Carousel.

April looked at Karen inquisitively.

Karen answered her stare, "The tournament is only allowing officials to be out in carts, but it's a very short walk. I was out that way this morning."

"Oh, well, if we must, we must," consented Carousel. The executive stood, finished his tea, and the women followed him as he headed for the door. "What ever happened to that biscuit?" he asked.

Karen shrugged. Carousel shook it off and led the way. April mouthed to her, "biscuit?" Karen shrugged again and they were off.

CHAPTER 20 – FIFTEENTH HOLE

140

The pole on which perched the running totals for both of the final two golfers now showed a reversed position. Patterson was now nine under par and Hanover was eight under. Scott looked at his name in the number two position and shook it off. No matter what happened, he was going to have his best round ever. It would be a day that would last the rest of his life.

Andrew was called to the tee first. He seemed more confident, if that was possible. Almost smiling. His silly cap with the pompom on top was jauntily tilted to one side. He stood in the tee box, like he was a model for some golf apparel catalog's closeout section.

Andrew knew he couldn't count on a birdie for this hole, a four hundred and fifty yard par four. The pin placement almost guaranteed a two putt as it sat at the lower level of a two-leveled green. What this meant was that if he hit the ball hard enough to get near the pin, the drop off between the two levels would send the ball rolling far past the pin. If he left it short of the drop-off, the first putt would also zip past the pin. It was perhaps the most difficult green on the course, particularly with this pin placement. A bogey wasn't out of the question and he was prepared for that. However, he was confident that Hanover would find the hole difficult if not impossible to par.

Andrew placed his ball on the tee and hefted his driver a bit. There was a slight bend in the fairway to the right, time for a fade. He would hit the ball with a little spin to let it follow the fairway to the right. To the left was an open area that connected to the fairway on fourteen. There was a hill where an old bunker had once occupied space, but it had grown in and the side of the hill was tall weeds.

He blasted his ball from the tee and it sailed down the fairway, taking its expected bend, landing two hundred and sixty yards from the tee. The audience applauded and he withdrew to the back of the tee.

Scott walked up. He found Sarah and blew her a kiss. She returned it. Did she care if he won? He didn't think so. He was so glad she was here. Yes, he'd be giving up his golf for a while, he had promised, but the experience of being a father, he was sure, would make up for it.

Not being in the lead position, he felt no small degree of relief. Scott really hadn't noticed how much pressure he was feeling until it was gone. He placed his ball down. The fairway was pretty wide open and the bend to the right would play well if his ball happened to slice. He took two practice swings then stepped up to hit the ball. The yellow duck with its orange beak and beady black eyes was looking out towards the fairway. Ready to fly.

He stepped up, drew back his club and knew as soon as the club hit ball he had nailed it perfectly. The ball soared straight out. It hit the fairway just behind Patterson's ball and to the left. The slight slice he had anticipated wasn't there and the ball cut across the fairway with a couple of more bounces. Ahead lay a sand trap and as the ball continued to roll, it fell over the lip of the trap with a little speed and disappeared from view. A line of trees edged the trap and prevented spectators from lining that portion of the fairway. Quickly, a few people scurried across the fairway to look at where Scott's ball had landed and pretty soon one guy was waving a hat and pointing to the ground. He was standing was almost parallel to the hundred and fifty yard marker. Three hundred yards in one hit but in the sand trap.

"You got a hold of that one," Paul praised.

"Unfortunately, it went where I aimed."

"Hitting off the sand should be no harder than hitting off the rough, Scott. You can still be on the green in two."

"Let's hope I have a good lie."

"Stop that pessimism, Scott. Good thoughts."

"Good thoughts," repeated Scott. He handed Paul the driver. As they walked down the fairway the crowd oozed along behind them until they were all in position to watch Patterson hit his second shot.

Andrew was still smiling. Hanover was going to make this easy. The guy was on the wrong side of the fairway for this green and in the sand to boot. All Andrew had to do was land on the green and he'd be able to two putt his way to a par.

Eric handed Andrew the five iron. He had always planned on leaving the ball on the right side of the top tier. From there, he'd have a lot of green to use for his first putt and would likely be able to get the ball within two yards of the hole on the lower tier for a relatively easy second shot.

He walked up to his ball and eyed a spot in front of the green he wanted it to land. He placed his club behind the ball and shuffled his weight to get his stance perfect. He had long ago learned that if he was positioned correctly, he could predict the ball's path within a couple of yards. He struck the ball with the grace of a professional golfer, a small piece of turf, following the ball into the air. The ball landed right where he had anticipated, rolled onto the green and stopped on the right side, about one yard from the slope down to the second tier. Perfect, he thought.

141

Ellie explained to Jason about the tricky two-tiered green and after a few questions, he felt he had the basics to comment intelligently on the situation.

"It looks like Andrew Patterson has found the one spot on the green that keeps him out of too much trouble. Another yard and the slope would have carried him off the green. A little shorter and he would have a tough time getting close to the pin on his first putt. The left side of the green presents the biggest challenge," continued Jason. "It is almost impossible to get your speed right hitting right at the pin. Too little and you're left at the top of the slope, too much and you roll right over the hole. Andrew Patterson knows what he's doing. Let's see how Scott Hanover does with his second shot. It's never easy to hit out of the sand."

142

Scott and Paul walked to where the crowd of onlookers, along with a couple of red-jacketed officials, had gathered. There was a collection of glum faces and Scott saw immediately why. The ball was sitting in a hole made by another golfers shoe print. The lie was nearly impossible. What's more, there was a slight lip on the side of the bunker nearest the fairway. It couldn't be more difficult. In order to get the ball out, he'd need to use a sand wedge and if he was lucky, he might knock the ball thirty or forty yards closer to the hole. A great drive wasted. Patterson had walked over to examine Scott's predicament. He nodded his head in false sympathy, shrugged and walked away.

Scott looked up and the large, red-jacketed man, who had shooed away the bee on thirteen, was looking down at him. He held a bag of ice to the back of his left hand and had a frown on his face. "Can I take relief from the footprint?" asked Scott.

He shook his head. "Play it as it lies. Sorry, that's the rule."

Scott took his sand wedge and walked into the trap. He wouldn't have the benefit of any practice swings in the hazard.

"Whack the heck out if it, Scott," was Paul's advice.

Scott hovered the sand wedge as close to the sand as he dared without touching it. He drew the club back like he was going to clobber the ball a hundred yards. He goal was to get far enough under the ball to lift it, and the sand around it, out of the trap and out as far onto the fairway as he could. He prayed it was enough.

He swung ferociously into the trap; the splash of sand obscured his vision as some of it fell back on his face. The hush from the crowd told him the whole story with having to look. He blinked the gritty particles from his eyes and wiped at his face with his sleeve. Sitting two yards closer to the hole, but still in the trap was the ball. While it was no longer submerged in the sand, it was very near the large lip at the edge of the trap. A good shot would get him out of the sand but maybe only a few yards closer to the hole.

He walked up to where the ball rested. He readied himself quickly, trying to gauge his stroke based on the swing he just made. Even if he got out now, he was still two strokes minimum from getting in the hole. Patterson would pick up at least one stroke, and without a miracle putt from Scott, likely two. He tried to banish the thought from his head. He let his club hover over the sand again and prepared to blast the ball and the little bit of sand under it as far as he could. His club sank deep into the sand and as the ball took off it bounced against the edge of the sand trap and rebounded backwards a yard behind where he had just hit it.

143

"A tough lie in the sand after his drive and now two strokes later, he still finds himself in the same trap. This has got to be eating Hanover up inside," said Jason Bernard. The video screen replayed the first shot in slow motion, the spray of sand almost obliterating everything. "Assuming he can get it out in one more stroke, Andrew Patterson would have picked up three more strokes on this hole and taken a four stroke lead. Perhaps too much for Scott Hanover to reclaim in the remaining three holes of this tournament considering the consistency that Patterson has been showing."

The camera was now showing a live shot of Scott. He was wiping his eyes again and looked back at his ball. His face twisted into an expression of confusion. He walked to where the ball had landed and looked at it with utter despair. He took a quick look around the sand trap, and then stepped out to consult with his caddy.

"A little confusion in the sand trap on fifteen," commented Jason.

144

"What's the matter?" asked Paul as Scott's look of confusion persisted. He almost whispered back, "That's not my ball."

"What?" asked Paul.

"There's no duck. It's a Nike ball. There's just that little swish and a number one on it. Oh man, I've really screwed up now."

Paul listened to what Scott said, walked over to the ball, and as he turned around he was smiling. "It's not your ball."

"What?" said Andrew Patterson from nearby. "Then whose is it?"

"The ball was buried in the sand, I couldn't see the duck, but everyone was pointing at it like it was my ball." He glanced around scanning the area behind the trap and there, lying next to a sand rake just outside the hazard, was his ball, neatly perched on the grass. It had rolled clear across the sand trap and the rake had neatly hidden the ball from a casual glance. It was easy to assume the ball in the sand was his. He picked up the rake and pointed at the ball, "This is mine."

"Then he gets some sort of penalty, right?" asked Andrew to the red-jacketed man with the ice pack on his hand.

"Well, there would be two stroke penalty for playing the wrong ball..."

"I knew it," said Patterson. Scott cringed at the thought. He quickly calculated the damages. Five strokes more for Patterson's lead.

"I hadn't finished," continued the large man, "However, since the strokes were taken while the wrong ball was in a hazard, there is no penalty."

"You mean I just play my original ball?" asked Scott.

"That's right. The last two strokes won't count."

"That can't be right," demanded Patterson. The man pulled out his pocket edition of the rules of golf and handed them to Andrew. Look it up for yourself. Page forty-one. Mr. Hanover is still lying one, ready to hit his second stroke.

Andrew flipped quickly through the book and his eyes scanned the bottom of the page quickly. He looked up, shaking his head in disbelief. "You lucky..." he muttered as he threw the book back at the official and stomped off across the fairway.

"Hey," said Paul, "Those Nike balls are good. Toss it here." Scott tossed the ball to his caddy. Paul pocketed it and pulled an eight iron from the bag. "This'll get you on, Scott," he said.

Scott walked to the far side of the hazard. The ball was sitting on the grass like it was on a tee. He took two practice swings then stepped up to his ball. The duck was once again facing the pin, laughing at him this time. "Nice joke," Scott said, "Now get on that green." He swung at the ball and it floated up and onto the front fringe of the green. It continued to roll and looked like it was going to disappear over the slope and roll off the green but it stopped, perched just on the edge.

"Nice shot," complimented Paul.

"If you can't be good..."

Paul completed the saying, "...be lucky!"

145

"What happened?" asked Sarah. "He must have hit that ball three or four times."

"I don't know," said Sally. She turned to the red-jacketed woman who was their escort. "Do you know what is going on?" she asked.

"I really couldn't tell you."

"He was playing the wrong ball," said a man from behind them. Sarah turned a man in a shiny blue satin Cubs jacket was holding an iPhone in his hand, a cord running to an earplug.

"What does that mean?" asked Sarah.

"Normally it would be a penalty, but since he was in the sand trap, he can just forget he played those other shots and play his original ball."

"How did he play the wrong ball?" asked Gina.

"Some idiot left a ball in the trap and the first people there saw it and nobody checked. His actual shot rolled right out the back of the sand trap."

"Thank you," said Sarah. "Good thing he didn't have to keep those shots."

"Oh yeah," said the Cubs fan, that Patterson guy seemed really pissed about it."

"Good," said Sarah with satisfaction. It was God's way of making up for the flubbed shot on the last hole, she thought. If God cared about things like that.

146

"What appeared to be a windfall for Andrew Patterson, has now resulted in both golfers sitting on the green after two strokes," said Lucy Penndel. Things certainly could have been much worse. If Hanover had hit the wrong ball after it left the trap, there would have been an automatic two-stroke penalty. If he had finished the hole with the wrong ball and started the next one, he would have been disqualified if the mistake had been discovered.

"It seemed apparent at first that Scott Hanover didn't realize he wouldn't be penalized for his mistake and the look of horror on his face was heart-breaking. However, the new lease on the hole should give his confidence a boost. I can't wait to see how this plays out. Back to you, Jason."

"Thanks, Lucy. Well, we're learning something new about this game with every hole. Back with the putts after this."

147

Andrew Patterson was the furthest from the hole. He had the slope to contend with. He just needed to get the ball to the next tier within two yards of the hole. Fortunately, where he was on the right side of the green, the difference between the levels was less than where Hanover was perched. There was also a little break to the left he could use. He wouldn't be able to hit straight at the pin, but if he got the distance right he shouldn't be more than two yards away. He lined up his putt and tapped the ball fairly lightly. It rolled down the slope picking up speed and caught the break which diverted the ball from spilling off the back of the green. His speed was perfect and the ball stopped one yard to the right of the hole. The crowd applauded his accomplishment of this difficult shot. He was more than satisfied. From there he had a straight shot into the hole.

Andrew walked up to where his ball was and looked at Hanover's lie. The ball was perched on the rim of the slope no more than two yards from the hole, but the steepness of the slope would make it impossible for the ball not to continue to roll right off the green. From there he would likely end up with two more shots to get it in. Andrew figured he could count on picking up one more stroke here, lengthening his lead to two.

He marked his ball and stepped back off the green in a line between the hole and his golden dollar marker.

Scott and Paul stared at the ball. "Another inch," said Paul, "and you'd be off the back of the green."

"I still may be," added Scott. "Anyway I can get some back spin on this ball?"

Paul laughed at the suggestion. "Just hit it as lightly as you can and aim straight for the hole."

"It'll just roll over it like the hole isn't there," pointed out Scott.

"It might and it might not. You saw Patterson's ball. This green is a little slower than you think. Just nudge it and hope it slows enough on the flat and that you aimed perfectly."

"That's the key," agreed Scott. "I have to be right at the hole."

"Here's what you do," said Paul and he gave Scott his suggestion.

"Really?" asked Scott.

"Hey, be the ball," he rejoined.

"You know, I've got nothing to lose." Scott let out a deep breath and searched for Sarah. She stood directly in back of the hole and she had fingers crossed on both hands. He looked at the ball and laid the putter behind it. No practice strokes here. They wouldn't make a difference. He stared at the putter and ball then twisted his head to see the hole then returned his gaze to the ball. He made a fine adjustment in the putter and checked again, readjusting a little back. A third check confirmed he was as perfect as he could be.

He closed his eyes and relaxed his grip on the club a little. Then he lifted his head, his lids still shut. There was a sudden hush over the crowd and this time the silence didn't bother him. He was no longer on the putting green of the fifteenth hole of George Dunne National Golf Course. He was no longer holding a golf club in his hand and there was no ball waiting to be hit. He was staring out his bedroom window, watching the beauty of the sunrise he had seen earlier that day. Sarah was behind him, holding him, reassuring him, loving him. She had her arms wrapped around him and her body next to his. It was almost like she was guiding his putt.

He didn't remember hitting the ball but with his eyes still closed he heard a chorus of people chanting, "yes, Yes, YES," louder and louder and a thunk followed by thunderous applause. Paul's heavy hand on his back snapped him out and his eyes opened wide. He turned to look at the hole but all he saw was Sarah clapping and jumping and screaming, "Yes, YES."

"It went in?" he had to ask.

"Scott, it was amazing."

"It had to be."

"Where the heck were you? It was like you were possessed."

"I think I was, Paul. I think Sarah just sank that putt."

"What?"

"I wasn't here. She was holding me, guiding me."

"Hey, whatever it takes. Look over at Patterson." Andrew Patterson's mouth hung open, his putter draped loosely at his side. His head slowly shook from side to side with disbelief.

"That look is worth it," said Scott.

"Yeah, ain't it pretty?" agreed Paul.

148

Jake Fischer was clapping as loud as anyone else. He watched Scott and Paul having their almost shouted conversation on the green. That shot was one in a million. Maybe not as impressive as a hole-in-one, but if he had hit the ball any harder, it wouldn't have gone in. The scariest part was when Scott lifted his head up with his eyes closed! He was smiling bigger than a Cheshire cat and seemed willing to put the putt in God's hand. The club's movement was almost imperceptible and the ball barely moved but it was enough and the sloped pulled it down. It picked up speed quickly but from the first moment one could tell it was headed straight for the hole. Too much speed and it would roll right over the hole and off the green. The ball did skip over the hole but managed to catch the back rim of the cup then dropped in with determination.

Scott and Patterson would be tied now, assuming Patterson made his putt. Five minutes ago, Scott was going to be four strokes behind, now he was tied. Jake felt for the contract in his jacket pocket, realizing that Hanover might just be able to do it. There was hope here. Scott could win.

149

Patterson walked slowly to his ball marker, the crowd still wild with excitement for Hanover's putt. He placed the ball down and picked up the coin. He had to wait maybe ten seconds before things quieted down enough for him to putt. With precision, he knocked the three-foot shot into the hole. The applause was a fraction of Hanover's but polite. He couldn't help but think that most of these people had gotten a certain pleasure out of seeing Hanover make that impossible putt. If only Hanover hadn't noticed he had the wrong ball, this would be over. But there were still three holes. Andrew would come back.

150

"Well," started Jason Bernard, "I don't think many people have seen a putt like that. Everyone here was saying the slope was too great for the ball to go in, but apparently nobody told Scott Hanover that. And with his eyes closed. I don't think I'll ever see anything as amazing as that again. At least not today."

Around the country millions of heads nodded in agreement. This guy was hot and there was going to be no stopping him. A day earlier, Scott Hanover had been no one of consequence. Today, he was working his way into a permanent spot of American golf lore.

"At nine strokes under par he and Patterson are not only tied on the course, but tied for a tournament record. He'd have to shave another four strokes off par to tie the professional golfing record for eighteen holes, but his bogey on fourteen helped to eliminate those hopes. But no matter what, we're getting a great show today."

151

There were a couple of dozen people already crowded around the sixteenth green when Karen, April and Tim Carousel finally trudged around the trees. There were even spectators waiting on the eighteenth green, several huddled around a tiny smartphone screaming and shouting and jumping.

"What is all that about?" asked Carousel.

"We'll soon find out," said April. She pointed to the tee and two golfers surrounded by a hundred peopled emerged from a space between the trees. "We'll be able to watch the last three holes live as they happen."

Carousel slammed his palm on the back of his neck. "I think something just bit me."

"Let me see," said Karen. She looked and only saw the bright red palm print. "No, nothing there, just an itch."

"Perhaps," he muttered, brushing a few gnats from around his face. "Probably would have been better off in the clubhouse." He looked around and sighed. "But we're here now. Nothing to do for it at this point."

Karen shook her head as she looked at April who was just as frustrated with Carousel. Still, they intended to get the most they could from his presence and him offering Patterson a contract with Callaway on live television could only help their client down the road.

152

Keith Kelly found the storage shed behind the clubhouse. The large sliding garage door was open and inside was a golf cart with a trailer attached. In the trailer was a dripping wetsuit, air tank, and mask and snorkel.

"Can I help you?" interrupted a voice?

Keith turned and saw a man in coveralls holding a wrench. "Looks like someone was doing some diving today," he observed.

"Yep, that was me. I think I made Kenny Chase's day."

"Who's Kenny Chase?"

"He's with the Golf Association. He needed a certain ball from a water trap. To tell you the truth I didn't think there was a chance I'd ever find it. Probably wouldn't have if it weren't for the duck."

"The duck?"

"Printed on the ball, like a rubber ducky. You know, Ernie's rubber ducky from Sesame Street."

"Why did he want it?" he asked. He often found that the more he acted ignorant of something, the more people wanted to explain to him about it. He was sure that the tournament wanted Hanover's ball for testing but he couldn't just ask this guy to tell him where the ball was now. He'd get too suspicious and clam up. But if he let him talk, it would all come out.

"Didn't tell me straight out, mind you, but I'm betting that Hanover fellow is using illegal balls. They didn't have any other logo other than the duck picture. Mighty suspicious, if you ask me."

"Wow," said Keith with an appropriate amount of awe. "That could get him disqualified, couldn't it?"

"Wouldn't be the first time a player broke the rules."

"Well, I'm sure this Mr. Chase will settle the matter," said Keith.

"Probably already has."

"What?"

"I saw him come back a few minutes ago. He had taken the ball to have some tests or something. Don't know exactly what he could get done on a Saturday, but he used to test balls for the PGA. He knows his stuff."

"I think I saw him, short guy with gray hair and pot belly?" he asked.

"Naw," corrected the diver, "Chase is tall, blonde hair, thin, wearing a red jacket. He was getting some coffee last I saw him."

"My mistake," apologized Keith as he tried to suppress his smile. "Well, I better get back to the clubhouse," said Keith, "I don't want to get into any trouble."

"No trouble at all."

CHAPTER 22 – SIXTEENTH HOLE

153

Ellie panned her camera down the sixteenth fairway and zoomed in on the sand trap guarding the left half of the green. "It's a fairly short par four," she told Jason, "but they definitely want their first shot to be on the right side of the fairway. It opens up about halfway down and with this hole being downhill, it should be fairly easy to par. If I know Patterson, though, he's going for the birdie.

"Because he's tied?" asked Jason, off air.

"No, because of the green. It's fairly flat and if he gets a good chip shot, which we know he usually does, he can get it within a few yards of the hole."

"And Hanover?" asked Jason.

"We'll have to wait and see. His approach tends to be inconsistent at best."

"Listen, we have about fifty markets on now. We're pretty much national and the station says we're getting tons of calls asking what this tournament is about and why don't they know who these two guys are."

"Aren't you telling them on the air?"

"With people tuning in all the time, it's hard to keep them all up to speed. But I am getting a lot of comments on my commentary."

"Good comments?" asked Ellie. She had a little caution in her voice.

"Of course. Mainly thanks to you and Freddy."

"That statistics geek back at the station?"

"You know him?"

"Yeah, he knows his stuff."

"Well, I couldn't be doing it without you."

"And to think," pointed out Ellie, "you didn't even want to come here today. An hour or two and we were going to be back in the studio editing your two and a half minutes of tape."

"I'll admit, I misjudged the whole thing."

"Does that mean you'll be out golfing with my uncle soon?"

"Let's not push it."

"Only three more holes and I don't have any idea how this is going to turn out."

"It's already turned out magnificent, Ellie. Keep up the good work."

"You too," she answered. She turned her camera to the tee. Scott Hanover would get to go first this time. He was still smiling from the last hole. Where had that putt come from, she thought? It was amazing, especially with him closing his eyes. It was like he was in a trance. The tiny leader board held aloft on a pole by some kid now had Hanover listed in the top position although both golfers were now nine under par. That would irk Patterson.

154

Kenny Chase sipped at his coffee. Hanover had gone and tied the score. If only Hanover had the sense to drop another stroke or two, Kenny wouldn't have to look.

He pulled the ball from his inside jacket pocket. It was still wrapped in the butcher paper and sealed with a bit of masking tape.

"What's in the package?" asked the man standing in front of him.

"Nothing," said Kenny, a little too quickly.

"Is that Hanover's ball?" he asked.

"Who are you?" asked Kenny.

"Keith Kelly. I'm a producer with USA Sports. You want to tell me what you found?"

"I really don't..."

Keith cut him off. "Don't lie, Mr. Chase. If you don't answer my questions I'll be forced to speculate. You wouldn't want misinformation to get out, would you? I know you sent a diver to the water hazard on the eighth hole and he pulled out a ball with a duck logo printed on it. The same kind o ball Scott Hanover is using. The ball he hit into the hazard this morning. I know you just returned from doing some tests. I know you used to check balls for the PGA. Now, Mr. Chase, do you want to answer my question or not?"

Kenny didn't want to answer his question but how in the world did he get all that information? He considered the options. If he went public with all he had, Bateman would fry him. If he answered Kelly, maybe he could get him to wait with the results until he could tell Bateman himself the news. "I haven't finished my analysis yet."

"You expect me to believe that?"

He plunked the halved ball onto the table. "It's in there. I was about to do a visual inspection. The x-ray showed nothing obvious in terms of an illegal ball."

"You had the ball x-rayed?" he asked. "Where?"

"At a veterinary clinic. Sometimes you can see a distinct inner core that is consistent with a doped, illegal ball. The best test is to put the ball in the club machine."

"The club machine?"

"It's a mechanical golfer. Hits any ball it tests with the same force so we can compare how far it goes. The PGA limits the distance allowed for balls when hit by the machine."

"Then how can you tell?"

"I had the ball cut in half. I'll visually inspect the material inside. Most balls have distinctive layers or colors. The doped balls have a material inside that is almost like a superball."

"You really haven't looked yet?"

"No," answered Kenny. "I thought that if Hanover wasn't close it wouldn't matter."

"Well it matters now," added Keith.

Kenny slid the package towards himself and peeled the tape off. He unfolded the paper and looked at the two halves sitting side by side. He picked up the one without the duck logo and turned it over. The surprise on his face did not go unnoticed by Keith.

"What is it?" he asked.

Kenny pulled a pocket knife out of his pocket and pulled out a small blade, then dug at the material in the ball. "I'll be," he muttered.

"Is it doped? Is Hanover using illegal balls?"

"It can't be," he almost chuckled.

"What is it?" demanded Keith.

He turned his attention to the other half and scraped lightly at the duck logo. The yellow flaked off in streaks as he scraped and slowly the word "Wilson" was visible. A little more work and he revealed "Titanium."

"What's a Titanium," asked Keith.

"A perfectly legal ball. The guys put the logo over the brand name. I went to all that trouble and all I had to do was scrape off one of those ducks. I'll be a monkey's uncle."

"But how is he doing so well? He's ranked last for God's sake," moaned Keith.

"I guess he's just having a really good day," answered Kenny.

155

"How are the contractions?" asked Sally.

"Nothing bad," said Sarah.

Gina glanced at her watch. "They are getting closer together. They're about eight minutes now."

"We need to get you to a hospital," said Sally.

"I just think the kid wants to see its dad play," suggested Sarah.

"Well, with any luck he or she will get to watch it on tape in a couple weeks," hoped Gina. The three laughed. Sarah saw Scott look at her from the tee. His smile was bright and hopeful. She didn't know if he was hopeful of winning, but she knew he had won the hearts of a bunch of these people here. It was evident, even to Sarah, that Patterson was a much better golfer, but Scott had luck on his side and he had her. If her presence could help, she'd be here, even if she did have to drop the kid on the eighteenth tee!

156

Scott looked down the fairway. He'd remembered playing this hole and ending up in the sand just in front of the green. He tried to think how Andrew Patterson would hit. Most likely he'd try to end up on the right side and approach the pin where there was an open spot in front of the green. If only he could be certain of where his ball was going, he'd do the same. If he aimed to the right and then added a little slice, he'd be in the trees. If he aimed left and had another great drive like on the last hole, the sand would be directly in his line on the second shot. If he aimed down the middle, anything could happen.

His safest bet was to go down the middle and hope for a little fade or a minor slice. The fairway opened up on the right side. If he did end up hitting it straight, he'd hope it would go far enough that the sand wouldn't be a problem on his approach shot. Then he could just plunk it up on the green with his pitching wedge.

He'd had good drives and bad drives today. Good chips, especially on the second hole, and bad ones. His putting had been great. He looked at his ball on the tee and his club. He picked it up and laid in on his right shoulder like a baseball player, waiting for the pitch.

He remembered the story of Babe Ruth pointing to where he was going to hit his home run. He tried to imagine the expression on the pitcher's face. Was he intimidated? Did he think it was a joke? But when Ruth hit that ball into the stands where he pointed, they all knew he was the best player of their time.

Scott looked at a spot down the fairway. There was a lonely yellow spot on the green carpeting of the fairway. A flower, maybe a dandelion that was growing low enough to escape the mower's blade. Maybe a piece of paper or a premature fall leaf. Whatever it was it stood out against the emerald carpet of grass and he could use it as a target. It looked approximately halfway between the hundred yard and hundred and fifty yard markers on the fairway. It was on the right side of the fairway where he hoped to be, but safely away from the rough. He took his right hand and pointed at the yellow speck.

"That's where I'm going to hit it, Paul," said Scott. Paul came up behind him and looked aver his shoulder where he was aiming.

"At that dandelion? Go for it."

"Hah," blurted Andrew Patterson. He was looking down the fairway, shaking his head. "You won't get within five yards of that spot, Hanover."

Scott let down his club and walked back to talk to Patterson. "You know, Andrew, on any given day when I might be out golfing, you'd be right. But today, on this hole, with this shot, I'll land within one yard of that flower out there. I don't know how I know it. But I can just feel it. It's like déjà vu. I've been at this very spot with that same lonely flower sticking up in the fairway before. And I know that's where my ball will land." Scott turned to walk back to the tee.

"You want to bet?" asked Andrew quietly. Scott stopped and turned. "A little side wager, nothing big, say a hundred dollars?"

Scott thought about it. Did he want to lose a hundred dollars to this guy? Would he lose? The feeling he had was so strong.

"I'm in for fifty," said Paul.

Scott grinned and walked back to Andrew. He shook his hand. "One yard from the flower."

"One yard," agreed Andrew.

Scott looked around. The red-jacketed official who was now acting as their starter was behaving as if he was oblivious to the wager. Likely it was strictly against tournament rules, but it appeared he didn't care what the golfers did between themselves. Maybe, Scott thought, the official wanted to see Patterson lose the bet as badly as Scott wanted to take that money from him. He walked back to his ball at the tee and pointed once again. The feeling was back. He imagined that instead of on a golf course fairway, he was in a baseball stadium and the flower was an empty seat in the right field bleachers. He warmed up by taking his practice swings like a batter would up at the plate.

Then, with all seriousness, he placed his club behind the ball, looked out to the fairway then back at the ball. He knew the shot required precision and accuracy, but most of all luck. But he also knew, by God he knew, it was going to land there. He pulled back and whacked the ball as hard as he dared.

The white ball soared and broke to the right with a vicious slice. The people gathered at that side of the fairway parted like the red sea and the ball hit the top of a tall tree with a crack that sounded at the tee a half second later.

"Hah," sounded Patterson.

"Wait," said Scott. A white object bounced out from the tree line, landed on the edge of the fairway and rolled right up to the yellow smudge on the field of green. The consolatory "ah" of the crowd was quickly replaced with cheers and applause as people realized what happened. Not exactly how Scott thought it would play out when he swung but when he saw the ball head for the trees, he prayed for that lucky bounce.

"That's out of bounds," complained Andrew.

"Trees are in play," corrected the official.

It was plain to see the ball was well within a yard, if not six inches but Andrew insisted they walk out to measure after his hit.

He placed his ball on the tee with unusual shortness and proceeded to hit five yards beyond Scott's ball with his usual precision.

"How did you know you'd hit it there?" whispered Paul as they started to walk out. "That was one heck of lucky shot."

"It had to land somewhere," answered Scott. "Why not there?"

"Man, are you some sort of witch or something? Or did you have someone standing in the woods there to through a ball out on the fairway?"

Scott raised his eyebrows and smiled.

"That's pretty cool," said Paul, "but if you keep doing it you're going to creep me out.

"Easy fifty bucks for you," Scott added.

"You keep it, put it in the kid's college fund."

"Thanks," said Scott, "I think I will."

157

Sarah tried her best to hide the pain from the two women but before she took too many steps she was almost doubled over. They rushed in to support her and Gina coached her, "Breathe, Sarah, breathe."

"We'll have to get you to the clubhouse, this is ridiculous. I'll have our escort call in for a golf cart."

"No," gasped Sarah. She held up a hand and the other two waited as she slowly stood up, taking some deep breaths. "It's over now. I'm fine between contractions and any doctor would tell me to wait, it could be twelve hours or more before I have this kid."

"Do you want to take that risk?" asked Sally.

"It's not a risk. I want to see Scott play this out. I want to be with him at the end. If I go to the hospital now, he won't finish. I know him. He'll leave the tournament and Patterson will win. Is that what you want?"

"Cecily can have her victory," Sally said. "I don't want your baby to be in danger."

"I'm fine," Sarah argued as she started to lead the women forward. "I'll decide when it's time to go."

Gina and Sally shrugged. Sarah was probably right and they likely had a long time before the baby would come. They'd defer to Sarah. They certainly wanted to see how things turned out as well and both knew Scott would drop his golf clubs in an instant if he thought Sarah was going to have the baby now.

They quickly walked to catch Sarah and locked their arms in hers and they all three smiled.

"It was neat how Scott's ball just bounced out of the tree like that," commented Sarah.

"Luckiest shot I've seen since, oh, the last hole," joked Gina. Their smile turned to laughs.

158

Andrew peeled a hundred dollar bill off the outside of the dozen or so bills in his money clip and handed it to Scott, shaking his head the whole time. He walked silently back as Scott prepared for his second shot. A nice perfect swing with his pitching wedge would put him on the green.

"Any idea where this one is going?" asked Paul.

"Haven't a clue," said Scott.

"How about in the hole?"

"Sure, then I'll know I'm dreaming."

He took two practice swings and then stepped up to his ball. The tiny dandelion was two inches away. Scott stooped down and picked the small yellow flower and searched the crowd. He found Sarah with Sally and Gina. He walked over to her and handed her the flower. He kissed her and she hugged him. "How am I doing?" he whispered.

"I'm sorry, said Sarah, "I've been watching that guy across the way pick his nose." They laughed. "I think you're doing wonderful. So does the baby." Scott looked down at her swollen belly; unaware of the contractions his future child was imposing on its mother. "Now go and play like a good boy," she insisted.

Scott walked back to the ball, retook his practice swings to the annoyance of Andrew Patterson and with his actual swing placed the ball about five yards from the pin.

The crowd applauded and some cheered the shot. Scott turned and looked at the woods to his right. He stared at the thick trunked oak tree that stood before him. "Thanks," he called out. The tree didn't respond but Scott forgave him.

Andrew stepped up to his ball and lined up his shot. He just needed to get a little closer than Hanover. He chopped at his ball and it rose high and straight, bouncing two yard from the hole and sticking tight to the soft green. Excellent, he thought. Let's see Hanover sink his putt from five yards.

159

"He's got a mixture of luck and good shots that seem to alternate with each other," pointed out Joe Caulkin.

Ted Lange nodded his head in agreement. "It's the bell curve. He's settled far to the left of average and doesn't want to move. He got momentum both with his actual game and it's overlapped with some of the luckiest shots I've seen. I think that's the third tree he's hit. If he were a pro, he'd be nowhere near nine under par at this point. He just keeps coming back."

"He just might win," said Joe. He had seen the look on Patterson's face when he handed the money to Hanover. News of the side bet on the tee had spread quickly through the crowd. Joe was relieved that the officials didn't do anything about it. He just hoped he get to see the same expression fifty times worse after this was all over.

160

"The boys are putting on a fine show," said Harold Frisk as they drove the cart to a position behind the sixteenth green. He tapped his iPad. "Look at that ball bounce out of the trees, right on the fairway. I wish my ball did that half the time I hit it into the trees. Heck, a tenth of the time."

Carl Bateman nodded in appreciation of the shot. "This is going to do a great deal for the Northern Illinois Amateur Golf Association. I'm sure we'll get membership inquiries all next week."

"Give me the information, I'll make sure my commentator gets it on the air, Carl."

"Really."

"Sure. We wouldn't be snatching up so many viewers if it weren't for you're little tournament. I'm sure we'll be able to make a contribution in support of your organization as well. My sales boy have been selling spots on the fly all afternoon."

"Wonderful," cackled Carl. He gave the information to Harold who called it in on his cell phone. As Hanover walked up on the green,

Patterson marked his ball with his giant golden dollar. Frisk disconnected and turned the phone off before slipping it into his pocket.

"Think Hanover can sink it?"

"No," said Carl.

"Why not, the boy's hot."

"Statistically I think only ten percent of putts from that far out make it in," he said.

"It's still not zero."

161

Scott marked his ball, picked it up, wiped a green smudge and checked it for any damage from hitting the tree. He should have done that before he hit his second shot but fortunately it looked fine. He lined up the duck with the hole. It was a straight in shot. No breaks or hills or slopes to deal with. Just hit it straight in.

"Straight in," whispered Paul like he was reading Scott's mind again. "Only not of those eyes closed trance things. Seriously, it's creeping me out."

Scott chuckled and drew his club back six inches and tried three practice swings. He stepped up and repeated the swing with his ball in front of the putter. It bounced a little as it took off and it looked like it was going in but it was slowing too fast. It rolled closer, slowed, rolled closer, slowed and seemed to balance on the rim of the hole. The crowd was silent and hopeful and everyone watched. With what seemed to be a desperate effort the ball rolled another fraction of an inch and, like a thirsty man dragging himself to an oasis in the desert, plunked into the hole.

Scott jumped in the air waving his club like mad. Paul was jumping with him and the roar of the crowd was enormous.

162

"Ten percent," shouted Frisk to Bateman. "Never go to Vegas, my friend."

163

"Another birdie for Hanover," screamed Jason in the control booth. He was jumping in place, his headphone cord threatening to pull out of the console. "I don't believe it. This guy just won't give up. If Patterson can sink his, they'll still be tied. If he misses, Hanover will be back in the lead but no matter what, it is still anybody's game. This is just incredible. I can't remember a more exciting, nerve wracking, suspenseful sports event in all my years on the air. Call your friends and neighbors and have them turn on their TVs. It's going to be a day to remember."

164

Jake Fischer punched the air and screamed, "yeah," as loud as he could and still he was unheard over the roar of the crowd. The excitement was thick and people were jumping and hugging each other and shaking their head in disbelief. As he looked around three seemingly calm figures caught his attention. He strained his eyes a little to distinguish them across the green and smiled as he recognized, Karen Blakely, April Weinstein, and their friend. They neither applauded nor cheered. One fellow clapped the tall thin man on the back a good thump that earned him a contemptuous glare for his trouble. "Yeah," said Jake again, this time almost whispering the word. He didn't want to be too excited, but if Hanover kept this up, he just might turn out to be his ticket back into the game.

165

It took the officials about a minute to quiet down the crowd so Andrew could attempt his putt. He knew he had the birdie but why did Hanover have to make his? He almost didn't. Andrew was having his best game ever and on any other day he'd be out in the lead alone, but this miserable snot was making him fight for every stroke.

He calmed himself down and lined up the putt, straight in, two yards. He did these in his sleep. He tapped the ball and with no doubt at all, it rolled into the hole. The applause was tempered in comparison to what Hanover had received, but Hanover was the underdog. People wanted to root for the underdog, supposed Andrew. It was human nature.

Still two holes to go, he said to himself. Anything can happen. He reached in and pulled out his ball.

166

Scott and Paul were still grinning as they walked along the paved cart path. Ahead was the large pond. Around it circled the seventeenth and eighteenth holes. A par three along the water followed by a par four long dogleg left. The pond lined the left side of both holes, cutting into the fairways, making the last two holes the most challenging of the course.

Scott noticed the strange rock ahead on the path. The gunning of a golf cart engine from behind startled him. He turned. The man driving the cart was busy talking to his companion. It was the same idiot who cost him a stroke on fourteen. Scott looked back at the path and the strange rock lurched forward. It was a turtle. The biggest box turtle he'd seen. The cart was heading straight for it. He broke into a sprint and yelled, "Stop!" as loud as he could. He waved his hands like a mad man. The startled man in the red-jacket gripped the steering wheel with white knuckles and jammed his foot on the brake pedal, the wheels screeching over the black top, smoking with the friction. Scott had reached the spot where the turtle was and reached out his hands to push against the front of the cart.

The cart's momentum had all but dissipated in the melting rubber of the tires and Scott barely had to touch the cart before it stopped.

"What the heck are you doing?" asked the now sweating man.

"Sorry," said Scott. "You didn't see him."

"See who?" asked the other man in the cart.

Scott bent down and grabbed the turtle's shell by the edges. He lifted it up for the men to see. "It would have made a pretty awful mess," commented Scott.

"A turtle?" asked the red-jacketed official.

"Biggest box turtle I've ever seen," said Scott.

"You almost got yourself injured over a turtle?" said Carl Bateman in disbelief.

"I wasn't thinking about getting hurt. Just didn't want the turtle to get hit," answered Scott. "I'll put him back in the water." The turtle had started to poke his head out from its shell and it was waggling his legs, trying to twist free from Scott's grip.

The crowd lining the back area of the seventeenth tee parted as Scott walked towards the large pond. He placed the turtle on the edge of the water and it pushed itself into the pond, sinking slowly into the murky depths. As he stood, the nearby onlookers started to clap, just a few at the start, then more. "The Duck saved the Turtle," yelled one clever chap. Scott smiled and waved as he hiked back up the embankment to the tee.

Ellie was standing there with her camera, apparently broadcasting the whole episode to golf fans across America. Scott waved into the camera. "Hi, mom," he shouted. He'd always wanted to do that.

CHAPTER 22 – SEVENTEENTH HOLE

167

Carl Bateman's phone rang with one of those distinctive ring tones that users could program. His song was "Just a Spoon Full of Sugar" from the movie "Mary Poppins." The music earned him a jolly chuckle from Harold Frisk. He put the phone to his ear. "Bateman," he spat. He remained silent for a moment then allowed his lips to part into a slight smile as he listened to the report from Kenny Chase.

"Good news?" asked Frisk.

Carl punched the End button on the phone and slipped it back into his jacket. "No news really. Nothing at all."

168

Andrew saw Karen Blakely approach. With her was another woman. She wore a suit like Karen's but lacked the bedraggled appearance. Her hair was a darker blonde with strands of gray and she wore it short but professional. She had a plastic smile on, one she saved for when she had to pretend to be happy. A tall thin man with casual attire also accompanied her.

"Andrew," started Karen, "I'd like to introduce Tim Carousel with Callaway Golf. He's very impressed with your playing today."

"Yes, you are a far better golfer than anyone else here. However, that Hanover fellow seems particularly lucky today," said Carousel as he shook Andrew's hand.

"I would have to agree with that assessment," said Andrew.

"And this is my boss, April Weinstein."

"Pleased to meet you," said April. Andrew took her limp hand. It was kind of slimy he noted. He let it go quickly.

"You play Callaway, I hear," stated Tim Carousel.

"Absolutely. Callaway Tour. Best ball I've found."

"Well, it certainly nice to know the person we might hire to promote our products is already on the team. I did notice that your clubs are custom made. That's quite a beautiful putter."

"It putts as nice as it looks," commented Andrew.

"May I see it?" asked Carousel. Andrew seemed a little shocked at the request. He never considered letting anyone else but his caddy handle his clubs, particularly the putter. Karen nodded vigorously behind Carousel's back. Andrew got the message and waved Eric Peters over.

"Putter, please," he directed the caddy. Eric responded without question and removed the encased putter from its slot in the bag. He carefully removed the cover and handed the club to Andrew. Andrew hesitated a moment then handed it to Carousel. Carousel examined it closed, lifting the head to his face and examining the solid jade head. He turned the club back around and took a putting stance, letting the club swing a few times between his legs. Then he handed it back to Andrew.

"Wonderful balance. Not a bit of wobble. My niece could sink a putt with that and she'd only seven," noted Carousel.

Andrew carefully handed the club back to Eric and shooed him away. Suddenly there was a screeching of a golf carts tires and they all turned to see Scott Hanover bending down in front of a golf cart. He stood and held what appeared to be a turtle.

"My, my," said Carousel. "What a silly thing to do."

"He does a lot of strange things," added Andrew.

"Yes, but you must admit, Mr. Patterson, when it comes to strange things your attire sets you apart from the other golfers."

"It is distinctive and different. I never do follow the crowd, Mr. Carousel."

"Quite right. Do your own thing, I always say. No need to pay attention to what anyone says about you."

Andrew looked at Carousel inquisitively. He couldn't decide if he had just been insulted or complimented. He chose to take the compliment and nodded. "We're about to tee off soon. I have a feeling this hole will settle this little contest once and for all. Eighteen will likely be icing."

"Well, I hope we can do business together, Mr. Patterson. I do believe I would find that quite enjoyable." He shook Andrew's hand again and walked off, sniffing the air a bit.

Karen rushed up and grabbed Andrew's arm. "That was wonderful. He really likes you."

"Well, why not. I'm pretty lovable," pointed out Andrew.

"You will win," said Karen cautiously.

"After this next hole, there will be no doubt as to who will win this tournament, my dear. It has all the elements that will add to Hanover's demise. It's over water, the pin is in very difficult position, and the distance is one of the hardest for a par three at two hundred and five yards. In fact it's the most difficult par three on the course. The man is getting tired and inconsistent, not that he ever had any consistency. I'd be surprised if his first shot wasn't in the water."

"I hope your right," prayed Karen. She let go of Andrew's arm.

Andrew gripped her arm, "Just you wait and see."

169

Lucy felt her cell phone vibrate in her pocket. It had to be Keith, she thought. He had the dirt on Hanover. She pulled the phone out and it was his extension. She connected the call. "Keith, are they going to disqualify him?" she asked.

She listened and her forehead wrinkled more and more with each second. Her shoulders slumped and her lower lipped dropped.

"He's absolutely sure?" she asked out of desperation.

She listened to the reply then muttered, "yes," before slipping the phone back into her pocket. "Why can't I be having a day like Hanover?" she muttered to herself.

170

Ellie's camera panned from the tee, across the water to the green. It was a very long green and the pin was tucked way at the back left portion. Behind it, the ground sloped off into a line of trees. "One can't rule out the psychological effect the water can have on a player," she told Jason. "I've seen Scott put one in the water today. If he plays it safe and keeps the ball to the right, he can run into trouble with the trees. He'll run right down that slope if he hits it too hard. If he's on the green but on the right side it may be difficult getting the ball in with two putts."

"What makes it difficult?" asked Jason.

"There are some strange hills and more bumps on the green than on a nudist walking into a beehive. Over a long distance they can send your ball in pretty much any direction. If you hit a twenty yard putt straight at the hole, you can end up five yards to either side of the hole if you don't read it just right."

"It looks like the water comes right up to the green on the front edge," said Jason.

"It does," agreed Ellie over her headset. "Andrew Patterson could pull the lead back, especially if Scott hits one in the water or too far into the trees."

"This game is never as simple as it looks," said Jason.

"Rarely," agreed Ellie.

She panned back but focused across the water at the eighteenth hole. "There is the next hole. It's just as challenging, if not more. Eighteen's one of the longest par fours and plays around the same water hazard as seventeen but even more so."

"I'll worry about that hole when they get there," said Jason.

Ellie put her camera back on the tee. Neither golfer was ready to shoot yet. The officials were busy trying to clear room as the spectators were crowding the small hole too much for their comfort. She would have to remember the "quack." If there was ever a hole where Scott needed it, this was it.

171

Scott found Sarah again. She was off to the right of the tee and had a great view of the green. "How's it going, Sarah?" he asked.

"Fine," she said, her voice pitched a few steps above normal as she smiled. She almost had to force the smile as a wave of nausea was slowly fading away. It had peaked as Scott had walked up to them but she managed to force it back down. Sally noticed and shot her a concerned look that Sarah ignored.

"Two more holes and we can go home."

"Right," she agreed, "home."

"Are you okay?" he asked.

Sally started to talk but Sarah grabbed her forearm and squeezed. "Just a little tired, but I'm having a great time watching. Hit a hole-in-one for me and the baby."

"One wasn't enough?" he asked incredulously.

"Well, I only saw that one on TV. It's not the same, is it?"

"I don't know if anyone has ever had two holes-in-one in the same round," pointed out Scott.

"So you're saying you won't do it?" said Sarah with a pout.

"I think I've already used up my lifetime quota."

"Please?" she begged.

Scott considered the request. "Well, if you give me a kiss, I'll do my best." He leaned over and kissed her. He had kissed Sarah perhaps thousands of times, but he never remembered a kiss like this one. Not even the first time they kissed outside her apartment door on their second date. It was a simple kiss, their closed lips meeting, the warmth of her skin caressing his nose and chin. His lips tingled with a tiny electrical shock. How long they kissed he didn't know. His arms slid around Sarah. Her left hand caressed the back of his head, and as they kissed, she let it slowly

284

slide down onto his neck and shoulder. They parted slowly to several whoops and hollers from the crowd. Out of the corner of his eye, Scott could even see Ellie's camera on them.

"Will that do?" asked Sarah.

"That'll do," said Scott. He stared into her eyes and saw a confidence and strength he had never seen before. He realized that for a moment, not only had their bodies been in intimate contact, but their souls had touched, combined, and drawn strength from each other. Then he realized he had seen that look in her eyes before. He had seen it in his own eyes the day he had proposed to her and again on their wedding day. He knew this day would be special as well.

He raised his right hand and brushed a loose strand of hair from her brow. "Thank you," he said almost in a whisper.

She whispered back, "I can feel it in you, Scott."

"I know," he answered, knowing exactly what she was talking about. "I know." He backed away and they separated from each other physically but there was no separating their spirits. He felt her presence more deeply than he did during his putt on the fifteenth hole. He wondered if she knew she was with him then. She had to know she was with him now.

"You're up, lover boy," said Paul and he handed Scott his five iron.

"Thanks," said Scott.

"You don't want me to kiss you too, do you?" he asked.

Scott looked at him and stuck out his tongue.

"Hey," said Paul as he put up his hands, "just asking. But I must tell you, Mary says I'm quite the..."

Scott stopped him before he could go on. "More than I need to know, Paul."

Paul patted his friends back.

"Any words of wisdom?" asked Scott.

"Just one," said Paul. His right arm shot up and as he started to talk what seemed like the entire crowd yelled, "QUACK!"

Scott stood and laughed and hugged his friend.

"Thought I'd forgot, eh?" said Paul.

"Never," answered Scott. The crowd settled and Scott walked over to the tee. He looked at Sarah. She smiled. He looked out at the pin, at the water. The tough part would be getting the ball near the pin. He needed a bit of a draw to roll the ball to the left as it hit the green. If he aimed straight for the pin, he'd likely land in the water. He remembered reading how to set up the club at a slight angle to get the proper spin for a draw. While he was quite good at unintentionally adding significant spins to his shots, doing it on purpose was something he had never practiced at. He was sure Patterson was quite good at it. But if he was going to give Sarah her hole-in-one, he'd need some sort of trick shot and there were no big trees to bounce off either.

He placed his ball on the tee so it sat only a quarter inch above the ground. He lined up the duck to the right of the pin. He stood and stared at the ball and tried to remember which way the club head had to tilt. It had to twist in a little if he wanted it to pull to the left. He took a couple of practice swings with the face turned in about three degrees. It didn't seem like a lot, but he didn't want to over do it. He stepped up to the ball then turned his head to look out at the green. He closed his eyes.

He reached for the connection to Sarah and felt it come alive. For a moment he thought he could also feel their child. Well, he thought, we'll just have to see what happens. He opened his eyes and took a deep breath. The scene was marvelous. A dark, glass-smooth pond to the left, full leafed trees with hints of yellow and orange and red lined the background. The grass leading to the hole was crisp and clean and mowed into contrasting diagonal checkerboards. The red flag on the stick lay limp and quiet. Hundreds of eyes stared at him, all waiting for one more great shot.

He looked down at the ball. The duck looked like it was crouched and ready to jump off the tee as soon as he hit it. Careful not to change the feel he had established with his practice swings, he drew back the club. As it neared the top of his back swing, his right wrist bent back and the left forward and the club head dipped a little, his hips had twisted around and his left heel had come off the ground as his left knee bent in. His instep on his right shoe dug deeply into the grass, ready to anchor him during his down swing.

A golf pro had told him once that as he swung the right foot should dig in, like he was passing a football. With sudden swiftness his body uncoiled. At the moment the club hit the ball it was as if a strobe had captured the moment of impact in a freeze frame photograph. The ball was squashed flat like a pancake, the duck tall and thin like in a fun house mirror.

If he hit the ball as he planned it would now be spinning counter-clockwise. His hips and his body turned to face the green and the ball sailed into the air. As it dropped it drifted ever so slightly to the left. It hit the front third of the green and bounced directly towards the pin. The ball had the right speed and spin and direction. Scott hoped it had the will as well.

The ball rolled and rolled and Scott stood frozen, unbelieving as he watched. From where he stood there was no way it couldn't go in. And with the abruptness on an ant being stepped on it stopped so close to the edge of the hole, it looked like a sneeze would sent it in. The applause was delirious and despite the amazing shot, Scott felt disappointed. He was so close. He should be happy with one 'ace' but his eyes started to tear up as he turned to Sarah. She was clapping and cheering with the rest of them. She certainly didn't seem disappointed. He turned further and looked at Andrew Patterson. His expression was priceless. He head was pitched forward, his mouth open, his cap crushed tightly into the fist that was his right hand. Andrew's head nodded from side to side and threw the cap on the ground. Scott's irrational disappointed faded quickly and he smiled. At least he wasn't going to make it easy for Patterson.

Scott stepped off the tee and waved to the crowd. They continued to cheer and Scott smiled in delight. He'd have to give Sarah her hole-in-one another day.

172

Alf Redding stared at the ball on the green through his viewfinder. Then he looked over the camera at the ball. Something didn't look right. He worked his way further along the green going along the back edge to get a different view of the hole. There were a couple rows of spectators crowded into the space around the green. Some of them were whispering among themselves, pointing at the green. Alf lifted the camera again to his eye and zoomed in. He clicked his microphone on. "Jason, do you see this?"

Jason Bernard looked at monitor three, Alf's feed. What he saw didn't seem possible. "I see it," said Jason off air.

"Somebody's in for a big surprise," noted Alf.

"Make sure you get his reaction when he sees it. I'll fill in Bob."

"No need," cut in Bob. "I see it too. Wow."

"Wow," echoed Alf.

173

Andrew held his right hand out. Eric Peters didn't notice it as he squinted at the white speck in the distance. "I thought it was going in," he muttered.

"My club," growled Andrew between clenched teeth. Eric snapped back to life and pulled Andrew's five iron out of the bag. Andrew snatched it from the young man's hand and walked up to the tee. He was beginning to think that some supernatural force was aiding Hanover. No one was that lucky. It was like the guy had won a hundred hands of blackjack in a row. Yeah, it was possible, but you'd have to play for years for it to happen.

He pushed his tee into the ground, and set his ball down, careful to show the logo for the camera. The crowd was quiet and he set the club down behind the ball. He had planned on parring this hole but if all he did was par, Hanover would have a one-stroke lead. Could he count on

287

Hanover falling apart on the last hole? The answer was no. He had to get close enough to birdie the hole. It would mean a little risk, but he was prepared to take it.

He picked out a spot near where he had seen Hanover's ball land. He looked down at his ball and layered his right hand onto the shaft of the club. His ability to concentrate was probably the most important quality that made him a great golfer. When he was swinging the club that was all he was doing. His body and muscles were so well trained that his swing was as consistent as a basketball player sinking free throws from the half court line a hundred times in a row. He knew where the ball would land. He knew how much spin it would have. What he had little control of was any bounce the green would impart. That was hard to read from two hundred yards away.

He swung and the ball rocketed out over the water and bounced to the left of where Hanover's ball had hit the green. It stuck in the green refusing to roll further. Somehow, he had found a soggy bit of turf and the ball had almost buried itself in the scrunched up sod. Worse yet, he was still twenty yards from the hole.

The crowd applauded courteously but he knew they were rooting for Hanover now. It was going to come down to the last hole. He had hoped to be leading five holes into the back nine but his plan had fallen away. The putt he had left was far from easy, but not impossible. It was within his ability. He had to make it. He needed it. Twenty yards.

Before he was even able to pick up his tee, the crowd was starting to flow down toward the green. Eric was standing behind him and took Andrew's club. Andrew walked off without a second look. Eric was fearful. He had never seen Patterson like this before. The man was seething under the surface. The one thing his game didn't take into account was luck. And Eric was beginning to realize that luck was an integral part of this game. If you didn't have a little bit of it, a good golfer would have a tough time rising to the top.

174

Sarah waited until Scott and Paul had walked past before she let a deep moan escape past her clenched teeth. Gina quickly checked her watch. "Six minutes, Sarah."

"I know," she groaned. "I know. I'm beginning to think my sister might have been wrong about a false labor."

Sally spotted a bench and they walked over to it and sat down. In a minute, the area was deserted apart from a few people sitting along the slope that led down to the pond. They had a view of the seventeenth green as well as the eighteenth hole. Sarah was drained after the last contraction and considered just sitting there for the rest of the tournament, but part of her wanted to be on the green when Scott knocked the ball in. The pain had faded and in the distance she could see Paul and Scott stop as they neared the flag. A red-jacketed man moved in. A sudden shiver gripped Sarah as a cold wind brushed behind her from the north. The rustle of the leaves around them was loud and growing. The wind headed for the green.

175

"I haven't seen anything like this before," said Paul. "The pin shouldn't be like that. Someone didn't put the stick in all the way."

As they had gotten closer to the hole it was apparent why the ball had stopped so suddenly. The pin was leaning forward and had trapped the ball next to the rim of the hole. Paul started to walk forward to reach for the pin.

"Wait," urged a voice. It was the red-jacketed official who had been Scott's nemesis in the front nine and had been chased by the bee earlier. He stared at the situation. "You have ten seconds."

"For what?" asked Scott. He heard the rustle of the leaves before he felt the wind. It was cold and stinging on the back of his neck.

The man was monitoring his watch, "seven seconds..."

The red flag on the pin whipped into the air and flagstick shuddered with the force.

"four seconds..."

The ball slipped slightly further into the hole.

"...two...one..."

One more gust of wind and the pin settled into its socket. The ball dropped all the way in.

Plunk.

No one knew what to do.

"Does that count?" asked Paul.

The official looked up at them. He was smiling bigger that a Cheshire cat. "It counts."

"That ball was at rest," shouted Andrew Patterson, "that's a penalty stroke."

The man in the red-jacket shook his head. "The player approached the hole without unreasonable delay and the ball fell in within the ten seconds allowed to determine if it was at rest. The player is deemed to have holed out with his last stroke."

"But the wind blew the flagstick. The ball was at rest," argued Andrew.

"Not according to the rules of golf, Mr. Patterson, rule 16-2. Congratulations, Mr. Hanover," said the official, "you have scored another eagle."

Andrew's mouth moved but nothing came out.

Scott looked at Paul. "Another hole-in-one?" he questioned.

"That's what the man says," answered Paul.

As if suddenly realizing they held the winning lottery ticket the crowd erupted in cheers. Hats flew into the air and the officials moved quickly to keep the masses from rolling onto the green. After all, there was still one golfer left to play to hole. Scott spun around searching the crowd. Where was Sarah?

176

"Freddy," muttered Jason under his breath, "has this ever happened before?"

"As far as I can tell, it's another first. This is the most amazing round of golf I've ever seen. Rule 16-2 applies. As long as the golfer doesn't take too long getting to the hole, even if an earthquake knocks it in, the ball is declared holed in with the last stroke played."

Jason returned to his on air commentary and explained the situation to the audience. "Scott Hanover, first by sheer luck and now with a little help from the wind, has accomplished a first in the world of golf. Two hole-in-ones in the same round of golf."

177

"Where did the ball go?" asked Sarah. She had seen it before the cold wind whipped over the flag. She made a visor of her palm and stared intently at the situation six hundred feet away.

"I think it fell in," said Sally.

"What does that mean? Does he get the hole-in-one?" she asked, excitedly.

"I think so," said Sally. At that point the crowd erupted in cheers. "Well I guess that confirms it then."

Sarah stood up. "I have to get down there." Tears were starting to flow down her face. "That was for me."

"What?" asked Gina. "You need to rest."

"Let's go," insisted Sarah. The two women were too slow to stop her and they chased her along the fairway, Gina struggling along as best she could with her brace.

178

Andrew closed his eyes and clenched his fists. He turned and forced himself not to stomp down the green. Twenty steps later he was at his ball. Eric swallowed nervously and gently pulled Andrew's putter from the bag. He didn't want to say anything, not even to try and console the man.

"You will need to tend the pin, Eric. I need to know exactly where the hole is," directed Andrew with an unexpected calmness.

"Yes, sir," answered Eric. He walked down the green, past the hole. He place Andrew's clubs on the grass beyond the fringe and walked back to tend the pin. He had never seen anything like that before and he wished he wasn't caddying for Andrew Patterson at this time. The crowd was calming down and the officials were doing their best to help get them quiet quickly.

Standing alone at the pin, Eric sensed the excitement electrifying the crowd. Hanover was making miracle shot after miracle shot. Twenty yards away, Andrew Patterson readied his putter for his shot. From where Eric stood, it would take a miracle of his own for Patterson to sink it. "In the hole, fancy pants," shouted a voice from crowd. Eric turned his head to see who it was. The voice in the crowd was lost among the dozens of faces nearby. Eric had always thought that Patterson's outfit was ridiculous.

Suddenly he heard shouting from another direction, then from all around. What was going on? "Move, you idiot," came the distinct command from Patterson. Eric turned to look across the green at Patterson. What was he talking about? Then he noticed that Patterson no longer stood over his ball, or rather, his ball was no longer there. Patterson's expression turned to horror and his priceless putter dropped carelessly to the ground.

There was quiet tap and Eric, frozen with the sudden realization of what had happened, looked slowly down. Patterson had putted while he was off daydreaming. The ball had rolled up and Eric, negligent in his duties, had not moved as the ball tapped against his left shoe. It was inches from the hole. Eric pulled the pin and moved his offending foot back, like the ball was burning his foot. He looked around and the red-jacketed official was holding up two fingers. What did that mean?

In what seemed like an instant, Andrew Patterson had stomped up the green. He looked at Eric, then at the official. Eric Peters, by allowing the ball to touch his foot, has just added two strokes to Andrew's score. Now, instead of being two strokes behind Hanover after seventeen holes, and still having a chance to close the gap, Patterson was now four strokes back. Four strokes. His widest gap so far. The only way he would win now was if Hanover really messed up eighteen or he dropped dead of a heart attack. In any case, Eric Peters had about three seconds to disappear from Andrew's sight before he would find Andrew's ball shoved down his throat.

Eric saw the look in his boss's eyes and realized that Andrew Patterson was no longer his boss. That it was unlikely he would ever get a job caddying for the pros. His carelessness and negligence was broadcast on television for anyone to see. He stepped back, letting the flagstick fall to the ground. Andrew stepped forward as if to follow the caddy and Eric turned and ran. The crowd parted for him and he disappeared through the break in the trees leading to the eighteenth tee.

Andrew walked back across the green to where his putter lay. He picked up the gold-plated shaft and walked back to his ball. The crowd remained silent, perhaps frightened. Patterson's expression was murderous. He stood by his ball, an eight-inch putt remaining. His hands trembled and the club shook until his grounded it on the turf. He closed his eyes to hold in the tears. This wasn't how it was suppose to happen. He was supposed to win today. He was the best golfer here and everyone knew it. Even Joe Caulkin wouldn't have been able to beat him today. Even with the two-stroke penalty he was having a great game. But Peters had spoiled it all.

Andrew opened his eyes and tapped the putt in the hole. He reached over and pulled it out. There was no applause, no acknowledgment. He walked to where his clubs stood. He shouldered the bag still holding on to his putter and tromped off to the eighteenth tee. He would finish. He would hope for a disaster for Hanover, but he would see his ball fall into the eighteenth hole.

"Tough luck," consoled a voice as he passed. Patterson's tunnel vision widened and he saw Joe Caulkin standing at the edge of the crowd, his left arm hanging in its sling. Andrew's expression didn't change and he continued on.

179

Scott and Paul watched as Patterson walked off. No one else made a move to follow him. "That was a two stroke penalty?" asked Scott.

"Yeah," answered Paul.

"I still would be two strokes ahead of him even without it."

"Hope you don't win by less than two strokes. He had no control over that. It was an accident. Just a stupid accident."

"You know, I feel sorry for him. Even though he is a jerk and all, he's one of the best at playing golf I've ever seen."

"You know the biggest difference between you and Patterson?" asked Paul.

"What's that?" asked Scott.

"He doesn't have any fun playing this game."

"I believe you're right."

"What a waste," Paul added.

CHAPTER 23 – EIGHTEENTH HOLE

180

"Is there a doctor here," screamed a frantic voice.

Scott turned, he couldn't see where it's coming from.

"I'm a doctor," shouted another voice.

"Over here," shouted the first voice again.

"What's going on?" asked Paul.

"Someone needs a doctor," said Scott.

"I heard that," sniped Paul, "who and why?"

Scott felt a grip on his arm, "Scott come with me." It was Jake Fischer. He was tugging Scott back along to the front part of the seventeenth green. Scott could see a crowd of people hovering and a man pushing his way in shouting, "I'm a doctor, I'm a doctor."

"What's going on?" asked Scott.

"Gina sent me to get you."

"What's wrong?" asked Paul.

"Come on," urged Jake.

Scott and Paul followed the man and he forcefully wedged them through the throng of people.

"All right," shouted the doctor, "Make room. Get these people out of here." On the grass, supported on either side by Sally Bernard and Gina Beck, was Sarah. He heels were dug into the turf and her knees up. Sally saw him arrive through the crowd.

"What's going on?" asked Scott. "Is she all right?"

The doctor turned to look at Scott. "What are you doing here?" he asked, confused as to why the golfer was there.

"She's my wife," he answered.

"Well," he started to explain, "she's going to have your baby."

"When?" asked Scott.

"Any minute now."

"That's impossible. She's not due for another couple of weeks," insisted Scott. "What's going on?"

Sally explained, "The contractions started getting worse and closer together. She was trying to get to the green to be with you when she nearly collapsed. Thank God Gina and I were here."

"What contractions?" asked a confused Scott.

"I didn't want to worry you, they've kind of been going on all day," added Sarah. "My water just broke and the doctor here says the baby is on the way out."

"You can't have it here," argued Scott.

"Can't move her now," interrupted the doctor. "Okay, Sarah, get ready to push."

"This is impossible," muttered Scott. He knelt beside his wife.

Sarah's face grimaced and she reached for Scott's hand. The red-jacketed woman who had been leading the women around burst through the crowd with a hand full of towels. The doctor spread some around. "Push," urged the doctor."

"I can't believe my baby is going to be born on the seventeenth green," said Scott. Sarah was now breathing rapidly, sweat was pouring off of her face. A bundle of jackets were propped up behind her.

"Come on, Sarah," urged Gina, "You're almost there."

"One or two more pushes," confirmed the doctor. "I can see the top of its head."

181

Alf Redding had his camera shouldered and as people saw him, they automatically spread and let him through. Suddenly there was a tug on the back of his coat and he almost fell down.

"Where do you think you're going?" asked Ellie.

Alf shrugged out of her grip, "Hey, there's a big human interest factor going on in there," he indicated to the crowd being held back by a dozen or so red-jacketed officials.

"There's a kid being born. Let them alone, Alf."

Alf clicked on his microphone, "Jason, you want me to try and get some footage of Hanover's kid being born?"

Jason's voice came over both of their headset, "Alf, is that you?"

"Yeah, boss."

"This is a golf tournament, not a reality show."

"What's the difference?" asked Alf.

"Ellie, can you hear me?"

"Yeah," she answered, realizing Alf's camera was pointed at her and Jason could see her on his feed.

"Have Lucy find out what the rule is here. Is there a penalty for delaying the match? Is Patterson still in this?"

"Sure."

"Alf, go find Patterson, I want to know what he's up to. Oh, and Ellie, if she does have the baby, ask if we can get a shot of the family."

"I'll see what I can do."

"Thanks," said Jason.

182

"What's going on?" Patterson asked the official standing with him at the eighteenth tee. "Can't we get this over with?"

"There's some sort of medical emergency," said the official.

"Why isn't Hanover here?" he asked.

"I don't know."

"If he's not here soon, you'll have to give him a penalty to delaying play. That's two strokes," he insisted. And I'm back in the game, he thought.

"There's will be no penalty, Mr. Patterson," answered a voice from behind him. Carl Bateman, President of the NIAGA removed himself from his golf cart. Another large, but seemingly more fit man got out from the other side of the cart. He held an iPad in his hand.

"The rules allow us to discontinue play for any reason we deem appropriate."

"What good reason does Hanover have?"

"His wife is giving birth."

"On the golf course? Why isn't she in the hospital."

"Apparently," added the other man, "she wasn't due for another couple weeks and she was out here watching her husband play. You must have noticed her following you two around. Only woman that pregnant here."

"Unbelievable."

"I suppose there is a chance," continued Bateman, "that given the circumstances, Mr. Hanover will not want to finish the round."

Andrew's eyes lit up at the prospect. He quickly subdued his excitement. "Well, it certainly would be understandable if he wanted to take his wife and child straight to the hospital. It would be the only sensible thing to do."

"Yes," agreed Bateman suspiciously. He and Frisk walked back to the golf cart and puttered back toward the seventeenth green.

183

Karen Blakely, April Weinstein and Tim Carousel stepped to the side as the golf cart rolled past them. They had heard through the crowd gossip that Hanover's wife was having her baby. They decided to try and track down Patterson. Karen realized that there was a great chance Patterson had already lost the tournament and she needed to talk to him.

They found him on the eighteenth tee. A crowd of people were in the area, awaiting the continuation of the tournament, most not aware of the events on the previous hole.

"Andrew," greeted Karen.

"Rotten luck there," consoled Carousel.

"Luck had nothing to do with it, it was my idiot caddy. I better not see him again. Certainly that moron's negligence can't affect any possibilities of a deal with your firm."

"We have no deal, Mr. Patterson," Tim Carousel pointed out. "I'm here to see the tournament. Miss Blakely's firm was asked to see if they might be able to produce a top amateur who we could deal with."

"Are you kidding?" asked Andrew incredulously. "I'm eight under par, even with the two strokes I lost due to that cretin. That's a sixty-four if I par the next hole. That's a great score. Most pros don't shoot that well."

"I understand, Mr. Patterson, "but Mr. Hanover is twelve under. He's a birdie away from tying the professional record for eighteen holes. Whom would you rather buy a ball from?"

"It's been all luck for him. Lucky shot after lucky shot. He hits a tree and it bounces back onto the green. A sudden wind gives him an eagle. That isn't a good golfer, that's a lucky golfer."

"Most of the people we sell to, depend on lucky shots, Mr. Patterson. If they think our balls will make them luckier, then we have an advertising campaign we can really sell."

April Weinstein cut in, "Our agreement was to provide Mr. Patterson. He's the one whose career will be taking him to the pros in record time. He's the one who should be winning." She realized the argument wasn't a great one, but it was all she had.

"Too bad you didn't sign up Scott Hanover," interjected another voice.

"Oh, no," moaned Karen. "Not you."

Jake extended his hand to Carousel. "Jake Fischer, I represent Scott Hanover."

"Really," said Carousel, drawing out the word with satisfaction. "I'm Tim Carousel, Callaway Golf."

"Pleased to meet you."

"You planned this all along, didn't you," said Karen.

"What are you talking about," asked April.

"I had trouble getting back into the grounds because I lost my credentials. He vouched for me. He just wanted me to get Mr. Carousel here so he could swoop in and steal Patterson's endorsement deal from underneath me."

"What can I say," added Jake, "I have a knack for being in the right place at the right time."

"Mr. Hanover certainly seems to be capturing the hearts of the crowd," pointed out Carousel.

"This guy is washed up," interrupted April referring to Jake. "He hasn't represented a client for over a year. You think he's any better at picking a spokesman for you now?"

"I pick the spokesman, Miss Weinstein, I can't control which agent represents him."

"What if Patterson wins?" injected Karen.

"If he wins?" asked Carousel. "He's four strokes behind. Well, I suppose that would be an amazing comeback, five strokes in one hole. He'd have my admiration."

"Just hold off on picking someone until the tournament in over," urged Karen.

"Fine with me," agreed Jake. The two women looked at him with surprise. Jake answered their stares, "He is ahead by four strokes."

"Yes, but his wife is having a baby. You think he's going to want to finish? I could score a double bogey on the last hole and still win," taunted Patterson.

"Mr. Patterson," said Jake, "Scott Hanover has already won in the minds of most people out here. You might end up the winner on paper, but he has already accumulated enormous respect, admiration, and displayed tremendous sportsmanship and ability. You'd win the tournament by default, but you won't win anyone's heart, let alone their wallet."

"They won't think that way when they find out Hanover is a cheater," interjected Karen.

"What?" asked the other four people simultaneously.

"The tournament officials found his ball in the water hazard on the eighth hole. They sent a scuba diver to get it. It's being checked as we speak. They think he's playing with non-regulation balls. He could be disqualified at any moment."

"That's ridiculous," said Jake.

"Well, we'll just see, won't we," taunted Karen.

"Well, good points all around," managed Tim Carousel. "Let us see how things finish out shall we. I think I would like to head toward the eighteenth green to wait this out, ladies and gentlemen." He started to walk along the fairway. Karen and April, realizing he was walking away from them turned and jogged to catch up, and hopefully lobby a little more for their client.

"You know, Andrew," started Jake, "at first I was pretty disappointed that Karen Blakely got to you first."

"What?" said Andrew.

"I thought you were my chance to get back in the game. Make a name for myself, but I've learned a lot today. Karen Blakely is your type of agent. I do hope you have a successful career, Mr. Patterson." Jake extended his hand.

Andrew stared at the offered hand in disbelief. He took it, not knowing if he'd get some sort of shock from a joy buzzer or other gag device.

"I'll tell you a secret," offered Jake, "Scott Hanover is not going to go play in any Pro-Am tournament. By default the offer will extend to the person who is in second place."

"Why wouldn't he take it?"

"Because he promised his wife this was going to be his last round of golf for a while. He's going to concentrate on his family and he can't do that and prepare for an event like that."

"Why are you telling me this?"

"To let you know that you are a good player. You need to work on being a better golfer."

Andrew looked confused. Jake smiled and started to walk back to the seventeenth green. He wasn't sure Scott was going to finish the tournament. He wasn't even sure Scott was going to be interested in any endorsement deals from Callaway or anyone. But he was sure that he wasn't going back to where he was a day ago, or a week ago or a month ago. He was going to someplace new. Someplace he hadn't been before.

184

"It's a girl!" shouted a voice. A huge cheer went up from the crowd and applause rippled around the area. Word quickly spread to the clubhouse where speculation and betting pools had spontaneously popped up and were now being settled. Nothing like this had ever happened in the history of the tournament and Jason Bernard was quite sure that it was a unique event in sports history as well. The monitor was replaying Scott and Sarah's kiss on the seventeenth tee and his amazing shot with the ball finally dropping in the hole with the help of the fortuitous breeze. As he watched the replay and saw Sarah and Scott staring into each others' souls, he noticed something he hadn't seen before. It was off to the side but it was apparent that Sally had noticed the camera and with a huge smile had mouthed the words, "let's try," as a secret message to only him and the eighteen million estimated viewers at the time.

He sat back and rocked in his chair, a huge smile infecting his face as well. "Yeah," he said quietly to himself, "let's try." A lot of things had come into perspective for Jason today. He could always come up with excuses not to start a family now. Sally had been patient but after today she'd be intolerable. He had always thought that if he could do this or do that, he'd feel he was ready. But there wasn't really anything he needed to do to make him ready to be a father.

As soon as he found her after the match he'd tell her yes. Today was as good a day as any to start.

<h2 style="text-align:center">185</h2>

Scott Hanover looked into his daughter's face and couldn't help but cry. Sarah had already beaten him to it and only the doctor seemed to be able to control his emotions. The umbilical cord had been tied with a shoelace and cut with a Swiss army knife sterilized under a lighter.

"What are you going to name her?" asked Sally.

Sarah looked at Scott. "We haven't really finalized anything. We thought we had a couple of more weeks to decide," she answered, "but I was kind of leaning towards Sally Gina Hanover."

Scott chuckled and was pleased to see the genuine surprise on the other two omen's faces. "It sound terrific," he agreed.

"That's not necessary," said Sally.

"You must have had other names picked out," added Gina.

Sarah looked at the other two women. "When I first a saw my daughter those were the two names going through my mind and she looks so much like a Sally Gina."

"What?" interrupted Paul, "like a wrinkly, bald, pink dwarf?"

Scott popped him a good one in the shoulder and Sarah laughed, "Exactly. In fact, if it was a boy, Paul would have been appropriate."

Ellie Burke worked her way through the crowd and Scott noticed her smiling and staring at Sarah and the baby. He walked over and stood beside her. "Ellie, meet my daughter, Sally Gina Hanover."

Ellie's eyes widened as she took in the name. "Good name," she said. "If you guys wouldn't mind, I promised I'd ask if we could get a shot of the new family. It turning out to be a huge deal. But don't feel you have to."

Scott looked at Sarah, "What do you say? Shall we share her with everyone?"

Sarah hadn't imagined her first moments with her child like this. She was supposed to be in the dimiy lit birthing room at Evanston Hospital, just her, Scott and their child. A quiet intimate memory that she would carry all of her life.

But things were not as she had imagined. This day had started with her resenting Scott for wanting to play in this stupid tournament and was ending with her being so proud of him. She had gained new friends and had seen Scott's determination to fulfill his promise to her. "Yes," she answered, "They should see the reason for all this fuss."

She handed the baby to Scott and he cradled her as if he'd been doing it all his life. Sarah was pleased to see the love in his eyes. She had no doubt that Scott would love their child, but seeing him express it so openly was heartwarming. Ellie pointed her camera at the couple seated on the fairway. "Smile, Sally," she said to the baby as the picture beamed across the nation. A flash from the crowd captured the scene as well.

186

"And here is Sally Gina Hanover, born today, on the golf course, to Scott and Sarah Hanover. I'm told she's a little early but baby and mother are doing fine," said Jason. "As to what happens from here, it's anybody's guess.

187

Ellie lowered the camera. The red-jacketed woman came up. The ambulance will be here in half an hour. There's a lot of traffic out there," she pointed out.

The sound of an approaching golf cart stole their attention. It was one of the grounds keeping carts with a trailer attached. In the trailer was a large mattress covered with blankets and a few pillows. The driver had a huge grin on his face. "Stole these from a couple cots in the equipment shed. Don't tell anyone," he winked, "but we do take an occasional nap after an early morning of mowing. They're clean and dry and warm. I'll give you a lift to the clubhouse."

"Sounds like a great idea," agreed Scott. "We can wait for the ambulance there."

Sarah looked at her daughter. The crowd near them was silent; many of the people had smiles on their faces. In their eyes she saw one question again and again. Is it over?

Scott passed the baby to Sally Bernard and he and Paul helped Sarah into the trailer of the golf cart. Sally walked over and handed Sarah's daughter to her. Scott jumped into the seat next to the driver. "Let's go," he said.

"Wait?" asked Sarah.

"Well, yeah," answered Scott.

"What about the tournament?" asked Sarah. She had asked the question everyone around them had wanted to ask for the last ten minutes.

"Heck with the tournament, I told you I'd stop golfing after she was born and there's no way I'm not going to the hospital with you guys."

"You do have a half an hour," pointed out Paul.

"It shouldn't take you that long," urged Sarah.

Scott looked into her eyes with a questioning gaze. "You want me to finish?"

"We, want you to finish," she emphasized. "Sally Gina doesn't want to have to wait to see you golf again."

"I suppose I could, if I'm not already disqualified," said Scott. "But..."

"I really want you to, Scott," said Sarah. "It's important to you and it's important to me."

"Besides," pointed out Sally, "you can't let Andrew Patterson win by default."

"She's got a point, Scott," agreed Paul.

Scott considered the arguments. He was well prepared to walk away from the whole thing. Holding his daughter in his arms had made him wonder why he thought giving up his silly golfing for a few years would be such a hardship. She had such an amazing effect on him. She was a part of him and he of her. He saw her future flash before his eyes; her first steps, starting school, her first date, college, her wedding, her having her own kids. What else could be as special as the little life he held in his arms?

"You're sure?" asked Scott.

"Go," said Sarah. "Win this thing. Do it for Sally Gina."

Paul shrugged, "Hey man, if it's for Sally Gina, you pretty much have to. I think it's illegal not to or something."

Scott looked at Paul. "Let's go."

188

Jason Bernard watched the expression on Andrew Patterson's face as Scott Hanover pulled up to the eighteenth tee, his chauffeured golf cart hauling a makeshift bed. Word had made it to the control booth that despite the recent birth of his daughter, Hanover was going to play the last hole. The crowd erupted in delight. Cheers roared and hats flew in the air. Patterson's disbelief was transparent, his heading rocking from side to side. Patterson's disbelief was transparent, his heading rocking from side to side.

"And Scott Hanover is going to finish the tournament with his new daughter along with his wife and Paul Bauer, his best friend and caddy cheering him on. Not to mention the hundreds of people crowded around this last hole of the George Dunne National Golf Course," announced Jason.

"This is certainly the hardest and longest of the par fours on this course, a true tester of these golfers' skills. To say that Andrew Patterson is out of this would be a little premature. As we saw on the last hole, it only takes one little mistake to make a huge difference in the score. I'm sure Patterson was hoping for Scott Hanover to drop out, but his family and friends have convinced Scott to finish the hole.

"The same water we saw lining the left side of seventeen, lines the left side of eighteen on the inside of the nearly sixty degree dogleg to the left. Sand traps line the right side of the fairway. Perfect distance on the tee shot is needed to stay out of either hazard and provide an open shot to the green that is protected by some overhanging trees on the right side.

"Scott Hanover's incredible hole-in-one on the last hole puts him three strokes away from tying the PGA record of fifty-nine for lowest score. A birdie certainly is not out of the realm of possibility, but very difficult on this hole. So far today, no golfers have birdied eighteen according to scoreboard, and only half a dozen have parred it. But from everything else we've seen today, if anyone can tie that record, it's Scott Hanover."

Jason watched as Scott Hanover and Paul Bauer conferred in the tee box. He opened his private line to Ellie. "Any chance we can hear what they're talking about?" he asked.

"No. I have the wrong kind of mike and it's getting a little windy, in favor of the golfers."

"Just thought I'd ask."

"You'll find out what they're thinking when we do," said Ellie.

"I suppose you're right."

189

The golf cart had been pulled around so the trailer faced the eighteenth hole. Sarah and her daughter were comfortably seated on the mattresses. The crowd had been pushed back behind her so she'd have a good look at Scott's tee shot, even though his back would be to her.

She was beginning to feel the effects of the delivery as the adrenaline wore off. It had taken more out of her than she wanted to admit and she really needed the rest. Sally Gina had settled into nursing under a blanket. Surprisingly, the little girl had not cried much at all but the doctor assured Sarah that her daughter was just fine.

Sally and Gina sat on either side of Sarah, both seemed to enjoy the prime viewing spot are were beaming with joy at being so close to their namesake. "Do you think Scott can lose?" asked Sarah.

Gina turned to answer her, "Only if he tries something stupid," she answered.

"Like what?"

"Like trying to hit over the water to cut off the dog leg."

"Cut off the dog-leg?" asked Sarah.

"You know, hit for the green as the crow flies, not following the fairway around," explained Gina.

"Why would he do that?"

"He wouldn't," said Sally. "He just basically has to finish the hole and he'll win. Andrew Patterson is going to finally lose and maybe that Cecily Waterston will go down a peg with him."

"But Scott said he wouldn't play in the Pro tournament."

"Oh, Patterson will get to go to that, but only as runner up, like Scott got into this tournament."

"Maybe he'll do as well in that one as Scott has done here," suggested Sarah.

"Maybe," chuckled Gina, "but as for this tournament, no way is he going to win."

190

Joe Caulkin was able to work his way to behind Andrew Patterson. While Hanover and his caddy conferred on the tee he whispered, "A personal check will be just fine," loud enough for Andrew to hear.

Patterson turned to see the smiling man, his casted arm still slung in front of him. "Game's not over."

"You're four strokes down. Big bird could beat you at this point."

Patterson shrugged, "Luck has a way of turning on people just when they least expect it."

"Then let's double the bet," said Joe. He surprised even himself with the statement, sure that Patterson would refuse such an offer."

"Okay," said Andrew. "Ten thousand dollars."

"You're insane," pointed out Caulkin.

"Losing a little of that confidence, Joe?"

"Not one bit." Joe turned to Ted Lange with sudden panic. "There is no way for him to lose, is there?"

"Hundreds of ways," pointed out Ted Lange.

"But he's on the outside of the bell curve. He's got to win" argued Joe.

"Patterson is right that anything can happen. The guy's wife just had a kid. He's lost the momentum he had on the last hole. His back nine, without the hole-in-one has been good, but not spectacular."

"But four strokes. He'd have to hit it into the water – twice. Or get stuck in a sand trap or duff it ten yards on his approach."

"All things that he has done before, and quite likely will do again."

"And I just doubled the bet."

303

"Relax, Joe, the odds that he'll lose are maybe only ten percent. Really, the only stupid thing he could do is try to hit it over the whole pond on the drive and cut off the dog leg."

"Why would he do that?"

"He wouldn't," said Ted. "No one is that stupid."

Then why, thought Joe, is Andrew Patterson so relaxed?

191

"I doubt that there is a single golf fan not watching this tournament right now. I got to say, Carl, you put on a good show," congratulated Harold Frisk.

"These are the top amateurs in Chicago," Bateman pointed out.

"It sure would be nice if this Hanover fellow could tie that record of fifty-nine."

"No way he can beat it," said Bateman, "He'd have to drive it over the pond onto the green. I don't think even a pro would try that shot."

"Not in a million years," agreed Frisk. "That would just be plain insane. Still, I've seen a lot of things I thought were crazy today."

"Well," continued Bateman, "I can guarantee you won't see that!"

192

Tim Carousel found a spot near the cart path leading back to the clubhouse from which to watch the final moments of the tournament. The whole thing with Hanover's wife having the baby had seemed such an unnecessary delay. What was she doing on the course so pregnant in the first place? Wholly irresponsible, he thought.

Karen and April had remained silent. They had both been praying that Hanover wouldn't appear on the tee, but there he was, talking to his caddy and getting ready to finish the tournament. They wondered what his wife thought, her husband still continuing to play even after she had just given birth. He had to be nervous now. He had to be in a rush. He would make a mistake. Andrew Patterson could still win this. They had to believe that. Without it, there was nothing else. Jake Fischer held the paper on Scott Hanover. April thought, why hadn't Karen thought to sign him too? You can't lose if you bet on all the horses.

Karen knew it would take a miracle for Hanover to blow this one. If only that caddy had been paying attention, a two-stroke lead was not impossible to overcome. Still, there was hope. There was a lot of water and a lot of sand and a lot of trees.

She tried her best to will Scott Hanover to mess up. It was perhaps useless with all the other people hoping he did well, but it was worth a try.

"We need to find out if they finished analyzing Hanover's ball," April told Karen. "If he's cheating, these people need to know now."

"Cheating?" asked a man standing next to her?"

"The tournament thinks he's using illegal balls," explained Karen.

"No we don't," interrupted another man. "As a matter of fact, we found out that Scott Hanover's golf balls are just fine, so stop spreading rumors."

Karen looked at the tall man with the red-jacket. His name tag read Kenny Chase and his expression showed the seriousness of his request. "He's not cheating?" she asked.

"Kosher as a pickle," added Kenny. "Now I'd like to watch him play this last hole if you don't mind.

"Be my guest," muttered Karen. Her last hope for a miracle had just been dashed. There was nothing she could think of that would turn this around now. Carousel would pick Hanover and Fisher. It just wasn't fair.

193

Paul held out the three wood to Scott with his left hand and placed his right hand on Scott's shoulder. "Just get it halfway there, Scott, two shots will put you on the green. Hey a birdie and you get your name in the record books."

"Not likely," pointed out Scott. "But it had been an incredible day. I'm glad you were here."

"Wouldn't have missed it for the world. I got a cigar waiting for you in the car, dad," he added.

"Isn't she beautiful?" asked Scott.

"Yeah, whatever," answered Paul with a smile then added, "most beautiful kid I've ever seen, Scott."

"Well, she's going to take a little while to grow into that face but she'll be a heart breaker for sure."

"You'll be beating them off with a five iron," agreed Paul. "Hey, do you think there is anyway you'll take that invitation to the Pro-Am?"

"No," said Scott. "First of all, today aside, I'm really not that good a golfer."

"Yeah, but it'd be fun, hanging out with all the pros, playing on the real nice courses," pointed out Paul.

"And I did promise Sarah."

"Well, there is that."

"And despite his being a jerk and dressing funny, Andrew Patterson deserves it more than me."

"What about Joe Caulkin?"

"If he hadn't have broken his arm, we wouldn't be standing here having this conversation and he'd likely be the one going."

"Yeah. Well, just one more thing to say."

"What's that?" asked Scott.

"QUACK!" roared Paul and the entire crowd. People began to applaud. A couple of guys even bowed down muttering, "we're not worthy, we're not worthy," in tribute to Wayne's World. Scott laughed and smiled and let a tear wet the corner of his eye. Gosh darn it, he had nearly forgotten about the stupid quack, but Paul hadn't and everyone seemed to be waiting for it. He looked out at the now stillness of the water. The dark green of the grass, the tints of fall colors creeping through the trees like splatters of paint. He looked up at the sky. It was crisp and blue. The clouds were brilliant white and very distinct.

He turned around and looked at his wife, his daughter buried beneath a blanket, nuzzled warmly against her mother. This was going to be his last hole for quite some time. He reached in his pocket and pulled out his duck logo ball and green tee, holding the tee against the ball with his middle and ring fingers. He inserted the combination into the ground until his knuckles barely grazed the close cut grass. He picked out his spot just to the right of the two hundred yard marker. Just the perfect distance for an easy three wood.

He drew his imaginary line to the ball and placed the club on the ground, then set his feet parallel to it. The crowd had become silent. Scott could imagine everyone holding their breath, awaiting his final tee shot.

He took his practice swing, getting used to the club. It wasn't as familiar as his driver had become. He took another, and a third. He stepped up to the ball ready to pop it neatly onto the fairway, hopefully not too far into the sand or hook it into the water. "What water?" he reminded himself.

He drew the club head back – then stopped. This wasn't right, he told himself. This wasn't how it was suppose to go. Something was wrong. It itched the back of his brain and he tried to remember what it was he was supposed to do. He looked out across the water at the eighteenth green and the crowds of people that had swarmed around it in the little space that was available.

Paul walked up and examined the puzzled look on Scott's face. "What's up?" he asked.

"How far?" asked Scott.

"How far what?" asked Paul.

"How far across that water."

Paul answered without hesitation, "Three hundred and fifteen yards."

"You seem pretty sure."

"I checked it out last week. Just did a little trigonometry off the scorecard. I even tried blasting a dozen water balls across."

"How many made it?" asked Scott as he turned to face Paul.

Paul grinned and shook his head. "None, Scott."

"Still, it's a lot shorter than four hundred and fifty yards."

"A lot wetter too," added Paul. He waited for Scott to say something else. Murmurs were running through the crowd now. "If you miss, that cuts your lead to two strokes. You don't want to play with that."

"I don't care if I win, Paul."

"Then just hit your three wood out there."

"I do care if I don't try. I will never ever be this close to something like this again."

"Probably not," agreed Paul.

Scott took a deep breath and held his club out to Paul. "Get me my driver."

194

"I can't believe this," said Jason Bernard. "He is going for it. He just handed his three wood back to his caddy and Scott Hanover is getting ready to hit his driver. One can only assume he will be going to try and drive the ball over the water hazard. Looking at the little map I have here, that has got to be well over three hundred yards."

"Three hundred and fourteen," came Fred's voice over his earphones. "On the fly. It's virtually impossible, even with the elevated tee. He hasn't hit anything close to that all day."

Jason swallowed and repeated Fred's words and added, "but it he does make it, his chance of entering the record books is virtually assured. If he misses, he'll automatically take two strokes off his four-stroke lead and open a window for Andrew Patterson to take this tournament from him. My God, I don't think I've ever seen anything so daring or should I say stupid. He doesn't need to take this risk. It's not like a half court shot when you're down by two at the buzzer, or a fifty yard Hail Mary pass from your own end zone in the final seconds of the playoffs when your down by five. This is seeing what he has inside him. Seeing if his incredible luck today will hold for one more shot. Or perhaps, it's never regretting not taking the shot. How many times have each of us wished we had reached just a little more when perhaps good enough wasn't really your best. If he makes the shot or misses it, it will be historic, but if he never even tries, it'll just be another tee shot in an amateur golfing tournament. What a place to be folks. What a place to be."

195

"What's he doing?" asked Sarah.

Gina was shaking her head, grinning, "He's going for it."

"What?" asked Sarah.

"He's going to try and hit it over the water."

"Oh my God," prayed Sarah. "You do it, Scott. I know you can."

307

196

Joe Caulkin buried his face in his palms. The idiot was going for it. He might as well write out that check to Patterson right now. He wanted to cry.

Ted Lange shook his shoulder, "Hey Joe, you know he has to try."

Joe nodded in agreement. He knew he would never do the same thing if he was in the same position, but he wasn't. Hanover had gotten further than he ever imagined. Further than anyone had imagined. He would go out in flames but he'd have no regrets. No, sir, not a one. "God have mercy," he added.

197

Andrew was confused at first, thinking that Scott Hanover was having some sort of problem, but then he saw the caddy slip three wood back into place and remove the driver with it's silly stuffed animal cover from the bag. He face grew into an enormous smile as he thanked God profusely for idiots like Hanover. He was still in this after all.

198

"I knew it," said Harold Frisk.

"The man's insane," said Carl Bateman.

"Yeah, but he's insane in front of millions of viewer on my network. I love it."

199

Ellie swallowed hard as she watched Paul Bauer exchange the clubs. Hanover was really going to try and drive over the water. She quickly focused her camera onto the far side of the pond. There was a yard or so of tall weeds and grass before the rough leading up to the green. It was simply impossible to do. But today, she thought, the meaning of the word impossible had changed.

200

Paul handed Scott the club with the cover still over the head. Scott looked at the figure of the plush gopher holding a golf ball. It was straight out of caddy shack, a bachelor party gift from Paul. Scott thrust the gopher high into the air. The crowd roared in delight. "Go for it," they shouted. "On the green."

A group of guys who maybe had snuck some alcohol into the forest preserve starting singing:

I'm alright,
Nobody worry 'bout me.
Why you got to gimme a fight?
Can't you just let it be?

The words and tune from the Kenny Loggins song that graced the closing credits of Caddy Shack spread through the mass of people like a fire. Scott bounced his gopher doll to the beat, conducting the crowd, feeling the surges of adrenalin flowing. This was his day and his moment.

He returned back to the tee and pulled the cover off the driver. He draped it across Paul's outstretched arms like he was giving his gloves to a butler. He turned forty-five degrees left in the tee box to face the flag. He stretched out his right arm with the club to line up his shot and let the club touch the ground about a yard behind his ball. As if on cue, the singing and clapping from the crowd faded out and was replaced by an awed silence.

He stepped over and lined up his feet and placed the club head behind the ball. He was going to hit with his practice swing. The most perfect swing there was. No matter how hard you tried, it always seemed like the practice swing was much better than your actual swing. Paul and he had often joked about Scott's need to take practice swings and occasionally Scott would allow his ball to be in the way when he took one. This was one of those times.

He closed his eyes for a moment and pictured in his mind the ball sailing across the pond and rolling onto the green. He could do it. He knew he could. He felt it. Something had given him the confidence or perhaps the stupidity to take the shot and he wasn't going to ignore it.

He looked at the ball, at the yellow duck with the orange feet and beak and black beady eyes. The song, Rubber Ducky from Sesame Street ran through his head for a moment.

Rubber Ducky, you're the one...

He smiled even more. "What water?" he said to himself one more time.

As he drew back the club starting the motion that would end with his ball leaving the tee for the last time that day, no one watching on the course, at the clubhouse, at the television station, or in any one of millions of homes breathed. More prayers were said in that second than the whole time the Titanic was sinking. Everyone, save perhaps Andrew Patterson, willed Scott Hanover to make the shot, the impossible shot that would cap an amazingly incredible day for Scott Hanover.

His left heel lifted from the ground and his left knee turned in. On the bottom of his field of vision his left shoulder appeared and pointed directly at his ball. The club hovered somewhere above his head, balanced and coiled, ready to strike. The next thing he heard was the plink as the club head stuck the ball and sent it out over the water. His body was facing the pin, his right heel now off the ground and his club hanging over his left shoulder. It was so fast, so perfect, he didn't even have time to feel it. "Oh my God," he muttered as the ball lifted higher and higher, further and further. The crowd gasped together. Those along the far left side of the water were the first to see the result of the swing; their view of shot from the side was not affected by optical illusions that could confuse one's depth perception. They saw first what Scott Hanover would realize a moment later.

His ball, beautifully hit, was going in the water. Alf Redding had his camera on the ball as it arced through the air. He hoped it would have the extra kick but as it started to fall the trajectory was clear.

A few in the crowd shouted, "No. No!" Many felt grief as if a love one had passed. They had wanted this for Scott Hanover more than anything in the world.

"It's wet, Scott," said Paul's voice from behind him. Scott remained silent. He pushed the ball with his mind as hard as he could. "Come on," he encouraged. "Get over there."

Andrew Patterson smiled. It was turning out to be a real good day.

CHAPTER 24 – THE MIRACLE

201

From where she sat, Sarah could see the ball was going to be short. She had so wanted him to make it. She felt Gina's hand on her shoulder, a comforting touch.

202

"What's that?" shouted someone around the tee.

Scott tried to focus his eyes on the dark water that the ball was heading for. There was a darker area, rippling like the ball had already fallen there.

203

Ellie, whose camera was still following the ball, captured perhaps the best shot of what happened next. The events of the next couple seconds would be replayed over and over for days to come. The possibility had occurred to no one and if anyone had suggested it, they never came forward.

Shortly after Scott and Paul saw the ball hit the water, they heard the slower traveling sound waves of the ball hitting something hard, similar to when an errant shot hit a cart path. The ball rose off the surface of the water with nearly the same speed it landed.

"Oh my God," repeated Scott.

"Holy Moses," added Paul.

Andrew Patterson's remark would be impolite to record.

Ellie zoomed in on the dark object sticking out of the water. It was a turtle shell and next to it, the turtle's head lifted out of the water for a moment, then he sank back into the shallow water of the pond. She remained focused on the spot, wondering if it would make a return appearance.

Then she remembered at the seventeenth tee. It couldn't be, she tried to convince herself. But once again, impossible was becoming a useless word on this day of miracles.

204

"That," grunted Harold Frisk to the slack jawed man sitting next to him, "was the turtle you almost killed."

Carl Bateman snapped out of his disbelief for a moment. "It can't be."

"It can if I say it is."

205

Karen Blakely's smile, that had broadened as she saw the ball heading into the water hazard, faded into incredulity as she watched the ball bounced high into the air off the surface of the water and land on the edge of the green, to stop three yards from the pin. "Jesus Christ," she let slip.

"Probably not too far off the mark," commented Tim Carousel.

April shook her head. From where they stood they couldn't see what had caused the ball to skip out of the water but seeing it wouldn't have helped them believe it any easier.

"Looks like it's over for your boy," stated Tim Carousel. "I think I'll try and track down that Jake Fischer fellow, see if we can work out some sort of deal here." He walked away from the two women, neither one of them seeming to have the ability to follow him.

"What was that?" asked April.

"It was a turtle," said a helpful golf fan watching the replay on his smartphone.

"A what?" asked Karen.

The short man with thick glasses, blue windbreaker and Cubs baseball cap held the tiny screen where Karen could see it. She stared at the image for a moment before feeling the staring eyes of the nerdy fan staring down her blouse. She shrugged her jacket over her chest and turned away from the man with disgust. "Get a life," she muttered.

206

From where he stood some three hundred and forty yards away, Scott couldn't see how close he was to the pin. It didn't really matter. He had done it. Had it been the turtle telling him to go for it? Prompting Scott telepathically that he had his back, so to speak?

His hands went to his head as he dropped his driver and took a step back. "Thank you, thank you, thank you," he said, perhaps to God but maybe to the turtle as well. Someone was looking out for him today.

Paul was standing next to him now, he left hand grasping firmly his buddy's shoulder. "That, my friend, was pretty cool."

"Hard shot to make," added Scott.

"Do you think you hurt his shell?"

"I don't know," answered Scott. "I hope not. If it was the same turtle I put in the water back on seventeen, he's a good-sized turtle. Pretty thick shell."

"Probably set his guts ringing like a bell," pointed out Paul.

"Ding, dong," agreed Scott.

207

Andrew Patterson squinted at the green. "Is he on? Is he on?" he kept asking with disbelief.

"It's on," answered a voice from behind him.

"That's impossible," said Andrew. "That can't be. It was going in the water. I saw it going in the water. That's not fair. It's not fair."

"The guy's got luck coming out of his ears," said the same voice.

"That's all it is," agreed Andrew without looking at the source of the voice. "Just pure and simple dumb luck. A one in a billion shot. It should have gone in the water."

"You never had a chance against this guy," said the voice.

"I played the best I could," said Andrew. He turned to look at the source of the voice. It was the large red-jacketed official that had been following them along the back nine. "What could I do?"

"Absolutely nothing," pointed out David Henson.

Andrew looked on the tee at Scott and Paul. A couple dozen people were crowding the golfer, holding out bits of paper for an autograph, others having his sign their scorecards that they had been keeping as they followed the two golfers. Andrew pulled out his scorecard. He looked at how he had come so close. He was leading at one point. He had the tournament in his hand. But that lucky son of a gun had taken it. It truly was his day today.

Andrew worked his way through the crowd of people, holding his scorecard in front of him. Scott was signing whatever was thrust in front of him, basking in the sudden but doomed to be short-lived celebrity that was thrust upon him. As he took Andrew's card from his outstretched hand the crowd silenced as they recognized Patterson. Scott signed his name and as he handed it back realized it was Andrew Patterson's card he had just autographed.

Andrew Patterson looked different. He didn't look defeated or disappointed or frustrated. He looked happy. "Congratulation, Mr. Hanover." He said sincerely.

Scott pocketed his pen and shook the outstretched hand. "It's Scott."

"Congratulations, Scott. It was truly an amazing shot. And congratulations on the birth of your child. A girl?"

"A girl, yes," answered Scott, still holding Andrew's Hand. "Game's not over, Andrew. I believe your up?"

"I'm not going to try that," he said.

"I didn't think you would. I'll see you on the green."

"Wouldn't miss it for the world."

Andrew turned and walked back to where his golf bag was. The officials were doing their best to keep autograph seekers away now. He sighed as he reached his bag and pulled out his three wood. The tournament was over in terms of who would finish first and who would finish second. But how he would come out was still to be determined. He could easily play the bitter perfectionist who felt he was cheated out of his victory, or he could be the consummate sportsman. He could realize that for Scott Hanover, this was a day that would come only once. Andrew had many victories in his future. He still had a better score than he had planned on. No one else was close to second place. He was sure that even Joe Caulkin would have had a tough time keeping up with him today. He wondered if playing against Hanover had an unintended affect on his game. Maybe Scott had pushed him to be a little better than usual. Perhaps he had shown Andrew that there was still a little more he could put into his game.

208

As the fans departed, satisfied with a scrawled name on a piece of paper, or directed back off the tee by the officials, the three, no four, women sitting on the bench to the side came into his view. He only saw Sarah's smile. Little Sally was sleeping now, satisfied with her first meal and obviously tired from the ordeal of being born. "You do that all the time out here?" asked Sarah.

"First time actually."

"Why did you even try? Even Gina thought you were insane to do it."

"I couldn't not try."

"Double negative," warned big Sally.

"I just had a feeling."

"Do you want to hold her?" asked Sarah.

"She's sleeping," pointed out Scott.

"If this crowd won't wake her, nothing will," she argued. Sally and Gina helped Sarah up and she passed the bundled baby to Scott. He held Sally Gina and couldn't help the tears that welled in his eyes. He was holding his daughter.

"Please clear the tee," announced the large red-jacketed man. "Mr. Patterson is up."

The crowd quickly left, realizing the quicker Andrew got on, the sooner they'd get to see what was going to happen next.

209

Jason Bernard sank back into his chair as he watched Scott take his daughter is his arms and the loving smile on his own wife's face. He had recounted the miracle drive five times for the viewing public and now Patterson was getting ready to make his hit. It had been a miracle.

It had been obvious from almost the moment the ball left the tee it was destined for the water and Jason had felt the adrenaline rush that had been supporting him drain for an instant, only to be replaced by amazement as the ball bounced off what he first thought was a rock in the water.

When Ellie zoomed in on the turtle he just kept repeating, "it's a miracle, it's a miracle." How else to describe it? Freddy had gone bonkers at the prospect that Scott Hanover was one stroke away from being alone with the lowest score in golf. A fifty-eight, fourteen strokes under par. And he did it having one bogey and two, possibly three eagles. Fred was trying to find out if anyone had even had two eagles in a round before, let alone three.

Then there had been the scene of Scott and Andrew shaking hands, exchanging words, like they were the best of buddies. What was that all about? It would have to wait until a post game interview. He hoped he'd be able to talk to Scott before he had to take his wife and daughter to the hospital. The police had reported that the ambulance had almost made it to Central Avenue and would be in the parking lot in a matter of minutes.

Despite the immensity of the moment, Jason had found the words to express the situation to the millions of television viewers. It was certainly different than reporting and editing things down back at the studio. He liked doing this. He liked it a lot. If only it wasn't golf, he kept telling himself with a smile. But still, today had been anything but boring. With only two golfers being followed the pace was a little slow as they trailed from shot to shot, but he and Lucy had managed to fill up the down time with interesting bits.

Ellie's camera was on Andrew Patterson getting ready for his tee shot. A man doomed to second place by circumstances outside his control and seemingly accepting of the situation.

210

Andrew couldn't help but keep thinking of Hanover's tee shot. He was so sure that it was in the water. It was in the water. Part of him was relieved the pressure was off. He could finish the tournament and when Hanover, as he hoped, turned down the invitation to the Pro-Am, he would accept graciously. He thought it ironic that Hanover had entered the tournament because of Joe Caulkin's injury, and now Andrew would be tempting a pro career due to another man's promise to his wife.

Cecily, he thought. Where was Cecily? Did she even know what was going on? Probably not. She was likely getting ready for their evening out to celebrate. She had never attended any of his golf tournaments and he didn't expect her to. She would be extremely bored. Undoubtedly she'd be disappointed that Andrew lost but excited he'd get to play in the Pro-Am. She was predictable that way.

He looked at his ball, drew back his club, and imparted a mild counterclockwise spin to the ball. It soared around the edge of the pond, landing on the fairway about halfway to the hole. The applause was there but tempered. Compared to Scott Hanover, his superb drive was like a duffed shot.

Andrew went back to his clubs and was surprised to see Jake Fischer standing there with the bag slung over his shoulder. "That was a nice thing to do."

"What? Not show up your client?" said Andrew.

"I do believe you told a joke, Mr. Patterson," laughed Jake.

"Well, I won't make a habit of it," promised Andrew.

"Looks like you could use a hand," said Jake, stating the obvious.

"Mr. Fischer, that would very nice of you." He handed his driver to Jake who found its slot in the bag. He walked up next to Andrew Patterson and the two started trekking down the fairway. Andrew thought how strange it was to have a caddy walk next to him. It was turning out to be an unusual day all around.

211

Paul pointed out the sight of Andrew and Jake jabbering as the newly hired caddy and his boss walked down the fairway. "Is that legal to change caddies?" asked Paul.

"Doesn't bother me," answered Scott.

"But he's your agent," pointed out Paul.

"I don't need an agent."

"Well, apparently, neither does Andrew Patterson. So why is Fischer doing it?"

"Because Andrew needed a caddy and it's a nice thing to do."

"I suppose," agreed Paul. He picked up Scott's bag. "You going to carry that thing all the way to the green?" he asked nodding at the sleeping infant.

"If Sarah lets me," he answered. He looked over at his wife. She had collapsed into near sleep, Gina and Sally offering her a drink produced by one of the officials. He walked over to her. "Mind if Sally Gina walks with me to the green?" he asked.

"I think she'd enjoy that," said Sarah with a smile.

212

By the time Andrew and Jake had reached Patterson's ball on the fairway they had both discovered some things in common that neither would have thought. They both loved crosswords, Stephen King novels, and Meg Ryan movies.

"Listen, Jake," started Andrew as they stood staring toward the green. "I can get out my contract with Blakely. You can be my agent."

"No, don't. Karen is very good at what she does. She'll do right by you."

"What'll you do if Hanover ducks the limelight like you think he will."

"Something will come along. That's how it's always been with me, something always seems to come along."

"Five wood," instructed Andrew. He suddenly realized that the well-trained Eric Peters had actually become an integral part of his golfing. He pondered giving the boy another chance. Maybe, he thought.

He lined up his shot, swung at the ball and sent it onto the green, a yard or two behind Scott Hanover's. Finish up with a par, he thought. Not bad.

213

"Get out there," urged April Weinstein.

"What?" asked Karen.

"Fischer's carrying Patterson's bag, you go out there and do that. He's your client."

Karen stared at he boss in disbelief. "Do you know what I've been through today? That wild goose chase you sent me on at the marathon landed me three tickets. I had to walk two miles in those shoes. I've ruined this suit, the blouse and the pantyhose. I had to use a payphone, for God's sake. I am not going to carry golf clubs. You can do it if you want, but I'm staying here."

April made an exasperated noise, gave up the argument and stomped off towards the clubhouse. There was no reason for her to be there anymore.

214

Scott and Steve caught up to Jake and Andrew halfway to the green from his second shot. The girls in the trailer had been ushered through and waited on the cart path behind the eighteenth green.

Andrew stopped to admire Hanover's daughter. "I suppose, she'll look a little more human in a couple of days," he consoled.

"I told you," said Paul with righteous indignation.

"Another joke, Andrew," commented Jake, "you'll likely find yourself being a little more human as well."

Andrew chuckled at the comment, "Touché," he agreed.

"This is Sally Gina Hanover, Andrew," introduced Scott.

"Pleased to meet you young lady. You sure picked a good time to make your appearance. You'll get to see your daddy kick my butt, and on your birthday to boot."

"You know I wasn't playing against you, Andrew," explained Scott.

"No, but I was playing against you. That's why I lost. And despite the frustration, it has been a great experience. Life altering one might say."

They had reached the green. "I hate to say it Andrew, but you're still away."

"Of course," sighed Andrew.

Scott took Sally Gina over to Sarah and she snuggled in. Scott pulled his Cayman Island penny from his pocket. He marked the ball and pocketed it.

Andrew marked his ball, picking it up to check for any damage and to clean it. He replaced it quickly, aware that the crowd was unwilling to broach any delay in the proceedings.

He lined up his putt. The green was fairly flat. He just needed to get close to the hole for a par. That was all he wanted. It was all he needed. He tapped the ball and it rolled up to the hole, broke a little left and stopped about six inches from the cup. He looked at Scott Hanover. He hoped that the man had noticed the break near the hole. Scott's ball was nearly on the same line and to ignore it would ruin any change he had of breaking the record. Furthermore, if Andrew were to mention it to Scott, he would give the golfer a two-stroke penalty for taking advice on the course. He didn't want to do that.

The crowd applauded Andrew's effort and he walked over and tapped his ball in for the par. More applause and Andrew removed his hat and waved to the crowd. He walked to where Jake Fischer was standing with his bag. Jake took the putter and slipped it back into Andrew's handmade cover, sliding it gently into the bag. He was glad his initial assessment of the man was wrong, or was it that the man had changed? Had a day of miracles not only affected Jake's life, but the life of a man who had known nothing but victories up until now? By accepting his defeat hadn't he truly won something better? Jake thought so. He truly did.

"Nice shot," said Jake.

Andrew turned and looked at him. For two years he had abhorred any comments from the several boys who had carried his bags. He had always thought such comments were redundant to say the least. Andrew already knew he was a good golfer. To have others express that opinion to him had always irked him before. He turned to Jake and said, "Thank you." Jake clapped him on the shoulder with a big friendly hand and smiled and nodded. The miracles continued.

215

"One putt to go," said Paul.

"If I make it," answered Scott.

"Do you have any doubts?" asked Paul. "You're here. There is no way that ball is not going in."

"You saw that break to the left in Andrew's shot?" asked Scott.

"Like he was giving you a free lesson on how to one-putt this hole."

"I rather think he was."

"Awfully nice," added Paul.

Scott knelt on one knee behind his ball and examined the turf. He couldn't see the break but he knew it was there. He stood and lined up his shot, aiming an inch to the right of the hole. If he missed, he would miss. One more shot and he could go home, or rather to the hospital, with his family.

His family.

What a concept it was. The crowd diminished to silence but Scott wasn't there with them. He was watching his daughter, years in the future, taking his too big putter and knocking a golf ball around the back yard. She was laughing and smiling and determined to hit it all the way across the yard.

He took his customary three practice swings to set the speed of the putt. He stepped up the ball, lining up the lines on the top of his putter to the spot he had picked out to the right of the hole. He drew the club back and closed his eyes.

The club swung forward and he heard the tap of the club and he held his breath waiting for the plunk of the ball falling into the hole. He never heard it. The roar of the crowd and the screams of Paul Bauer from several yards behind him deafened his ears to the final confirmation. He opened his eyes and his ball was nowhere to be seen. He breathed and swallowed and collapsed to his knees. His exhaustion was sudden and unexpected. He buried his face in his hands and his body shuddered with pure joy.

Paul and Jake were suddenly standing next to him. They helped him up.

"Are you okay?" asked Paul.

"I'm fine," he answered. Scott walked over to the hole and picked up the ball. He tried to hand it to Paul but he pushed it back.

"You keep it," he insisted.

"No," answered Scott, "this would not have happened without you. Sell it on eBay if you want, but you've earned it."

Paul took the ball. "I'll never sell it."

"Your loss," joked Scott. The two friends hugged and Paul held the ball in the air to the delight of the crowd.

Scott glanced toward Sarah and Sally Gina in the golf cart. He handed his putter to Paul. "I've got to go, buddy."

Paul took the club. "Go. I'll talk to you later."

<h1 style="text-align:center">216</h1>

"Don't let him go," screamed Jason into Ellie's headphones. She slipped the headphones down around her neck as her camera pointed at the new family bouncing away in the golf cart. Jason did deserve to interview the man who had just golfed a fifty-eight, but Hanover's family had first claim on him today.

She turned her camera to Paul, slipped her headphones back on and clicked her microphone. "Here's a guy with the inside story," she said. "Interview him."

Jason was silent a second thinking over the possibilities. From his booth he could see the Hanover's golf cart racing through the crowd to the waiting ambulance. Any port in a storm, he realized. "Give him an earphone and a microphone," he ordered. Ellie was quick to reply.

"And here, with a point of view rarely seen in these events, is Scott Hanover's caddy, Paul Bauer," introduced Jason.

"Just call me Zorro," said Paul.

CHAPTER 25 – NINETEENTH HOLE

217

Sally and Gina arrived from the kitchen carrying trays of steaming chicken wings, egg rolls, cocktail wieners and breaded cheese sticks. "Get your heart attacks here," said Sally, smiling as she set her tray on the coffee table.

Surrounding the table sat Sarah with little Sally Gina, enjoying her evening meal courtesy of her mother in a very nice glider rocker with matching footstool. On the sofa, Scott, Paul and Jake dug hungrily into the food earning disgusted looks from the women.

Sally and Gina sat on the settee to their right, taking an appropriate portion of the snacks as they settled in to watch the big day on television.

A lot had happened in the last four weeks and this afternoon was the culmination of those events. "Here it comes," announced Jake as the television coverage of the tournament broke away for some commercial announcements.

Andrew Patterson appeared on the screen, walking slowly across a green on a beautifully manicured golf course, dressed in a slightly toned down version of his playing attire. "I'm Andrew Patterson. I have the great distinction of being the guy Scott Hanover beat when he scored his record breaking round of fifty-eight. One thing I learned was never to underestimate your opponents luck. The other thing is that if you can't be lucky, use Callaway. I wouldn't be on the course with anything less." He stopped by a ball sitting several yards from the hole. The camera changed perspective to reveal the Callaway logo on the ball then returned to show Andrew. He had his gold handled jade putter in his hand. With total nonchalance, he backhanded the ball, the hole behind him, and miraculously the ball rolled right into the cup.

"I wonder how many takes that took?" said Paul.

"Shh," warned Gina.

The scene was replaced with a picture of a box of a dozen Callaway Tour balls and five words printed below them which were echoed by the announcer, "All the way, with Callaway."

The ad was replaced by an SUV driving jauntily through a muddy back road. "Too bad you didn't end up with a piece of that," said Scott to Jake.

"Ah, that's okay. Karen Blakely did end up working pretty hard to convince Tim Carousel that since you weren't available, Andrew would be the man they wanted. After all, he was who they were after in the first place."

"Still, he should have been your client," added Gina, "April had no business sending Karen out like that."

"Hey, at the time, given my recent history, it was a wise business move. Besides, I do better with the little guy."

"Oh, I think this is it," said Sarah as the SUV ad faded out and the dark, mirror-like surface of a pond filled the picture.

The camera panned to a figure sitting on a log. As he turned to face the camera, the friends gathered in the living room cheered the appearance of Paul Bauer. "Shh," shushed Paul.

Paul on TV started, "When history is being made, a golfer doesn't need to have a caddy who's unprepared. I'm there with his clubs, his balls, his tees and a little friendly advice." The camera panned down to the log he was sitting on. Next to Paul sat a very large turtle. "And for my assistant, I use only the best." Paul now was holding a short, green can. "Turtle wax. Guaranteed to give you the perfect bounce on the golf course and the longest lasting, shine on your car." The replay of Scott's drive on the eighteenth hole from the month before played. The caption explained to the few watching who didn't know what the event was, what had happened. The scene cut back to the tee and there in the background, while Scott and Paul celebrated, tucked into Scott's golf bag was a can of turtle wax, thanks to some sort of digital imaging magic. The scene cut back to Paul sitting by the pond, "When you need extra protection for your car, or, your turtle." He was now holding up the turtle. The turtle wax logo replaced their picture and the announcer reiterated the message to run out and buy turtle wax now.

The people in the room applauded. Paul stood and took his bows.

"That," said Scott to Jake, "was a stroke of genius."

"Well, it's nice to know I still have the old instincts."

"He's got more than that," said Gina. "Are you going to tell them now or shall I."

Jake chuckled. "Gina and I are engaged." Gina pulled out her left hand. A sparkling diamond ring had appeared on the third finger. The stone was significant but tasteful. She stood and walked to Sarah so she could get a look without disturbing the now snoozing Sally Gina. The little girl had been able to sleep through most everything. Scott attributed it to her first day of life at a golf tournament.

The television returned to the coverage of the Callaway Pro-Am Tournament. Jason Bernard was summing up the tournament so far. "You must be pretty proud of Jason's career taking off," Sarah said to Sally.

Sally blushed and smiled. "He never liked golf and now they got him working the pro tournaments. But come next summer he'll need to find something a little less demanding."

"Why?" asked Sarah.

"Oh, it's probably too early but I have to tell somebody and you're all like family to Jason and me," she began to explain.

"You're not," demanded Gina.

"We are," exclaimed Sally. "I'm due July 4th if you can believe it."

"Oh, Sally," cried Sarah, "I'm so happy for you. For the both of you."

"You hang around enough babies those old instincts to procreate kick in," she explained.

Congratulations spilled from around the room, accompanied by hugs and kisses.

"You'll be next," Paul warned Jake.

"Someday," agreed Jake. "Lot of things I still have to work out."

"Well, just stay my agent," urged Paul.

"You got it," answered Jake. He turned to Scott. "How about you. I have half a dozen offers for you if you're interested."

"I really don't have the time or desire, Jake," said Scott. "I've got my memories of that day and to sell them just doesn't seem right. Paul can sell them all he wants, but I'll keep things the way they are."

"Had to ask," apologized Jake.

"We thank you for your concern," said Sarah. "I'm just glad to have Sally's dad around every weekend."

Scott looked over at the trophy sitting on the mantelpiece. Hanging above it was the plaque from the USGA recognizing his record setting round. Next to that was a picture of Scott and Sarah and Sally Gina on the golf course, sent to him by an anonymous photographer. His mind drifted back to that moment. It had been a really good day.

AUTHOR'S NOTES

Thanks for taking the time to enjoy my "Golf Fantasy" as I've taken to calling it. George Dunne National Golf Course is real and I've played it many times. I did take some liberties with some of the holes to help with the story but for the most part, the course is as Scott and Andrew played it. As many golfers know, even though a lot of Scott's shots seemed incredible, none of them are impossible.

I hope I haven't broken any USGA golf rules or at least interpreted them in the spirited they were intended.

I did make up the NIAGA and the tournament and the USA Sports Network. Any other similarities to actual people or organizations are totally coincidental.

Special thanks to Rachel and Dan Mitchell for their early read through and suggestions and encouragement. Much appreciation to Rick Shoenfield for his thorough proofreading and corrections.

Thanks to my brother, Rich, for getting me out on the golf course all those early mornings in college. It's still as fun now as it was then.

James Hosek

ABOUT THE AUTHOR

Dr. James Hosek, DVM was born in Chicago, IL, and grew up in Stickney, IL. He attended Thomas Alva Edison Elementary School and J. Sterling Morton West High School. He received his B.S. And D.V.M from the University of Illinois. He currently has a house call practice on the north side of Chicago and is the owner of Merrick Animal Hospital in Brookfield, IL. He is married and has two boys, hopefully future golfers. He also has been adopted by two cats, Sonyonia and Hedwig. Apart from writing, he enjoys, gardening, woodworking, and photographing mushrooms.

Made in the USA
Charleston, SC
23 August 2012